Death at Saint Patrick's Cathedral
Anthony P. Mikle

APC Publishing – Columbia, SC
ISBN 978-0-578-45427-6
Library of Congress Control Number: 2019902884
Death at Saint Patrick's Cathedral | Anthony P. Mikle.

Available Formats: eBook | Paperback distribution

Dedication

I would like to acknowledge and thank the following:

To my family for your unconditional love and support.

To a long list of friends who encouraged me to write. It was through your suggestions, with the help of the various details, this novel was developed. Most importantly, it was through your honesty, and those who slashed and edited many drafts that this mystery connected.

To the many priests, deacons, religious sisters and brothers of the Catholic faith and other religious denominations whose lives were an inspiration for some of the characters. Be true servants of our Lord, not judgmental, but ones who show compassion and forgiveness — I hope this is found in this novel.

To one of my favorite places to visit, the great City of New York, the setting for this novel.

Finally, to all who will read this novel, may it bring knowledge and understanding into the mysteries of the Catholic faith while at the same time keep you turning the pages to discover "who did it?"

Mercy triumphs over judgment.
James 2:13

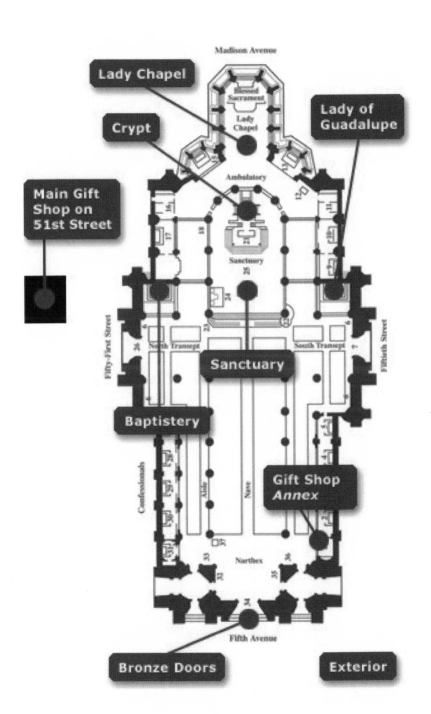

Lady Chapel

Crypt

Lady of
Guadalupe

Main Gift
Shop on
51st Street

Sanctuary

Baptistery

Gift Shop
Annex

Bronze Doors

Exterior

Chapter 1

"He's dead!" Hector Rivera yelled, hoping someone would hear him. "He's dead!" He screamed a second time with no response. Bending over the mutilated, bloody body lying half off the front pew, Hector placed his hand on the neck of the person to confirm there was no pulse. He tried to turn the body and saw what remained of the bloody face of someone he was quite familiar with, Monsignor Steven Triplett, Rector of the Cathedral. It was his boss.

As the maintenance director for Saint Patrick's Cathedral in New York City, Hector had just arrived for work early Saturday morning. He was to begin cleaning the cathedral for the necessary preparations for Holy Saturday and the Easter Sunday Masses. The stripped main altar covered by an enormous high bronze canopy—the Baldacchino—the empty sanctuary, the opened tabernacle, and the absence of lit votive candles around the various statues and side altars in the church were a few of the reminders of the Good Friday services the day before.

Frantically, he pulled his cell phone out of his jacket and immediately dialed 911.

"This is Hector Rivera, the Director of Maintenance Operations at Saint Patrick's Cathedral. I... need... help! I need to report a death." He could hardly get the words out of his mouth.

"Where are you?" The 911 operator couldn't completely understand Hector's foreign accent.

"I am at Saint Patrick's Cathedral between 50th and 51st Streets on Fifth Avenue. I just found the body of Monsignor Steven Triplett. You need to send a medical team and the police!"

"Are you sure the person... a Mr. Stefan Triplett is dead?" asked the operator.

"Yes! It is Monsignor Steven S-T-E-V-E-N Triplett—a Catholic priest—the rector of the cathedral." Hector was frustrated. He slowly spelled the first name to the operator who sounded like she was chomping on some gum. "He has no pulse. He is lying here in the front pew of the church. I just arrived for work and found him dead."

The operator remained calm but struggled with Hector's accent spelled the name back to him. "Monsignor Steven S-T-E-V-E-N Triplett is the deceased."

"That's correct." Hector was relieved she now had the proper name and spelling.

"I've notified the NYPD and EMT, and they're in route," the 911 operator informed Hector.

"Thank you." Hector looked at Monsignor Triplett. He wondered who could have done this to him.

"I need you to stay on the line with me until the police officers arrive," the 911 operator calmly explained to Hector.

"Okay. Would you please contact Lieutenant Will Palmer and ask him to come to the cathedral?" Hector asked. Having grown up together in Brooklyn, he and Will would occasionally run into each other and catch up on what was happening in their lives. In fact, Hector just saw Will yesterday afternoon at the cathedral's Good Friday 3:00 p.m. service. He was praying that Will was on duty today.

2

"I'll try my best. The police and EMT are asking which doors they should use to enter the church?" The operator asked.

"The side entrance on 50th Street. It will be the quickest and closest to Monsignor." Hector was shaking.

"I will relay this information to the response team," the operator said. "Let me get some more information from you before the officers and EMT arrive."

"I don't know anything more, except it looks like Monsignor Triplett lost a lot of blood." Hector's eyes filled with tears as he stared at his boss' body.

"Are you the only one in the church?" The operator asked.

"Yes, I believe so." Hector remembered everyone was out of the church the night before when security locked the doors at 10:00 p.m. All of a sudden, he thought he saw a shadow coming from the narthex of the church near the choir loft stairs. It was too hard to see with just the overnight lights reflecting from the walls. But then he heard what sounded like footsteps.

"What do you mean?" The operator asked.

"I'm not sure if I'm alone. I thought I saw someone and heard footsteps coming from the front of the cathedral... near the bronze doors. Maybe I'm not the only one here," Hector whispered.

Hector had no intention of seeing if anyone else was in the cathedral. One murder was enough. He did not want to be the next. While the 911 operator was still on the phone, he cautiously walked to the church's side doors on 50th Street and nervously pulled out his keys to unlock it. These unique ten-foot doors are framed by a 30-foot wooden facade door. The entrance door has an intricate woven hand-carved frame around it specially made for the cathedral. Hector wanted the police officers and emergency medical team to be able to get in.

"Do not touch anything," the emergency operator warned. "Even the smallest possible piece could be evidence. Please

3

leave it for the investigators and the crime scene technicians."

"Okay, I understand."

"Lieutenant Will Palmer is on the phone, and I'm going to patch him through to you," the operator continued.

"Thank you," Hector responded, and within a few seconds, he heard the familiar voice of Will.

"Will, this is Hector Rivera. Sorry to get you up so early." Hector looked at his watch and saw it was 7:35 in the morning.

"That's okay. The 911 operator told me there's been a death at Saint Patrick's."

"It's… it's Monsignor Triplett!" Hector felt powerless.

"I just saw him yesterday afternoon at the Good Friday service!" Palmer exclaimed.

Hector was frantic. "You need to come immediately! You have to be the investigator in charge since you know him and are Catholic. You're not going to like what you see. Monsignor Triplett's body is in the front pew and really looks bad. Someone really did a number on him."

"I'm getting in my car right now and will be there within fifteen minutes. When the police come, and the EMT arrives, tell them not to touch anything. And the same goes for you!"

"Don't worry. I won't touch a thing. Enter the cathedral on the 50th Street side. I unlocked those doors."

"Thanks for the information. See you soon."

Hector relieved Lieutenant Palmer was on his way. He walked over to the body and carefully reached inside Monsignor Triplett's jacket and removed a small black leather notebook from the inside pocket. He took the notebook and placed it in the pocket of his jacket. Seeing blood on his hands, he panicked and quickly wiped them on his pants.

He heard the sirens blaring right outside the door and knew the police had arrived. As they entered the cathedral, Hector motioned for them to come over to the front left pew in the main part of the seating area in the nave of the cathedral. As

4

they looked at the body that appeared to be a priest, they were horrified at his condition. They immediately noticed the blood on the bludgeoned face, body and pew.

Two EMT workers arrived and proceeded to the police officers with what looked like several bags. They placed disposable gloves on their hands preparing to examine the body. They checked and confirmed that there was no pulse. One of them made the Sign of the Cross and said a quiet prayer for the priest. They realized there was nothing more they could do. They noted the hour and pronounced the victim dead. The police called the Medical Examiner and the Crime Scene Unit and within a few minutes received confirmation that both would be there in 10 minutes.

Hector, hearing the news, "I've been in touch with Lieutenant Will Palmer, and he asked that nothing be touched until he arrives. He said he was on his way over."

"I'm Police Officer Justin Lang, and this is my partner Officer Maria Snow. We need to begin the investigation. We want to ask you a few questions if we can?"

"That would be fine." Hector was still shaking.

They all stood at the far aisle of the south transept surrounded by scaffolding and construction materials that obscured the height and depth of the largest Gothic cathedral in the nation.

Officer Lang noticed that Hector had blood on his pants and was shaking. "First, are you okay?"

"I'm fine, just never expected to come to work and find my boss dead."

"What time did you arrive?" Officer Lang pulled out his notebook to take down the information.

"Monsignor Triplett asked me to be here at 7:30 this morning. I arrived a few minutes early. I was to meet him and discuss the preparations for the Holy Saturday celebration taking place tonight at 7:00."

"Is this the normal time you would come to the cathedral?"

"Not every day. Most weekdays I'm here by 7:00 a.m. I very seldom work weekends, unless Monsignor Triplett asks me."

"How did you enter the cathedral?" Officer Snow was gathering some preliminary details for the detectives.

"I came in through the entrance off 51st Street. I got off the subway on 51st and walked the two blocks to those doors." Hector pointed to the carved wooden doors opposite from where the officers had entered. "With all the construction going on, it's the easiest and safest way for me to enter."

Hector continued. "After I was in the church, I locked the doors and walked behind the side Altar of the Holy Family to turn on a few more lights. I entered the sanctuary and saw the huge cross that was used in last night's Stations of the Cross service lying on the floor near the front steps. I knew it needed to be put back in the sacristy. As I was looking out to what I thought was an empty church, I saw a black coat in the first pew. Since I locked the cathedral last night after everyone had left, it surprised me to see the coat in the pew. I thought maybe someone had left it. I didn't expect to see Monsignor Triplett!"

"Are you sure you were the last person in the church last night?" Officer Lang asked.

"Yes. I didn't hear or see anyone. I went through the church with security and rechecked to make sure all the doors were locked before I left." Hector confidently recalled his actions last night.

"I see a security camera. Can we see what's on it?" Officer Lang asked.

"With all the scaffolding and reconstruction, the system isn't connected." Hector informed the officer.

"Has there been anyone else in the cathedral since you arrived?" Officer Lang continued with the questioning.

"As far as I know, there's been no one. But I thought I heard something coming from the area where the stairs go to the choir loft." Hector pointed to the area near the main entrance of the cathedral. Additional scaffolding obscured the view of the choir loft and more than 7,800 pipes for the gallery organ.

Officer Lang immediately called the dispatcher to find out where their back-up was. He knew the cathedral needed to be searched. The dispatcher informed him they were two minutes out, along with Lieutenant Palmer.

"Are you the person who normally opens the cathedral?"

"Yes, but the construction supervisor, if needed, could open the cathedral. Their work sometimes begins as early as 6:00 a.m., and I don't get here until 7:00 a.m. But since this is Holy Week, they haven't been here since Thursday," Hector said.

"Is the cathedral supposed to be open to the public today?" Officer Snow asked.

"It's supposed to open to the public at noon today."

"You have four hours or so to clean the church before it opens?" Officer Snow was mentally developing a schedule of the cathedral for today.

"Yes, Monsignor Triplett wanted our work completed by noon?"

"Our?" Officer Lang asked.

"Two more workers are coming here at 8:30 this morning."

"Do you know the rest of activities in the church for today?"

"I believe the Easter flowers should be delivered at 9:00 a.m., and the choir is scheduled to rehearse at 10:30 this morning. I can verify this by checking the schedule posted at the front entrance." Hector pointed toward the massive, bronze front doors that were recently refurbished and reinstalled. Each weighed over 9,000 pounds but surprisingly when built were so well balanced that it only takes a single hand to open one.

As Hector continued speaking with the police officers, two medical examiners arrived. They both carried several bags as they made their way to the deceased. They immediately set their bags down. While the EMTs and medical examiners exchanged information, Hector, turned pale and fell forward grabbing the side of the pew before sitting down.

"Are you okay, Hector?" Officer Snow asked.

"Sorry, I just lost my balance." Hector still felt lightheaded as he began to comprehend what had taken place. The cathedral was now a crime scene, not unlike ones he had seen in many of the network dramas filmed in New York City.

"Let's get one of the EMTs to look at you." Officer Lang waved for one of the EMTs to check Hector.

"Believe me, I am fine." Hector tried to reassure them.

"Let's just be safe and have them do their job," Officer Snow insisted. For the next few minutes, The EMT's checked Hector out. Physically they found nothing wrong.

Crime scene investigators came over to talk with Officers Lang and Snow and give them a preliminary report. "There was blood on the body and the pew from the head injury. There was a spatter of blood on the floor. We followed a trail of blood drops from the front center pew where the body was found, up the sanctuary steps, but it stopped at the end of the carpet. We also found numerous overlapping and smeared partial footprints in front of the pew. We still have to take prints and photographs of the scene. The medical examiner is here."

"I'm Alicia Webster, and I've just examined the deceased. It looks like someone beat him with some sharp object. In checking his wounds, my guess is the blows to the head killed him. Given the temperature of the body, I would estimate the time of death in the last four hours. Knowing the temperature is only 55 outside and not much warmer in here, this is my best guess at this time. Once the chief medical examiner looks at the body more closely, she'll be able to give a more accurate time and mode of death. Do you know if the deceased was on any medication?" Alicia turned and asked Hector. She wanted this information to conclude her preliminary report.

"He had high blood pressure and was taking something for it. But I am not sure. I know last night he was coughing more than normal. Do you want me to go over to the parish house and get one of the priests?" Hector asked. He then thanked the EMTs for checking him out.

"Let's wait for Lieutenant Palmer." Officer Lang advised as the two additional police officers entered the cathedral.

"Do you know who has keys to the cathedral?" Officer Snow asked.

Hector wasn't sure. "I think Sam Tolden, the Director of Administrative Services, could answer your question. He takes care of those things."

Just then Lieutenant Will Palmer entered. As he looked around the semi-dark gothic church lined with scaffolding, he heard a few familiar voices and walked to the first pew in front of Saint Patrick's statue.

"Jesus, Mary and Joseph!" Lieutenant Palmer saw the body of Monsignor Triplett. "Who would do such a thing to a priest... and the day before Easter?"

"There are a few who may have thought about it," Hector answered.

"I am so sorry, Hector." Lieutenant Palmer wondered what Hector meant. He clearly made a mental note to ask him about it later.

"I don't know what to do? This will be a shock to everyone this Easter. The priests and staff need to know. Someone needs to tell His Eminence, Cardinal Flinn." Hector became more upset and agitated.

"First, are you sure you're okay, Hector? You look a little shaken up. Do I need to call to get you some medical assistance?" Palmer knew that the EMTs had checked him out but saw Hector's hands were trembling.

"I'm fine! I appreciate everyone's concern. It's just difficult to believe Monsignor Triplett is dead!"

"Hector, if you're sure you're okay, then please give me a few minutes with the police officers and also with the emergency medical team. I've been assigned as the senior investigator, and once I've talked with the police officers, I'm going to need to ask you some questions."

"I'm glad you're in charge. I'll sit over here, wait and pray." Hector pointed to the right.

"While you are praying, I could use your help with the investigation. You mentioned you think you know some individuals who may have wanted Monsignor Triplett dead. I need you to make a list of those people." Palmer pulled out his notepad, tore off two sheets of paper and passed them to Hector along with a pen.

"I'll try." Hector maneuvered his way around the poles of the scaffolding, to a pew close to the side Altar of the Sacred Heart in the south transept where the image of Our Lady of Guadalupe is prominent. He knew the little black notebook in his pocket contained the names of several people who may have wanted to harm Monsignor Triplett, but until he was alone, he couldn't look at it. Whoever did this must not have known about or been able to find the notebook Monsignor kept.

Officers Lang and Snow brought the other police officers and Lieutenant Palmer up to date on the information they had gotten from Hector. The EMT workers realized their work was done, and they packed up their equipment. The emergency medical team gave a preliminary report to Lieutenant Palmer and left. The CSU investigators continued to place various markers for any blood found in the sanctuary leading all the way to the first pew. The photographer began documenting the scene. Upon closer examination by the lieutenant and officers, the trail of blood appeared to end at the carpet in front of the archbishop's chair, approximately twenty steps from the main altar. Looking over the area, the officers also noticed one of the ornate bronze candlesticks missing from the bare marble altar.

Lieutenant Palmer looked up from his notes to see his partner arriving. With a Starbucks coffee in one hand and a

10

half-eaten donut in the other, the young Detective Patrick Sabor joined the investigators at the communion rail.

"Did you bring coffee and donuts for everyone?" Palmer asked—already knowing the answer.

"I wish I could have, but I thought maybe you got some from the church. Don't they have coffee and donuts after church?"

"You're a walking cliché, Pat," Palmer muttered under his breath, looking at his partner. Despite being a little distracted sometimes, Palmer did see potential in Detective Sabor.

"Can't deny that." Sabor gave a grin before finishing his breakfast in two bites. He stretched his neck as he looked up to see some of the cross-ribbed vaults visible over 100 feet above the sanctuary. Despite all the interlocking scaffolding, he was able to see the morning light coming through some of the stained glass windows. He looked down the long aisle and noticed pews removed and chairs in several areas. Saying nothing, he reached for his notebook, ready to work.

After the introductions, Detective Sabor was brought up to date on the investigation.

"I want two officers to canvas the church checking all the doors to make sure they are all locked. The Director of Maintenance Operations is sitting in the pew over there. He thought he heard a noise by the front doors. Let's check that out. I want to make sure we're alone. I want officers posted at the side doors, so no one else can enter the cathedral until we complete the investigation. Report anything back to Detective Sabor," Lieutenant Palmer instructed the four officers.

Officers Lang and Snow began to canvas the cathedral to ensure it was totally secured. Anything suspicious or appearing out of the ordinary needed to be reported immediately since there was the possibility of someone hiding in the cathedral. The other two officers positioned themselves at the entrance doors on 50th Street allowing no one in or out. Little did they know these side doors would become the center of attention for some hungry reporters.

Pulling Detective Sabor aside, Lieutenant Palmer advised, "Follow the blood. Make sure everything gets photographed. In the meantime, I need to see if these are all the lights that can be turned on. It is very dark in here."

Palmer remembered reading an article from *The New York Times* about the restoration work at Saint Patrick's. The article mentioned the extensive work being done both inside and out. At no time would the cathedral close. The enormous amount of scaffolding covered the 2400 seat church and rose 100 feet inside to the ceiling and over 300 feet outside covering the two front spires at the entrance of Fifth Avenue.

Surveying the cathedral, Palmer noticed the number of the church lights covered or shielded by the scaffolding. The scaffolding covered over fifty percent of the church and was assembled with a complicated crisscross pattern of horizontal and vertical bars that ran above the side aisles to the sanctuary. It was enclosed with visqueen to contain most of the dust and debris.

Because of the plastic, many of the windows were not visible resulting in little natural light. The seventy stain glass windows illustrating the life of Christ and various saints in the cathedral that usually illuminated the interior, but they were covered. One of the largest windows, the Rose Window above the gallery organ, was obscured. This 25 foot window contains over 10,000 pieces of glass depicting numerous angels. Palmer wanted every light that could be on, turned on, especially since it was an overcast, drizzly day with thunderstorms predicted later in the afternoon. The contractor had strung lights under the scaffolding, but it was still not enough, so the lieutenant motioned for Hector.

Hector made the Sign of the Cross, put the pen and paper in the front pocket of his pants and returned to Lieutenant Palmer.

"Hector, show me where the light switches are. Can we turn every light on in the cathedral?"

12

"Lieutenant, they're in the usher's room. But with the restoration work, I'm not sure any more can be turned on. I came in this morning and turned the switches on at the Altar of the Holy Family. I was instructed two days ago not to touch any breakers with tape over them," Hector explained.

As they walked up the two marble steps to go around the back of the sanctuary, they passed the Altars of Saint Andrew, Saint Theresa, the Pieta, and the small chapel dedicated to Our Lady before they entered a large room used by the ushers. There on the wall were several labeled light switches. All of them were on. Within the usher's room, there were three smaller rooms. One was marked maintenance, another marked electrical, and the third marked restroom. As Hector opened the electrical room, there were three large electrical panels. They checked each panel. It looked as if almost all the breakers that could be turned on were on. Hector flipped a few more on hoping this would help brighten up the interior of the cathedral. When they left the usher's room, instead of going back the way they had entered, they turned right, underneath the scaffolding, passed the Altar of Saint Joseph, and the chancel organ before they reached the front of the sanctuary. Neither could see any difference in the lighting.

"Do you know if there are any more electrical panels?" Palmer asked.

"I know there's a panel down in the priest's sacristy. But they only control the electrical on the basement level." Hector responded.

"I'll eventually need to see that room and the electrical panel." Palmer, saw Sabor motioning for him, and asked Hector not to move.

The lieutenant walked over to Sabor. "This is all the lighting that we can get. We need more. Call the precinct and see what they can send."

"Will do, Boss." Detective Sabor replied.

"I'm going to question Hector Rivera. We grew up together in Brooklyn. I want to verify the information he gave the 911 operator. I asked him for names of possible suspects. Then we need to take the best course of action to notify the resident priests and staff of a death in one of the most recognizable churches in the United States."

"Don't forget the cardinal."

"Just what I wanted to do this Saturday, meet with the cardinal on the death of one of his priests. I'll be able to remove this from my bucket list!" Palmer tried to make a joke.

"I'm glad you'll be doing it. I haven't been to church in a long time, and I'm not sure how I'd do in the presence of the cardinal," Sabor confessed. "Looks like it will stay on my bucket list."

"He's like all of us. He puts his pants on one leg at a time. We'd better get back to work. Let me start with Hector."

Palmer went to back to Hector while Sabor made the call for more lights

"Hector, would there be any reason for one of the candlesticks to be missing?" Palmer pointed to the altar where Hector focused his eyes and realized a candlestick was gone.

"No. I don't remember one missing last night, or I'd have said something to one of the priests! With so much restoration, I'm surprised there haven't been more things missing."

"Are they always out on the altar?"

"Normally, both candlesticks stay on the altar. But I'm surprised they weren't removed after the service last night since the altar should be completely bare. On Good Friday, the focus is on the cross, not the altar." Hector wondered if the candlestick was used as the murder weapon.

Palmer walked around the sanctuary while Hector remained in place. The lieutenant suddenly stopped, circled one of the marble pillars and looked down. Something shiny caught his eye. He went over, bent down to see what it was and noticed a brass candlestick. He called Detective Sabor to come and take a look which Sabor immediately did. As they

14

were looking at the candlestick, they realized it was just like the other one on the altar. The difference was that there were patches of dried blood on top mixed with what looked like pieces of hair and skin. The CSU investigators were called over to dust for fingerprints. They both knew it would be further inspected back at the crime lab.

"Get plenty of pictures before it's moved," Palmer instructed Sabor, as he returned to resume questioning Hector.

The coroner arrived from the NYC Office of Chief Medical Examiner. Doctor Sara Brown was one of the best medical examiners in the country. She had seen all types of deaths in her twelve years with the OCME's office, the last three as its director. With her expertise, she had testified many times in court to explain the causes of deaths. Born and raised a New Yorker, she would take charge of the removal of the body and the autopsy. As she came close to Monsignor Triplett, Hector recognized her from the local news. Detective Sabor and members of her medical team were bringing her up to date.

"Hector," Palmer asked, "you arrived here about 7:30 this morning to meet Monsignor Triplett. Is that correct?" Lieutenant Palmer pulled out his notepad. Hector moved his eyes away from the first pew and the body to give his attention to the Palmer's questions.

"Yes, that's correct. I rechecked the cathedral doors to make sure they were all locked last night after the Good Friday Stations of the Cross... around 10:00 p.m. As I was leaving, Monsignor Triplett reminded me—more like ordered me—to come at 7:30 this morning. He said he had a few additional things he wanted me to do for tonight's celebration."

"Were you supposed to work today?"

"Normally I don't work Saturdays, but I have always worked and helped set up on the Saturday before Easter," Hector knew all the work it took behind the scenes to get the cathedral ready for Easter Masses.

"What time is tonight's Mass?"

15

"Eight o'clock. Do you know about the Easter Vigil celebration?" Hector was eager to share.

"I know it begins at dark, and it's very long. But I haven't been to one since I was a high school senior behind in the required service hours when I was asked to serve it." Palmer couldn't help reflecting on his years as an altar boy almost twenty years ago.

"It's the most beautiful of all celebrations we have in the church." Hector's eyes brightened as he spoke. "Yes, it's long, but it's where the fire is lit. The tall Easter candle is lit. Those who have been studying the faith are baptized, received into the faith and confirmed. It's where we hear the story of salvation in the readings and then celebrate and receive Holy Communion. It's special."

"It seems you enjoy this service," Palmer remarked.

"I do. It's more than a service. It's a celebration. It's the story of our faith. It's very special." Hector reverently shared his faith. "That's why I came back early this morning to help with the preparations."

"I'll have to come again one Easter." Palmer knew when he had served during Easter, he didn't have the same excitement that Hector expressed and probably never would.

Hector's enthusiasm didn't relent. "I wish you would. You'll find the joy in celebrating what our faith is all about— resurrection and salvation!" Hector loved embracing the faith of the Catholic Church he had been baptized into and lived all of his life. He was looking forward to returning for the celebration tonight.

"I need you to focus on when you came in this morning, or tonight's celebration will not happen." Palmer turned the page on his notepad.

"As I told the officers, I arrived about 7:25 this morning. I took the number 6 subway into the 51st Street subway station and walked to the side church doors on 51st. With all the construction, this was the most practical entrance. I unlocked the door, entered and re-locked the door. I walked behind the

16

Altar of the Holy Family to turn on a few more lights. As I waited for Monsignor Triplett to arrive, I entered the sanctuary and saw the huge cross that was used in last night's Stations of the Cross service lying on the floor near the front steps. I knew it had to be moved. I walked over to pick it up. As I turned, I noticed something black hanging out from the front pew and saw something dark on the floor. Then I went down the sanctuary steps, over to the pew and discovered the body."

"Did you touch him?" Palmer asked.

"Yes, I checked to see if he had a pulse on his neck."

"Did he?"

"No... no, he didn't. His face was down, so I turned him over a little to see the face. Once I saw it, I knew it was Monsignor Triplett. I pulled out my cell phone and called 911. If you look at the phone, it says the call was made at 7:32 a.m." Hector explained as fatigue was setting in.

"Did you touch any other part of his body besides his head?"

Hector was hesitant. He knew what was in his coat pocket. "I touched his coat when I tried to turn him over." Hector needed to say something if they found his fingerprints on the coat since he had removed the small black notebook.

"You mentioned Monsignor Triplett had some additional work for you to do. Do you know what that was?

"I'm not sure. He was to tell me this morning. I have two additional maintenance staff workers coming. I knew we would probably be cleaning what we were able to reach, including the stations of cross and some of the many side altars that were visible. Some had become construction storage areas. Monsignor Triplett wanted it cleaned and looking good for the cardinal, the many parishioners and tourists who are here for Easter. We'd be very busy, especially when the flowers came and the florist started placing them around the church. The florist knows the approved plan from

17

the archdiocesan liturgy office." Hector tried to include all he could to explain his job and Monsignor's requests.

"You told the officer the flowers are being delivered at 9:00 a.m.?"

"I believe so. That information is on the board at the main entrance if you want me to check." Hector pointed to the main doors facing Fifth Avenue.

"Do you know where the flowers are coming from?"

"No, I don't. I would imagine Monsignor Triplett knew, or one of the other priests, or the head volunteer."

"Do you know who is in charge of the volunteers?"

"Sorry."

Palmer was frustrated that Hector didn't know. "Would the priests know?"

"I'd hope so. Do you want to go over and ask them?" Hector hoped he would get a break from the questioning.

"In a few minutes. Could you go check to make sure the times are correct?"

Hector walked down to the board of scheduled activities for the cathedral and confirmed the time. He returned to the lieutenant who was standing in the sanctuary and reported the times were correct.

"Hector, you told me that there were people who may have thought about murdering Monsignor Triplett."

"Yes, I can think of a few. I've written their names down for you." Hector pulled the list out of his pocket where he had his keys.

"Would you have any grudges against Monsignor Triplett?" Palmer asked.

"I would, but I wouldn't kill him. Why would I kill him? With his death, I could lose my job." Hector revealed.

"What do you mean?" Lieutenant Palmer asked.

"There's always a fear when a new rector is appointed that he can fire any of us and come in with a new staff."

"I don't think you have anything to worry about, Hector. You've been here for so long, know the place well, and have worked your way up to being the director, so I doubt you'd be fired." Palmer reached for the paper in Hector's hand. "Is that the list?"

"Yes, it is."

"Are you on the list, Hector?"

The question surprised Hector. "No... no... I'm not." He knew the list was incomplete. There were only a few names on it—those people he felt really had a hard time with Monsignor Triplett and possibly wanted him dead. Then he felt the notebook in his pocket.

"Thank you, Hector, for your help." Palmer took the list from him, looked at it and then placed it in his pocket. He knew he'd have to return to the list after he informed those living in the parish house of the death of one of their priests.

"You mentioned that two additional maintenance workers are coming?" Palmer asked.

Hector looked at his watch. "Yes, in about 45 minutes."

"Do they have keys to get into the cathedral?"

"Yes, they do. They've been working here for the last twenty years. They were hired together." Hector remembered the day each of them started.

Pulling the list of names out of his pocket, Palmer looked at the paper. "Are their names on the list?"

"No." Hector didn't put them on it for there were others he knew who had bigger grudges against Monsignor Triplett, himself included.

"Why not? Should they be?"

"Monsignor Triplett didn't pay us what he should have, and we were always complaining about this among ourselves. But he was very fair in giving us time off for our families and some additional cash when he could. This sometimes helped make up for the proper payment we should have had." Hector tried to give reasons he and the other two maintenance workers were not on the list.

"I need to write their names down." Palmer slowly turned to a clean page in his notepad.

Without hesitation, Hector blurted, "Oscar Martinez and Luis Hernandez."

"Thanks. When they come in, I'll need to question each of them."

"I'm sure they'll cooperate. They come from good families. They're good workers." Hector wanted Palmer to know they were decent individuals.

"Can I prepare things now so when Oscar and Louis come, they will know what to do?"

"Not yet. The crime scene cleaners will sanitize the crime scene first. Once they are done someone from the Crime Scene Unit will inform you of when you can start cleaning.

Hector relieved he wouldn't have to clean up the blood.

"Besides the additional maintenance workers coming this morning, the flowers and volunteers coming at 9:00 and the choir practice at 10:30 a.m., was there anything or anyone else scheduled for the cathedral? Palmer asked again confirming what he had already been told.

"Not that I am aware of. The cathedral is supposed to open at noon today."

"That's not going to happen. There's too much to work to be done here." Palmer was insistent on this point.

"Then we need to go over to the parish house, wake up the priests and call some people," Hector suggested.

"Before we that, I want to ask about the priests in the parish house. Can you tell me who is there?"

"Besides Monsignor Triplett, there are three additional priests in the parish house. The two associates are Father Juan Morales and Father Luke Crumbley. There's also a retired priest, Monsignor James Black."

Palmer wrote down their names. "Hector, would any of them have any reason to be in the cathedral late last night or early this morning?"

"I doubt it. Good Friday and Holy Saturday are the only two days in the year when there's usually nothing going on in the morning. There's no morning Mass or anything happening in the church before noon. I'd imagine they're all resting. As I said, tonight's service with the cardinal will probably go until midnight, and all the priests in the parish participate."

"If my memory serves me correctly, the cardinal lives alone?"

"Yes, his residence is next to the parish house where the priests of the cathedral live. Both buildings look alike, but the cardinal's house has the papal flag hanging outside, showing where the popes who have visited the cathedral have stayed."

"I'd appreciate it if you'd take me over to the entrance of the parish house. I'll need to ask you a few more questions after I've informed the priests and the cardinal of Monsignor Triplett's death." Palmer knew he wasn't looking forward to telling the clergy.

"I can." Hector felt relieved that the questioning from the lieutenant ended, for now. Palmer asked him to take a seat in the front pew.

As Hector was leaving he saw Detective Sabor lift the missing candlestick from behind the pillar. Hector knew the area. It was one of several blind spots in the cathedral where the pillar blocked the view of the altar from the congregation.

"It looks like this could be the murder weapon," Sabor suggested as he took the candlestick to the crime investigators. He was wearing pink rubber gloves he received during cancer awareness month last October but had not used.

"Nice gloves." Palmer couldn't resist the comment.

"My last pair."

"Bag and ID it," Palmer directed.

The officers at the south transept doors escorted members of the NYC Office of Chief Medical Examiner in with the gurney and black bag for Monsignor Triplett's body. As they walked under the scaffolding, they looked up at the Gothic arched ceiling and the beauty that surrounded this edifice of faith, as they look down they were shocked at the mutilated body of a priest lying on the front pew.

In the meantime, Sara Brown walked over to see Lieutenant Palmer to share her initial review.

"Sara, look at this candlestick. Could this be the blunt object used on Monsignor Triplett?" Palmer pointed to the plastic bag Detective Sabor held in his hand.

"It's possible. It could have made those blows to the head and neck, but I'll have to run some forensic tests to make sure. Visually, I would say yes, but I'll know more once I make some comparisons of the markings," Sara explained.

"Was there anything unusual as you began your inspection of the body?" Palmer asked.

"It looks like someone hit him over the head and then on the face with a blunt object. I'm not sure how many times. There are small cuts on his hands, possibly from trying to protect his face from the murder weapon. With the temperature in the church and the temperature outside, I estimate the time of death within the last two to four hours, but I'll have a more definite time after the autopsy. Rigor mortis has set in. They are taking blood samples to see if all the blood on him is his. I'll be able to give you a further report on that tomorrow."

"Thanks, Sara."

"Anytime Lieutenant. That's why I get paid the big bucks, especially on a Saturday," Sara quipped. She returned to the body to make sure her team did everything correctly. The police photographer was still taking a few more pictures.

"Before you remove the body, I'd like to go through the pockets of the deceased," Palmer requested.

"We're done. Just let us know when you're finished, so we can move him." Sara turned to consult with her team.

Putting on rubber gloves, Palmer patted the first front trouser pocket and discovered the monsignor's well-worn rosary. Checking the other front pocket, he removed a set of door and car keys fixed together on a large ring with two medals of Saint Patrick and Saint Stephen. As he held them, a single key, one not on the ring, fell to the ground. An unusual key, Palmer examined it as he called for one of the CSU investigators to bring evidence bags. In one bag, he placed the ring of keys, another bag the rosary, and in the third bag, he put the solitary key.

"What type of key is this?" Palmer asked.

"It looks like an old safe key," the investigator remarked with confidence.

Finding nothing more in the pockets, Palmer was finished. The medical team placed the body in the black bag and onto the gurney. They carefully avoiding the taped area around the smeared footprints, as they left through the doors they had entered. Monsignor Triplett was on the way to the morgue for the required autopsy by the state of New York.

Hector watched, shocked and saddened knowing that Monsignor Triplett's body was spending this Easter in the morgue. He hoped and prayed God had forgiven the rector's sins.

"Lieutenant Palmer, Officers Lang and Snow checked every door. The only door open is the 50th Street door we've been using it to enter and exit. What do you want them to do next?" Detective Sabor asked.

"It'll probably be useless since so many visitors have touched the doors, but let's get the CSU to dust all the handles and locks. Maybe we'll get lucky, and a fingerprint or two pulled will lead us to the murderer." Palmer wished the case could be solved that quickly.

"It's worth a shot. The officers say there's a bit of a crowd, probably tourists, lingering outside, but with the rain, they are not staying around," Sabor reported. "I'll have more crime scene tape put up and have our men in blue keep the onlookers moving."

"Detective Sabor, have Officers Lang and Snow help you. I want to make sure there's no other entry into the cathedral besides those doors. Go up and down all of this scaffolding and make sure there are no other entrances or exits. Let's call in more officers and post them at the various doors. No one in or out until we've walked every inch of this place to make sure we have missed nothing. While you oversee this, I'll be over at the parish house interviewing the three priests and hopefully the cardinal. Call me if there is anything to report," Palmer directed.

"Will do."

"Detective Sabor, if the media shows up, which they will shortly, let them know a statement will be made at 11:00 a.m. Hector is going to show me the entrance to the parish house. Once he does, then I want him to come back here to help you open any doors you may need opened."

"I understand," Sabor responded.

Little did anyone know the secrets inside and outside the cathedral.

Chapter 2

Hector and Lieutenant Palmer followed the removal team and Monsignor Triplett's body out the side door of the cathedral to the hearse. Hector had mixed emotions as he watched the black bag on the gurney. He found Monsignor Triplett a holy, spiritual person but a terrible boss. He was sad he hadn't thanked him for all his help. But at the same time, he was often frustrated with Monsignor Triplett for how thankless and callous he had been to him.

The police placed more crime scene tape across the doors of the church. They woke up a couple of homeless people and tried to question them. Their breaths reeked of alcohol; the officers realized they knew nothing. At the sight of the police tape, more people gathered outside. Rumors began to circulate as the tourists and locals asked the officers what had happened. The police remained quiet. It was only a matter of time before the media crews arrived to report the incident.

As they passed the cardinal's residence, Hector suggested, "Lieutenant Palmer, when we get to the parish house, we need to have someone go over to the cardinal's house and notify His Eminence, Cardinal Flinn."

"Hector, I'm surprised he didn't hear the sirens." Palmer smiled.

"I think the scaffolding has really limited the visibility to look out any of the windows in either of the residences."

"But he should have heard the sirens. Do you even know if he's home?"

"Lieutenant, I know he was here last night. Like I said, for the priests, this is a day to sleep in. Besides, sirens in Manhattan are common here on Madison Avenue."

"Once I get into the parish house, I'll have one of the priests contact the cardinal. If he's home, I'll ask him to meet us. I'll question each one individually about their whereabouts last night. What time did you tell me the service for Good Friday was over, Hector?"

"I don't think I told you. It was over at about 9:00 p.m. However, the church wasn't locked until 10:00 last night. I, along with the volunteer guides, had to ask a few people, mostly tourists, to leave. Thankfully, the police were around to help out. They're some of New York's finest officers."

Hector opened the door and heard the street cleaners. It was a typical Saturday morning on Madison Avenue, with light traffic, a few runners, and several street vendors staking out their spots. As they walked outside under the scaffolding to the parish house, it amazed Lieutenant Palmer at the complexity of the assembled scaffolding that covered the entire city block.

The parish house had the same exterior as the cathedral. Palmer noticed the cornerstone was dated 1880. They approached the entrance, and the lieutenant rang the doorbell.

After a few minutes, a man appeared at the ornate wooden door. He was not happy to be disturbed so early in the morning. He recognized Hector opened the glass storm door.

"I'm Lieutenant Palmer." He showed his badge and credentials. "Do you mind if I come in?"

"Please, come in."

Before he entered the house, Lieutenant Palmer thanked Hector for all of his assistance and asked him to return to the cathedral and help Detective Sabor.

"I'm Father Luke Crumbley. Is there a problem Lieutenant?"

"I'm sorry to bother you this morning, Father, but I need to talk to all those living in the house, and, if possible, Cardinal Flinn. It is extremely important. Would you contact Cardinal Flinn and those in the house?" Lieutenant Palmer asked.

"It will take me a few minutes. Please come in." Father Crumbley showed him to what they called the living room.

"Thank you." Lieutenant Palmer entered the room through two French doors. Examining the room, he realized this was more than just a living room. He looked at the two old, faded couches and four high-backed chairs, with its built-in bookcases, and noted the room décor had not changed in probably thirty years. It was filled with various religious statues of Jesus, Mary, and Saint Patrick, and pictures of past events at the cathedral that should be in a museum. There were no indications of individuals keeping anything personal in the room.

As Lieutenant Palmer waited, his cell phone rang with a call from Detective Sabor.

"Well, while the officers were going up and down on the scaffolding, they discovered that it is possible to go from one end of the cathedral, across the narthex, and back down the other side without ever being on the ground. What I'm saying is someone could have killed the priest, made his or her way up the scaffolding and hidden up top. Now we're trying to see if there are any exits or entrances from the outside to the scaffolding. We haven't found anyone or any entrances. It would be helpful if the supervisor of the construction company was here," Sabor suggested.

"Let me see if I can get a name for you. The priests are being awakened, and they're trying to get in touch with the cardinal."

"Lieutenant, we'll keep searching. Hector has just returned. I want to ask him if he knows of any openings within the ceiling."

"Keep me posted. I hear someone walking down the hallway."

"Will do, Boss."

As their conversation ended, Father Crumbley returned to the room fully dressed in clerical attire of black pants and shirt, with a white collar under his chin.

"I've been in touch with Cardinal Flinn, and he's preparing to come over. I've awakened Monsignor Black who will be down shortly. Father Juan does not seem to be in his room. I placed a call to his cell phone, but he didn't answer. He sometimes goes out for a morning run. I went to Monsignor Triplett's room, and he was not there—even though his door was left open, which it usually is not. I've never known him to keep his door open," Father Crumbley was visibly concerned.

"Thank you for your assistance. Is this room used much?" Palmer asked.

"No, our community room is one floor up. We use this room to meet people who come to the parish house after hours." Father Crumbley explained which rooms were on this level of the house, including the kitchen, library, laundry room, an extra storage room and bathroom.

"How does everyone get from this house to the church?" Palmer was curious to ask this energetic young priest.

"There's an underground passage between the parish house and the cathedral. That passage leads to the sacristy."

"And where is this passage in the house?"

"It's in the basement, one floor down. I'd be happy to show it to you."

"Not right now."

"Lieutenant, can I get you some coffee, hot tea or a glass of water?"

"Thank you. I'd like a glass of water if it's not too much trouble."

"I'll be right back with one." Father Crumbley walked out of the room down the hallway to the kitchen. Monsignor

Black, who was walking toward the living room, passed him in the hallway without saying a word.

Monsignor James Black at 81 years old had really no choice in being at the cathedral. Unfortunately, he had made some rather controversial statements that angered a few of his former parishioners who went to Cardinal Flinn about removing him from Saint Monica's Church. The cardinal was forced to do something and to make it look good for all parties, so he accepted the monsignor's retirement. Monsignor was placed at the cathedral primarily to hear confessions and offer Mass when needed. He wanted to remain as active as possible in his priesthood in whatever days he had left on this earth.

Entering the room, Palmer introduced himself. "I'm Lieutenant Palmer from the NYPD. I'm sorry to have awakened you so early this morning."

"I am Monsignor James Black. I was up, just not dressed. You're out early. What's happened?" Monsignor Black slowly moved toward the lumpy couch.

"I'll explain everything when all the priests are here."

"Good luck trying to get everyone together. This is a house that does not get together." Monsignor Black was surprised at the words that came out of his mouth.

"Why do you say that?" Palmer was very curious.

"It's a house of misfits. The cardinal sent us all here for one reason or another. For me it was a reward, so he says, for years of service I've given to the church—fifty. I think it was more of a punishment to move me from where I lived on the upper east side of town to here. I enjoyed my time uptown. Now I feel I've been put out to pasture since I was forced to retire."

"I'm sorry to hear that."

Father Crumbley walked in with a tray of cups, a pot of coffee and a glass of water. "Here we go. Just brewed some of our favorite coffee. You sure you won't have a cup, Lieutenant?"

"Thank you. As much as I'd like a cup of coffee, I'll pass and keep my doctor happy. I'll be happy with a glass of water. Thank you, Father Crumbley."

"Monsignor Black, can I get you some coffee?" Father Crumbley asked.

"Thanks."

Father Crumbley poured two cups of coffee and passed one to Monsignor Black while taking a sip from the other. He heard another person coming down the hall.

"Good morning, Your Eminence!" Father Crumbley respectfully stood straight up as the cardinal entered the living room.

"Good morning. I got here as quickly as I could. When you called me, I had just returned from the NBC studios. They were interviewing me for a segment to air tomorrow morning on the *Today Show*. What a nice group of people," Cardinal Flinn explained.

Father Crumbley made the introductions. "Lieutenant Palmer, this is His Eminence, Cardinal Flinn."

"Cardinal, nice to be formally introduced." Palmer attempted to extend his hand.

Father Crumbley stopped the lieutenant. "You should address the cardinal as His Eminence."

"My apologies, Your Eminence. I don't know if you remember me, but we met a few years ago."

"I may have." As the cardinal shook Palmer's hand, he looked at what seemed a familiar face and wondered where they had met.

"It was dealing with another case at Blessed Sacrament Church." Palmer knew when he mentioned Blessed Sacrament Church, the cardinal would remember removing the pastor for stealing the Sunday collection. The NYPD had worked with the archdiocese and set up surveillance where it was discovered the priest had stolen more than $100,000 over the course of a year.

30

"Yes, now I remember you." Cardinal Flinn exchanged looks with Palmer. He also recalled the assistant district attorney, Jennifer Gibson, who refused to work a deal with the priest to avoid a prison sentence. He knew she left the district attorney's office and started a private practice prosecuting several organizations, including churches that were found to have misused funds. Jennifer represented a local electrical contracting company, and the results of that case could have a damaging effect on several highly placed people.

"I'm in charge of the investigation." Palmer was pleased the cardinal remembered him.

"Has something been stolen from the cathedral?" The cardinal nervously asked as he helped himself to some coffee and took a seat in one of the high-backed chairs.

Lieutenant Palmer did not respond to the cardinal's question but waited for the other members of the house to arrive. Looking at his notepad, Palmer asked, "Father Crumbley, have you been able to get in contact with the other priests who live in the house?"

"I've tried to contact Father Morales and Monsignor Triplett. Neither one has returned a call to me. Do you want me to try again?"

"Yes, please. If we don't hear anything, I'll need their numbers." Palmer stood patiently by a bookcase filled with books that could be as old as the building.

Father Crumbley dialed both of the numbers. "They both have gone to voicemail," Father Crumbley reported as he sat next to Monsignor Black.

Palmer knew at least one would not answer, but was surprised Father Morales was not responding. He found it odd in this age of technology that a priest wouldn't return the call. He couldn't stall any longer in telling them the news of Monsignor Triplett's death.

"Let me get right to the point. The reason you've all been gathered is to inform you of the death of Monsignor Steven Triplett."

Immediately the cardinal and each priest made the Sign of the Cross. Then the cardinal prayed, "Eternal rest grant unto Monsignor Steven Triplett, O Lord."

The priests responded. "And let perpetual light shine upon him."

The cardinal continued. "May his soul and the souls of all the faithful departed, through the mercy of God, rest in peace."

The priests concluded, "Amen."

"I can't believe he's dead!" The announcement of the tragedy visibly shook the cardinal. He tried to stand but was unable to do so.

"I am so sorry to inform you, but someone found him in the cathedral. Your maintenance director, Hector Rivera, was the one who found him at 7:30 this morning when he came to work." Lieutenant Palmer noted the reactions of the cardinal and each priest.

"How did he die?" The cardinal asked as he took out his handkerchief to wipe his tears from his eyes.

"It looks like someone murdered him. I know this is a shock, but I have to ask each of you where you were last night from 9:00 p.m. until now?" Palmer looked at each of the faces of the priests.

"I was at the Good Friday evening Stations of the Cross service that ended about 9:00 p.m. I came back to the parish house and watched a little TV and went to bed. When you're 81, there's not much more you can do," Monsignor Black answered.

Cardinal Flinn gave his answer. "I also was at the Good Friday evening Stations of the Cross, and when it was over, I went out to dinner with friends at Patsy's on West 56th Street. I took a cab back and returned around 11:00 p.m. and went to bed. I knew I needed to be at the NBC studio by 6:00 this morning."

"I'll need the names of your friends and any receipts you may have, Your Eminence." Palmer recorded the information.

"I'll be more than happy to provide those to you." Cardinal Flinn was very cooperative.

"And where were you, Father Crumbley?"

"I was also at the Good Friday Stations of the Cross. I was on call for the hospital, carrying the beeper. As the service ended, I received a call to go to Lenox Hill Hospital to anoint one of our parishioners, Fred Morris. After I left the hospital, I then got a slice of pizza and got back to the parish house by midnight. I remember I turned on the TV, and *The Tonight Show* was on with Betty White. I just woke up about an hour ago."

"Was Monsignor Triplett at the Good Friday Stations of the Cross?" Palmer looked for information and continued to take notes.

"Yes, he was. He was the one who did the reflection after the 12th Station. It was a great reflection." Cardinal Flinn recalled the words of Monsignor Triplett reminding us we all have our own crosses to bear, and if we can carry them well, they will be lifted from us so that we can enjoy everlasting life.

"Did any of you talk or see him after the service?"

"I did," Father Crumbley quickly responded.

"I also did. I even invited him to come to dinner with me." Cardinal Flinn got up from his chair.

"I saw him, but he seemed a little agitated. He told me he had to see someone and would be back to the house shortly," Monsignor Black revealed.

"Did he tell you who he was going to see, Monsignor Black?"

"No, I'm sorry, Lieutenant, I don't know who it was."

As the lieutenant looked at him, he could also see the distress on the Monsignor Black's face with the news of Monsignor Triplett's death.

"Could anyone tell me about the other priest who is not in the house?"

"His name is Father Juan Morales. Father Morales is our Spanish-speaking priest who takes care of the Hispanic ministry for the cathedral. He has been here for the last three years. He is well-liked among all in the cathedral," Father Crumbley shared with a bit of envy in his voice.

"Is he normally around?"

Father Crumbley continued. "Sometimes. He pretty much comes and goes as he likes. I think he does what Monsignor Triplett asked of him, but he's not always around. He has various meetings in the evening, and the meetings are not always here." Father Crumbley knew more than he was willing to say.

"Does he always spend the night here?"

"Most of the time," Monsignor Black said. "His room is across from mine. Last night I got up in the middle of the night, and I found his door open and the light on, but he wasn't in his room."

The cardinal listened to what the two priests were saying about Father Morales, unsure of what to think of his absence. He wondered where Father Morales could be, knowing of his past struggles that could jeopardize his priesthood. He knew he need to talk with him.

Cardinal Flinn, worried where this conversation was going, interrupted the lieutenant. "I am sorry to ask, but I need to let our communication director know of the death and begin to prepare a statement. Can I make a call for him to come over?"

"Yes, Your Eminence, by all means. I think this would be important since the news media is gathering. I've set up a press conference at 11:00 a.m. Shortly our public relations person will be here to guide the police commissioner and others on the protocol we will need to use."

"Father Crumbley, can I use the library to make the call?" Cardinal Flinn asked.

"Yes, go right ahead." Father Crumbley replied with a worried face.

34

Cardinal Flinn excused himself from the room to call Donald Armenti, the Director of Media and Communications, for the archdiocese. A former news reporter and Director for NY1, the local television news channel for the last five years, Armenti managed all the public relations for the archdiocese. The cardinal also wanted to call one of his auxiliary bishops, Bishop George Newsome.

Palmer, concerned they were hiding something from him about this priest, pushed to get an answer. "I'd like to return to the question I asked about Father Morales. Is it unusual that this priest can't be reached by cell phone?"

Again, Father Crumbley was first to respond. "I know he sometimes turns his phone off if he's in a meeting, but he's been good about returning calls, especially if the matter is in regarding one of our Spanish-speaking parishioners. Usually, when I've called him, he calls me back. I'm a little surprised we aren't hearing from him. Do you want me to try him again?"

"Let me ask a few more questions. Does Father Morales have a car?"

"No, he doesn't have a car. Most of the time he uses the subway." Father Crumbley wished he could leave the room.

"Or someone comes and picks him up," Monsignor Black added, not revealing any more.

"Do you know of any place he would have gone last night or this morning?"

"If he's not out for a run, he could have gone to the gym. I know Father Juan is an active member of Planet Fitness on 55th Street," Father Crumbley explained. "Sometimes I see him with gym clothes and a bag in the evenings or first thing in the morning. Do you want me to find the number and call and see if he's there?"

"Is there any other place he goes?" Lieutenant Palmer continued his questions, noting the answers.

"For breakfast, he often goes to the Starbucks in Rockefeller Center. He sometimes returns with muffins for us." Father Crumbley mentioned.

"If we don't hear from him in thirty minutes, we'll have the police locate him."

"I'll be more than glad to contact these two places and see if he's there," Father Crumbley offered.

"Make those calls to see if he's at either place." Palmer was uncertain if either priest was telling him the whole truth.

Father Crumbley got the number for Planet Fitness and had to do some web searching for that particular Starbucks. He called both. Both businesses announced Morales' name, but no one responded. He could only wonder where Father Juan was and what he was doing.

Chapter 3

The Michelangelo Hotel was on the corner of 7th Avenue and 51st Street. It's a convenient location for those who come to New York to see the sights or for those who have business in Manhattan. With so many hotels in the city, lovers could always find a place to meet.

Father Juan Morales stayed at this hotel since it was walking distance from the cathedral. Thanks to his grandmother's inheritance, he could afford the $425 a night. He had decided that after Good Friday Services at the cathedral, he would meet a friend at the hotel, have dinner and spend the night.

As Father Juan Morales rolled over in bed, the gentle touch of Father David O'Hara greeted him.

Five years ago, Father O'Hara was a newly-ordained priest whose first assignment was at the cathedral. After arriving at the parish house on the first of July, he was anxious and enthusiastic to minister to the parishioners. He heard it would be very challenging, and he thought he would be capable in his new role, not realizing what he would encounter as the new and naïve priest.

Monsignor Triplett met Father O'Hara on his first day and showed him his room, right beside the rector of the cathedral. As he tried to settle into the assignment, Monsignor gave him a list of responsibilities "for the newly-ordained," along with another list of procedures and rules for the house. Monsignor

Triplett emphasized the special position the cathedral had in the city and the universal church. He also explained to the young priest that the cardinal, his schedule permitting, liked to join the rest of the cathedral priests to feel a part of the community.

Monsignor Triplett was very specific in explaining the responsibilities of each of the associates in the parish. He wanted them to know and clearly understand that he was in charge and that he knew what was best for them. Monsignor let Father O'Hara know he would help him every step of the way.

As Father O'Hara reviewed the lists, he thought some tasks would be unpleasant, but the rest he would enjoy.

For the first sixth months, Father O'Hara could not make a move without Monsignor Triplett knowing or granting permission. During the time at the cathedral, Father O'Hara slowly lost the joy for the priestly ministry. He became very bitter and unhappy in his assignment until the beginning of his third year when Father Morales, another newly-ordained priest, was assigned to the cathedral.

When Father O'Hara heard the news of Father Morales' coming to minister to the Hispanic community, he knew his list of duties would change, and he'd be given what Monsignor Triplett called the "assistant to the rector" responsibilities. He also knew about some of these duties from the priest who held that position, Father Ron Shaw. Monsignor Triplett often commented on Father Shaw's abilities in carrying his duties perfectly. Unfortunately, no one realized the toll it took psychologically on his life. When Father Shaw left, he was given a six-month sabbatical to discern his future in the priesthood.

Father O'Hara wouldn't let the same thing happen to him. He felt comfortable and confident in carrying out the duties as the "assistant to the rector." Monsignor Triplett appreciated his enthusiasm and often complimented him.

Father Morales' experience with Monsignor Triplett was not as smooth. Father Morales had high hopes that as the new associate, he and the rector would bond. He also knew he wanted a good first experience as a new priest. Unfortunately, he found Monsignor somewhat intimidating and critical. Monsignor Triplett was thirty years older and lacked the patience to mentor him. As hard as he tried to have a brother-to-brother priestly friendship, it seemed more like a distant relationship of a nagging father to a wounded son. Father Morales turned to Father O'Hara for advice. Quickly their relationship developed, and they became another secret in the parish house.

"Let me tell you the best way to handle Monsignor Triplett." Father O'Hara looked into the blue eyes of Father Morales. "Ignore him and go about doing what you do best. You're a good priest and well-liked. Don't let him get to you."

"Easy for you to say. You're out of the cathedral parish house. I'm now the 'assistant to the rector' and have all the duties you had, along with the Hispanic ministry. I'm not doing them as well as you did either. He misses you. I can never measure up to you." It was painful for Father Morales to admit.

Father O'Hara tried to give some reassurance. "Listen, as long as you take care of what he asks and don't let his secrets out, he won't bother you with our little secret."

"It's just so hard. He keeps track of everything. You watch, he'll find out about our getting together tonight—if he doesn't know already," Father Morales complained.

"We've been meeting like this for almost two years now. Do you remember the first time we made love?"

"I remember our first time. It was right in the cathedral parish house. We thought the monsignors had gone to dinner, and we were alone. You came into my room and kissed me and as much as I had tried to resist the temptation, I gave in. I felt so alone, and you were such great support to me."

"Yes, you remember well," Father O'Hara kissed his lover.

"But do you remember what happened next?"

"Yes, Monsignor Black came back into the house looking for his glasses, he saw us kissing!

"And then do you remember what happened?"

Father Morales remembered it well. "Yes, the next time the three of us were together, Monsignor Black informed us he knew of our relationship. He didn't condone it. But he pulled no punches with either of us. He had his own needs. We knew from then on we had to be extra careful while in the parish house."

"I had to bring him a bottle of Scotch now and then. As far as I know, Monsignor Black hasn't said anything to anyone. But Monsignor Triplett could see the bond between us when we lived together, and he must have asked for a change in assignment for me. We knew one of us would get reassigned sooner or later."

"How lucky for you, David!"

"Yes, lucky for me. I got moved to a more stable parish, but unfortunately under the eyes of Bishop Newsome!"

"But it hasn't kept us apart, and I think it's made us better priests." Father Morales smiled.

"I agree. Juan, you covered your tracks this time, didn't you?"

"Yes, no one saw me leave. After the Good Friday service was done, I went back to the parish house and put on my running clothes and carried a small bag to look like I was off to Planet Fitness in case anyone asked. I didn't run into anyone. And you?"

"I did the same. When Bishop Newsome came into the house, I had on my running clothes and carried a small bag! I told him I was meeting some friends at the gym."

"I can say we've had some physical exercise since we've come together," Father Morales said as he kissed Father O'Hara.

"Indeed, we have, and maybe we need a little more."

"First, I need to go to the bathroom." Father O'Hara jumped out of the bed and stepped over their clothes scattered on the floor.

They had looked at their individual schedules months ago trying to coordinate a time to meet. They knew this would be the only time they'd be able to see each other for several weeks.

Last night they had arrived almost thirty minutes from one another. Father Morales reserved the room. He checked in using the fake I.D. and paid cash for the room. Once he had the room number and key, he sent a text message to his lover letting him know. He brought a bottle of their favorite wine and some cheese. He realized housekeeping had forgotten to put glasses in the room, so he called down and asked for two wine glasses and two additional pillows.

When Father O'Hara arrived, they embraced and slowly took each other's shirts off. But a knock on the door interrupted them, and a voice on the other side said 'housekeeping.' When Father O'Hara opened the door, he was caught off guard. He recognized the name on the hotel badge.

"Do you need some money for the tip?" Father Morales hollered.

Hearing the voice of Father Morales, the young man looked puzzled. He had heard the voice before. He was trying to place it. Before anyone could say anything, Father O'Hara quickly took the items, tipped the boy a twenty and closed the door wondering what the young man knew. He decided not to say anything to Juan to spoil their evening. He hoped the tip was enough to buy the young man's silence.

As he brought the glasses over to the table, he poured the wine, and they made a toast to their love for each other. They ate some cheese and watched the eleven o'clock news. After a few minutes of kissing, they continued taking each other's clothes off reaching the bed, making love, entwined in each other's arms. That's where they had spent the last seven hours.

As Father O'Hara entered the bathroom, Father Morales knew he'd better check his phone. Since neither one of them was on duty for emergencies at their respective parishes, they'd left the outside world behind to concentrate on their love for one another.

When Father Morales turned on his phone, he had three voicemail messages from Father Crumbley and a text reading "IMPORTANT."

"Shit!" Father Morales knew something must have happened.

"What's wrong?"

"Father Crumbley has been trying to call me—and I've missed all his calls. He texted me with the word 'IMPORTANT' in capital letters, and when he does that, it's telling me my ass is in trouble—Monsignor Triplett is looking for me."

Father O'Hara looked directly into Father Morales's eyes. "Call him. You're working yourself up without knowing why Father Crumbley is calling you."

"You're right." He picked up his phone and made the call.

"What do you think it could be on Holy Saturday morning?"

"I have no idea."

Father Crumbley answered his phone call.

"Luke, Juan here, what's so important?"

"Father Morales, it's so good to hear from you." Father Crumbley had stepped out of the living room without the lieutenant, cardinal or any of the priests hearing him. "Are you on your way home?"

"Shortly." Father Morales heard the anxiety in Father Crumbley's words.

"The cardinal and police are here in the parish house. I have some very sad news to tell you—Monsignor Triplett has been… murdered," Father Crumbley struggled with the word *murdered*.

"Holy shit! I'll be there in fifteen minutes!"

"I'll hold off telling the cardinal and police as long as I can. You owe me," Father Crumbley spoke softly, and the call ended.

"Did you hear that?" Father Morales asked Father O'Hara.

"Yes, Monsignor Triplett is... dead...." Father O'Hara struggled with the words.

"That's what he told me. I need to go. What am I going to say?" Father Morales was confused as he tried to gather all his clothes. "What clothes should I put on, my gym ones or my black pants and shirt? I don't know what to do."

"I'm going to take a quick shower. You start thinking about what I need to do and say. We need to have our stories match." Father Morales moved toward the bathroom to take a shower.

As Father O'Hara watched the person he loved enter the bathroom, he wanted to shower with him but knew this was not the time. He had to figure out what their story would be. He turned on his phone, and there were two phone calls and a text message from Bishop Newsome—GET HOME NOW. The bishop knew he'd been out all night.

Chapter 4

Holy Name of Jesus Parish was located in Upper West Side, at 96th Street and Amsterdam—a rather large parish with its own parochial school where George Newsome had been both pastor and Vicar General for the archdiocese for ten years. As Vicar General, he was director of priest personnel for the archdiocese.

Two years ago, Monsignor George Newsome was named Auxiliary Bishop of the Archdiocese of New York. Upon his appointment as a bishop, with the consultation of Cardinal Flinn, he remained at Holy Name of Jesus, and a new pastor was appointed. Bishop Newsome knew the pastor he wanted, and, with a bit of negotiating with the priest and the cardinal, he was able to assign one of his former associates, Father Matthew McFadden. There was a good friendship between them, and Newsome knew the expansion of the physical plant would continue to move forward in this vibrant and growing parish.

However, there was a caveat placed on the appointment of Father Matthew McFadden as pastor. The cardinal would select the associate parochial vicar for Holy Name of Jesus Parish. The cardinal wanted Father David O'Hara moved from the cathedral to provide the young priest a good place and a new beginning for him.

Father O'Hara was assigned to the cathedral as a newly-ordained priest. He was well-received when he first arrived and, like any new priest, was under the watchful eye of the rector and the cardinal, who at times was not always an easy boss. With the lack of affirmation from the hierarchy, Father O'Hara's enthusiasm deteriorated so he searched and found it elsewhere.

As one of the five auxiliary bishops of the archdiocese, Bishop Newsome knew of Father O'Hara's past. He had been discussed among the bishops and cardinal at past personnel meetings. The cardinal was very fearful Father O'Hara could become a liability for the whole archdiocese.

Two years ago, Bishop Newsome had spoken to Father O'Hara and Father Morales after discovering their relationship. He sent them away for psychological evaluations, and when they returned, Bishop Newsome required each of them to meet with one of the local psychologists the archdiocese used. Both priests appreciated Bishop Newsome's support. He wanted them to commit to their priesthood and fight the temptation to continue their intimate relationship with one another. He promised he would talk with Cardinal Flinn and Monsignor Triplett to improve the situation in the parish house.

With the constant nagging from both the cardinal and Monsignor Triplett, it became clear that the only real support for Father O'Hara and Father Morales was from each other. They moved their relationship out of the parish house to wherever they could be alone together, being as discreet as possible. They assured themselves it was not only to protect themselves but also for the good of the Roman Catholic Church.

In the archdiocese, there were over six hundred priests. Bishop Newsome over the years had interviewed over half of them and mingled with the rest when he visited the parishes for the Sacrament of Confirmation or other special events. The bishop knew the appointment of Father O'Hara to Holy Name of Jesus was not the worst, nor the best, of choices. When Father O'Hara moved into the parish house, Bishop Newsome talked with Father O'Hara about the importance of brotherly community. He also encouraged having a good working relationship with the parishioners of Holy Name of Jesus. The bishop asked Father O'Hara to stop any of his previous activities that might jeopardize his ministry as a priest.

It was not easy to be the Director of Priest Personnel, Bishop Newsome would say because of the numerous ethnic backgrounds and diversity of the priests serving in the archdiocese. Despite the challenges and difficulties, he handled the responsibility well. He had developed a system where each of the six auxiliary bishops along with Cardinal Flinn, was responsible for a geographical area of the archdiocese. They knew the priests assigned to the various parishes. When a priest needed a change or would be asked to move, the protocol required that bishop to consult Bishop Newsome, who would then look at possible assignments and bring the suggestions to the next personnel board meeting.

Cardinal Flinn was extremely thankful for and depended on Bishop Newsome. At the monthly meeting with the cardinal and bishops, Bishop Newsome reviewed concerns about various priests. He did it in such a way for the bishops to offer input and to help them seek possible solutions for some of the disgruntled priests, as well as for the good of the archdiocese. The cardinal and bishops, for the most part, would agree with the suggested assignments Bishop Newsome presented. Many times, Bishop Newsome said he felt like a manager trying to make sure each bishop's team had the players—the priests—they wanted for a good, healthy spiritual season. The cardinal was the owner putting his stamp of approval on the changes made. On the first of June, he announced the priests' new assignments to start the first of July.

Bishop Newsome always found it a balancing act to match the priest with his various gifts and talents with the right parish. There seemed to be a continual crisis with a priest or priests. There were the priests who would not speak with one another while living in the same parish house, creating tensions, not only between the two or three of them but also within the parish community. The letters of complaint came to his desk on these problems. There was the parish where the pastor was seen as a kind person by parishioners, but ruled like a dictator, giving orders to his associates who were expected to obey without any discussion. There were those priests whose gifts were limited but needed, and the bishop tried to find a parish house where they would be accepted by a pastor who knew of their limitations. He had letters from pastors wanting the other priest to move out and letters from the unwelcomed priests saying their gifts were not being used at the parish and seeking another assignment. There were priests who had gotten in trouble. Some who even spent time in jail had paid their dues to society and needed to be placed somewhere. There were also a few priests who were just not happy. They would not be happy in any assignment but were ordained for the archdiocese and had to be placed. The list of reasons priests needed to be changed, removed, sent away for a psychological review, or even the chance to seek further studies, seemed endless. All of this came to the attention of Bishop Newsome, who was often overwhelmed by this responsibility. Then there was the very unexpected — the death of a priest. Bishop Newsome was about to get the call about an extraordinary death.

He was sleeping comfortably when Bishop Newsome's phone rang awakening him from a wonderful dream of retiring to a Caribbean islands and having a small parish community to lead. Checking the time on the clock by his bed, he was surprised to see it was 8:30 a.m. He located his glasses, and checked the caller ID. He knew it was important—it was Cardinal Flinn.

"Dominique, good morning." Bishop Newsome spoke to Cardinal Flinn, as he struggled to prop himself up in the bed. "What brings you to call me on Holy Saturday morning?"

"Good morning, George. I'm so sorry to bother you, but I have some rather sad news to tell you." Pausing to catch his breath to say the words, the cardinal continued. "Monsignor Steven Triplett has been murdered."

Without saying a word, the bishop's heart sank in disbelief as he almost dropped the phone. He took a deep breath and uttered, "Oh my God! How did it happen?"

"It happened in the cathedral. I don't have all the details yet. I need you to call the other bishops to let them know. There will be a press conference at 11:00 this morning."

"I will call them and relay the information." Bishop Newsome, saddened by the news, tried to control his emotions.

Changing the subject, the cardinal asked, "I need to know if the associate, Father David O'Hara, is there?"

"I'm not sure. I'm just getting out of bed. It was the one day I could sleep in."

"I'm sorry…. I need you to get up and go to his room and see if he's there," the cardinal insisted.

Bishop Newsome was confused by what the cardinal was asking of him. "Why is this so important? You don't think he killed Monsignor Triplett, do you?"

"I don't know. All I know is Father Morales is not here, and Father Crumbley can't reach him. If he's not here, I am wondering if Father O'Hara is there?" Cardinal Flinn continued to question.

Bishop Newsome attempted to remain calm. "Let me get dressed, and I'll call you right back once I've gone to his room."

"Thanks. I need to call Donald and have him come to the parish house to prepare for the news conference today."

"I'll be back in touch with you in five minutes." With those words, Bishop Newsome hung up the phone, made the sign of the cross as he remembered Monsignor Triplett, got out of bed and slowly began to dress, saddened by the news of the loss of a friend and good priest.

When Bishop Newsome was pastor of Holy Name of Jesus, he converted the fourth floor of the parish house into an apartment of several rooms to be used for family and friends who came into the city. Once he became Bishop, he moved to the apartment which gave him the additional privacy he needed. Remaining in the parish house, he had community when he wanted. What he particularly liked about the apartment was having a small private chapel where he could celebrate Mass under the beautiful stained-glass window of Our Lady. His simple chapel contained a small altar with a picture of Christ with the crown of thorns around his head, hanging above the tabernacle for the Blessed Sacrament. Two small chairs sat along the back wall. In the center of the room, he knelt on a prie-dieu he had received at his priesthood ordination. He would come into the chapel with the many burdens of church personnel and place them on the altar asking for the divine assistance needed. He was thankful for the peace he found when he entered each morning before going to the chancery, the administrative offices of the archdiocese. Today he had no time for the solace, and it would be hard to find peace with the news he just received.

Quickly the bishop walked down to the third floor where he heard music coming from his former suite, now occupied by Father Matthew McFadden. Bishop Newsome knocked on the door and heard Matthew say "just a minute" before he opened the door.

"George, good morning." Father McFadden was surprised by the bishop's early morning visit.

"Good morning, Matthew. Sorry to bother you, but I just received a call from the cardinal with terrible news... Monsignor Triplett has been... murdered."

Father McFadden was shocked by the news, made the sign of the cross, and spoke with reverence, "May his soul rest in peace." He then looked at the bishop with tears in his eyes. "How did it happen?"

"The cardinal didn't say. He just wanted me to see if Father O'Hara is here. Have you seen him this morning?"

"I'm just getting up. I haven't been out of my room." Father McFadden became confused with this question.

"Would you walk with me down to his room?"

As the bishop turned to go, Father McFadden offered, "He usually keeps his door closed, but I'm not sure if he locks it at night."

"We'll find out."

Together they walked down the hallway, its walls filled with pictures of events throughout the 100 years of parish life.

Once at the door, they knocked and called out Father O'Hara's name. They heard nothing, so they tried a second time. Once again there was silence; the door was locked.

Bishop Newsome looked at Father McFadden. "Do you have the keys I gave you to the rooms down here?"

"They're in my desk drawer. I'll be right back." Father McFadden walked almost in a sprint back to his room.

"They should be marked," the bishop hollered after him, hoping it wouldn't take Father McFadden long to locate the keys.

Moments later, Father McFadden was sprinting back to Bishop Newsome holding the keys and raised the one marked for Father O'Hara's room. Without a word, he passed the key to the bishop who placed it in the keyhole and with a deliberate turn unlocked the door. The bishop opened the door to find a rather spacious, uncluttered room for a young priest. Everything looked like it was in its place. There was a crucifix hanging over the made bed, a stack of books on the nightstand, the top of the desk organized with a family photo next to his laptop computer, but no sign of Father O'Hara.

It frustrated the bishop at the absence of Father O'Hara. "Why isn't he home?"

Father McFadden wanted to defend Father O'Hara. "He goes away on his day off, but today is not his day off, so I don't know where he might be. But I could probably guess with whom."

"Father Morales?" The bishop had hoped for a negative response.

But Father McFadden broke eye contact with the bishop. "I would say that would be a good guess."

The bishop responded in rather a disappointing tone, "I need to call the cardinal and let him know. Then I am going to call Father O'Hara."

"Before we leave Father O'Hara's room, let's see if there's anything here that could tell us where he might be. While you make the phone calls, I'll go prepare breakfast for us and meet you in the kitchen." Father McFadden knew with the news of Monsignor Triplett and the missing Father O'Hara this was going to be a long Holy Saturday.

Together they looked over everything in Father O'Hara's bedroom. They glanced over his dresser and found several rosaries, a couple of white insert collar tabs for his shirts and several receipts from the local food store. They went to his desk and saw the printed schedule of the parish calendar. After the Good Friday Service, Father O'Hara had written the word *overnight* with a smiley face. Troubled by what they saw as they looked at each other in shock, and saying nothing, the bishop and Father McFadden walked out of Father O'Hara's room.

The bishop was upset as he returned upstairs to his suite praying for the Holy Spirit to give him the strength to make the calls he needed before trying to sit down for breakfast.

In the meantime, Father McFadden locked the bedroom door, walked down to his room and wondered what the future held for Father O'Hara. He returned the keys to his desk and went to the kitchen to cook breakfast.

Bishop Newsome felt a tightness in his stomach as he made the call to Cardinal Flinn. "Dominique, George here." As he sat in his oversized recliner, Bishop Newsome explained, "David is not here. I saw Father O'Hara leave last night telling me he was going to meet a few friends at the gym, but it does not look like he returned. Let me see if I can find him."

After a brief silence, "George, this is not good. Give me a call back." Agitated, the cardinal needed to get back in the living room with the lieutenant before the Director of Media and Communications for the archdiocese arrived. Before hanging up, the cardinal added strongly, "FIND HIM!"

Knowing the cardinal would not give him much time to find Father O'Hara, Bishop Newsome leaned forward in his chair and went through the contacts on his cell phone. He placed a call to Father O'Hara. The bishop heard it ringing, hoped the priest would answer, but instead it went straight to voicemail. Worried and frustrated, the bishop left a rather strong message to call him as soon as he received this message. Then he did one more thing—he sent a text to Father O'Hara — *GET HOME NOW!*

Chapter 5

Father Crumbley went back to the living room after hearing from Father Morales and returned to his chair, but didn't have a chance to speak as Lieutenant Palmer was continuing his questioning. "Did Monsignor Triplett have any family?"

"He has one brother who lives on the East Side of town," Monsignor Black stated.

"Do you know how I can get in touch with him?" Palmer knew one of the difficulties of his job was notifying family.

"I believe we have the phone number on our community bulletin board in the kitchen. Monsignor Triplett had asked each of us to have a number on the board to call in case of an emergency. Let me check." Wanting to be of assistance, Father Crumbley got up from and headed to the door.

"Father Crumbley, while you're checking, would you also see what phone number Father Juan left in case of an emergency?"

Lieutenant Palmer was now alone with Monsignor Black and still seeking more information. "Do you know Monsignor Triplett's brother?"

"Yes, his name is Thom. I have met him a few times. Nice guy. I believe he works as an independent attorney near Wall Street. He does very well. He's been here a few times for dinner. He was married, now divorced. Very sad that his wife left him. I believe he has two boys. I think they're both married. If I remember correctly, Monsignor Triplett told me yesterday that his brother was coming over this morning, and they were going out for breakfast," Monsignor Black nervously stated.

"Do you know what time they were going to meet?"

"I believe it was to be 9:00 this morning."

"So there are no other relatives?"

"None I would know of."

"How long has Monsignor Triplett been here?"

Monsignor Black continued to provide information with some uncertainty. "I'm not sure; I want to say he arrived a year before I came. And I've been here for the last five years. But you could ask the cardinal and the other priests. They would probably know exactly when he started this assignment."

Palmer was pleased with the information and noticed how nervous Monsignor was and asked one more question, "Monsignor Black, is there anyone else who is usually here on Saturday morning?"

"Sometimes Steven, that is, Monsignor Triplett, would have the housekeeper, Emma Pickle come in for a couple of hours. I know on Friday when she was leaving, Monsignor said 'enjoy the weekend' and wished her a happy Easter."

They both stopped talking when Cardinal Flinn and Father Crumbley entered the living room. As they returned to their previous seats, each was ready to share more information.

Cardinal Flinn informed everyone, "Donald Armenti, our director of media and communications, is on his way over. He should be here shortly."

Palmer replied, "That's good since the commissioner of police will be here before long, too. I'm expecting the public relations liaison for the city to come here as well. Her name is Karen Zirpoli. If you don't mind, let me give her a quick call." Palmer pulled out his cell phone before the cardinal had a chance to respond. It was only a quick ring before Karen picked up and informed him she was on her way over to the cathedral.

As Palmer placed his phone in his pocket, Father Crumbley approached him. "Here's the number for Monsignor Triplett's brother. His name is Thomas, but he likes to be called Thom. He's a few years younger than Monsignor."

"Thank you. I need to notify Monsignor Triplett's brother." Palmer took a deep breath and excused himself to the hallway. He placed the call and hoped the brother would answer. After the third ring, he heard a voice say to leave a message, and he would be back in touch as soon as possible. Palmer identified himself and left the message to return his call immediately. He knew if he didn't hear from the brother within the hour, he would have to send uniformed officers to his residence. Palmer called the precinct and gave the number to the dispatcher with the instructions to locate Thom Triplett's residence and send an officer over to inform him of the death of his brother.

Returning to the living room, Palmer flipped through the pages of his notepad. "Father Crumbley, was there an emergency number to call for Father Morales?"

"Yes, it's for another priest in our diocese, Father David O'Hara, and here's the number." Father Crumbley passed a sheet of paper with the phone number to Palmer.

"Thank you. Did you try the number?"

"No... no... I didn't. Would you like me to?" Father Crumbley wasn't certain he wanted to make the call.

"Yes, if you wouldn't mind." Palmer returned the paper. "Who is Father David O'Hara?"

"Father O'Hara is a former associate here at the cathedral." Monsignor Black responded.

"They were associates here for one year." Father Crumbley excused himself and went to the kitchen. He had just finished talking with Father Morales and was trying to give him time to get home. Father O'Hara's phone went to voicemail, and

Father Crumbley left a message of six words in a rather strong tone: "Juan needs to get home now!"

"Where is Father O'Hara now?" Palmer looked to Monsignor Black for the answer.

"In a parish uptown, Holy Name of Jesus," Monsignor Black answered.

As Father Crumbley re-joined Palmer, he shared, "There was no answer, so I left a voice message."

"Does anyone know which florist is bringing the Easter flowers and who is the person in charge of your volunteers?" Palmer searched for more details.

"Yes, I can answer both questions," stated Father Crumbley, relieved at the change of questions. He was about to give the information when the lieutenant stopped him.

"I'd appreciate it if you'd call those individuals. Inform them that the delivery of the flowers can't be before 2:00 p.m. and that no one can decorate the cathedral until then. The CSU investigators will need an additional six hours in the cathedral before we can let anyone in." Palmer looked intently at the priests and waited for their responses.

"Let me do that right now. I'm sure neither will be happy. What can I tell them, Lieutenant?" Father Crumbley asked.

"Tell them there has been an emergency here, and the cathedral will not open until 2:00 this afternoon."

Father Crumbley excused himself again. He returned to the small 1950s kitchen with outdated appliances and bright green metal cabinets. They would all be replaced—a part of the total restoration of the cathedral. He located the parish directory and phone book that was stacked on the small metal kitchen table and looked for the number of the florist, realizing he already had it in his cell phone contacts.

"Now, I would like to question each of you individually." Palmer continued. "Is there some additional meeting space that's available?"

"There is a small library you could use," the cardinal suggested.

"Thank you, Your Eminence. That would be great if you could show me the room. I'd like to start with you?"

"That would be fine." Cardinal Flinn stood slowly and prepared to walk toward the library.

"Monsignor Black, would you and Father Crumbley remain here? I would appreciate it." Palmer's cell phone rang. This time it was Harold Timberbank, the police commissioner. For the last three years, Harold was very much the mayor's man who was always at the forefront of any crisis. He would enjoy the publicity from this one.

"Excuse me a moment, Your Eminence." Palmer stepped into the dimly lit narrow hallway again.

"Commissioner Timberbank, I was expecting your call."

"Lieutenant, I'm on my way down to the cathedral. Where are you?"

"I'm in the parish house behind the cathedral where the priests live. I'm getting ready to interview each of them. Detective Sabor is in the cathedral handling the crime scene investigation. The coroner has already removed the body. We have police officers stationed at all the entrances, and no one is allowed in at this time. I've set up a news conference for 11:00 a.m."

"I'll meet you in fifteen minutes—where is the entrance to the house?" There was an urgency in the commissioner's voice.

"It's on Madison Avenue. It may be hard to find because of all the scaffolding. It's the house on the corner of 51st and Madison. The house next to it on 50th and Madison is the cardinal's residence. The cardinal is in the parish house with all of us. He has already contacted their director of media and communications to come to the parish house." Palmer was sure his directions and information were correct.

Commissioner Timberbank continued. "I'll need to meet with him, and so will Karen Zirpoli. Do you know if she's on her way?"

"I've spoken with her, and she should be here shortly."

"Okay, I'm on my way. I'll see you shortly." And the phone went silent.

Focusing his attention back on those present, Lieutenant Palmer returned to the living room, apologetic, "Sorry for the interruption. Commissioner Timberbank is on his way over. Now, Your Eminence, if we can go to the library. After I've questioned you, then you, the commissioner and your director of media and communications can meet."

"That would be fine." Cardinal Flinn straightened his pectoral cross around his neck, adjusting it to hang below his heart and slowly walked down the hall to the library.

Father Crumbley walked out of the kitchen and met Palmer in the hallway. "Well, the flowers are coming at 9:00 this morning. The store didn't answer their phone. The head of the volunteers to help with the decorating will contact the others to come at 2:00 this afternoon."

"What's the name and number of the florist?"

"We purchase all of our flowers from Harvest Wholesale Florist."

"Let me get a uniformed officer over to the store, so we don't have a problem with the flowers coming and no place to put them." Palmer made a call to Detective Sabor to make the arrangements.

Father Crumbley returned to the living room.

Cardinal Flinn and Lieutenant Palmer entered the library, and each took a seat around a big oval table that could easily seat ten people. The dark-paneled room was filled with an assortment of old and relatively new books, magazines and papers. In the one corner, an antiquated computer with a huge tube monitor and an old dot matrix printer collected dust. It looked like the place where priests left behind whatever items they didn't want to take with them.

"Cardinal Dominique Flinn. Is that your correct title?" Palmer pulled out his notepad and began to take notes.

"The correct title would be Dominique Cardinal Flinn, Archbishop of New York."

"I'm confused, your title is Cardinal, but you are the Archbishop of New York?"

"That's correct. Cardinal is an honorary title given to archbishops of large metropolitan archdioceses. Three years ago, the pope bestowed the title of cardinal upon me. Does that help?"

"It does. My understanding of the hierarchy from my high school class on the church is slowly coming back to me," Palmer remembered.

"Where did you go to school?" The cardinal was curious to know a little about the lieutenant's background.

"I went to Saint Agnes High School for Boys on 87th Street and West End Avenue. Sad it has closed. I understand it was bought and turned into luxury apartments."

"Yes, it was a sad day to have to close that and other archdiocesan schools. The Marist Brothers and priests had done a good job, but enrollment dropped, and expenses were just too high to keep it open." The cardinal was reminiscing, too, when Catholic schools had been the preferred education.

"How long have you been Archbishop of New York, Your Eminence?" Palmer continued.

"Eight years."

"Where were you before you came to New York?"

"I was Bishop of Cleveland for ten years."

"And before being Bishop of Cleveland...?"

"I was an auxiliary Bishop in Cincinnati for five years."

"So how many years have you been, if I am correct with my next word–ordained–for the church?"

"Since my ordination to the priesthood, it will be thirty-nine years in June."

"And twenty-three years as a bishop or archbishop? Am I correct in the way I asked that question?"

"You are. I will celebrate my twenty-fifth in a year and a half."

"Congratulations, Your Eminence. I believe you have been good for New York City." Palmer interjected his opinion as he flipped the notebook page.

"Thank you, Lieutenant. I appreciate that. I do love the city."

"Let's continue with my questions. How long have you known Monsignor Triplett?"

"I've known him since I arrived here eight years ago. He was one of the priests instrumental in my installation as the Archbishop of New York."

"Was Monsignor assigned to Saint Patrick's when you first came?"

"No... he wasn't. I moved him from Saint Mark's Parish in Brooklyn and made him rector here after my second year. I knew he was one who would be well-received by the parishioners, could handle the day-to-day operations of the cathedral, deal with the general public, and be a great help as we looked to begin the restoration of the church and parish house." The cardinal stared forward as fondly remembered the first conversation he'd had with Monsignor Triplett.

Palmer was curious. "Did he meet your expectations?"

"I would say that, for the most part, he did a good job as rector. He had to deal with many unexpected situations as we started this restoration project. I think it has taken its toll on everyone involved, including me."

Palmer looked for more information. "What do you mean?"

"We had gone 'round and 'round about what was going to be done and how it would be paid. Saint Patrick's Cathedral is one of the best-known churches in the world. Every year more than five million people of every different nationality and faith pass through the doors. Some come just as tourists, but many more come to participate in the life of the Church – as we will see tonight and tomorrow. Regardless of the reason people visit this magnificent cathedral, our doors must be open to them as they are welcomed to open their hearts to God."

"You have a good message." Palmer had heard this before from the cardinal's past news interviews. "Was this the message Monsignor Triplett was also conveying?"

The cardinal folded his hands. "Yes... yes... he was. But since the scaffolding has gone up, it has caused nothing but disruptions. And, unfortunately, loss of income to the cathedral. It's been hard for Monsignor Triplett to pay the operational expenses. I know he was trying to make some budget cuts as he had shared his thoughts on what he was going to do."

"What was he going to do?"

"I believe he was going to eliminate some positions in the cathedral and reduce other positions to part-time." The cardinal unfolded his hands and cast his eyes downward.

"Do you know what positions?"

The cardinal looked up. "I am not sure. He had a well-thought-out plan, and he was working closely with the director of administrative services."

Palmer looked through his notepad. "A Sam Tolden. Is that correct?"

"Yes, he is the one who is handling the operational finances as the administrator for the parish. I am sure you will want to talk to him," Cardinal Flinn suggested as he looked out the window and saw an ambulance pass by with sirens blaring.

"I want to talk with him. Your Eminence, do you have access to the cathedral from your residence?"

"Yes, I do—through the back of my house. There is a door and a short hallway that leads to another door to the sacristy designated for my vestments."

"Are you the only one with access?"

The cardinal thought for a moment. "Again, I am not sure. I know I am the only one who has a key to the door to get into my residence."

"Let's get back to Monsignor Triplett. Do you know of anyone who would have a reason to kill him?" Palmer looked intently into the eyes of the cardinal.

"No one... no one I know would want to kill him. But I know he had some people who did not always agree with him. I always enjoyed my time going over to the parish house to see Monsignor. I will miss our talks, and the times we got together. There were not many with my schedule, but when we had time, they were refreshing. He helped me to be not only a better person but also a better leader for the archdiocese. I must say it was his honesty with me, and I think my honesty with him, that helped form our relationship." But the cardinal knew Monsignor Triplett had kept things from him.

Palmer turned to another clean page of the notepad. "I need to ask you about the other priests—first, Monsignor Black. What can you tell me about him?"

"This is an interesting story," Cardinal Flinn continued. "I was the one who moved Monsignor Black to the cathedral, and Monsignor Triplett was not happy even before the move was made. The two of them put aside their differences and became friends. In fact, I think sometimes it has been good for both of them to be together. Monsignor Black, as a senior priest, has so much wisdom, and as we age, we sometimes do not always express ourselves well. This is what happened with Monsignor Black. He was in a great parish, Saint Monica's on the Upper East Side, and was loved, but had made a couple of controversial remarks from the pulpit. *The New York Times* wrote about him. Before long, the parish he had been in for 30 years was asking him to retire and be removed. He had done it to himself, but I offered him a place here at the cathedral. It gave him a place to continue to minister to the people of New York, and it gave me the opportunity to place a new pastor in the parish."

"Do you think there would be any reason Monsignor Black would want to kill Monsignor Triplett?" Palmer needed to ask for the record.

Troubled by the question, the cardinal responded with his own question. "Are you thinking one of the priests may have been the murderer?"

"I need to rule out everyone, including you, as we begin the investigation."

"No, I would not know of any reason Monsignor Black would want to kill Monsignor Triplett. If anything, I believe Monsignor Black was a help to Monsignor Triplett in the parish and the parish house." Again, Cardinal Flinn defended Monsignor Black.

Palmer heard the affirmation for Monsignor Black. "What do you mean?"

"I believe if someone needed sacramental attention, especially with the Sacrament of Reconciliation, Monsignor Black was there to help, more so than the young associates he had. Monsignor Triplett told me the other priests were not always around."

"Are you saying Monsignor Black was around the parish house and was available to help when the two associates were not?"

"That is one way of looking at it. Associates or Parochial Vicars, as we now call them, sometimes are young, naïve and fresh out of the seminary with great ideas but no pastoral experience. In some ways, the associates' assignments for the first few years provide them the practical training they need, but do not get, in the seminary to allow them to be good priests. It is a reality check for what the priesthood is all about. I know Monsignor Triplett was somewhat hard on them, but I also know in talking with past associates of his, when they were assigned as first-time pastors, they were thankful for his leadership. I just don't think these two associates appreciated his leadership." The cardinal knew much more after sitting through many personnel meetings, but he wasn't ready to share anything more than what was asked by the lieutenant.

Looking at his notes, Palmer once again looked squarely at the cardinal. "Are you referring to Father Juan Morales and Father Luke Crumbley?"

"That is correct."

"Do you know of any reason, besides not liking his leadership, either one of them would want to kill Monsignor Triplett?"

"There is a brotherhood, a fraternity of priests. As brother priests, young or old, of whatever ethnic background, or whatever college or seminary we come from, rich or poor, just like the apostles, we respect one another. For we have all received the call to be the best servant to our Lord. Because of the call, there is a working relationship, and that is not to say we won't have disagreements. Each of us has different gifts and talents. Each of us touches others with the Gospel message in his own way. Just look at how the apostles were. There was a fraternity with them, yet they were all independent using the gifts and talents God had blessed them with sharing the Gospel message." The cardinal tried to avoid the question.

"I understand everything you're saying, Your Eminence. We all have our favorite priest or priests. But you didn't answer my question. Would either priest want to kill Monsignor Triplett?"

The cardinal struggled to respond. He first grabbed his pectoral cross around his neck and taking a deep breath answered, "To be totally honest with you, I'm not sure."

"Why do you say that?" Palmer followed his line of questioning.

"At the last meeting with my auxiliary bishops, one of their names came up as a possible move, and the request had come from Monsignor Triplett."

"And who was the priest?"

"It was Father Juan Morales." Just as the cardinal revealed a name, there was a knock on the door.

Palmer looked toward the door. "Yes."

Opening the door, Father Crumbley poked his head in. "Sorry to bother you, but Father Morales called and is on his way back to the parish house. He said he'd be here in fifteen minutes." It had been fifteen minutes since Juan had called, and it was the perfect opportunity, Father Crumbley thought, to see if the cardinal was okay.

Palmer seemed pleased with the news. "Thank you. When Father Morales arrives, would you have him go to the living room and remain there."

"While I'm here, do you need anything?"

"No, thanks. Would you please close the door on your way out?" Palmer was not one who liked to be interrupted, especially during an interview. It distracted him from his line of questions.

"Again, I apologize for the interruption." Father Crumbley quietly closed the door. He wondered if the cardinal would thank him or chastise him later for the interruption.

Palmer focused on his last question. "Your Eminence, you were saying something about Father Morales... that Monsignor Triplett wanted him moved. Why was Monsignor making this request?"

"I am not sure. He was talking with Bishop Newsome, my Director of Priest Personnel, who probably knows the reason. The last time I met with Monsignor Triplett, he told me everything was fine with his associates."

"How long ago did he tell you this?"

The cardinal tried to remember the conversation. "Maybe three weeks ago. We'd gone out to dinner."

"And when did you find out he wanted Father Morales moved?"

"It was at my meeting with the auxiliary bishops on Tuesday before the Chrism Mass, and Bishop Newsome told all of us of his request."

"Just one more question for Your Eminence. Were you going to move Father Morales?" Once again, Lieutenant Palmer looked directly into the eyes of the cardinal.

There was a moment of silence in the room, then another knock on the door before the cardinal answered this important question.

Chapter 6

"*Get home now* was the text message Bishop Newsome left for me. He knows I didn't sleep at the parish house last night," Father O'Hara told Father Morales who walked out of the bathroom after taking a shower.

"We're both in trouble." Father Morales sat on the bed with the towel in his hand, water still dripping off of him. "We need to get our stories straight before we leave here."

Father O'Hara took the towel and started drying Father Morales, uncertain of how Father Morales would respond. "The bishop knows, the cardinal probably suspects it, and those at the cathedral parish house know. Neither of us was where we should have been last night. We can't make up any story. We have to tell them the truth." Father O'Hara tried to assure Father Morales as he looked into the eyes of the one he loved.

"So we're going to tell them that after Good Friday services we planned on meeting. We checked into the Michelangelo Hotel, had some cheese and wine, and made love to each other until this morning? Is that what you want to tell the two people we promised obedience? Are we really going to tell that to the person who told us not to have any physical relationship with one another anymore?" Father Morales looked away and took the towel to finish drying himself.

Father O'Hara tried to remain calm. He slowly made his way out of bed and fumbled to find his clothes. "I don't think we have any other options. It'll go better for both of us. It is the truth, and Scripture says, 'the truth will set us free.'"

Father Morales nodded slowly without turning his face toward Father O'Hara.

"I think it's important we tell them we turned off our cell phones because we didn't want to be disturbed. That will be the reason they could not get in touch with us." Father O'Hara explained the plan as he moved toward Father Morales.

Father Morales was worried. "It is the truth. I didn't want anyone to get in touch with me when I was with you. Do you realize what this could mean for us? It could be the end of our priesthood!"

"Relax, it's not going to end our priesthood."

"If the truth comes out, it will devastate my parents, my family!" Father Morales nervously moved as he looked for his clothes.

"Coming out is never easy." Father O'Hara remembered when he did.

Father Morales took a deep breath, turned, and looked directly at Father O'Hara. "You know I haven't come out. I'm struggling with it all!"

"Like I said, it's not easy and not always accepted, but it does take some pressure off you." Father O'Hara tried to reassure Father Morales.

As he collected his clothes, Father Morales asked, "Remind me, how did you tell your parents?"

"It happened by accident. One day I was home... it was in my first year of priesthood. I had taken the day off to spend with my parents. We were watching TV, and there was a reference to a gay couple on one of the sitcoms. My dad was outraged. 'How could this filth be on TV? Why are we watching it?' He yelled at my mom and me as he stood up and turned off the TV. He couldn't understand about two men in a relationship with one another.

Before my dad could leave the room, I told him something like, 'What if I'm in a relationship with another guy? How would you react?'

My dad was surprised by my words. 'Did you say 'IF'? You aren't, are you?'

Knowing I could not back down, the words finally came out, 'I am gay.' And with his face as red as a tomato, and a few explicit words, he asked me to leave," Father O'Hara recounted the event as if it was just yesterday.

Father Morales saw the confidence in Father O'Hara. "What did you do?"

"I got up, kissed my mom and left. I walked to the subway station, got on the B line, and transferred to the number 4. I cried the whole way back to the cathedral."

They had never really talked about their families, so Father Morales had to ask. "What is your association with your father now?"

"I have a family who loves me for me — but it's not the close relationship I would like it to be. It took time just to get it this far. A few days after I came out, my mom phoned me and asked if I would come back to the house. My parents wanted to speak about what I'd said to them. Nervous and uncertain about what they would say, I went home where I had grown up."

I talked with my mom first. We talked about everything, including my so-called 'relationships' with girls. I had girls who were friends in high school and dated them, but I was never really in love with any of them. It was all for show. My real love was a boy named Jimmy. She knew who he was. My mom just cried, but at least we were talking.

When my dad came home from work, we sat and talked. He couldn't, and still doesn't, understand homosexuality. He broke down and cried too, wondering what he had done wrong. He blamed himself. I tried to reassure him it wasn't his or anyone's fault. It just happened. At the end of the conversation, he told me he loved me. I was thankful for the words even though my father had a hard time convincing himself he truly loved me. Then he said since I was a priest who took the promise to remain celibate, would I? Not knowing what to say, I agreed I would.... He believes I have." Father O'Hara was thankful to finally tell his story.

Father Morales didn't move; he saw the relief in Father O'Hara's eyes and smiled. "After kicking you out, why did they have you come back to talk to you?"

With a little more confidence in his voice, Father O'Hara responded. "They had gone to see Father John Mastermonico, their parish priest. He listened and assured them that I was their son who needed their love. 'The best you can do for him is to simply love him,' were Father John's words. You know John. He helps others to be positive."

"Yes, Father John's a positive and popular pastor. Was there a sense of relief when you returned to your parents' home?"

"It helped, but there still remains a look of disappointment when I go home," Father O'Hara sadly answered.

Father Morales feared his own confrontation with his parents. "It would all be a disappointment in my parents' eyes."

"You've never talked to me about your parents. What are they like? Are they as wonderful as you are?" Father O'Hara asked with a smile on his face as they both sat at the foot of the bed.

Father Morales was so proud of his parents, "Alicia and Jose' Morales are two of the hardest-working parents you could ask for. My dad works two jobs—in a grocery store during the day and cleaning an office building three nights a week. My mom loves cutting and styling hair. She's been working out of the house for years now, and most of the neighborhood come to her for their haircuts. Together they have made a better life for my three sisters and me. If you walked into their house, you'd see it's filled with statues and holy cards. They are the traditional Mexican Catholics. There's always a candle lit in front of the Blessed Mother statue. Since

70

I was born, they have prayed I'd become a priest. They knew how much I loved the church and were thrilled when I was accepted into the seminary. My ordination day was one of the happiest days of their lives. I think if they could have lit every votive candle in Saint Patrick's they would have—it was their way of saying thanks. The day was one continuous celebration in the neighborhood. I was really feeling loved."

Father O'Hara saw a side of Father Morales he didn't completely know until now. "I remember your ordination day. I remember when the cardinal announced you would be assigned to the cathedral. I was excited that we would have a chance to get to know one another a little better. I never got to know you in the seminary since I was three years ahead of you. Even though we talked, you had your friends, and I had mine."

"You upperclassmen never really associated with the underclassmen!" Father Morales joked as he thought back to the seminary days.

Father O'Hara, sensed the release of tension in the voice of Father Morales. "And look at us now!"

"I was even one of the servers for your ordination! The cardinal was thrilled to be ordaining five new priests that day."

Reminiscing, Father O'Hara turned his head and looked at Father Morales. "One of the happiest days of my life."

Father Morales quickly added, "And yet two of those ordained have already left."

Father O'Hara was somewhat surprised at this statement, "We know why they left—like you and me, they also struggled with the promise of a celibate life. They both found partners who made them happy, which they needed in their lives. Neither one of them was happy in the seminary. They both thought happiness would come by being ordained priests. It didn't, and they both knew within that first year that they weren't really called to the vocation of priesthood."

71

"I'm glad they found happiness." Father Morales smiled and then struggled to find words for his own actions. "But I love the priesthood even as I struggle with the whole man-made rule of living a celibate life. I don't want to leave what I have been called to do."

"So you wouldn't think about leaving the priesthood?" Father O'Hara posed the question for the first time.

"No, I love being a priest. And I love you. And I struggle knowing what we are doing is wrong. Have you ever thought about leaving?"

"No, I love my priesthood, and I love you. I have the same struggle as you do." He wished he could challenge someone in authority who would listen to him about celibacy. But he knew if he did, he'd be suspended and even possibly removed from the priesthood—a vocation he felt called to.

Father Morales got up from the bed. "I never thought when we were assigned to the cathedral it would be like this. You seemed so mean."

"I was just giving you a hard time," Father O'Hara just smiled.

"How good it's been to have you in my life." Father Morales looked intently at Father O'Hara.

"How good it's been for me, too." Father O'Hara now realized that if he and Father Morales wanted to remain priests, they would have to end their physical relationship. "So your mom and dad don't know about us?"

"No... no they don't." Father Morales was emphatic. He walked over to the dresser to brush his hair.

Curious, Father O'Hara asked, "Would you tell them?"

Father Morales thought a long moment before speaking. "If it's to come out, I would want to let them know. I would want them to hear it from me. It will be another blow to them. Right now, I don't want to see any more disappointment in their eyes. David, when I do come out, I am afraid of the shame I will bring to my parents, my sisters, and the neighborhood. I just don't know if I can tell them."

Walking over to Father Morales, Father O'Hara tried to reassure him. "You don't have to do it today. You don't have to do it tomorrow. In time, you will know when to tell them."

It was at that moment they both wanted to give each other a kiss and hug but decided it best not to.

Father Morales walked toward his clothes. "I do need to call my parents and tell them about the death of Monsignor Triplett." He searched to find his phone but was still unsure of what clothes he was going to put on.

Father O'Hara's voice was filled with urgency as he checked the time. "I need to call mine, too, but we don't have time. We need to go."

"I'll wait until I get back to the cathedral. I'll find out more once I get back." Father Morales began to get dressed.

Father O'Hara started putting on his gym clothes. He looked around to make sure he had picked up everything in the room and the bathroom.

"What will happen to us, David?" Tears now streamed down Juan's face.

"The cardinal and the bishop will probably send us on a sabbatical, require us to get some counseling, or who knows what they will do! But I don't see it as the end of our priesthood." Father O'Hara was skeptical as he stuffed things into his gym bag.

"But you and I both know we're not living the teachings of the church. Look where we are and what we've done." Father Morales pushed away his tears.

"True, we're not following the church teachings. We are letting ourselves rely not on God's strength and graces but on our insecure and insufficient strength of each other. As consenting adults, it is this sin that gets us in trouble, and the sinner must seek forgiveness every time our faith is weak. The sinner, if truly sorry, should be forgiven."

"But only if we choose to sin no more. Do you? Do you choose to sin no more?" Father Morales asked although he

73

didn't really want to hear the answer. He found his socks and sat on the edge of the bed to put them on.

"Don't you forgive the sinner when he or she comes to you in confession?" Father O'Hara was avoiding the question.

"You know I do, just like you. But the penance is to go and sin no more." Father Morales took a deep breath.

"And does the sinner return?" Father O'Hara asked.

"He does. And I must forgive again when the sinner comes telling the same sins from the last confession." Father Morales remembered. We were taught not to play judge, but to direct and help the person to rely on God's strength and graces rather than the temporal things of this world."

"So must you and I. If we want to be true to our priesthood, then we have to listen to what we are saying to one another. We need to ask for forgiveness. I plan on doing that when I see the bishop. It's the passage in John's letter that comes to my mind: 'If we confess our sins, God is faithful and just and will forgive us of our sins. He will purify us from all unrighteousness.'"

Father Morales was surprised. "How'd you remember that verse?"

Without hesitation, Father O'Hara replied, "It was one of the Bible verses I had to remember for our high school retreat."

"As the father in the Prodigal Son showed great compassion, so do I. I should do the same," Father Morales stated with some conviction in his voice. He had known this discussion between the two of them would take place one day. It was time to put their vocations above the relationship; he thought as he finished putting on his black pants and his black clerical shirt.

"So will the hierarchical church. Why are you putting on your blacks?" Father O'Hara asked with some confusion.

"If I'm going to go back and have to face the cardinal, I want him to see me as one of his priests of the archdiocese and for him to know how much my priesthood means to me." Father

Morales buttoned his shirt, looking for the white plastic collar.

Father O'Hara once again calmly suggested, "You need to relax. It won't be good for you to go back wanting to confront the cardinal. Instead, you need to humble yourself to find the peace that God can bring as we stop our physical relationship. If you would like, I'll go back with you to the cathedral."

"No, I don't think that would be a good idea. You need to go back to Holy Name of Jesus and face the bishop."

"We're going to get through this together." Father O'Hara still continued to reassure Father Morales but was uncertain how they would actually get through this.

"Tomorrow we'll both be at our parents'. I hope it will be a good opportunity for each of us to appreciate their love." Father Morales was now more aware of Father O'Hara's relationship with his family.

"So do I," Father O'Hara reiterated. He knew how much he wanted the unconditional love of both his parents.

"You know, even if we can't see each other, we are going to have to stay in touch today and tomorrow." Father Morales put on his shoes. He then looked about the room to make sure they each had what they brought. "David, remember, I'm supposed to leave on Monday for Rome. Do you think I'll be able to go?"

"Sure, you will. I miss you already. You'll hear from me." Father O'Hara knew how excited Father Morales was for this religious pilgrimage.

"It's my first trip to Rome and the Vatican. I'm looking forward to seeing Italy with a few parishioners. They are looking forward to seeing me celebrate Mass at Saint Peter's and the other churches the cardinal was able to arrange for them, and I may have just messed it all up." Father Morales tried to hold back the tears in his eyes.

"Juan, you're worrying too much. Take some deep breaths and relax. You can't go back as a wreck. This will draw suspicion to you." Father O'Hara started to rub his back.

"You know this will be in all the papers, 'Rector at Cathedral Murdered,'" Father Morales said.

Father O'Hara tried to reduce the stress of the moment. "Yes, but that story will have more readers than 'two priests screwing one another on Good Friday.'"

"That's not funny at all."

"I love you, Juan."

"I love you, David. But we need to leave."

"Not before I give you another kiss and wrap you in my arms one more time." Father O'Hara embraced Father Morales. He wondered if it would be the last time that they would be together.

Father Morales pushed himself away from Father O'Hara. "I'm sorry, but we don't have time for this. I said I would be back in fifteen minutes. I'm already late. Put on your shoes, so we can get out of here!"

"You need to get a copy of the bill for both of us, so our stories will check out." Father O'Hara sat back on the bed to put on his tennis shoes.

"Smart thinking. When I return the key to the front desk, I'll ask for a copy of the bill."

"Juan, who do you think killed Monsignor Triplett? I mean he was a strict son of a bitch but kind of a father to both of us. I sure wouldn't have killed him." Father O'Hara closed his gym bag.

Father Morales gave some thought to the question. "Nor would I. I'm not sure who would have. It seems for the last couple of weeks with me he was even more demanding than usual. He had me go to two different hospitals and visit all the Catholic patients. He never asked me to do that before, but I went. I just think he wanted me out of the house."

"I remember one time when he sent us all to the hospital. He wanted everyone out of the house, including Monsignor Black. We all went," Father O'Hara recalled.

"I'm not sure if he was just under a lot of pressure from the restoration at the cathedral or what. But lately, when he came back into the parish house, he just wanted to be alone," Father Morales added.

"Alone, no. He didn't want to be alone. He was never one to want to be alone when I was at the cathedral. But he didn't want to be around his associates. We are not his type. He would rather be alone, with a certain female." Father O'Hara continued putting on his running suit.

"Who are you talking about?" Father Morales was startled at this information.

"I'm talking about Emma Pickle."

Father Morales almost laughed. "The housekeeper? You've got to be kidding me!"

Father O'Hara smiled. "I think their relationship started as I was leaving. I'm not sure if it's still going on."

"I see nothing of a relationship between the two of them," Father Morales held in a laugh.

"I think there was one, believe it or not—they also had a place to go." Father O'Hara continued. "Not far at all from the cathedral where Monsignor Triplett usually has lunch once a month."

"Where? What am I missing?" Father Morales couldn't believe it.

"Does he still go on the third Thursday of the month to Women's Republican Club for lunch and meeting with the Knights of Columbus president? What's his name?" Father O'Hara stood up ready to go.

"You mean Charles Hawthorne???"

Charles had been the president of the Knights of Columbus for the last four years. His way of communicating with the rector was with a monthly luncheon at a quiet place. For the last three years, the Women's Republican Club had been the site where they met, in its small but pleasant dining room just a block from the cathedral over on 51st Street.

"Yes, that's his name," Father O'Hara replied.

"I'm not sure, since I'm usually at the hospital on Thursdays, and we're all on our own for lunch that day since Mrs. Pickle cooks the evening meal. Don't you remember?" Father Morales looked at his cell phone to make sure he didn't have any messages.

"Yes, I do. But didn't you ever notice how happy she is in preparing and serving the evening meal even though she's working late?"

"I guess so. I never really paid attention. I've been too worried that Monsignor Triplett was going to bite my head off for something I might have forgotten to do."

"Well, when I was there in my last year, on the third Thursday of every month, Monsignor Triplett would go to the Women's Republican Club and have lunch with Charles. Monsignor supposedly would hang around until he got a call from Emma. Once she had a key for their room, they would meet, do their thing, and then Monsignor returned to the parish house, usually around 4:00 p.m. As I was finishing up with the Legion of Mary group, I would see him walk right by the office windows on his way to the back door of the parish house. A few moments later Emma normally followed."

"I don't believe it. I know she's a widow, but having an affair with Monsignor Triplett! I haven't seen this at all! Why didn't you tell me all this when you were at the cathedral?"

"I thought you should find out some things on your own. It looks like you missed this one." Father O'Hara couldn't help being a bit sarcastic.

"Yes, I did, and now I'm just wondering what else I've missed." Father Morales zipped up his light windbreaker.

"Do you want me to start talking?"

Father Morales once again checked the time on his phone. "No, we need to go."

"Check the bathroom and make sure there's nothing left in there. I'll recheck the room." Father O'Hara checked his gym bag to make sure he had his electric razor and pulled his phone charger out of the wall socket.

With a clean sweep of the bathroom and with a few drops of wine left in the bottle in the bedroom, it seemed everything Father O'Hara and Father Morales brought had been picked up and placed in their gym bags. They gave each other one last kiss and left the room.

Entering the elevator, the two priests were greeted by two gentlemen who were dressed in gym clothes ready to take an early run in the city. Each gave a nod, uncertain if someone might recognize them.

As they entered the hotel lobby, Father Morales stopped at the front desk while Father O'Hara walked over to the coffee station for a cup of black coffee.

"Can I please have a copy of my bill for room 1260?" Father Morales gave his key to the muscular, foreign front desk clerk.

"Give me just a moment." The clerk looked up the room number. "It is paid in full, sir."

"Yes, I know. I just need a copy of the bill to show I was here, and the room was paid for."

With a few strokes on the keyboard, the clerk printed a copy of the bill. Trying to remember if he had seen Father Morales before, the front desk clerk handed it to Father Morales. "Here you go. I hope your stay at the Michelangelo was enjoyable, and you will come again."

Looking over at Father O'Hara, Father Morales responded, "Fine... it was fine." He thanked the desk clerk who was still trying to place the guest. Father Morales walked over to Father O'Hara to grab a cup of coffee himself.

"Here's a copy of the bill for the room. We need to take a picture of us together with it," Father Morales advised.

"Let's do it. Hold your hand over the name on the bill. We don't want to divulge that information," Father O'Hara suggested as he took out his cell phone.

"No, we don't. He wouldn't think it was funny."

They each pulled out their phones and took a picture of themselves with the bill in front of them and the clock in the lobby behind them. The picture would support their story and provide an alibi if needed.

Walking out the doors, they felt the coolness in the air and the threat of rain as they headed toward the cathedral. They said their goodbyes at the corner of 6th Avenue and 51st Street.

Father O'Hara realized that he had been told to get home over thirty minutes ago. He wanted to make a stop before he went back to Holy Name of Jesus, but it would have to wait.

Father Morales continued toward the cathedral, seeing again the scaffolding covering the cathedral with the two spires reaching through the clouds up to the sky. It was at that moment he remembered the Led Zeppelin song, "Stairway to Heaven." He wondered if Monsignor Triplett had made it.

As Father Morales reached Fifth Avenue, he saw the various media trucks trying to find parking spots so they could set up all the lights, cables and satellites for broadcasting. He knew the death of the rector would probably be the number one story for the city today. His thoughts, however, were focused on Monsignor Triplett's little black book. He had seen him intently looking in it several times. Many people who saw Monsignor with the notebook speculated that it contained the stories and lies of numerous individuals. Father Morales could only wonder if his name were among them.

Chapter 7

Hector Rivera, wanting to remain strong but emotionally drained, was still trying to comprehend Monsignor Triplett's vicious murder. As he slowly walked under the scaffolding that covered the exterior of the parish house to the side doors of the cathedral, he found reporters gathered from all the major news stations, including the local station NY1. The police instructed him to say nothing to anyone. He shielded his eyes to avoid the harsh lights of cameras. The hoard of television trucks aimed their antennas directed toward the gray-blue sky, and their reporters positioned themselves to capture the best angle for the proper shot. They were intent on broadcasting the news of the death, or were they? He tried to listen to one of them but saw the police officer who was guarding the door motioned him to enter. Hector kept his head down and made sure he didn't trip over any of the television cables. He knew he better get inside before someone asked a question.

Hector commented to a nearby police officer. "Thank you. It looks like you'll have your hands full keeping them out. Do they know there was a murder in there?"

"They know a body came out of the cathedral, and there is a press conference at 11:00 a.m. Right now, they're doing a lot of speculating and hoping they will be the first ones to break the news." The officer replied as he opened the cathedral door.

"Good luck." Hector proceeded inside and, to his surprise, saw it was twice as bright in the cathedral than before he left. It seemed during the short time he was away, additional lamps used at a football stadium had been brought in and were placed in strategic areas where the scaffolding blocked the normal lighting. The police officers were trying to locate places to connect and direct the lights where needed.

Detective Sabor called to him, "Mr. Rivera, can you come over here?"

Hector saw the various police markings on the floor, and he walked carefully as he approached the first pew where the body of Monsignor Triplett was found. The CSU, identified by their shirts and jackets, were still dusting for prints. Some pulled prints off the pews and surrounding area while others made notations in their notebooks. It was the photographer who was snapping pictures rapidly that caught Hector's attention. The man stood out from the rest with the various cameras and equipment draped over his shoulder as if he were a paparazzi photographing a major star.

Hector eagerly asked the detective, "How can I help you?" With his hand firmly on the pew, Sabor began his questioning. "Did you know that this pew is not bolted down?"

"With the construction going on, not many pews are." Hector wiggled the pew to confirm.

Sabor crouched down to further exam the pew. "But this one seems to have been bolted down. Someone has cut the screws, and it looks like it was recently done."

Hector moved next to the detective, squatted down to get a better look, and was surprised at what he saw.

"Do you know any reason for this?" Sabor looked at Hector.

Hector was confused. As he looked back at the detective, he tried to offer a possible explanation. "I don't know. The pew was there last night in the spot where it is right now. Maybe the construction company tried to move it out of the way and wasn't having any luck, so they cut the screws."

"It looks like someone tried but couldn't finish removing the screws." Sabor stood up.

"Well, I know they had a real hard time removing the screws in many of the wooden pews before they put up the scaffolding."

Detective Sabor made a note in his notebook. "Do you know if any objects or materials were found under any of the pews and removed from the cathedral by the workers?"

"Just a lot of stale chewing gum." Hector grinned. "It was disgusting."

"Probably every church would say that about their pews," Sabor displayed a guilty smile, remembering he had placed his share of gum under many church pews during his teenage years.

"Part of the restoration is securing the pews to the floor with all new hardware. It looks like the construction crew didn't finish this one. I'm surprised since they knew everything had to be safe before the crowds of people came here for Easter." Hector added, "I know the ushers advise those entering the pews to be careful."

"Hector, I need a couple of doors opened. Could you follow me along with Officer Lang to the doors?" Sabor asked as he motioned for Officer Lang.

"No problem." Hector looked disappointed. He really wanted to find out what, if anything, was under the pew. "Where's the door you want opened?"

"In the sacristy below the altar," Sabor indicated.

Hector carefully led the way for the detective, Officer Lang, and one of the CSU investigators, taking them in front of the statue of Saint Patrick underneath the scaffolding and around the back of the main altar down the steps to the door of the priests' sacristy. It surprised the investigators to find the crypt that entombed some notable Catholics, including eight archbishops.

When Sabor entered the sacristy, he saw a huge room and counted 40 single-door closets around the perimeter of the rectangular room. Some doors had signs on them, either a priest's name or a description of the contents. Additionally, there were four chest-high cabinets, each six feet by three feet. In each of the cabinets, there were a series of thin drawers on two sides and on the other side, there were two doors. This was the room where all the liturgical vestments, vessels and supplies used for the cathedral celebrations were stored. The detective pointed toward the door in question, which looked like all the other doors, but with one distinction—an exit sign above it. "Where does this door lead?"

"This is a secret hallway that takes you to a hidden staircase that leads to passages that run the length of the cathedral and continue to the attic and two towers. The door is kept locked for safety reasons. The only time it's unlocked is for the firefighters to conduct safety inspections. You'll notice the graffiti marks they made after their inspections." Hector explained as he turned on an additional set of lights. "We seldom go up there."

"Has the door been dusted for prints?" Detective Sabor turned and asked Officer Lang.

Officer Lang, a ten-year member of the NYPD, confidently replied, "Yes, it has."

"Once it's opened, I want it dusted on the other side before any of us goes in," Sabor instructed.

Sabor then turned toward Hector. "Who would have a key to this door?"

"I'd say all the maintenance personnel, and there's probably one with Sam Tolden. I'm not sure if the priests, or anyone else, has one. A spare key is in the cabinet behind the sacristy door in case of an emergency," Hector explained as he carefully thumbed through his many keys to find the one needed to open the door.

Hector placed his key in the door. Slowly he turned the key and opened the creaking door. He located the switch that turned on a single light revealing a passageway that led to a flight of marble stairs. He then moved out of the way.

Before the crime scene investigator could begin, Sabor stuck his head in at the door entrance. "Hector, do you know how many stairs there are to the top?"

"I don't. Does it say anything on the side wall by the stairs?" Hector asked. "In these old churches, we find all kinds of notes written on walls."

"It doesn't." Sabor looked around the confined area. He then stepped out and motioned for the crime investigator to dust for fingerprints.

"Is this the only entrance?" Sabor asked.

"Yes." Hector carefully pulled out his key without touching the door. The way the crime investigator began to work intrigued him. He had wondered if it was like all those television drama shows he liked to watch.

Detective Sabor had a fear of heights from childhood, when he was stuck, for what seemed like an eternity, on the top of a roller coaster. Now he motioned for Officer Lang. "Officer Lang, once the area is dusted for prints, call Officer Snow and ask her to meet you here so you two can go up the stairs."

"Yes, sir," Officer Lang responded. He radioed for Officer Snow to meet him in the sacristy and gave her directions.

Sabor was specific in his instructions to Officer Lang, "I need you both to go up, check it out, and see if there is any connection at the top to the scaffolding in the church. I need to know if someone could get on the scaffolding by climbing these steps."

Officer Snow entered the priests' sacristy, and Officer Lang repeated the directions for their task. They worked cautiously, uncertain of what they would discover.

As the crime investigator finished dusting the door, Officer Lang pulled out his flashlight and made sure it was working properly. Officers Lang and Snow slowly and carefully ventured up the stairs to the top. Detective Sabor watched until one of the investigators asked him to return to the front pew.

Then Sabor yelled up to the officers, "Let me know what you find, Officer Lang. I'm needed back upstairs in the church." He motioned for Hector to follow him back upstairs and sit close to the front pew.

Sabor approached the investigator at the front pew. He pointed to a spot on the pew where Monsignor Triplett was found. As Sabor bent down to look, he discovered what appeared to be two letters written in blood. Each seemed to be an uppercase letter; it was hard to decipher.

As he pointed to the bloody letters, Sabor was confused at what he saw. "What do you make of this?"

The investigator was also puzzled. "I'm not sure. I think it looks like an S and an A, but it's only a guess. What do you see?"

Sabor looked at the mysterious writing again. "I would agree, but then again it could be a C and an O with blood running through it to make it look like an S and an A. If it was the deceased who did it, what was he trying to tell us?"

The investigator half-jokingly responded, "That's why you're the detective."

Sabor didn't respond to the investigator's remark. He stood and pulled out his cell phone to get a picture of the cryptic message. Once he finished taking pictures from several angles, he forwarded them to Lieutenant Palmer with the simple message, "Discovered on the front pew. What do you see?" Putting his phone back in his pocket, Sabor instructed the investigator, "Get the photographer over here to take proper pictures of the mysterious writing."

"Will do," the investigator realized how serious Sabor was.

Looking around, Sabor continued with his instructions. "We'll have to remove the pew carefully. Do we have the right tools?"

"I believe we do," the investigator answered with confidence.

"If we don't, let me know. We may have to get the construction company to move it. I don't want anything to happen to it, especially to those bloody letters."

"I understand."

Suddenly, from out of nowhere and echoing in the church, a voice yelled, "Detective Sabor, can you see and hear me?"

Sabor turned his head quickly and looked up, wondering where the voice came from. He noticed four red hats with long tassels hanging from the ceiling. These ornate, wide-brimmed hats with tassels, called *galeros*, are given to cardinals to acknowledge their exalted positions. After their deaths, the hats are traditionally suspended from the ceiling. As the voice called out again, Sabor turned his head toward the Gothic-arched openings of the triforium. He saw Officer Lang, wave. "Yes, I see you now."

"Detective Sabor, you need to climb up the stairs. There's something you must see. We need someone to do fingerprinting up here, too!" Officer Lang spoke with urgency.

Sabor now had to face his fear of heights and hesitated. "I'll be right there." He instructed one of the CSU investigators and Hector to come with him.

As they went back downstairs to the priests' sacristy and through the passageway to access the concealed steps, Sabor asked Hector and the crime investigator to lead the way up, so they would not see the fear in his eyes. They both proceeded carefully and with no hesitation.

Bravely, Sabor took a couple of deep breaths, gained his composure and began the climb up the staircase. He counted each step, but lost track after 100, and slowly ascended to the top. When he reached the top, he took another deep breath and focused his eyes on Officer Lang.

Officer Lang approached the detective quietly to see if he was all right. Sabor assured him he was. Then Lang showed how the scaffolding was almost connected to the balcony.

There was less than a foot between the stairs and scaffolding.

Detective Sabor looked towards the place Officer Lang was pointing. "Could someone who was at the back of the church have made his way to this spot and climbed down the stairs?"

"But the door was locked!" Hector quickly responded.

"Yes, but you can unbolt it from the inside to get out and re-lock it," Sabor reminded everyone.

"The person would need a key to the door. Where would the person have gone? We checked everywhere." Officer Lang looked over the balcony.

Detective Sabor didn't want to spend any more time so high up. He turned towards Hector. "When we get down from here, show me where the emergency key is located."

"I'd be happy to. You can get to the offices from the sacristy. The door is not obvious since it looks just like the one for the vestment closet. When you open the door, there is a small hallway to another door which leads to an entrance for the parish offices on 51st Street." Hector was trying to be helpful and thorough.

Sabor took another deep breath and appeared confused by Hector's description.

Hector saw the confusion on Detective Sabor's face. "Once we get down from the scaffolding, I'll show it to you. Even though it leads to the office, you must have a key to get into the office area since that door is always locked."

Surprised by Hector's information, Sabor responded, "Is there also a door to the parish house?"

"Yes."

Moving closer to the stairs, Sabor directed the crime investigator. "Dust the area for fingerprints on those doors. If our murderer was up here and went down into the office area, at least we have the point of exit, and possibly the point of entry into the locked cathedral."

As another inspector was coming up the stairs, Sabor let him know what they needed and asked, "Do you think you have any clean fingerprints from the pew or the key that fell out of the priest's pocket?"

"Well, it looks like we have lots of smudges, but we did obtain a couple of prints that look like a thumb and finger. It may take a while to see if any prints match with those we have in the computer." The investigator reported as he prepared to dust for prints in the area requested.

"We may need to fingerprint the entire staff, all the priests, and even the cardinal." Sabor unexpectedly announced.

"In the old days, we could have given them an Easter present—dyed fingers." The CSU investigator made a half-hearted joke knowing today they use a more sophisticated and accurate electronic method.

"Funny!" Sabor responded with a half grin on his face. "I thank you for your input."

"Just trying to help," the investigator returned a half smile.

Before climbing down, Hector looked out of the small arched opening and noticed Oscar Martinez and Luis Hernandez trying to get into the cathedral, but an officer stopped them.

"Detective Sabor, my two maintenance workers are at the side door. Can they come in?" Hector pointed to the two men.

"Officer Lang, please radio the officer at the door and have him escort those two men talking with him to sit in two separate pews in front of Our Lady of Guadalupe until I get there," Sabor directed. He looked at his watch and noted the time of their arrival—8:20 a.m.

When Oscar and Luis entered, they noticed the many investigators, police, and placement of additional lighting in the cathedral; it was a hectic scene. Oscar was asked to sit in the third pew, and Luis was asked to sit several pews further down. As they took their seats, both men wondered what was going on and were uncertain of the unfamiliar faces present.

Sabor slowly walked down the stairs. When he reached the bottom step, he felt that knot in his stomach subside. Hector followed him and walked over to show the detective the emergency key for the door that led to the secret staircase and walkway. Before opening the cabinet, it too was dusted for prints. Once dusted, Sabor opened the cabinet and discovered the key was missing.

"Hector, do you remember the last time you looked in this cabinet?"

"I don't remember if I ever have. I have my key." Hector was surprised by the empty space.

"Who knew about the extra key?" Sabor continued to gather information.

"I'm really not sure. The priests, staff in the cathedral, and maybe the construction workers. This would be a question for Sam Tolden."

Detective Sabor quietly closed the cabinet door and looked at Hector, "Do you have his number? There are a lot of questions he needs to answer."

"Yes. Would you like me to call him?" Hector wanted to be the one to tell Sam.

"No, I think it best if I call him. What's his number?" Sabor took out his cell phone ready for Hector to give him the number.

Disappointed, Hector searched for Sam's number on his phone and passed it to the detective.

Sabor entered the number into his phone. "What's his name again, Hector?"

"Sam Tolden." Hector then asked, "What about Oscar and Luis?"

The detective wasn't ready to make the call nor was he immediately concerned for the other maintenance workers. "First, Hector, would you show the crime scene investigator which door leads to the office and which door leads to the parish house?"

Hector walked past five closet doors of vestments to the sixth door. The investigator dusted it for fingerprints, then opened it and found exactly what Hector was talking about — a small hallway leading to another door, which was also dusted for prints.

Sabor proceeded through this door into the hallway and tried opening the office door — it was locked.

"Hector, do you have a key to this door?"

"I do." Hector pulled out his set of keys to locate the correct one.

"I need you to open the door and not touch the other side." Sabor noted that Hector, it seemed, had access to a lot of areas of the cathedral buildings.

Hector placed the key in the door. "For security, there is an alarm attached to the door, and I don't have the code."

Sabor motioned for Officer Lang, who called the dispatcher that an alarm would be activated shortly.

Hector opened the door. A loud shrieking alarm blared right at the office entrance. Officer Lang told the dispatcher to locate the alarm company, inform them of the false alarm, and find out how to disengage.

Detective Sabor, holding his free hand to one of his ears, looked at the others who were doing the same, raised his voice and sarcastically remarked, "This alarm will wake a few people. I hope I didn't interrupt Lieutenant Palmer's tea with His Eminence, the cardinal!"

Chapter 8

"Who's knocking at the door?" Lieutenant Palmer turned abruptly at the same time an alarm went off.

Father Crumbley bolted into the room looking nervous. Both Palmer and Cardinal Flinn got up from their chairs. "I'm sorry to interrupt you both, but the office alarm has been set off. Someone needs to see why."

"I'll go." Palmer quickly reacted. "Your Eminence, if you would please remain and give some thought to that last question I asked you."

Stuffing his notepad into his pocket, Palmer asked Father Crumbley to show him the entrance to the office. The two men left the library and walked single file through the narrow corridor down a flight of stairs to the locked door where the only light came from the alarm pad blinking away.

Father Crumbley found the light switch to the single light above and quickly flipped it on.

Palmer placed his hands over ears, pleading, "Father Crumbley, please turn off the alarm and open this door!"

Father Crumbley quickly pushed the five buttons to deactivate the parish office alarm and silence returned. Then he pulled out his keys to unlock the door to the parish office. Once the door was opened, Palmer entered the passageway to find Detective Sabor and Hector waiting at the office entrance.

Sabor greeted Palmer with a smirk on his face. "Boss, sorry for the interruption. I wanted to give you a break with the cardinal."

"Didn't you see the alarm keypad?" Father Crumbley directed his question to Hector.

Hector was embarrassed. "I don't know the code."

Detective Sabor, came to Hector's defense, sarcastically asking, "Was the code on one of the statues of Saint Patrick?" Without waiting for an answer, he turned and got serious with his partner. "As you can see, the buildings do connect. There's a door in the sacristy, and this corridor connects the cathedral to the parish offices, and as you now know, the corridor continues to the parish house."

Father Crumbley went over to the light switch and turned on another set of lights. As they walked down this corridor from the sacristy entrance, they first noticed the stairs and elevator to the second floor. As they continued, they saw a series of offices and meeting rooms that led to a glass-enclosed reception area. The waiting room was a modest size with six chairs next to the outside door of the offices where a receptionist sits in front of the glass window to welcome and direct visitors. Palmer and Sabor looked down the office hallway to see if there was anything out of the ordinary.

Detective Sabor instructed Officer Lang, "I need you to get Officer Snow to come here, and then the two of you need to go carefully through each office."

Immediately, Officer Lang radioed for Officer Snow to come to the sacristy.

Palmer continued gathering information. "Father Crumbley, who has keys to the offices?"

"Lieutenant, I don't know. That would be something you would have to ask Sam Tolden. If it would help, I could start a list of who I think has keys." Father Crumbley wanted to make himself useful.

"Please do. We need to a get a hold of Mr. Tolden. I need his number. Do you have it?" Palmer looked at Father Crumbley.

"I can easily get it." Father Crumbley was prepared with paper and pen.

"I have it. Hector just gave it to me, and I was about to make the call." Detective Sabor announced.

Lieutenant Palmer gave his take-charge look. "Let me call Mr. Tolden. I have a few questions for him that need some answers." He desperately wanted information that only the Director of Administrative Services could provide.

"Here's the number." Sabor quickly wrote the number down for Palmer.

Officer Lang greeted Officer Snow, along with two CSU investigators. "Open every door. Make sure no one has entered or is in any of the offices. You're looking for a possible murder weapon or any disruption in these offices. Let me know if you find anything suspicious." Detective Sabor barked his instructions at the four of them as they put on the proper gloves.

Father Crumbley watched the officers, pulled out his office key, and gave it to Officer Lang.

Palmer was skeptical that anything would be found in the offices since the alarm had been activated. He knew there must have been a point of exit for the killer, but was uncertain if it had been through the office building. He wondered how many more avenues of entrance there were into the cathedral. "Father Crumbley, are there any other buildings that connect to the cathedral?"

"The cardinal's residence has access to the cathedral."

"Could you show me where it is?"

"I can show you, but we need to go back into the cathedral." As Father Crumbley led Palmer and Sabor back through the passageway into the sacristy, he showed them the second alarm keypad that was somewhat concealed by a statue, not of Saint Patrick, but Saint Jude.

"You may want to learn about this saint." Father Crumbley looked at Detective Sabor. Sabor was surprised by the comment but said nothing as he pulled out his notepad.

Palmer still looked for explanations. "Father Crumbley, who has keys to this door into the sacristy?"

"I believe only the priests, office staff and the maintenance personnel."

"So the sacristy is a room where there is access to the parish office and parish house without going outside?" Palmer wanted to confirm that detail with Sabor.

Father Crumbley explained. "Yes, that's true. But the parish office has an alarm—the parish house does not. I know Monsignor Triplett was looking into getting an alarm for the house, but I don't think there was any money for it."

"And the cardinal's entrance?" Palmer asked. "The cardinal informed me he can get from his residence down a passageway to his vesting room... sacristy? Did I say the word correctly?"

"Yes, the cardinal's sacristy where he vests for liturgical events at the cathedral is a level up." Father Crumbley again tried to help. "I can show you."

Palmer and Sabor followed Father Crumbley through the priest's sacristy up the stairs, turned right, walked behind the main altar, and stopped at the first door.

"This door, the cardinal's sacristy, will lead you to the cardinal's residence." Father Crumbley pointed to the door with the cardinal's coat of arms on it.

"Is the cardinal the only one who has a key to this?"

Father Crumbley hesitated before he answered. "I'm not sure. I don't have one. But again, you would have to check with Mr. Tolden."

Father Crumbley turned around looking into the church and was struck by how this was unlike any other Holy Saturday morning at the cathedral. Instead of people decorating for Easter, the cathedral was filled with police who occupied the entire building and grounds.

"Thank you, Father Crumbley. I'd like for you to go back to the parish house and inform the cardinal once my officers have finished inspecting the parish offices, I'll be back as soon as possible." Palmer looked at Father Crumbley, who was more interested in the activity in the cathedral. "Father, did you hear me?"

"I... I... certainly will." Father Crumbley slowly walked off as he continued to watch the police, surprised by how bright it was in the cathedral.

Palmer watched Father Crumbley leave, appreciative of his assistance, yet noticing the hesitancy in some of his answers. Detective Sabor was approached with information from one of the CSU investigators. Palmer, while he had the chance, called Sam Tolden.

"Hello," a muffled voice came from the phone, sounding like the person had been awakened from a sound sleep.

"Hello. Is this Sam Tolden?" Palmer asked as he found a quiet place in Our Lady's Chapel.

"Yes, it is."

"This is Lieutenant Palmer of the NYPD. Are you the Director of Administrative Services for the cathedral?"

"Yes, I am." Sam Tolden became more alert.

Sam Tolden had been Director of Administrative Services for the last two years. His twenty-five-year marriage to Jean had failed. He had two children in college, Michael and Meghan. After almost thirty years of working for the accounting firm of Earnest and Patrick, he had become unexpectedly unemployed. A faithful member of the cathedral, despite living in Hoboken, New Jersey, Sam had served on the parish finance council. When the administrator position became available, he quickly applied and was hired immediately. He was hired immediately. He was well-liked by Monsignor Triplett and over time was given more and more authority. Authority he used to his advantage.

"How can I help you, Lieutenant?" Sam asked as he grudgingly turned over in his king-size bed.

"I'm here at the cathedral, and I'm sorry to inform you that Monsignor Triplett is dead." But Palmer never found it easy to inform family or friends of the death of a loved one.

"O my God! How… how… did it happen???" Immediately Sam's eyes opened wide, as he sat up in the bed and moved the hand of the woman lying next to him off his chest.

In his usual calm voice, Palmer responded. "We're still investigating. I'd like you to come to the cathedral as soon as possible. There are some questions I need answered. How long will it take you to get here?"

"I can be there in an hour." Sam Tolden answered hurriedly, looking at the woman next to him and wondering how this was going to all play out.

"The sooner, the better." Palmer's tone conveyed real urgency. "When you arrive, it would be best to come to the parish house front door and ask for me."

Sam was thinking of the other priests in the house and fearing one of them may have been injured. "I understand. Is… is… everyone else all right?"

"Do you mean the rest of the priests?" Palmer sensed real concern in Sam's voice.

"Yes, the priests and… and… the cardinal?"

"They were not injured. Just stunned by the news."

"I'll see you in an hour." Sam abruptly ended the conversation and began to dress quickly. Looking at his phone, he realized he'd missed a call from last night, and there was a voicemail. Sam listened to the message, "He has the money." Startled, he knew the voice. He looked at the woman who loved him and wondered about their future.

Palmer left the chapel, walked past the cardinal's sacristy and noticed Sabor finishing his conversation with the CSU investigator. Sabor informed Palmer, "The crime scene investigators got the additional lighting needed to help with their work. Where the deceased was found, it looked like someone was trying to cut or saw the pew bolts off. Very strange. When they finally moved the pew, they noticed something even stranger that you need to see."

Palmer pleased with the news, told Sabor, "Tolden will be here in an hour. Let's hope he has some new information."

Hector walked over to the detectives while Palmer was still trying to figure out which cathedral staff members had keys to those doors. "Hector, do the maintenance personnel have keys to the priest's sacristy doors and the cardinal's sacristy?"

"I believe we all do, but we can't enter their homes. That takes different keys which only the priests and cardinal have." Hector remembered the conversation with Monsignor Triplett about the reason certain doors were keyed certain ways. Hector never fully understood why.

"So... can you open the cardinal's sacristy?" Palmer asked as they walked towards the door. "I understand it goes to Cardinal Flinn's residence."

Hector immediately took out his keys, unlocked and opened the door. They entered a small room with several closet doors. At the end was a door with an exit sign over it. Palmer opened it and walked into the dark, musty corridor that served as a passage from the cardinal's residence to the cathedral. He found the light switch which turned on a single light that helped guide him to another door with the cardinal's coat of arms on it. He tried opening it, only to find it locked. Upon returning, he asked Hector to once again lock the cardinal's sacristy door. Palmer was amazed and confused by the number of doors and hallways within the structure of the cathedral property.

As Hector locked the door, Palmer asked, "Hector, do you know if there is a set of master plans for this block of buildings?"

"I've never seen any," Hector quickly answered. "If there are, I'd think Mr. Tolden would have them."

"Detective Sabor, is there anything else you need from Hector?" Palmer asked.

"Not at this time," Sabor responded.

"Thanks for your assistance, Hector." Palmer allowed Hector to return to the work that needed to be done.

Sabor continued to update Palmer. "The two additional maintenance workers are here, and I need to interview them. I still need to contact the supervisor of the construction company."

As they walked towards the stairs that lead to the priests' sacristy, Palmer explained his tasks. "I need to finish interviewing the cardinal, and I still have two of the three parish priests in the house to question. The third was missing but has been located and is on his way back."

"I'll locate the construction supervisor and call you once I'm finished." Detective Sabor knew the company had posted several signs both inside and outside the cathedral to advertise their business. The blue and white signs containing the company logo, address, and telephone number were some of the best free advertisements one could get with the number of people who passed the cathedral every day.

Sabor paused. "While I have you alone, I want to talk about a possible escape route."

"What are your thoughts?" Palmer stopped to listen.

"If the murderer, or murderers, were in the church when Hector arrived, they could have easily used the scaffolding to move from the bronze front doors through the hidden passageway, down the stairs into the sacristy, and gone through the office door... provided they knew the alarm code and turned it off." Sabor knew from past investigations this was speculation.

Palmer was surprisingly impressed with the observation from Sabor. "Anything is possible at this point."

As they approached the priests' sacristy stairs, their conversation was interrupted by the arrival of Father Crumbley who informed Palmer the cardinal was waiting. The cardinal had told Father Crumbley that he would use the time to make a couple of calls. Sabor, irritated by Father Crumbley's interruption, turned, excused himself and left.

It was Palmer who walked with Father Crumbley through the passageway to return to the parish office building where they stopped at the reception desk. On the counter was the church bulletin which Palmer picked up. He discovered the cathedral staff included bookkeepers and secretaries, as well as religious education directors, a youth director, and a lay ministry coordinator, some choir and music personnel, and a few others although he did not understand the titles beside their names. He asked Father Crumbley to write a list of the offices and the people who worked in each. Grabbing a sheet of copy paper, Father Crumbley started making the list.

Palmer reviewed his notes. "Father Crumbley, I have in my notes there's choir practice this morning. Do you know if this is still on?"

"Yes, it's supposed to happen at 10:30 a.m. I'm singing "The Exsultet" tonight and was going to practice with them. Even though a deacon would normally sing it, the cathedral's permanent deacon doesn't have a strong singing voice for it, so I volunteered." Father Crumbley expressed great joy in himself for his role at the Easter Vigil. "The Exsultet," the Easter Proclamation, was a beautiful hymn of praise he humbly looked forward to singing.

Palmer dismissed the priest's obvious enthusiasm for singing and informed Father Crumbley, "The practice will have to move to after 2:00 p.m."

Father Crumbley was understandably disappointed as he hesitantly responded. "Our choir director, Dr. Andy DiBrisco and... and... the organist Brian McManius... they won't be happy." He finished writing the list of offices and the names of those who occupied them and gave it to the lieutenant.

Palmer thanked Father Crumbley and continued to give him more directions. "I need for you to call the choir director and organist when you go back to the parish house. Then inform the cardinal I'll be back shortly. Thank you for your help."

As Father Crumbley looked for the phone numbers he needed, he wondered how these musicians would react to the news of Monsignor Triplett's death. He was even more concerned with how they would react to the change of time for choir practice. Neither DiBrisco nor McManius seemed pleased when they left after last night's Good Friday service. Father Crumbley had heard from a choir member leaving practice that Dr. DiBrisco, a perfectionist, was disturbed by the mistakes made by the organist.

Before leaving the office building, Palmer thanked Father Crumbley again. Father Crumbley gave a half-hearted smile and watched one of the crime scene investigators approach the lieutenant. The investigator wanted Palmer to inspect two of the offices.

"Did you find something?" Palmer eagerly responded as they walked to the first office door. He opened the door and turned on the light.

The maple desk and credenza, along with the two high-back leather chairs, were filled with files, invoices, and miscellaneous stacks of papers. Palmer did not need to pull out the list to know who occupied the office. It was confirmed with the degree hanging on the wall. He had just spoken with him.

The CSU investigator gave his partial report to Palmer. "There seems to be some blood on the carpet near one of the chairs and beside the desk. It looks new. Pictures and samples were taken of both spots. We're still bringing in more equipment and the luminal to see what else the carpet reveals."

Palmer looked intently at the bloodstains, paused and looked around again. "Something tells me the person who occupies this office needs to answer some questions. And he might just have something to do with this murder."

"Wait until you see the second office!" The investigator was eager to show Palmer his discovery. He led the lieutenant down the short hallway around the corner to the next office.

They entered office number two, and Palmer wrote in his notes that it was larger and much neater.

The investigator began his explanation. "Once again, blood is here on the carpet next to the heavy metal visitor's chair in front of the desk. It also looks fresh. The one thing different

101

from this office compared to the rest of them is there was nothing in the trash can. All the rest of the cans had trash."

Palmer looked closely at the bloodstains, thinking out loud. "It's too bad we can't ask any questions of the person who occupied this office."

"It seems there is also blood around the desk chair. But I couldn't find any on or around the desk legs." The investigator had marked off the area.

Palmer walked around the office of Monsignor Triplett. The bookshelves and walls were filled with accomplishments, awards and pictures of various civil and religious leaders including the mayor, governor, senator of New York and the three cardinals he served with. On the wall behind the desk chair was the exquisitely framed decree for his honorary title of Monsignor. Also hanging on the wall was a letter from Mayor Bloomberg welcoming him as the new rector of the cathedral, and a picture of Monsignor Triplett with Pope John Paul II at the Vatican. As he looked at the nearly empty desk, he noticed three words written on Monsignor Triplett's yellow legal tablet— *key, stone* and *annulment*. Palmer wondered if this could be a clue to Monsignor's death. Pulling out his notepad, he wrote down the three words: *key, stone* and *annulment.*

"Have you taken any pictures in here?" Palmer looked at the crime scene investigator.

"Not yet."

Palmer interrupted the investigator. "Get the pictures and blood samples. Once you're finished, make sure you bag this notepad as possible evidence." Palmer believed this was not an office, but a conference room where Monsignor Triplett must have met with people. He wondered where his working office was.

As he checked his watch, Palmer calmly informed the investigator, "I'm going back into the parish house. When you're finished with the offices, please let me know."

Needing some fresh air, Palmer exited the office building to 51st Street where he noticed the cathedral gift shop across the street. People were outside looking through the huge glass windows as they waited for the shop to open so they could purchase some last-minute Easter items. As he turned the corner onto Madison, two individuals sat holding a cardboard sign asking for help. When he passed them, he radioed for one of the officers to come and escort them off the property. He also called the squad room and asked for additional detectives since the list of those who needed to be questioned was growing. Walking to the parish house entry, he ran into a young, obviously anxious, individual carrying a duffel bag.

"I'm Lieutenant Palmer, and you are?" He looked into the priest's red eyes.

"I'm Father Juan Morales."

"Good to have you home." Palmer observed at a nervous young priest as Juan entered the four-digit code to enter the parish house. "I need you to take a seat in the living room with the other two priests. I'll speak to you shortly." Palmer was pleased to know the priest he needed to question had just walked into the parish house.

Father Morales approached the living room, and suddenly realized he was still carrying his duffel bag. When he entered the room, he was wary of the reception he would receive. Father Crumbley was finishing a conversation on his cell phone, and Monsignor Black was sipping a cup of coffee. The expressions on their faces and the haunting eyes looking at him were enough to tell him of their disappointment. Trying to avoid any further eye contact with either of them, Father Morales dropped his duffel bag and looked down. He was uncertain what to do or say. He calmly walked over to the window to see a cab driver dropping off a local reporter. As Father Crumbley put his phone in his pocket, total silence prevailed in the room. Father Morales waited for one of the priests to speak. But when neither did, he knew he had to make the first move. His trembling voice muttered, "I'm sorry."

Monsignor Black knew the young associate was scared but seemed sincere in his words, even though this was not the first time this had happened. "Juan, you have issues to deal with, but right now we have to share with you what we know about the death of Monsignor Triplett. Why don't you come over and sit on the couch?" Monsignor Black spoke as if talking to a son.

Father Crumbley walked over to Father Morales to hug him, knowing he was hurting. Father Morales simply started to cry. Together they went over to sit on the couch.

Monsignor Black and Father Crumbley shared what they knew about the death of Monsignor Triplett. Each one helped the other when the words became too hard to express. They realized the impact that Monsignor Triplett had in each of their lives.

While the conversation was going on in the living room, Palmer returned to the library and apologized to the cardinal for the interruption.

"That is quite all right." The cardinal felt a little tired. "I used the time to make a few phone calls to some priests and a few of the archdiocese personnel about the terrible news."

As Palmer took a seat at the ornate mahogany table across from the cardinal, he looked directly at the Archbishop of the Archdiocese of New York, "Your Eminence, I hope you had time to think about my question. Were you going to move Father Morales?"

With his hands folded, he slowly moved his thumbs back and forth pensively. The cardinal looked at the lieutenant and explained, "I was planning to move Father Morales after I talked with him."

"It appears you'll have your chance. He just walked into the house with a gym bag in his hand." Palmer opened his notebook, speculating to himself that the priest had been out all night.

"These are discussions as a bishop and cardinal that I do not enjoy but must have." Cardinal Flinn spoke calmly, but the wrinkles on his forehead showed the difficulty he had with these conversations.

"What discussion is that?" The lieutenant observed the difficulty the cardinal had in answering these questions.

"Inappropriate behavior from one of the sheep I shepherd." Cardinal Flinn's voice softened.

"What do you mean?"

"I think it best if you talk with Father Morales before I do. It should be his story to tell you." Cardinal Flinn slowly removed his handkerchief from his back pocket to wipe his face.

"I'll respect what you say, Your Eminence, but if there is something to help this investigation, I have to know." Palmer tried to be compassionate in his words and facial expressions, but he wanted and needed answers to help him with the investigation.

"I will talk with you further about this once you have talked with Father Morales." Cardinal Flinn heard the parish house doorbell ring, hoping it was one of the individuals he had called, so he might have a break from the lieutenant's questions.

Palmer reviewed his notes. "I'll interview Father Morales next."

Before they could continue their conversation, someone knocked on the door. Father Crumbley slowly opened the door and made eye contact with the cardinal and lieutenant. He told them the police commissioner had arrived with the Director of Media and Communication for the archdiocese, Donald Armenti.

"Thank you, Father Crumbley. If you could find a place for the police commissioner and your communication director to meet, I'd appreciate it. We'll be out in just a few more minutes." Palmer instructed, unhappy with the interruption.

Returning his attention to the cardinal, the lieutenant wanted to dig deeper. "Did Monsignor Triplett confide in you?"

"I am not sure what you are asking. I had great respect for him, and I believe he did for me. I would ask his opinion, and he was straightforward with me. Confide might not be the correct word—it was trust. I think this is why we were able to get along so well with one another. I trusted him in the decisions he made here at the cathedral." Cardinal Flinn answered while recalling the advice Monsignor Triplett had offered.

"Would he have confided in someone else?"

Without hesitation, the cardinal responded, "Yes... Bishop Newsome."

"How can I get in touch with Bishop Newsome?"

"I can call him for you if you would like."

"Is he far from here?"

"He is on the Upper West side at Holy Name of Jesus Parish off 96th."

"Before we end our conversation, can you tell me anything else about Monsignor Triplett that might help the investigation?"

As the cardinal straightened his pectoral cross around his neck, he thought for a moment before speaking. "His only living relative is his brother. I know Monsignor was having some personal financial problems, but I am not sure where they came from."

Palmer was surprised at this information. "And how do you know this?"

"He told me about it several years ago." Cardinal Flinn watched as the lieutenant wrote on his notepad again.

"Do you know if he had any medical problems?"

"He had high blood pressure. He was taking medication for it and informed me that as long as he took the medication, he would be fine," the cardinal explained. He knew the last time he had discussed it with him, the doctor had increased

Monsignor Triplett's medication, as his blood pressure was higher than the doctor liked.

Seeing the cardinal becoming more relaxed with the questions, Palmer knew the next question would be difficult, so he looked directly at the cardinal. "As the owner of this parish house, I need your permission to examine Monsignor Triplett's living quarters."

Confidently, Cardinal Flinn was quick with his response. "You have my permission to examine any of the rooms here at Saint Patrick's. I expect everyone to cooperate with you fully in the aftermath of this tragedy. If you have any problems, please let me know."

"Thank you, Your Eminence, for your cooperation. I know you have much to do, but I would ask that if you think of anything, anything at all, please call me on my cell phone." Palmer gave him his business card. He then closed the notebook and stood out of respect for the cardinal.

"I will be more than happy to." The cardinal accepted the card and carefully placed it in his pants pocket as he slowly tried to stand.

Palmer looked at this important man in the Roman Catholic Church and felt the weight that must be on his shoulders. He reached over to help the cardinal stand. The cardinal appreciated the assistance and thanked him. "These bones are getting old."

"We're all getting old," Palmer remarked as he picked up his notepad. "Before you go, Your Eminence, I have one more question. Do you have a key to the doors in the cathedral?"

"I have a key I use to get into the office and the cathedral." Cardinal Flinn moved toward the door. He was thankful this interview was ending. Then looking at the lieutenant, he said, "It opens the doors I need to get into."

Palmer followed the cardinal to the door. "If I have any more questions, where will I find you?"

"I was going to go back to my residence and work on a statement with Donald Armenti, but I must first say hello to

107

the police commissioner. Maybe it would be easier if the communications people meet in my residence. I have a conference room I can make available," Cardinal Flinn suggested.

"Thank you again, Your Eminence." Lieutenant Palmer shook the cardinal's hand and opened the door.

As the men turned to walk down the hallway, they both heard the police commissioner and Donald Armenti coming up the stairs, discussing the protocol for the press conference.

"Commissioner Timberbank, I believe you know His Eminence, Cardinal Flinn?" Lieutenant Palmer began the introductions although he already knew the answer as they returned to the library.

The commissioner replied, "Yes, Your Eminence, I'm so sorry for your loss. Donald and I were working out the details for the press conference. Normally, we would have the press conference at the station. But since many of the reporters have all gathered outside, if it's okay with you, we'll conduct it in the cathedral. With the cold and damp weather and the possibility of rain, I think it would be easier to get everyone in place and make the necessary statements. But we won't take any questions. We'll update the press as information becomes available. I suggest a possible second press conference at city hall at 4:00 p.m. We'll move out of the cathedral, so you'll have time to prepare for Easter. I'm sure it's probably one of your busiest days. How does this sound to you, Your Eminence?" Serving in his third year as commissioner, and twenty-fourth year in the New York police department, Timberbank was a highly respected, take-control person who was a stickler for details.

"It sounds fine." The cardinal saw Donald nodding slightly, indicating his approval of the commissioner's plans.

"Are you going to take care of the location in the cathedral for the press conference?" Commissioner Timberbank looked at Donald Armenti, who was about a foot shorter than the commissioner.

Donald knew that was his cue. "Yes, I was suggesting we do it about halfway down the center aisle, avoiding the sanctuary and crime scene area. It will also show much of the restoration."

"I like the location," the cardinal added. "We can enter from the sanctuary, make our way toward the podium and leave without having to face any reporters afterward."

"Is there anything else we need to discuss?" the commissioner asked as he looked toward the other three.

Cardinal Flinn suggested, "I want to offer the conference room in my residence for us to meet prior to the press conference."

Commissioner Timberbank confirmed the suggestion. "Thank you. First, I want to talk with the lieutenant and detectives and then see the crime scene."

"Okay. Commissioner, if you are finished with Donald, I would like his assistance with the formal statement from the archdiocese." Cardinal Flinn stretched his head to make eye contact with the commissioner.

Commissioner Timberbank directed his question to the cardinal. "Yes, I believe we have covered everything at this point. Your Eminence, I presume it will be something I can read?"

Cardinal Flinn was quick to reply, "Yes, and we will make it available for the media."

"When you have the statement ready, I want to run it by our public relation liaison, Karen Zirpoli. She should be here shortly. We can have her look at it with you and Donald," the commissioner suggested.

Mr. Armenti interjected, "I have no problems regarding who reads the statement. I want to make sure we agree with the facts as we know them now. And from what I've been told, these are the facts: that around 7:30 a.m. this Saturday morning, Monsignor Triplett's body was found in the cathedral. By all indications, someone murdered him. The Archdiocese of New York is cooperating fully with the New York City Police Department. We pray for the soul of Monsignor Triplett and his family. Do we have their names?"

"There is only one living family member, his brother, whose name is Thomas although he goes by Thom." Cardinal Flinn remembered Monsignor Triplett mentioning him.

"Thank you." Armenti made the notation and continued. "And his brother, Thomas or Thom. Your Eminence, would you like to say something about the Easter schedule?"

"Good idea." Cardinal Flinn appreciated the insight of his communication director.

"The Mass schedule will remain the same, and I will celebrate the Easter Vigil and Masses the good Monsignor would have celebrated. Perhaps that can be added to the statement?" The cardinal asked. As he did so, he bowed his head momentarily and realized how important the upcoming ordinations to the priesthood would be now that there was one less priest in the archdiocese.

"I would recommend you do so for the parishioners and visitors in the city this weekend. Be assured, Your Eminence that there will be additional uniform officers around the cathedral tonight and tomorrow." Commissioner Timberbank looked at Palmer to make sure it would happen.

"Thank you, Commissioner."

"I look forward to your statement." Commissioner Timberbank placed his hand gently on the cardinal's shoulder. "Again, I'm sorry for your loss."

Cardinal Flinn appreciated the commissioner's gesture and words. "Thank you. The official statement from the archdiocese will be ready within the hour. When you are finished, you are welcome to come over to my residence."

The commissioner appreciated the cardinal's invitation.

The cardinal politely said his goodbyes and walked towards the living room with Palmer.

When Cardinal Flinn entered, he looked to see how the priests were doing—noticing each was sitting by himself. He announced he would like to meet with them once they all had been interviewed. Palmer then asked Father Morales to follow him to the library. The cardinal looked Father Morales in the eye as disappointment radiated from both of their faces.

The cardinal returned to his residence and wondered what information Father Morales would reveal.

As Palmer approached the library, one of the crime scene investigators told him all the parish offices were cleared. There was nothing new to report. The blood samples had been taken to the crime lab for analysis. Palmer could only speculate whose blood was found and was eager to interview the occupant of the cluttered office.

Chapter 9

Before walking up the seven brick steps to the back door of Holy Name of Jesus Parish House, Father David O'Hara nervously located his key for the metal door which needed a new paint job. Struggling to get the key out of his pants pocket, he prayed a Hail Mary asking for the strength and guidance he would need when confronted by the other two residents. When he opened the door, his hands were shaking... the time for thinking was over. As soon as he entered the large kitchen, Father O'Hara met Bishop Newsome and Monsignor McFadden sitting at the kitchen table. He resisted looking at them. But once he did, Father O'Hara realized they knew.

"Good Morning, Bishop..." Father O'Hara fretfully began. But before he could get another word out, he was interrupted.

"David, I need you to go to your room, do whatever you need to do to get yourself cleaned up and in your clerics. Then meet me upstairs in my study." The bishop spoke with a calm but forceful voice.

Father O'Hara felt the knot in his stomach. He looked at the bishop and nervously replied, "I'll be there in fifteen minutes." Without saying another word, he took his gym bag, left the kitchen and went to his bedroom.

It surprised Monsignor McFadden how quickly the mood changed with the entrance of Father O'Hara. "You didn't even give him a chance to speak!"

The bishop, unhappy with Father O'Hara's actions stayed calm. "I didn't want to hear anything from him, since, at this moment, I am thoroughly disappointed in him."

Monsignor McFadden knew one quality he admired about Bishop Newsome was his ability to remain calm when trying to help someone. He held in his anger to avoid making a reactionary decision. Knowing the bishop needed to talk it out, Monsignor continued, "What are you going to do?"

The bishop didn't answer right away. He pushed his coffee cup aside and dropped his head to the table for a few seconds before he looked at Monsignor McFadden. "That is the million-dollar question, and I better come up with the best solution, or it may cost the archdiocese." The bishop knew the scandal the archdiocese could face if what he thought had happened became public.

"I know in past situations, we sent priests off for six-month sabbaticals. A separation from one another for a period of time may be good for both. It would give them a chance to pray and discern whether they can live celibate lives. Is that what you're thinking?" Monsignor McFadden hoped the bishop wouldn't be too harsh.

The bishop slowly stood, clutching the kitchen chair. He wanted to throw the chair across the room but knew he had to remain calm. "Right now, I'm not thinking. I need to calm myself down. I thought this was all put aside in his life. Now I fear their relationship may be more important than their priesthood. I'm not sure a six-month sabbatical will do either of them any good. But a separation would remove the problem from the archdiocese."

Having seen the struggle in the bishop's eyes many times before and knowing how proactive Bishop Newsome had been with other priests and personnel in the archdiocese, Monsignor McFadden chose his words carefully before he spoke. "Be calm in your approach with David. He is well-liked and has the potential to be a good priest. Do you really need to decide today? You are good at being the caring father, and tomorrow is Easter." Monsignor McFadden cautiously pleaded again for Father O'Hara.

The bishop looked at his friend and sighed. "You're right. I need to listen and remain calm. I suppose I could wait until after Easter to make a decision with the cardinal." He moved slowly to the hallway door, and his mood became very meditative. "I think before David comes to my office, I'll go to my chapel and pray to the Holy Spirit for guidance."

"I'll be praying for you." Monsignor McFadden cleaned off the table preparing to return to his room to work on his Easter homily.

The bishop turned to enter the hallway. "Thanks. I'll see you for lunch. Are we still going out?"

"Yes, we have reservations at your favorite place Paola's. Monsignor cautiously asked, "Is David still invited?"

"I'm sure he'll let you know after our conversation if he wants to join us." The bishop took a deep breath as he started down the hallway and passed Father O'Hara's room, where he heard the shower running. Monsignor McFadden was right with his words. Priests who showed inappropriate behavior with adults were given sabbaticals to a treatment facility for an evaluation. The center provided the recommendations. Then the bishop, or the religious superior, would determine the next steps for the priests. Often it was outpatient therapy that could take several months or years and included periodic review meetings with a panel of priests. The bishop had his successes, but there were also the failures. But this case was different for Bishop Newsome. He had guided Father O'Hara through his discernment to priesthood. They had a long-standing personal relationship.

The bishop walked up the steps to his suite and the first room he came to was his favorite—his chapel. He entered, knelt and prayed.

David O'Hara was the third son of Todd, now a senator, and Kristen O'Hara. When Bishop Newsome was Father Newsome, he was the pastor at Saint Teresa of the Infant Jesus Parish on Staten Island where the O'Hara family faithfully attended church each Sunday. David graduated from the parish grade school, number one in his class. He was an altar server all the way through his senior year of high school. Active in the church youth group, he attended many local and national events. In his senior year, his peers voted him as the Outstanding Youth in his class.

Father Newsome spoke about the life of a diocesan priest many times at the O'Hara family home or when David was serving at the altar. Father was planting the seed hoping that David would be open to the call. They had many talks and developed a trusting friendship. After graduating from high school, David seriously considered entering the seminary.

When David discussed his plans with his parents, it troubled his father. He had hoped David would be the one to succeed him in the family's import-export business. David had worked many summers with his dad, but his heart was never in the business. He knew his two older brothers would be much better at it. David tried many times to tell his dad this truth, but was afraid of seeing disappointment in his dad's eyes. With his father focused more on his bid for senator than on his son's emotional dilemma, David was thankful for the relationship he had with Father Newsome.

When David was caught by the police in his first gay sexual encounter, it was Father Newsome he called. The priest had kept the secret between the two of them. He knew David's parents, and Father Newsome was uncertain of their response if they found out. Now, kneeling in his chapel, the bishop remembered that night and wondered if not telling David's parents had been a mistake. Years had passed, and now Bishop Newsome was faced with perhaps another scandal for the church and the crisis of a priest who would not remain celibate.

As Bishop Newsome knelt, he looked up and asked for Christ's strength, as he had done so many times before. He would spend as much time in here as he possibly could, asking for guidance on the decisions he would make for the church. A knock on the door interrupted the bishop. He ended his prayers with the "Our Father," stood, and composed himself. "Come in."

As Father O'Hara opened the door to the chapel, the light shown on the silhouette of the young man. For the bishop, it was not a priest but the young altar boy he had known over the years. Standing at the door, dressed in his black clerics, David was fearful of taking a step. He waited until the bishop spoke. For as many times as he had sat with the bishop in his suite, this time would be different.

"Let's go to my office." Bishop Newsome stood and motioned for David to follow him to the next room, which was his home office. It was cluttered with books, file folders, and papers. The bishop moved a stack off one the two chairs. "David, please take a seat." Bishop Newsome motioned for David to take a seat in front of the desk. The bishop went over to his desk and moved another stack of folders on the desk so he could better see David. He then turned on the desk lamp which brightened the room. He purposely sat behind the desk instead of his normal recliner since he knew this discussion would be in his role as a bishop rather than as a friend.

"Thank you," David nervously said. As the bishop sat in the straight-backed chair, Father O'Hara noticed the great tension in the man he admired.

Bishop Newsome leaned forward with his hands clasped and turned the ring on his finger. It had been a gift from David's family when he was consecrated as bishop. He looked directly at Father O'Hara and with a tone of voice that seemed sterner than usual began. "I need you to be totally honest with me, David. There can be no bullshit. I need to know where you were last night. If I find out your story is not the total truth, then I will be forced to take even harsher action with you. You must realize how difficult this is for me... as your friend, your former pastor, and now as your bishop."

Father O'Hara had a difficult time looking at the bishop as he listened. He was ready to speak but couldn't because of the dryness in his mouth. He simply bowed his head in remorse.

The bishop slowly leaned back in his chair and waited calmly for Father O'Hara to say something.

Father O'Hara raised his head, wet his lips, leaned closer to the desk, looked directly at the bishop and spoke with a quiet voice. "I realize your difficulty, and I'm very sorry that I am putting you in this situation." He wet his lips once again and took a deep breath. "I'll tell you the truth about everything. And when I am finished, I'll want to go to confession to you for my sins." Relieved to get the words out, Father O'Hara sat back in the chair, nervously waiting for the bishop to respond.

Bishop Newsome returned upright in his chair, pulled a yellow tablet from a stack of folders, and with pen in hand was ready to take notes. "Let me hear the truth, David."

David had no choice but to tell the truth. He prayed Father Juan Morales was doing the same.

"As you know, I left here last night with my gym bag telling you I was going to the gym, but I... I... never went to the gym." Father O'Hara gained his strength to speak, and told the bishop the truth about his first sin from last night. Looking directly at the bishop, he continued. "I went to the Michelangelo hotel to meet Father Morales. We set this up a few days ago. We hadn't seen each other in several weeks. He arrived first and then called me to tell me what room he was in."

"What was the room number?"

"It was 1260. Why is it important?" Father O'Hara was surprised by the bishop's question. He removed his

117

handkerchief from his back pocket to wipe his lips and forehead.

"Just curious." The bishop wrote it down. "Continue... with the truth."

"I spent the night with Juan. Since neither of us had any commitments this morning, we turned our cell phones off so we wouldn't be disturbed. We told no one that we were getting together. We knew it was forbidden, but we wanted to be together and see each other before Easter. When I turned my phone on, saw your text and heard your voicemail, I knew we were in trouble and had to tell the truth. We can no longer hide our feelings for one another. I... we... have to face the consequences. Now you have the truth." Father O'Hara was relieved, although tears formed in his eyes and a feeling of shame showed on his face. He took his handkerchief and wiped his eyes and blew his nose. He then held the handkerchief tightly and formed it into a ball in his hand as he slowly made eye contact once again with the bishop.

Seeing that Father O'Hara had composed himself, the bishop asked, "So is this the story Father Morales will be telling the cardinal at the cathedral?"

"I told him we had to tell the truth. I was very emphatic about this. I hope he's doing just that. He's worried and scared. He told no one he is gay, and he's terrified about how his parents will react. You know how difficult it has been for mine."

"Your parents have never talked with me about your sexual preference." The bishop turned his eyes away from Father O'Hara and reviewed what he had written. He wanted to make sure he had all the facts and was ready to ask a few more questions when his cell phone rang.

"Excuse me for a minute. I need to take this call. Before I answer, I'm asking you to sit in my chapel and pray." The bishop was hoping to see remorse by the priest as he pondered what the punishment should be. He knew he must

118

be fair. Many times the priest had given himself a punishment more severe than the bishop had considered.

Father O'Hara slowly got up, thankful for the interruption, and held on to the chair before taking the steps to go next door to the chapel. As he entered the small room, he knelt down on the same prie-dieu the bishop had used earlier. He looked up at the face of Christ. As he did, he felt his phone vibrating and wondered if it was Father Morales. He was afraid to look.

Bishop Newsome got up from his chair, closed the office door, and looked at his phone. He realized it was the cardinal on the other end. "Bishop Newsome speaking."

"George. How are things at Holy Name of Jesus?" The cardinal asked, trying to make light conversation before dealing with the situation of Father Morales and Father O'Hara.

The bishop was thankful for the good relationship he had with the cardinal. "Not how I thought I would be spending Holy Saturday morning. How are things at the cathedral?"

The cardinal sat in his oversized recliner and kicked off his shoes. "I have just finished being questioned. Now they are questioning the other priests in the house. Not my typical Holy Saturday morning either. I believe they want to talk with you, too."

"Me? Why me?" The bishop was quite surprised.

"Because I told them that Monsignor Triplett confided in you."

"Thanks for the heads-up," the bishop sarcastically remarked, unsure of where the conversation was going as he pulled a yellow tablet off the desk and sat in his recliner.

"Did Father O'Hara come back to Holy Name of Jesus?" The cardinal asked.

"Yes... Yes, he did." The bishop felt a sense of relief because he believed Father O'Hara had shared the truth with him, but uncertain what the cardinal knew or didn't know.

119

The cardinal realized how difficult the conversation would be, knowing the relationship between the bishop and Father O'Hara. "Did you talk with him?"

"I just finished listening to his story. I sent him to the chapel to think about an appropriate punishment for himself?"

"Were they together?" The cardinal was searching for more information.

"Yes... yes, unfortunately they were." The bishop struggled to get the words out. "They were at the Michelangelo Hotel."

"What are you going to do?"

Bishop Newsome hadn't even thought of what the proper punishment should be. "I don't know. What are your thoughts?"

Surprised by the bishop's response, the cardinal sat up in his recliner. "I need to talk with Father Morales. Let me listen to his story and see if it matches what Father O'Hara said. I think I have a way to remove him from the cathedral that will be seen as positive for him and will not cause any harm to the church. I just do not need another scandal. Neither the church nor any of us needs this type of publicity. Dealing with the murder of Monsignor Triplett is enough headline for now."

The bishop could hear the disappointment in the cardinal's voice, for he knew how much the cardinal tried to be a good shepherd to his priests. Before the bishop could respond, the cardinal lamented. "Why today, of all times? Could we not have one Easter where the focus was on the Risen Christ rather than on the sins of our priests?"

Bishop Newsome had similar feelings as he listened to the cardinal. "Okay. I'll ask Father O'Hara to meet with us at the chancery on Monday."

"How about Tuesday?" The cardinal knew he already planned to be away with some friends. "Hopefully, I am taking Monday off and will not be going in."

"Tuesday it will be. What are you thinking for Monsignor Triplett's funeral?"

"I have to talk with his brother. Monsignor Triplett's body will need to be released from the coroner's office, so I would say maybe as early as next Thursday or as late as Saturday."

Bishop Newsome returned to his desk and located the archdiocesan calendar. "I'm just looking at the archdiocesan in-house calendar and see we are both away next Saturday."

The cardinal knew of his commitment next Saturday. "I have to return a favor to Cardinal Johnson in Boston and promised to speak at the seminary. What wonderful timing!"

"You will be treated to a good meal." Bishop Newsome joked, knowing how much the cardinal enjoyed good food.

"You are right." The cardinal quickly returned to the issue at hand. "I will be back in touch after I have spoken with Father Morales."

"I'll look at options we have for these two. They are well-liked where they are serving. They just need to keep their zippers up. As much as you and I have both talked with them, I thought they would have listened." Bishop Newsome was thoroughly frustrated with these two priests.

The cardinal detected the bishop's frustration. "We need to keep talking with them. And let us pray to the Holy Spirit to give us the guidance we need."

"Indeed! Let me know how your talk goes with Father Morales and if you reach any decision." The bishop looked at his desk and realized he had other issues that needed resolving if he were to have any time away after Easter.

The cardinal moved to his desk and sat down in his chair facing his computer. "I will. Right now, I need to work on the statement for the press conference. Talk with you soon."

As they ended their conversation, Bishop Newsome returned to his notepad and reviewed the information Father O'Hara had told him. He wanted a few more facts but realized this time he could no longer protect Father O'Hara from his indiscretions.

Father O'Hara was still in the chapel wondering what was happening with Father Morales. He couldn't resist any longer and checked his phone. There was a call from his mom. He had mixed emotions. He wanted to talk with his mom but also wanted to hear from Father Morales.

While kneeling before the Blessed Sacrament and trying to remain calm, a fear suddenly came over him that made him realize that everything he had worked for, prayed about and was living for would change. He knew Bishop Newsome would continue to ask questions to get all the facts. He had to be prepared; he knew his future was uncertain. He looked at his phone again, hoping he would hear from Juan, but there was no message. He thought about sending him a text, but he heard the bishop approaching and quickly put the phone away.

The bishop walked into the chapel with his yellow pad ready to continue. "Father O'Hara, please sit." The bishop took his seat in his normal chair. Bishop Newsome loved his simple chapel containing a small altar, a tabernacle for the Blessed Sacrament, two chairs along the back wall, and a kneeler in the center of the room.

"I want to ask you a few more questions and, because of the seriousness of your situation, it probably is good we are doing this in front of the Blessed Sacrament allowing the Lord's presence to give both of us the strength we need to find a proper resolution." The bishop looked at the Blessed Sacrament and then at his yellow pad, feeling calmer being in the chapel.

"Like I said, I've told you the truth." Father O'Hara reassured the bishop as he sat next to him.

"I am thankful for your honesty, David. But I'm not sure it will save you this time. Do you understand what I am saying to you?" Bishop Newsome voiced was filled with great concern as he placed his hand on David's shoulder.

"Yes..." Father O'Hara spoke nervously as tears began to form again."

"Was this the first time you were at the Michelangelo Hotel?"

"No, it wasn't." Father O'Hara easily said, believing the bishop already knew the answer

"How many times would you say you've been there in the past year?"

Father O'Hara, wiped away the tears from his eyes, held his head down and used his fingers, trying to remember the times they had met. "I believe it's been... three times."

"And every time Father Morales made the reservation?"

"Yes."

"And every time the reservation was under his name?"

"No, he didn't use his name."

"Was it under your name?" The bishop looked directly at Father O'Hara hoping it had not been.

"No." Father O'Hara felt a knot slowly build in his stomach.

The bishop was confused. What name did the priest use? He cautiously asked, "Each time the reservation was under a different name?"

"No... no... it was the same name." Father O'Hara nervously responded, fearful of the next question.

"Do you know what name Father Morales used to register at the Michelangelo?"

Father O'Hara looked at the bishop, knowing he probably already knew the answer to his own question. He figured that once he said the name, there was nothing the bishop could do or want to do for him.

"He used your name."

Chapter 10

Father Juan Morales nervously sat in the library waiting for the investigator to question him. He had to tell the truth. He knew there would be another questioning session with the cardinal, probably more difficult than with the investigator. He only wished he knew what was happening with Father O'Hara.

As he was waiting, he reflected on his encounter with Monsignor Triplett last night. Before the Good Friday service, Monsignor Triplett had entered Father Juan's bedroom for a chat. As the monsignor sat down on the unmade bed, he saw the gym bag. He also saw Father Juan nervously sitting at his desk, making sure the computer screen was not visible and then quickly turning it off.

"You're going to the gym?" Monsignor Triplett asked out of curiosity.

"I was planning on going out after the Good Friday service." Father Morales looked directly into monsignor's eyes making the statement, knowing it was a lie.

"Cut the bullshit. You're going to meet him, aren't you?" Monsignor Triplett shocked Father Juan with those words.

Father Morales avoided eye contact as he tried to move things cautiously from his desk into one of the drawers. "Going to meet whom?"

"You think I am blind. I knew what was happening when Father O'Hara was here. You can deny it all you want, but I know. Don't deny you two are lovers." Monsignor Triplett bit his tongue, not wanting to explode as he asked the question.

"We did nothing here to bring shame to the Catholic Church. We have always tried to stay away from each other. We know it's wrong, but the truth is... the truth is..." He would get the words out finally—"We love each other!" There it was... he had said it. For the first time, Father Morales was emotionally expressing his true feelings for Father O'Hara. As he looked at Monsignor Triplett, there was a brief sense of relief but a nervousness of uncertainty.

There was that moment of silence between the two as they looked at one another. Monsignor had seen the signs before with others, but this was different. For the first time, Father Morales was admitting it.

"Then I need to give you some advice," Monsignor Triplett began. "I don't care what you do with your personal life, but when it interferes with your professional life and becomes public knowledge—which it will—I will have no sympathy for you." As much as he wanted to show compassion for his associate, he couldn't. He had to be the one to try and try again to show how this behavior could hurt Father Morales, the church, and others if continued. To make sure Father Morales heard him, Monsignor repeated it: "When it interferes with your personal life and becomes public knowledge... you will be removed from your position for the good of the parish and the good of the Universal Catholic Church."

Father Morales always respected the insight he had received from Monsignor Triplett. But now that he had told him the truth, he defended his actions by standing at his desk and confidently saying, "I'm not letting it interfere with my priesthood. In fact, I think it's making me a better priest! I have someone I can share my joys and struggles with."

"That may be, but one day you and Father O'Hara will get caught. You need to end it tonight!" Monsignor spoke with a voice of authority as he stood and looked directly at Father Morales.

Father Morales didn't want to hear what Monsignor was saying to him. Again, he tried to defend his relationship with Father O'Hara. "We hardly see one another. Each of us is so busy. We talk on the phone but have not had the chance to get together. Now we have an opportunity to meet tonight because nothing is happening in the church tomorrow morning."

Monsignor was not moved by what he heard and became more frustrated in his attempt to help Father Morales. "You don't get it. All it's going to take is one person... just one person... seeing something inappropriate between the two of you, and... he took a deep breath... it's over... it's over for both of you. You will be shipped away to some institution. You will be separated from one another. You may even lose your priesthood. Is he worth it?" Monsignor Triplett bluntly asked.

"But I love him. He has been the best thing in my priesthood. He has helped me to grow as a person. He has helped me to grow in my faith. All you do is demand and order me around. You have never listened or even cared about me as a person or as a priest," Father Morales insisted.

Monsignor Triplett tried to understand and walked over to Father Morales, "I do care, but in a way that will make you stronger as a person of faith. I have made sure you have a good structure, so you will have the tools you'll need to go out and minister for years to come and hopefully be able to mentor others."

"These are the first words of affirmation I have heard from you." Father Morales' eyes began to fill with tears as he looked at the monsignor.

"Affirmation has never been one of my strong qualities," Monsignor Triplett said.

"With all due respect, you are a terrible mentor. Haven't you seen how depressed I've been? This was not what I was called to, having you as a dictator over me." Father Morales saw the opportunity to express his feelings to Monsignor Triplett.

It was a familiar word to the monsignor. "You're not the first to call me a dictator. I'm sorry if you feel I've been a dictator to you, and I'm sorry to hear you are depressed. But you've hardly talked to me either. I may have given you things to do, but I don't feel I required too much. It's just that the last few weeks have been difficult for me." Monsignor acknowledged his own shortcomings, as tears rolled down his face. "Will you forgive me?"

At that moment, Father Morales was dumbfounded. He had never seen Monsignor Triplett cry and only a few times show any emotion at all. After giving him a piece of his mind, now all of a sudden, he felt sorry for Monsignor.

"Monsignor Triplett, these last weeks have been difficult for me also... As a priest, I forgive you, but I cannot forget... You are a good priest, but you don't treat your associates as your helpers or even as your friends. We are more like your servants." Father Morales couldn't believe that he was being so blunt and honest with Monsignor Triplett.

Monsignor needed to sit down. He returned to the bed and took a deep breath before speaking. "Again, I am sorry if you've felt used as an associate. Thank you for having the courage to speak to me openly. I always want my associates to do so. Sorry if I never communicated that to you."

Father Morales sat back down in his desk chair, speechless over how the conversation had gone. He became more sympathetic as he listened to Monsignor Triplett.

Rubbing his hands together, Monsignor Triplett looked at Father Morales. "Juan, there are some things happening here I should probably make you aware of. Once we get past Holy Week, and you return from Rome, I'll fill you in. Then I think we should have a meeting with all the priest and get some

127

things out in the open to help us all be better ministers to the community and to one another."

"I look forward to it." Father Morales remained calm.

"I do have to tell you something that may have an impact on your future here at Saint Patrick's. I have requested a move for you. Do you want me to talk to the cardinal about you staying?" Monsignor realized this was one of the few times he had ever told one of his associates that he had requested a move. He was pleased with himself in doing so, uncertain if it was the right decision.

Father Morales didn't know what to say or do. He took a moment, looked at Monsignor Triplett and asked, "Can I think on this? Can we talk before I leave for Rome?"

"Sure. I want you to be happy and a good priest. I want to help, but you also must be willing to make sacrifices. One of these is by staying home tonight," Monsignor Triplett strongly suggested.

"I don't know if I can. I... I need to see David... Father O'Hara."

"We cannot be people of the flesh. We have to rise above it. You need to ask for God's strength and graces before you leave this house. I hope you will." Monsignor Triplett got up slowly from the bed. "I'll see you tomorrow. I have to go back over to the cathedral." And with that, Monsignor left the room and headed to the cathedral.

That was the last conversation Monsignor Triplett and Father Morales had.

Now sitting and waiting for the investigator, Father Morales wondered what the future conversations would have been like with Monsignor Triplett if he had been able to stay at Saint Patrick's. He was feeling the loss of someone who had, for the first time, opened up to him, as he had to Monsignor. He was mentally asking himself several questions. What if he hadn't gone out last night? Would he remain or leave the cathedral? What was he going to tell the investigator regarding the things happening at the cathedral? Why had

Monsignor gone back into the church last night? Why hadn't he asked Monsignor?

Father Morales was still engrossed in these bothersome questions when the door opened, and Palmer walked in, wondering where to begin his questioning with Father Morales.

"Hi. I'm Lieutenant Will Palmer from the New York Police Department." He showed his badge to Father Morales.

"I am Father Juan Morales." He stood, knowing they had already met, but thought it important to introduce himself again.

"Are you aware someone murdered Monsignor Steven Triplett sometime last night or early this morning in the cathedral?" Palmer began as he put away his badge and took out his notebook. He took a seat across from Father Morales.

Nervously Father Morales sat back down. "Yes, I was told that when I called and spoke with Father Crumbley."

"I need to ask you a few general questions and, even though you are not a suspect at the moment, you do have the right to an attorney if you would be more comfortable with one present."

"I don't think an attorney is necessary."

And so Palmer began. "When was the last time you saw Monsignor Triplett?"

"We were together for the Good Friday services yesterday evening. Once the service was over, a little after 9:00 p.m., I left the cathedral and returned to the parish house. Monsignor Triplett came into my room, and we had probably one of our best conversations since I was assigned here to the cathedral."

"Where were you from the last time you saw him until you returned this morning?"

This was the question Father Morales dreaded answering, and he knew he must be as honest as possible. Closing his eyes and taking a deep breath, he calmly said, "I left the parish house around 10:00 last night and walked to the

Michelangelo Hotel. I spent the night there. I received a call from Father Crumbley about an hour ago, and he told me what had happened. I got dressed and walked back to the parish house."

Palmer noticed that Father Morales was forthcoming with his answer, but there seemed to be a few details missing. Looking directly at him, he asked, "Why were you at the Michelangelo Hotel? "

"I booked a room there to meet a friend." It surprised Father Morales how calmly the words came out of his mouth.

"So, you were not alone last night?"

"No... no, I wasn't."

"Who was the friend you were meeting?"

"It was Father David O'Hara."

Lieutenant Palmer could not hide his stunned expression as he looked at Father Morales. He wrote the name of the priest down. "Where is Father O'Hara now?"

Without hesitating, Father Morales responded, "He went back to Holy Name of Jesus Parish where he lives."

"I'll need his telephone number and address." Palmer now realized that he was talking with a priest who was having a relationship with another priest. This raised more questions in his mind as he tried not to judge Father Morales.

"I'll be more than happy to give it to you." Father Morales pulled out his phone and located Father O'Hara's information. He then handed the phone to the lieutenant who copied the information

"Who paid for the hotel room?" Palmer returned the phone to Father Morales.

"I did." Father Morales was hoping he wouldn't have to answer anything more about it but knew there was more he could say to answer the question.

"Do you have a receipt?"

"I do. But... there... there is a problem. I did not register under my name." Father Morales started to sweat.

Palmer saw how uncomfortable Father Morales was but continued to question. "Whose name did you register under?"

"I registered under the name of... George Newsome."

"That name sounds familiar. How do I know it?" Palmer was trying to remember.

"It's... it's the name of one of the auxiliary bishops of New York City." Father Morales waited for the lieutenant's reaction.

The lieutenant was more curious as the conversation continued. "Why did you use his name?"

"Because he told us, more like forbid us, not to see each other. This was one way we could defy him," Father Morales retorted. "We had tried so hard for such a long time to remain just friends, but the friendship developed into something the church would not accept." Father Morales was surprised at what he had just revealed and looked at the lieutenant who was writing away. He was feeling some remorse now in his anger toward Bishop Newsome.

It took a minute to review his notes before Palmer asked another question. He looked at Father Morales, who was looking away. "Does he know you used his name?"

"I'm not sure." Father Morales knew the bishop had no idea.

"Is that the receipt from the hotel will say?" Palmer kept pressing the point.

"Yes! I can even show you a photograph of Father O'Hara and me holding the receipt." He located the picture on his cell phone and showed it to Palmer.

"I still need a copy of the receipt." Palmer was stunned at the priests had bothered to take a picture.

"I have it in my bedroom." Father Morales stood and was about to move toward the door to retrieve it, hoping for a break from the lieutenant's questions.

Palmer saw Father Morales moving out of his chair. "Where are you going?"

131

Father Morales was about to open the door, "To get the receipt."

"That's not necessary right now... you can get it later." Palmer didn't want the questioning to end. "Please sit back down."

Startled by Palmer's tone, a disappointed, Father Morales, returned to his seat, uncertain of the lieutenant's next question.

"What time did you get to the hotel?"

"I arrived first, and it was between 10:15 p.m. and 10:30 p.m."

"What time did, Father O'Hara arrive?"

"It was before 11:00 p.m. I know this because we were together when the eleven o'clock news started."

"Did you stay in the hotel room the whole night?"

Father Morales fiddled with his hands and felt a little uncomfortable as the questioning continued. He took another deep breath before saying, "Yes, we remained in the room the whole night."

Having asked these questions to others, but never to a priest, the lieutenant tried to remain emotionless. "Is there anyone else that can vouch for where you were last night?"

"The only people I saw were the front desk clerk who registered me and the one man who gave me a copy of the bill. Someone from housekeeping came to the room to bring us pillows and glasses, but I don't know who it was. And I didn't see him. Father O'Hara was the one who answered the door when housekeeping arrived."

"Do you know the names of those working at the front desk?"

"No, I don't." Father Morales became confused and disappointed that they hadn't thought to get their names.

"Is this the first time you've been at the Michelangelo?"

"No... it's not."

Again, shocked but remaining calm, the lieutenant continued with the proper line of questions. "How many times have you been there?"

Father Morales knew this question would be one of the hardest to answer. He wanted to tell the truth no matter what. Again, he took a deep breath. "I think this was our third or fourth time."

"Were those working the desk the same for you at the other times?"

Father Morales could not understand why the hotel desk clerk was so important to the investigation. "I'm not sure."

"Would those who registered you on Friday and saw you on Saturday remember you?"

"I don't know."

"Would you mind if I take your picture to see if they would remember you?"

"Okay…, but they wouldn't have recognized me as a priest."

Palmer realized what Father Morales meant. "You're welcome to remove the collar."

Father Morales pulled the white plastic tab from his black clergy shirt and opened his shirt for the picture. Palmer took two photos with his cell phone. If necessary, he would have to follow up on Father Morales's story to remove him as a possible suspect.

"What was your relationship with Monsignor Triplett?" The lieutenant continued turning the page on his notepad.

"When I first arrived at the cathedral, I was afraid of him." Father Morales was thankful there seemed to be no more questions about the previous night. He proceeded to tell the lieutenant the whole story of the last conversation he had with Monsignor Triplett. "So in answering your question about our relationship, I would say it was not that great, but it was getting better."

Palmer reviewed the information Father Morales gave him about Monsignor Triplett. "What were you going to tell the Monsignor about staying or moving from the cathedral?"

"Honestly, I wasn't sure what I would tell him. I was looking forward to another conversation with Monsignor Triplett even though I left last night when he asked me not to."

"So you were disobedient to your superior?" Palmer was unsure if he was using the right word.

"I guess that's one way of looking at it. He is my immediate boss."

"Don't you face the consequences of the disobedience with the cardinal?"

"Yes, I believe I do."

Without being judgmental, Palmer asked outright. "Would you have any reason to kill Monsignor Triplett?"

"No, there's none. I may have been angry with him or even disagreed with him, but I would never have wanted him dead." Father Morales responded with the strongest voice yet as he looked directly at the lieutenant.

"Would you say the priests of the archdiocese liked Monsignor Triplett?"

"Yes, very much so. He could get things done."

"Is there anyone you know who would want Monsignor Triplett dead?"

"There were a few people. Monsignor kept a black notebook in his pocket with names of people, and I believe he would write remarks besides their names."

"Did you see this black notebook last night?"

"Yes. It was in his suit pocket when he came to talk with me. He had it with him when he said he was going back into the cathedral."

"He told you he was going back into the cathedral?"

"Yes. As he left my room, he said he needed to go back into the church. He didn't say why, only that he was going. As he left, I noticed Monsignor looked a bit worried."

"So he had the black notebook as he was leaving your room to go to the church?" The lieutenant asked again making sure he had the information straight.

"I believe so. I don't know if Monsignor went into his room after he left mine or went straight over to the cathedral."

"Would he have gone through the offices to get to the church?"

"I would imagine so. Or he could have taken the underground passage. Do you know about that?"

"Yes. I'm aware of it." Palmer quickly responded. He wanted to return the focus to the black book. "How do you know about this black notebook?"

"Because I would see him writing in it, and I often wondered if he was writing something about me. I was always afraid of what he had in it." Father Morales cautiously informed the lieutenant, wondering what was written about him.

"Who knew about this black book?"

"I would say probably everyone on staff because he would bring it out during staff meetings. None of us knew what he was writing in it, but I think we all assumed our names were there. He didn't allow anyone to see it."

"All you know, then, is Monsignor Triplett had this small black notebook and wrote names in it to keep track of things about different people."

"I'm only guessing, but I think so." Father Morales was now worried he might have said too much.

Palmer took a few moments to review his notes as Father Morales thought about the black book and those whose lives could be affected if its contents were revealed. Father Morales never heard the next question from the lieutenant until he repeated it a second time. "Is there anything else you can tell me about Monsignor Triplett?"

Father Morales thought about the question and revealed to the lieutenant, "He had told the staff at a recent meeting he had high blood pressure, and the doctors were trying to regulate the medicine. He also mentioned that one of the side effects was a constant cough, and at times, he would have short coughing spells. He didn't like medicines."

"Is there anything else?" Palmer looked at Father Morales and wondered what his future would be.

"I can't think of anything else." Father Morales felt exhausted as the interview was ending. He was also getting nervous about seeing the cardinal.

Palmer saw the fatigue on the young priest's face. "I think I've asked all the questions I have at this time. If I need to, I'll be back in touch with you. Please do not talk with anyone from the media and do not leave the property. Do you understand?"

Father Morales heard the strong words and simply responded, "I do."

"You have been most helpful." Palmer closed his notebook, stood and contemplated the next person to interview.

Father Morales stood, said nothing more to the lieutenant, and slowly walked from the library to his room to call his parents and let them know of the death of Monsignor Triplett. As soon as his mom answered the phone, he heard her voice filled with excitement that her son, the priest, was calling.

"Mama, good morning," Father Morales began.

"Good morning, are you getting excited about Easter?" Alicia Morales asked.

"I am, but I need to tell you and dad something." He paused for a moment and then said, "Monsignor Triplett was murdered last night in the cathedral." He waited for his mother's response, and it was what he expected.

"Hail Mary, full of grace..." Alicia Morales started praying.

"Mama, please listen. Let me continue, and then you can pray. I don't know all the details. When I find out more information, I'll let you know." Father Morales was short with his mother, the effects of little sleep.

"Okay son, but how are you?" Alicia was eager to know. She worried about her son but had prayed many years that the Lord would bless her with a son as a priest. He did, and she was so thankful. Juan could do no wrong in her eyes.

"I'm fine. Just sad for Monsignor Triplett since he was really looking forward to Holy Saturday."

"He's having a great Holy Saturday in heaven." Alicia was a devoted Catholic who tried to get to church for Mass as often as she could.

Father Morales wasn't surprised by his mother's comments. He loved his mother and wished he had as much devotion to the faith as she did. "I guess so, but what a shock it will be for the parish!"

"I know. We're coming to your Mass tomorrow. Will you still have the 8:00 a.m. Mass?"

"Mama, I don't know," Father Morales quickly responded.

"You sure you're okay?" Alice asked, not liking how her son responded.

"I'm okay, mom. When I know more, I'll call you. Pray for me, Mama, and pray for Monsignor Triplett." Father Morales knew he needed to reassure his mother.

"I always do, son. I love you," Alicia said.

"I love you too. Tell Dad I love him."

"I will son."

"I have to go." Father Morales knew he was being less than honest, and he just kept thinking about seeing the cardinal.

"Goodbye, son. Be good." With those words from his mother, the phone went dead.

Father Morales wondered if he should call Father O'Hara as he waited, but instead decided it was time to pray for Monsignor Triplett. He knelt at the foot of his bed and opened his black prayer book, a special one that his parents had given him for his First Communion. He prayed the Glorious Mysteries of the Rosary, thinking about another black book.

Back in the library, Lieutenant Palmer was sitting with his own notebook open after questioning Father Morales. He focused on the black notebook of Monsignor Triplett—its contents and its location. The lieutenant wondered if anyone had discovered it in the cathedral. If not, he would have to search Monsignor Triplett's bedroom and his office. He called Detective Sabor to see if the precinct sent over more detectives.

"Have them come to the parish house. I need their help to interview the two remaining priests," Palmer explained.

"Will do. Hector is concerned about getting the cathedral cleaned," Detective Sabor said.

"What is he doing?"

"I'm looking at him sitting in the pew, and it looks like he is praying; his head is down. Or maybe he's fallen asleep. Do you want me to check?"

"Let him be, Sabor. Are the three maintenance workers separated from one another?"

"Hector is separated from the other two."

"You and I need to interview them and see if their stories match up." Palmer insisted.

"Sounds good. Is there something you're not telling me about the maintenance workers?" Sabor asked.

"I'm not sure yet. In the meantime, when Monsignor Triplett's body was removed, did anyone find a small black notebook on or around him?" Palmer hoped someone had discovered it.

"Not that I'm aware of. Is it missing?"

"No one has discovered a small black notebook?" Palmer asked again hoping for a positive response to his question as he continued with the investigation.

"No, I'm looking over the evidence and don't see any notebook." Sabor reassured Palmer.

"Call the coroner's office and see if they found a black notebook on him?" Palmer requested. There was a sense of urgency in his voice. "Sounds like our deceased may have been writing about his employees."

"I'll do it right away. I am getting ready to send Detectives Jabowski and Pantera over. Do you need anything?" Sabor asked.

"Yes, send CSU over to seal off Monsignor Triplett's bedroom. Once the detectives arrive, I'll brief them on questioning the other two priests. Then I'll walk back over to the cathedral," Palmer informed Sabor.

Detective Sabor hesitated. He knew Lieutenant Palmer would not like his comment. "The media is gathering. There are some hungry reporters wanting the story first. They'll be trying to question you."

"They can wait!" Palmer snapped back with his answer. He has not in the past, nor now, going to allow reporters to hamper the investigation. "There are still a lot of people we need to interview, and the CSU needs to finish their work. Have they given you any indication of how much more time they need?"

"It looks like they're progressing at their normal diligent speed, given they've only been working for about two hours. The front pew where the deceased was found is still in place. Is it going as evidence?"

"Yes, it needs to be removed." Palmer insisted.

"Okay. Let me call the coroner's office and ask about the black notebook, and I'll see you over here shortly."

When Sabor called the coroner's office, they told him there was nothing more in the pants or shirt worn by Monsignor Triplett. But they told him of an inside hidden pocket in his suit jacket that contained $5,000 in cash.

Detective Sabor called Lieutenant Palmer immediately with this new information. "Boss, I just talked to the coroner's office and no black notebook. But there was $5,000 in cash in a hidden pocket of Monsignor's jacket. Why would he be carrying that much money?"

139

Palmer was noticeably surprised and concerned. "Good question. I wonder where he got that kind of money. It's another twist in this case. I'll see you shortly."

Palmer placed his phone in his pocket and walked down the hall to the living room to wait for the two detectives. He asked the priests present which bedroom Monsignor Triplett's and found out its location on the second floor. He wondered if the small black notebook would be there or had the murderer taken it. This mysterious black notebook may hold some answers to the person who had a motive to kill Monsignor Triplett. And the big unanswered question, why did he have that $5,000 on him?

Chapter 11

Lieutenant Palmer was reviewing his notes when he realized he had not called the parish housekeeper, Emma Pickle, to come to the cathedral parish house. He asked the priests if one of them would get her number. Father Crumbley got up, went to the kitchen and pulled off the entire sheet of parish employee's phone numbers from the community bulletin board and gave it to the lieutenant. Thanking him, the lieutenant then walked to the library and made the call.

Emma Pickle's phone rang playing her favorite college fight song in a high volume, but she rested peacefully in bed without responding to the first sounds of the phone. She was in a deep sleep. A sleep she badly needed this week, especially since yesterday had been a long day and night for her.

Financially, things had always been difficult in the Pickle family. Emma with only a high school education, knew six years ago that she had to find a part-time job. She went to her pastor at the time, Monsignor Triplett, asking if there was anything she could do in the parish. Unfortunately, he had nothing for her, but he gave her names of individuals who might have work for her. Two of them hired her to come once a week to do some housekeeping. It was a beginning but not enough. Finally, through an employment agency, she got a job working as part of the banquet staff at a small, private club.

Shortly after Monsignor Triplett was transferred to the cathedral, the parish's housekeeper retired. He remembered Emma and knew she would be perfect for this part-time position. With the support of her husband Roger, and son, Jonathan, she accepted the position as housekeeper. For five years, she scheduled her day, so she could be home early in the afternoon when Jonathan came home from school.

As good Catholic parents, the Pickles did everything possible to keep Jonathan in the parish elementary school. Emma's income helped. Jonathan struggled in school and was being bullied by older and bigger boys. The school administration, teachers and parents worked to rid the school of the scourge of bullying. Unfortunately, as much as the school had tried, Jonathan could not escape some of his classmates who were mean and cruel to him. This was only the beginning of his problems.

Four years ago, sadness came to the Pickle family with the unexpected death of Roger. Emma, now a widow, wondered how she would survive without his support and his income. Monsignor Triplett, aware of her financial struggles, increased her hours to help supplement the small life insurance policy which helped to maintain the apartment where she and Jonathan lived. Emma was so thankful for the job and the care Monsignor Triplett had shown to her and Jonathan.

Emma had her hands full as Jonathan became more and more rebellious. Her son was about to turn seventeen in four days. When his dad died unexpectedly, Jonathan's world seemed to come to an end, just as his teenage years were beginning. His dad had been his best friend. They did everything together. Both had a great interest in football whether it was college, admiring the University of Notre Dame or professional, cheering on the New York Jets. Through the generosity of one of Roger's friends, they could attend some Jets' home games. Everything changed the night Jonathan's dad was murdered.

Roger was leaving work at the grocery store and on his way to the subway station. He walked down the same alley he had walked for years. Suddenly, two adolescent thugs came out of the shadowy alley and asked for his wallet. Roger refused. He had just acquired two tickets on the thirty-yard line for the next Jets home game—the best seats he'd ever had.

The police report said he was beaten terribly. He tried desperately to crawl out of the alley. Finally, one of his co-workers found him and called 911. Roger suffered massive blows to the head and lost a great deal of blood. Within ten minutes of the EMTs arrival, he died. They did all they could. The killers had stolen his wallet, watch, and wedding ring.

When the police officers came to the Pickle apartment that night, Jonathan, then thirteen, answered the door. Hearing the news of his father's death, Jonathan ran to his room, slammed the door, curled up in a fetal position on his bed and cried until he was exhausted. He had just lost his best friend, mentor and father.

Since his father's death, Jonathan had seen a few psychologists, but none seemed to be able to make any progress with him. Jonathan struggled with depression, fears, and loss. The only one who seemed to get through to him was Monsignor Triplett. They shared the same interests, especially talking football after Sunday Mass. Emma, in desperation, reached out to Monsignor Triplett and asked if he would be willing to come to the apartment and talk with Jonathan. After the first visit, Monsignor Triplett and Jonathan tried to meet once a week.

As Jonathan reached the mid-teen years, some of his classmates made fun of the relationship he had with Monsignor Triplett. A few of them had seen Monsignor teaching Jonathan to drive. Jonathan slowly began to distance himself from Monsignor Triplett despite Monsignor giving him a car for his sixteenth birthday. Jonathan felt very torn. He appreciated his friendship with Monsignor Triplett, but like all adolescents, he needed acceptance by his peers. When his classmates didn't accept him, Jonathan responded with a rebellious attitude.

Five days before Monsignor Triplett was murdered, Jonathan tried calling him to see when they could meet. He wanted to get Monsignor's advice on whether to stay or to leave the apartment. Jonathan was so upset with his mom and her actions. It had been over four months since Monsignor Triplett had heard from Jonathan. But because it was Palm Sunday, he, unfortunately, had a previous commitment and didn't have the time to meet with him. This infuriated Jonathan. After school the next day, Jonathan packed a bag, took all the emergency money his mom had hidden in the Pillsbury cookie jar and left home.

Except for one phone call to Emma telling her he was safe, there had been no communication. But his mom knew where to find him. He'd never risk losing his job. He had done this before, and as the story of the prodigal son, she knew he would return home when the time was right, seeking forgiveness.

Emma was working more and spending less time with Jonathan who was feeling lost, alone and abandoned. She didn't know what to do. She missed Roger and mourned him daily, wishing he was with her to provide the guidance Jonathan needed. But her tears would not bring him back. As much as she worried about her son, she started to love and live again. She was moving on with her life.

Emma had been at Saint Patrick's all day yesterday serving the traditional noon meal of her seafood casserole to the cardinal and the priests. She took a break to attend the 3:00 service and then finished in time to attend the evening Stations of the Cross. In between services, Emma made sure each of the priests' rooms was cleaned, and she laundered any dirty clothes they had. She was taking the following week off. When she left, she was exhausted. "The Notre Dame Fight Song," her ringtone, finally woke her from her deep sleep.

As she was opening her blurred blue eyes, trying to locate her glasses on the nightstand, she finally answered her phone.

"Hello." Emma had no idea who was on the other end of the phone call.

"Is this Emma Pickle? I'm Lieutenant Palmer of the New York City Police Department."

"Yes…. is this about my son?" Emma prayed for good news that they had located him.

Not understanding the question, Palmer wanted to make sure he was talking to the right person. "Are you the housekeeper for the cathedral?"

"Yes, I am. Did something happen at the cathedral?"

"There has been a… a murder," Palmer began.

"A murder? Who… who... was murdered?" Emma felt shear panic as she tried sitting up in the bed feeling the arms of Sam around her.

Palmer heard the panic in her voice and tried to convey the name in a quiet tone… "Monsignor Triplett."

There was a long pause as if for a moment time had stopped, "O my God!" Emma tried to hold back her tears, but she was physically shaken by the news and dropped her phone.

Hearing the clang of the phone drop on the floor, Palmer waited until he heard her breathing and in a softer tone of voice asked, "Mrs. Pickle, are you okay?"

"Sorry, I… I can't stop trembling."

He realized how upset she was. "Would you like me to send a police officer over?"

Emma took a deep breath, wiped away the tears and sniffled, "I've lost a dear friend."

Trying to be sensitive to Emma, but wanting her to come down to the cathedral to be questioned, the lieutenant once again asked if he could send a police officer over to pick her up.

Emma again said it would not be necessary.

145

The lieutenant then inquired, "How long will it take for you to get to the cathedral?"

Emma didn't know what to say as she looked at Sam who was mouthing the words 'thirty minutes.' She finally responded to the lieutenant's request. "I'll be there in thirty minutes."

"If you need more time, Mrs. Pickle...."

Mrs. Pickle quickly responded, "Thirty minutes should be plenty of time."

"Please come to the parish house and use the main entrance door. Just identify yourself to the police officer," Palmer directed.

"Yes... yes... I will." Emma confirmed while looking for some tissues.

Palmer had another question. "Why were you asking about your son?"

"I'll tell you when I see you. I really need to go." Emma ended the call abruptly. She looked right at Sam who seemed to be aware of the news.

"Sam, Monsignor Triplett is dead!"

As Sam turned toward Emma, she could see that he knew something about this.

"What do you know about this? How could you know something?" Emma demanded answers from Sam as she looked him directly in the eyes.

Sam, reached out to Emma. He wanted to take her in his arms, but Emma didn't accept Sam's invitation. He tried not to look hurt as his arms fell to his sides. He calmly responded. "The lieutenant called me a few minutes before he called you. That's all the lieutenant would say. I promised to arrive as soon as possible."

As she realized the grief she was experiencing, Emma placed the phone back on the nightstand. "What are we going to do? Monsignor Triplett is dead. What am I going to do?"

146

Sam, folded his hands and raised himself from the bed trying to calm her. "You need to stay calm. What's there to tell? We were together the entire night."

"Yes, we were together last night. It was a mistake. Monsignor had told me so. Now the police are going to question you and me about Monsignor's death, and I will dishonor that good man by admitting to being with you, Sam!" Emma was crying uncontrollably now. The death of her husband, her missing son, her betrayal of Monsignor Triplett all flashed through her mind at once and left her totally distraught.

"A mistake?" Sam exclaimed.

"A mistake!" Emma echoed.

Sam sat frozen in bed. He couldn't believe what he was hearing. Confused and at a loss for words, all he could utter in a whisper was, "He was a good man."

Sam tried to reach for Emma's hand again, but she pulled back and picked up her phone to call Jonathan. Before she was able to make the call, Sam reached for her shoulder and turned her toward him. He looked at her face and saw through her tears how lost she was. "I love you, Emma. I always will—remember that."

Emma didn't know what to say as she looked into Sam's red eyes. She was struggling with the news of Monsignor Triplett's death and didn't know where her son was. The last four years had been so difficult for her. Now Emma was looking at someone she could share the rest of her life with, but now she was uncertain if she had any real feelings for Sam.

She took a deep breath, knowing what she had to say. She slowly moved farther away from Sam. "Sam, we can't continue our relationship. It's not right. I've got to think of my son first."

"But I love you, Emma." Sam pleaded with her.

Emma held Sam at arm's length and stated what they both knew was true. "You love being with me, but you don't love

147

me for a long relationship. You're never going to leave your wife. I know that too, and deep down you know you won't. You need to go back to her. And I need to work on repairing my relationship with my son."

"Emma, you don't mean that?"

"It's over, Sam. There can be no more us. What we're doing is so wrong. What we're doing could cost us our relationships with our families and our jobs. We have to end it now."

Sam seemed uncertain what to say. "We can't hide the fact that we spent the night together. Jean thinks I stayed in town to get caught up on work since I have next week off, and the kids will be home."

"I'm sorry, Sam. It was a mistake. Go back to your wife, your family." It was painful for Emma. She had feelings for Sam but knew what she was doing now was right for her and her son.

Sam, searched for some empathy from Emma. "You know this is not what I want."

Emma tried to remain strong. She could not look at Sam for fear she would weaken. "I need to get dressed, call my son and get over to the cathedral. Call Jean... call your wife."

"What are you going to tell your son?"

"The truth... that I need him to come home as soon as possible. I need to tell him face-to-face about Monsignor Triplett. I pray this won't be too overwhelming for him. First his father, now Monsignor Triplett." Emma knew her son was still having a hard time with his dad's death.

Sam was confused about Emma's reaction to Monsignor's death. He watched her pack what she'd brought to the hotel into her bag as if she were stuffing the relationship he thought they had into a box. How could she switch so quickly from being his lover to this woman who demanded that it end because the monsignor was dead?

"I need to call, Jonathan." Emma repeated as she moved to the bathroom.

Of course, her son, Sam thought. He was realizing it was all about her son. Sam struggled with her son. The relationship struggled because of her son. It's ending because of her son.

But he also knew Emma was right. Jean had all the money, and he had used that as a handy excuse to stay married and yet cheat on her. If it were true that the money was all that mattered, then why, Sam wondered, did Emma's devotion to her son make Sam immediately think of Jean.

He picked up his phone and saw Jean had left a text. He decided to call her. Jean loved being in the limelight with the various charity commitments she had been involved with over the years. After Sam was let go from Earnest and Patrick law firm, Jean was happy to become involved in the various charity activities of the archdiocese. She wasn't too concerned about Sam's paycheck. It was more his position and accessibility to the cardinal that Jean was thankful for. Throughout their marriage, it was Jean who was the one who made the decisions for the family, especially the girls. Sam was glad she did because he couldn't always handle the stress.

Ever since he started the relationship with Emma, Sam and Jean spoke less and less to one another and rarely spent any time alone. Since their two girls were off at college, the guest room became Sam's crash pad when he came home late. Despite the lack of communication and rarely seeing one another, deep down inside he always felt that no matter what he did wrong, she would be right by his side. Today he wondered if that would hold true.

As the phone rang, he knew Jean needed to hear about Monsignor Triplett's death from him.

"Hello," Jean answered but was agitated by being awakened from a restless night.

"Jean, good morning," Sam began. "I need to let you know some sad news… Monsignor Triplett has been murdered."

"O my God!" Jean was shocked. "When, how, where did this happen?"

"I'm not sure. I wanted you to hear it from me. Once I know more information, I'll call back."

Jean, was uncertain what to say. "Thanks for the call. Monsignor Triplett sure did appreciate you. I'll always be grateful to him for giving you a job."

"So am I. I know we were supposed to leave tomorrow afternoon with the girls and drive to Myrtle Beach, maybe we should postpone the trip." Sam suggested but was uncertain what it would accomplish.

"Of course, we can always go another time, and the girls will understand. Let me make some calls." Jean looked for the folder with all the vacation information.

"Jean... Monsignor Triplett loved each of us and thought we were a great couple, but we've drifted apart lately, and it's my fault. I'm... I'm sorry."

"I'm sorry too." Jean held back her tears as she tried to remain strong. "Let's talk when you get home." She did not want to have this conversation over the phone, and she was uncertain if her husband was even alone. She had hints that he was seeing someone, but she never confronted him about it.

"I'll see you soon."

But Jean had already ended the call before she heard those words.

Chapter 12

"So he used my name!" Bishop Newsome tried to control his anger as he sat in his chapel with Father O'Hara. "Why my name?"

With his eyes down and hands shaking, Father O'Hara spoke, softly. "It was our way of getting back at you. It was dumb. It was wrong. I am so sorry." He was more fearful now of the bishop's reaction.

Looking directly at Father O'Hara, Bishop Newsome was irate. "How stupid are you? Didn't you think someone would recognize the name?"

Taking a deep breath while keeping his head down, Father O'Hara responded, "Like I said, we weren't thinking. All we knew was we wanted to be together. In some ways, we were just mad at you. It was our way of expressing our anger in a non-threatening way. Does that make sense?"

Bishop Newsome held back his anger. "None of it makes sense to me. Right after Christmas... the three of us had a conversation about your relationship. You told me then...." Bishop Newsome paused. He was frustrated that he was still dealing with this issue. He leaned forward. "Do you remember the conversation?"

"O yes, I remember the meeting." Father O'Hara recalled it well.

"How long has this been going on since then?" Bishop Newsome was fearful of the answer.

"We probably met three or four times."

"All at the Michelangelo?" Bishop Newsome raised his voice, as he sat back in his chair, shocked by what he had just heard.

"Yes."

"And you used my name each time?"

"We did."

Bishop Newsome could not contain himself any longer... "Do you realize you have put me in one of the most difficult positions I've ever been in? After everything I've done for you, you are willing to risk your priesthood?" Bishop Newsome cried out, unable to remain calm as he looked at the scared priest.

"I know... and I'm sorry... I'm... very... very sorry. If there is one mistake, I keep making over and over again, it is the weakness of the flesh. I love my priesthood, but the temptation of the flesh is sometimes stronger than the graces of the sacraments." Father O'Hara spoke softly and painfully, his voice full of remorse.

"Do you not know how much I care for you?"

"I know. I'm sorry, but the flesh is weak. I am weak." Father O'Hara answered with tears in his eyes as he finally looked directly at the bishop.

Bishop Newsome realized he had to place the church's needs ahead of his friendship. He had to face this crisis within the role of being his bishop. "God forgives. God seeks to change. You must make the change. You must seek higher than what is here on earth. This life on earth is all temporary. You must work towards what will be everlasting." He continued to look forlornly at the young priest. He knew he had to make a decision. With authority and a heavy heart, he gave Father O'Hara his decision. "David, I will have to send you away. I'm not sure where or for how long. These acts of defiance cannot continue. The archdiocese does not need another scandal to make the news. Even though you are two consenting adults, it's not right in the eyes of the Church. I condemn the sin, but I can forgive the sinner. Do you understand?"

Father O'Hara had heard many of the words the bishop had just said to him before. But for the first time, he heard he would be sent away—something he had not expected. Confused and obedient to the bishop, he humbly looked at this mentor and remorsefully said, "I understand. I must amend my life. I hear your words. You have said them many times to me."

"These words you must not only hear, but you, as a priest, must live them. And so must Father Morales." Bishop Newsome searched Father O'Hara's face to see if he was really getting through to him.

Wiping the tears from his face, Father O'Hara said, "This time, I hear what you are saying... I say so often to those who come to me in confession with sin, 'go and sin no more.'"

Bishop Newsome once again tried to make eye contact with Father O'Hara. He wanted to give him even more to think about. "Live these words also, David. How I miss the opportunity to hear confessions. It was what really kept me in touch with parishioners and their needs. It also helped me to see what temptations the devil was using to influence others. Lust has a great hold on people whether it is pornography in magazines, sites on the Internet, or the actual act. Many are struggling with this sin. The devil has found a way to bring temptation and for people to fall into temptation. We need to resist his temptation and encourage others to resist – that's why confession is so important."

Father O'Hara sat up straight, removed his handkerchief from his pocket, placed it over his face to wipe away the tears and calmly asked, "Bishop, will you hear my confession now?"

The bishop, surprised by the request, moved forward to get out of his chair. "Let me get my purple stole."

Bishop Newsome stood and got his purple stole from the closet. The stole is the symbol of the authority of the priest, and the color purple expresses a penitent heart.

While waiting, Father O'Hara sat and examined his conscience—the first step in making a good confession. It had been several months since Father O'Hara had gone to confession. He realized that besides his relationship with Father Morales, and the dishonesty with which he had treated the bishop, he had been negligent with praying the necessary universal prayers for the clergy, the Liturgy of the Hours. He also recalled he drank too much alcohol and gossiped about others.

When Bishop Newsome returned to his chair, Father O'Hara knelt in front of him and made the Sign of the Cross. His movements were very deliberate. This was important for him. He confessed his sins—the second step in making a good confession and asked for forgiveness and for the graces that come from the sacrament. Despite the great relief of having unburdened his soul with confession, he sat in anticipation of the penance the bishop would give him. He knew it would not be an easy penance, but he would accept it—the third step in making a good confession. He wanted to feel the weight of it all off his shoulders, so he nervously waited for what seemed like an eternity.

Finally, the bishop prepared to give Father O'Hara a penance—the fourth step in making a good confession. He began with a story from scripture. He reminded Father O'Hara of the story of the woman who had committed adultery. Jesus had told her to go and sin no more. "You must do the same," telling Father O'Hara. "For your penance, I ask you to offer the Masses you will celebrate this Easter for those priests who have influenced your life. Name them, so they may be examples for you in the life you want to live. I ask you to pray a rosary each night for the next seven days, in addition to the prayers required by the church which you have been negligent about. Embrace these prayers. Let the Lord speak to you. Use the rosary to meditate on the mysteries of our faith. While you delve into these mysteries, meditate on your priesthood and your future. End the rosary with the prayer to Saint Michael, asking to cast out the devil and the evils he brings to our world. Will you fulfill this penance that I am asking of you?"

It was a moment before Father O'Hara could speak. "I will try with the help of God." Once again tears streamed down Father O'Hara's face. He now fully understood his actions had serious consequences that would require changes in his life. He knew the penance given to him would help.

Bishop Newsome, pleased with the response from Father O'Hara, wanted to give final words of reassurance. "God will indeed help you, but you must be committed to a life of prayer. I'm trying to help you with this penance."

Holding his head up, he made eye contact with the bishop. "Thank you, Bishop."

"Now, please say your Act of Contrition for me as I absolve you of your sins." This is the final step in making a good confession.

Father O'Hara, still kneeling in front of the bishop, began the Act of Contrition. "O my God, I am heartily sorry…"

Bishop Newsome extended his hand, placed it on Father O'Hara's head and said the Prayer of Absolution: "God the Father of Mercies, through the death and resurrection of your son has reconciled the world to yourself. Through the forgiveness of sins, may God give you peace, and I absolve you of your sins in the name of the Father, and the Son and the Holy Spirit... Amen."

When Father O'Hara stood, the bishop also rose, and they embraced one another. Then, the bishop said, "Will you hear my confession?" Father O'Hara was surprised at this request, knowing that he had inflicted so much pain upon the bishop.

The bishop quietly passed the purple stole to Father O'Hara and then knelt before him with humility seeking forgiveness for his sins.

As the bishop ended his confession, there was once again the exchange of peace between the two of them. "Let us have a joyful Easter." Bishop Newsome hoped that what had just transpired within the last hour would help make it a joyful Easter for both.

"Thank you." Father O'Hara, still filled with so much emotion, was not totally aware of the words he had spoken to the bishop. He knew during many times of uncertainty that the Holy Spirit guided him with the words to speak during the sacrament of reconciliation.

The bishop's next words broke his peaceful thought. "I have forgiven you for your sins. And although I am under the seal of confession and can never share them, you must know because your actions are public...." There was a definite pause as the bishop continued, "I have to take some action."

"I know... and I know you will be fair." Father O'Hara prepared to leave the bishop's suite and return to his room. Once again, he thanked the bishop for his pastoral approach. Knowing the bishop supported him, he could make a change. Although it would be tough, this time, he was willing to do what was necessary for his priesthood. As he gently shut the bishop's door, he was also shutting the door on his affair with Father Morales.

Walking toward his room, Father O'Hara knew he needed to sit and pray the first rosary he was asked to do from his confession. After the rosary, he would call to see how Father Morales was doing. Father O'Hara went to his dresser and picked up the rosary his parents had given him. He knelt and began to pray.

Several miles away Monsignor David Stone sat in his apartment. His head was throbbing. He had just got out of the shower, the second one he had taken this morning. Shaken from the events of the last three hours, he tried to focus on his Easter homily, contemplating on the message he would preach tomorrow morning.

For six years, Monsignor Stone had served as judicial vicar for the archdiocese. According to canon law, specifically canons 1419 and 1420, the judicial vicar is the one who "constitutes one tribunal with the bishop and has the ordinary power to judge those cases not reserved to the bishop." As the canon lawyer for the archdiocese, he worked on behalf of the cardinal to help priests, deacons and religious in the laws of the church. In this position, it was also his responsibility to see that the bishops, priests and deacons within the diocese were carrying out the church laws. The position allowed him to have the trust and confidence of the cardinal. In many cases, he provided the cardinal with necessary information and a course of action.

Although he was not assigned to a parish, Monsignor Stone helped at the neighboring church, Saint Jerome's. This allowed him to feel part of a faith community and to celebrate Mass and assist with other sacramental duties as his schedule permitted. It was in these moments that he was able to show compassion and mercy as Jesus did many times when faced with difficult situations.

Because of the tremendous amount of work in the tribunal, and the strict confidentiality with it all, Monsignor Stone was given one of the archdiocesan apartments to reside. This allowed him the privacy he needed to be able to bring work home for the archdiocese and the freedom from the daily challenges of a parish. He was blessed to have a housekeeper who came once a week to take care of cleaning, laundry and shopping.

But with all the advantages that came with this important position, there were the disadvantages of knowing the many wrongs carried out by the clergy of the diocese, and at times the injustices of the church. The burden of knowing the peccadilloes of his fellow clergy and trying to remain loyal to the church had become increasingly heavy for him.

Monsignor Stone had felt very fortunate to be in the position of the judicial vicar. While the work in the tribunal was monotonous and boring for some priests and laity, he found fulfillment in the good he did to help the people of the church. However, lately, it was causing anxiety and sleepless nights for him.

Early in his priesthood, Monsignor Stone got into trouble. When the former cardinal found out, he provided counseling, and the incident was dealt with in a professional manner. He thought the matter had been forgotten. But a priest mentioned the incident and informed Monsignor Stone, he had pictures to prove of it. It infuriated Monsignor Stone! Even though the incident was not serious in nature, it was a blemish against his record.

When he became the judicial vicar, Monsignor Stone had access to his personnel file, and he removed the information that blemished his name. Since the previous cardinal had died, he thought no one else would remember, or know, about his past transgression. This morning he found out differently.

Instead of having the chance to sleep in this Holy Saturday morning, he had agreed to meet with the priest of the archdiocese who knew about his situation. Surprised that the priest wanted to meet on Holy Saturday morning, Monsignor Stone agreed to meet him at the cathedral at 6:00 a.m. to discuss not only the incident in Stone's past but another delicate church matter as well.

So on Holy Saturday morning with a brisk 55 degrees outside and dark clouds above, Monsignor Stone dressed casually, walked down to the 138th Street subway station and took the twenty-five-minute subway ride into Manhattan. After exiting the station, he stopped by Starbucks and bought a cup of hot coffee and something to eat. He checked his watch. He didn't want to be late or make this priest any more upset than he already was.

After finishing his breakfast, Monsignor Stone continued walking at a quick pace down Fifth Avenue and remembered the previous day's conversation. As careful as he had been throughout the last 35 years of his priesthood, this one incident would haunt him again. He had never seen the pictures. He wondered how terrible were they? He was heartbroken that his good friend, and priest, had kept them when he thought they'd all been destroyed.

The priest informed him the pictures were stored in a safe, and the key for it was hidden. He would be happy to disclose both the location of the key and the safe, provided Monsignor Stone was willing to do a favor in return. Monsignor Stone was eager to get the incriminating pictures, but ethically he wondered if he could do what was asked of him.

Feeling the pressure, Monsignor Stone knew he had no choice but to meet and discuss the particular request with the priest. He had to find a way to convince Monsignor Triplett there would be no winners if any of this information were ever discovered. The repercussion of this favor upon the church and the marriage annulment process would be heard in every diocesan tribunal. He would be stripped of his responsibilities and the amenities from it. But if the truth be told, he would miss parish life more. He desperately wanted to get the pictures back.

Now almost three hours later and still shaken, he was grateful for the receipt from the coffee shop. It could be a good alibi. He erased the phone message about the early morning appointment, took a shower and continued his effort to minimize with ice the injury to his head. Scared and confused, he sat in his apartment rubbing the back of his neck, trying to remember the details of what had happened when suddenly his cell phone rang.

Chapter 13

Lieutenant Palmer heard his phone ringing in his pocket and pulled it out, noting it was a number he had dialed a short time ago.

"This is Lieutenant Palmer of the New York Police Department."

"This is Thom Triplett. I was just informed of my brother's death. I was asked to call you for the details." As he stood next to the police officer, Thom was visibly shaken with the unexpected news.

"Yes, Mr. Triplett. Your brother Monsignor Steven Triplett was found dead in the cathedral this morning. I'm so sorry."

"How did it happen?"

"We've just started the investigation and are far from having all the answers to this case."

"The coroner's office took his body to the morgue. By state law, an autopsy must be done before we can release the body," Palmer explained. "I know this must be very difficult for you, but I have some questions that need answers to help with the case. I can come to your residence or have the officer bring you to the cathedral. After we talk, I'll have someone escort you to the morgue."

"I was going to meet my brother for breakfast at 9:00 this morning. I just saw him last night! I was his family." Thom remembered out loud, not listening to all the lieutenant said.

Hearing Thom crying on the other end of the phone, Palmer spoke again. "I'd like to arrange a time where I could come to your place of residence to ask you some questions."

"If you don't mind, I'd like to come to you." Thom tried to compose himself.

"I can ask the officer to bring you to the cathedral parish house."

"That won't be necessary. I've been there many times. Give me thirty minutes, and I should be there." Thom thought maybe he should have taken the lieutenant's offer to go with the officer in the squad car, but decided against it. He wanted to be alone.

"Come to the front door of the parish house. Just tell the uniformed officer present you're to report to me."

"Again, I'm sorry. You are lieutenant...?" Thom was still in shock and disbelief that his brother had died.

"Palmer, Lieutenant Will Palmer. Again, my condolences. I'll see you shortly."

Once the call ended, Thom thanked the officer and escorted him to the front door. Thom closed the door and cried. He walked to his favorite chair and sat. He wept for the loss of his best friend and brother. He looked up at the bookshelf and saw the last picture taken of him and his brother. Tears flowed down his face. He tried to compose himself; he knew he had to call the person he had dinner with last night.

Palmer put his phone back in his pocket. He always felt a terrible knot in his stomach when he had to notify the family of a death. He was surprised Thom wanted to come to the cathedral and was worried about his reaction to the news.

As soon as he was off the phone, Detectives Maria Jabowski and Gabe Pantera arrived with the CSU investigator.

"You okay, Lieutenant?" Detective Jabowski asked.

"I... I will be. It's never easy to inform the family of the death of a relative. As many years as I've been doing this, it's the one part of being a detective that gets me in my gut. You'll find out, detective." Palmer knew Jabowski had only been a detective for six months.

Lieutenant Palmer regained his composure and asked each detective to interview the two remaining priests—Father Luke Crumbley and Monsignor James Black. One would use the living room while the other would meet in the library. Palmer discussed various questions to ask the priests, including any information they may obtain about a small black notebook Monsignor Triplett carried with him. He reminded them to take careful notes and if there were anything he needed to follow up on, to let him know. Once they completed the interviews, he asked them to find him and to give a full report.

Meanwhile, he informed the police officer at the door to let him know if Sam Tolden, Emma Pickle or Thom Triplett arrived. Having briefed the other detectives and police officers, Palmer went with the CSU investigator to Monsignor Triplett's bedroom and sealed it off. They both left the parish house to return to the cathedral.

Detective Jabowski went into the living room and asked for Father Luke Crumbley. Once he identified himself, they moved to the library.

Father Luke Crumbley was a priest of great concern for the archdiocese. Five years earlier, he had been accused of sexual abuse with a fifteen-year-old on a parish youth camping trip. The individual who was accusing him claimed Father Crumbley waited until he and the youth were alone, then molested him. The allegation was found to be "credible" by the church authorities which meant only that Father Crumbley and the accuser were present on the same trip. However, "credible" sounds much like "guilty." The church struggles with its own definition of what "credible" means. The cardinal, following the church protocol, removed Father Crumbley from his assigned parish, suspended his priestly faculties and allowed him to live in a diocesan-owned property. Father Crumbley became depressed, felt abandoned and isolated from the priests of the archdiocese and the church authorities. In time, and after the report of a private investigator hired by Crumbley's family, the accuser admitted it was all a joke that had gone wrong, as another scout had put him up to it. Cardinal Flinn placed Father Crumbley in a new assignment at Saint Patrick's Cathedral. He knew Monsignor Triplett would help Father Crumbley adjust to the return of his priestly ministry. Father Crumbley knew that although the accusation was proven false, doubt remained among the many people who knew about the initial accusation.

After making every effort to exonerate Father Crumbley, Cardinal Flinn became one of Father Crumbley's supporters. Whenever he could, the cardinal defended Father Crumbley, particularly against the comments of organizations, which tried to name Father Crumbley as a sexual abuser. Father Crumbley was thankful for the cardinal's support.

As Father Crumbley sat down in the library, he immediately told his story to Detective Jabowski. He knew, if she hadn't already done so, she could just Google the details.

"I am so sorry to hear about this. Are you still being harassed from this accusation?" Detective Jabowski began as she pulled out her notebook ready to write.

"It's not ended but gets better each day. Being here at the cathedral has been a help," Father Crumbley said.

"Why do you say that?"

"First, all the priests here know what has happened to me, and they also know it could easily happen to them. I feel the support, especially from Monsignor Triplett. I will miss his words of wisdom, defending me, and being my confessor."

"So, you would describe your relationship with him as a friendly one?" Jabowski asked.

"I would not say friendly, but more of a father-son relationship. His advice and guidance for the last two years have helped me remain focused on my priesthood and ignore those who tried to hurt me in my ministry."

"Could you give me an example?"

"Are you familiar with this group called SNAP—Survivors Network of those Abused by Priests? This group can be relentless. Even when a priest is exonerated, they are still after him, hoping to catch him in the act. Monsignor Triplett confronted a SNAP member. It did not go well for the young man, but Monsignor Triplett said his peace, and I've never heard another thing from SNAP about me. I do feel a debt to Monsignor Triplett." Father Crumbley had tears in his eyes as he spoke honestly.

"Could you expand on what you mean 'it was a father-son relationship' with Monsignor Triplett?"

"He was the father—the boss. Like a father to a son, he would criticize me for something and then in the next sentence praise me. At first, I was afraid of him, but after he started to defend me, I wasn't afraid to speak my mind, especially at staff meetings. While everyone else may have been afraid to ask the questions, I wasn't. I've gone through a lot and have grown from the false accusation ordeal. I think in many ways Monsignor Triplett was thankful to have someone who would speak up. I think we had a good relationship."

"Did you know about his little black notebook?"

"I did. Monsignor Triplett was not one to use a computer for anything. He believed everything should be written down. So he would write in his little black notebook, just like you're doing with me in this interview. It was his way of remembering things."

"Have you seen what's inside the notebook?"

"No, I have not, but the rumor was Monsignor Triplett wasn't always pleasant with what he wrote about people in it."

"Do you know where the notebook is?"

"I don't. I would presume Monsignor Triplett had it on him. I never remember seeing him without it. I had heard he slept with it, but in all probability, he may have put it in his safe."

"There is a safe in his bedroom?"

"I believe so."

"Do you know where in his bedroom?"

"I believe in his closet. There's one in my bedroom closet to secure personal documents."

Detective Jabowski made a note to let Palmer know about the safes in the rooms.

"Where were you last night from the time you came back here until this morning?" Jabowski asked.

"As I told Lieutenant Palmer, I was the priest on call for emergencies. When I checked the messages, there was a call to go to Lenox Hill Hospital to anoint one of our parishioners, Fred Morris. I went and afterward got a slice of pizza and returned to the parish house by midnight. I remembered I turned the TV on and *The Tonight Show* was on with Betty White. I don't remember when I fell asleep, but I woke up about an hour ago," Father Crumbley explained.

"How did you get to Lenox Hospital?"

"I took the subway."

"Was the parishioner alert when you saw him?"

"He was."

"Do you know what time you were with him?"

"It had to be close to 11:00 p.m."

"Did you get a receipt for the pizza?"

"No, I didn't."

"Would you have any reason to want Monsignor Triplett dead?"

"No, I didn't. As I said, Monsignor Triplett really helped me remain faithful to my priesthood when I had thought I wouldn't return to the ministry."

"Father Crumbley, Lieutenant Palmer asked you to make a list of those who work in the parish offices. Were you able to complete the list?"

"Yes, I was." Father Crumbley pulled the list out of his pocket to pass to Detective Jabowski.

"Thank you."

"Is there anything else you can tell me about Monsignor Triplett?"

165

"He and his brother had been the best of friends, but I know since his brother's divorce, there seems to be a little distance between the two of them."

"What do you mean?"

"It was almost like his brother, Thom, had thought Monsignor owed him something. Does that make sense?"

"I'm not sure." Jabowski put a star beside the names of Thom Triplett and Monsignor Steven Triplett. "What would Monsignor Triplett have that he owed to his brother?"

"I wish I knew."

"Is there anything else that you would like to tell me?" Detective Jabowski was concluding the interview.

"I've probably already said too much," Father Crumbley said.

"No, you have been most helpful. I have to ask you to remain in the house and if there are any additional questions, make yourself available."

"I'll be in my room. I need to write a new Easter homily." Father Crumbley excused himself thankful he had been of assistance, but now, alone in his room, he wept.

Detective Pantera remained in the living room and pulled out his notepad to interview the elderly priest sitting across from him. Monsignor Black had been a true leader in the archdiocese during his active ministry. For over twenty-five years, he served as superintendent for the diocesan schools. There were 312 schools in the archdiocese at the beginning of his tenure — at the end only 258 schools. He tirelessly promoted Catholic education and saw the many fruits of the schools within the city. It was disappointing when enrollment dropped, and the school had to be closed. He took those decisions personally and eased the pain many days with a bottle of good Scotch.

While serving as school superintendent, he lived at Saint Monica's Parish. On the weekends, he regularly assisted in the parish by providing the sacraments to the parishioners, and the parishioners loved him. His homilies related current events to the Scriptures. His popularity was not lost on the pastor, Monsignor Edward Walsh. Though they were classmates, they were not the best of friends. Each of them tried to be hospitable to one another, but many knew it was all a facade.

Unexpectedly, Monsignor Walsh at the age of fifty suffered a massive heart attack and died on Sunday evening while watching *"Sixty Minutes."* The cardinal, unaware of Monsignor Black's drinking, appointed him pastor of the church while he continued as the archdiocese school superintendent. Monsignor Black had mixed emotions when he the cardinal called him to accept the assignment. This was not the way he wanted to be named a pastor. Even with the additional responsibilities, he still wasn't satisfied, and would turn to the bottle of Scotch for comfort. One day, a few years back, the bottle got the best of him, and the cardinal invited Monsignor Black to retire.

As he waited for Detective Pantera to start, Monsignor Black reflected on his last conversation with Monsignor Triplett. He realized he could easily name suspects in the murder.

Detective Pantera completed the standard questions: his full name, length of time as a priest, the various assignments he had, and how he had arrived at the cathedral, his whereabouts from last night until this morning. The questions that followed took on a much more serious tone.

"You've been at the parish house for three years and living in retirement. Correct?" Detective Pantera asked and recorded the information in his notepad.

"That's correct."

"And do you have any responsibilities being here?"

"I assisted Monsignor Triplett whenever he asked, and when I was available, I would hear confessions, anoint the sick, and celebrate weekday or Sunday Mass. It allows me the opportunity to feel needed, and I think the people appreciate my being here."

"Are you happy here?"

"I'd say for the most part. Like any parish house, there are some good things, and then there are things I would want to change. But since I'm not in charge, I would say my peace, and then keep my peace with them. I accepted what Monsignor Triplett, or the cardinal, wanted and moved on. At my age, it's not worth the fight."

"It sounds like you and Monsignor Triplett had a good relationship."

"I think for the most part we did. In many ways, I was his extra set of eyes in the parish house since we are all a bunch of misfits living here."

"What do you mean?"

"I mean we have a gay priest, a priest who was falsely accused of sexual misconduct, an alcoholic priest and then there was Monsignor Triplett. Not your normal house."

"Could you expand on this?" Detective Pantera asked turning the page on his notepad.

"I think it is obvious that Father Morales is the gay priest. Father Crumbley is the falsely accused priest, and I am the alcoholic priest."

As Detective Pantera wrote this down, he heard Detective Jabowski in the hallway and excused himself from the living room. As a practicing Catholic, at least on Christmas and Easter, Monsignor Black's remarks intrigued the detective. He needed Detective Jabowski in the room as he continued to question Monsignor Black, wondering what other surprises he might reveal.

Chapter 14

Turning the corner onto 50th Street to return to the cathedral, Lieutenant Palmer took in the brisk air of mid-April. He was amused at the number of satellite trucks and reporters already in position trying to be the first to break the story. As a result, there was a great deal of speculation about the reasons for the CSU and detectives' presence. The city police officers were saying nothing.

Recognized by the officer as he approached the side doors, Palmer entered with little notice from the reporters. Officers Lang and Snow saw him, as did the two maintenance workers who were still seated separately and still waiting to be questioned.

Hector had left his seat to go to the bathroom in the usher's room. He quietly took the little black notebook out of his jacket and thumbed through it. When he saw his name at the top of one of the pages, he read the nice comments Monsignor had written about him. He also read about a mistake he'd made and wondered if he could tear out that page of the book but decided not to. He was already in enough trouble just holding onto the book.

As Hector turned the pages, he was stunned at the information he read. Monsignor Triplett remembered the good, the bad, the ugly, and almost everything in between, on those who worked at the cathedral including the deacons, priests, bishops and even the cardinal. There were even a couple of pages about the construction company doing the restoration work. What he read revealed a few enemies of Monsignor Triplett. Suddenly he realized the time, figured he had seen enough and nervously closed the black notebook. He quickly placed it in his pocket and returned to the pew in front of Our Lady of Guadalupe.

Hector saw Lieutenant Palmer talking with the police officers. Officers Lang and Snow brought Palmer up to date as the CSU were still working away. The pew where Monsignor Triplett was found had been tagged for evidence, covered in plastic, and unbolted from the marble floor. Four investigators were carefully removing it from the cathedral.

"Hector," Palmer said, "would you come here?"

Hector uncertain whether Palmer knew if he had the black book, made the Sign of the Cross to indicate he was finished praying. He got up and walked slowly toward the lieutenant.

"Hector, in just a few minutes, Detective Sabor and I will interview the two maintenance workers. This probably won't take too long. CSU has just about finished in the altar area, and once they're done there, I believe you'll be able to start cleaning this area."

"That will be good. I've got a lot to do before the flowers come," Hector said.

"But before I let you go, I need to ask you some additional questions."

Unsure of the questions he was about to be asked, he felt the notebook in his pocket and wondered what he should do. "What do you need to know?" Hector asked.

"Do you know anything about the black notebook Monsignor Triplett kept?"

"Yes, I know he had one, and sometimes I would see him making notes in it, especially when he was talking with the supervisor of the restoration project."

"When you found Monsignor Triplett this morning, did you take anything in his pockets?"

Hector knew he had to turn over the notebook. Nervously, he removed it from his coat pocket and saying nothing about it, gave it to Palmer. The lieutenant told Hector to place the notebook on the pew. Then, the lieutenant took a pair of latex gloves out of his pocket and carefully put them on before touching the notebook.

"Hector, you have tampered with possible evidence." Palmer was noticeably annoyed with Hector as Officer Lang walked over with an evidence bag.

"I am sorry, Will. I should have told you right away I had it. I should never have taken it out of his jacket. How did you know I had the notebook?"

"I didn't.... Why did you take it, and why didn't you tell me?"

"I knew Monsignor Triplett made notes on all of his employees, and I just wanted to see what he said about us."

"And what did you find out Hector?"

"Monsignor Triplett had some enemies as well as information about a few who may have wanted him killed."

"Thank you, Hector, for turning it over. I am, however, going to have to ask you not to say anything about what you have read in the book. By taking the book, you could be considered a suspect in the case. Until your story is verified, you are a suspect and can't leave the cathedral. Officer Lang will watch you while you do the cleaning. Do you understand what I'm telling you?"

"I didn't kill Monsignor Triplett! I could never kill a person! You have to believe me! I just wanted to find out what was in his notebook about me." Hector fearfully explained his actions.

"What did he say about you?" Palmer skimmed the notebook and saw some of the names Monsignor Triplett had placed in it.

"He said I was one of the best workers he had at the cathedral. He was thankful that I was always honest with him. He then had the words 'budget cuts—one less maintenance worker.' I don't know if he was going to let me go or someone else because of budget cuts!"

"So you knew nothing about the budget cuts?"

"Nothing."

"And from what you read, could you tell me who had the most negative comments?"

Hector was still afraid, but he knew he had to speak. "He had a lot to say about the supervisor from the construction firm, Jared Quinn — something about wrong invoices."

"Anyone else?"

"Sam Tolden wasn't one of his favorite people nor was Cardinal Flinn. You need to read those pages carefully."

"I will. But in the meantime, let's get your name cleared and your story checked out." Palmer closed the notebook and placed it in the plastic bag Officer Lang was holding. He knew he would have to spend more time looking through it.

"One more question, Hector. If you were asked about the budget cuts and had to let one of your assistant workers go, which one would you have told Monsignor Triplett to terminate?"

Hector was startled at the question and hesitated to answer. "I... I probably would have told him I need them both. Just look at this place and how dirty it is with all this construction. We're having a hard time keeping the place clean, and if he was going to let one go, it would be even harder. I hope he would've listened to me and found another way to cut the budget."

"But if he had to let one worker go, who would it be?"

Hector feeling pressured, reluctantly answered. "If he pushed the issue, then I'd say Luis Hernandez because he could always work for his brother even though he doesn't want to."

"Hector, did you see anything in the notebook about Luis Hernandez?"

"Yes... yes... I did. Monsignor Triplett thought he was drinking on the job but couldn't prove it."

172

"Do you know if he was drinking?"

"Unfortunately, when things weren't going well at home, Luis liked to put a little rum into his afternoon coke to help take the edge off of having to go home," Hector revealed, "but it never interfered with his work. In fact, he and Oscar are the best workers I've ever had. It would be hard to lose either one of them."

Palmer accepted Hector's answers and then shared the information about the press conference. He asked Hector to make sure the area was accessible for all those who would be attending. "You may want to move some chairs, so no one can move any farther than the podium since this is still an active crime scene. And open the front doors closest to 50th Street at 10:30 a.m. allowing the press time to position themselves before the press conference at 11:00 a.m."

Hector understood the instructions and would make sure the podium from the sacristy was moved to the center aisle in the center of the cathedral.

Now Palmer had another thing to worry about during the investigation. He motioned to Officer Lang. "Officer Lang, I want you to stick with Hector as he makes the preparations needed to start cleaning the church and for the press conference."

Checking his notepad, Palmer informed Detective Sabor of a couple of items. "Let the CSU know the front, side doors on 50th Street of the cathedral will open at 10:30 a.m. for the press to enter and set up. Make sure we have police officers at those doors checking credentials and a few others stationed around the podium area. I'm going to have you interview the maintenance worker, Oscar Martinez, while I interview Luis Hernandez. Be sure to ask about Martinez's family where he was last night until this morning. Also, ask about his relationship with Luis Hernandez. Find out if he knew about Monsignor Triplett's black notebook. Hopefully, we can get this done in the next twenty minutes."

"Will do. I'm on it."

Detective Sabor talked with the lead CSU investigator and one of the police officers giving them the instructions for the upcoming press conference.

The three of them walked down the side aisle where the maintenance workers were sitting, and Palmer asked for Luis Hernandez. He identified himself by raising his hand. Sabor walked toward Oscar, introduced himself and informed him he would conduct the interview.

Lieutenant Palmer, with the crime scene investigator, walked a few pews farther and stood in front of Luis, holding the bag containing Monsignor Triplett's notebook. As Luis saw it, he began to tremble in fear, wondering if Monsignor Triplett had written something about him.

"What's wrong?" Palmer asked. "It is Luis correct?"

"Yes... yes... Luis Hernandez." Shaking, he spoke softly and slightly nodded his head.

"Why are you trembling?"

"Is that... is that... the... the notebook from Monsignor Triplett?"

"Yes, it is. Does that make you nervous?"

"I don't know what's in it, but I know Monsignor would pull it out when he would see me."

"I don't know what's in it either. Is there something that would worry you?"

"I'm not sure," Luis replied.

"You're not sure? Do you want to find out?"

"Not really."

Palmer gave the bag containing the notebook to the crime scene investigator who walked back to the evidence area, cataloged the notebook and put it in one of the plastic storage bins with the rest of the evidence. The lieutenant then went through several routine questions and asked, "What time did you arrive at the cathedral?"

Luis was nervous when asked this question. He wasn't sure he should tell the lieutenant that he and Oscar had come earlier than they were supposed to. But he wanted to tell the truth, so he explained. "Well... Oscar and I arrived almost an hour earlier than we were supposed to be here. We were going to surprise Hector and try to have some of the work done, so we could get out early. But when we arrived, we heard Hector yelling the words 'He's dead,' and so we left."

"How did you get in?"

"We slowly opened the side door on 50th Street and entered by the gift shop. But once we heard Hector yelling, we got so scared that we left through the same door and locked it. Then we waited down the street at a coffee shop 'til we were supposed to come to work."

"Why didn't you go to Hector when you heard him yelling?" Palmer asked.

"We were afraid to get involved." Luis knew he had to be totally honest.

"I'm confused. You didn't want to get involved when you heard Hector yell, but you came back?"

"We were afraid if we didn't come back, we would even be in more trouble."

"Why do you think you would be in trouble?"

"Because Oscar and I both have police records."

"What were arrested for?"

"We sometimes have a few too many beers. A couple of times, we got kicked out of bars and asked not to come back. One time it landed us in jail. Monsignor Triplett paid for the lawyer and provided the bail money for us to get out of jail."

"Nothing else?"

"No, that's it. We learned our lesson. Monsignor Triplett put the fear of God in us. Monsignor said that if it ever happened again, we would lose our jobs and stay in jail. He reminded us of this often. It helped me, and I think it helped Oscar."

"What time did you get off work last night?" Palmer continued with the questions.

"I left at 5:00 p.m."

"Alone?"

"No, Oscar and I left together."

"And when you left where did you go?"

"We took the subway back to my house. We stopped to get a couple of beers, and then Oscar and I sat outside and drank them before he went home."

"Is that where you stayed for the rest of the night?"

"Yes…" Luis took a deep breath as he told the truth.

"So you stayed home until you came to work this morning?" As Palmer made notes, he knew he would have to check the arrest records of all three of the maintenance staff.

"I was home."

"And where is home?"

"It's in Brooklyn off of Winthrop Street."

"Is there someone there who could vouch for you?"

"Yes, my wife, Isabella."

"What's her telephone number?"

Luis, who couldn't remember his own number, looked in his cell phone contacts to find his wife's and gave it to Palmer. The lieutenant placed the call and verified they were together last night after he got home from work. He and Oscar had a couple of beers, and then Luis fell asleep in his chair and came to bed about midnight. He got up at 6:00 a.m. and his wife remembered hearing the time on the radio in their bedroom. She was worried Luis was in trouble, but Lieutenant Palmer assured her he was only asking routine questions. When he got off the phone, he continued to question Luis.

"When was the last time you saw Monsignor Triplett?"

Luis paused a moment, trying to remember. "I saw him yesterday afternoon right before I left. I just finished cleaning the chapel, and he came in and sat down. He looked a little nervous. I thought maybe it was just everything happening on Good Friday."

"Did you talk with him?"

"I just told him I would see him tomorrow, and he said don't come before 8:30 a.m."

"Would that have been a normal response from Monsignor Triplett?"

"He was always telling me when to come and when to leave. Sometimes I would work eight-hour days, and other times it would be as little as five-hour days."

"Did you like this?"

"Not really. Money is tight, and when he would cut my hours, it was added pressure at home with the wife yelling. When she did, I just left and spent money we didn't have drinking which is what got me in trouble," Luis disclosed.

"Was Monsignor Triplett a good boss?"

"For the most part, I would say he was more of a priest to me then boss. Even when he cut mine and the other maintenance staff hours, he felt sorry for us. I think it was Sam Tolden who was making him cut our hours."

"Why do you say that?"

"I just don't think Mr. Tolden liked us. The rumor was he was thinking of getting rid of all of us and hiring a whole new maintenance staff."

"Why do you think he was going to do that?"

"One of the construction workers said something about doing the maintenance while they were here. He said it would be easier not to have us around."

Surprised with those words, Palmer pressed for more information, "Do you know who said it?"

"I would have to see him when he comes to work. I don't remember his name. I think he was just trying to frighten me, but I know Oscar and Hector were worried. I kind of was worried too, but I think Monsignor Triplett would have told us first before he would have let one of us go. That was the kind of person he was."

"Would you have any reason to want Monsignor Triplett dead?"

"No... no... As I said to you... I saw him more as a priest who cared about us. He... he helped Oscar and me when we got in trouble with the law. I was shocked when I walked back

177

in to find out he was the one Hector had yelled... was dead."
Luis' lips quivered with those last words.

"Do you know of anyone who would have wanted to kill him?"

Luis pulled himself together. "I know he and the main supervisor of the construction company were not getting along. I would see them yelling at one another. That's the only one I can think of."

"Is there any other information you may have that would be helpful to this murder investigation?"

"I'm not sure who will get in trouble with what I'm about to tell you, Lieutenant, but I know Monsignor Triplett was giving all three of us—me, Hector, and Oscar—money under the table. It was coming out of his pocket to help us when we could not work our eight hours."

"Monsignor Triplett was giving you cash?" Palmer was startled at this new information.

"Yes, $50 bills."

"What did you do with those?"

"I enjoyed a few extra beers at home—never at a bar."

"How often were you given money on the side?"

"Almost every payday."

"How often did you get paid?"

"Twice a month."

"How was the money given to you?"

"Usually, when we picked up our paychecks from Monsignor Triplett, he would give it to us then."

"How much was given?"

"Usually it was a $100 or $200. Again, it just depended on the work pay period."

"Did Monsignor Triplett always give you your paychecks?"

"Most of the time. It was his way of checking in with us and letting us know who the boss was."

"When he didn't give you the paycheck. Who would?"

"Mr. Tolden."

"Would he give you extra money?"

"No… no… in fact, he sometimes questioned the hours we submitted. But Hector would always defend us."

"Yet you left the cathedral today when you first came in."

"Hector is a good boss, but he has been known to show his anger. I was just afraid he had shown it when he yelled 'he's dead 'in the cathedral. "

"Had he shown his anger to you?"

"Only once and once was enough. I had done something stupid in not finishing cleaning and left the supplies out, and he got all angry about it. I think it was just a bad day for him. Like I said, Hector is a good boss."

"Did you ever see him get angry with Monsignor Triplett?"

"Just once, it was a long time ago when we first started working here. Hector was promised more money than what he was being paid, and when he received his paycheck, he let Monsignor Triplett know it. Turned out it was the parish bookkeeper's mistake. Hector really felt bad about showing his anger and apologized to Monsignor Triplett several times, but I don't think Monsignor forgave him."

"Why do you say that?"

"I think because it was something he could hold over Hector. Monsignor Triplett had this influence on Hector, like he did with Oscar and me."

"Did he use that influence?"

"Not with me."

Palmer rechecked his notes, making sure he had covered everything he needed to ask. "If you think of anything else, here's my card with my cell phone number on it. I think you should find Hector and see what work you can begin. You don't need to discuss anything you told me with Hector or anyone else. If I have any more questions, I'll call you." Palmer took down his number.

Luis was still unsure if he had said too much, but he was glad he told the truth, knowing what he had faced when he

179

didn't. He followed the Lieutenant's directions and went to find Hector.

Palmer called the station and asked the officer at the desk to pull any criminal records for Hector Rivera, Oscar Martinez and Luis Hernandez. He needed to know more about these men and see if Luis was telling the truth.

Detective Sabor came over to Lieutenant Palmer and filled him in on the information Oscar Martinez provided. Their alibis for last night and when they first arrived at the cathedral seemed to check out. However, the big difference in their stories was that Oscar never mentioned any criminal record, nor seeing Hector angry. He said they left the cathedral because they were fearful Hector was the killer when he yelled out the words, 'He's dead.'

Sabor followed up on Oscar's alibi. After calling Oscar's wife, Teresa she verified Oscar was drinking at Luis' house and came home last night. They both live in the same neighborhood. Oscar said he got home about 7:00 p.m. and stayed home the rest of the night. This morning, he and his wife got up at 5:00 a.m. and prayed together before Oscar left for work. She said there were lots of family members who would say the same thing. She wanted to know if Oscar was in trouble, and Detective Sabor said not at the moment. He would have Oscar call her as soon as possible. She seemed really upset and then made the comment that seemed odd, 'Monsignor Triplett had this coming to him.' She wouldn't say any more. She had said too much already.

"Will, do you want me to pursue this with her and Oscar?" Detective Sabor thought he might be on to something.

"I do, but first let me ask you a couple of questions? Did he mention anything about Monsignor Triplett giving him money?"

"Yes, he did. In fact, he said he was getting almost $200 every pay period for almost a year. He said it was because they were not working as many hours as Monsignor Triplett wished they could be."

"So if Monsignor Triplett was paying them this extra money, where was he getting it? It seems this mystery deepens."

"Who else was getting paid like this?" Sabor questioned.

Before Palmer could answer, his phone rang. It was Detective Jabowski asking Palmer to come back to the parish house since several people were looking for him, including Commissioner Timberbank, who, according to Detective Jabowski was not happy.

"Would you be happy if you were the chief working on a Saturday?" Palmer joked. "I'll be over shortly."

Palmer placed his phone in his pocket and then asked Sabor, "Before you question Oscar about his wife's comment, have you been able to get in touch with anyone at Delfino Construction?"

"No... I left a message."

"Luis gave me the name of the head supervisor for this restoration project, a Jared Quinn. Let's see if we can find him and get him to come to the cathedral. You and I are going to have to interview him together."

Palmer's head was spinning. It had been less than two hours, and he was already discovering a different side of Monsignor Triplett than what he saw the night before. There were so many questions to be answered. It seemed the more people who were interviewed, the more unanswered questions he had. He tried to make some sense of it all before heading over to the parish house again to face an angry police commissioner.

Two of the CSU investigators came to Palmer and said they were finished in the sanctuary. They told him the crime scene cleaners were almost finished sanitizing the area where the pew was and wherever they found blood. He asked how much time CSU still needed. They couldn't give a definite answer, but informed Palmer of the areas they were still working.

In the meantime, Hector moved the podium to the center aisle to the space that was designated for the press conference. On his way back up the aisle, he noticed the absence of the first pew and the spots of blood gone. He stopped and said an "Our Father." With a heavy heart, he did not move until one of the CSU investigators told him that he could begin cleaning the sanctuary.

Hector retrieved the necessary supplies to start the task and grateful for the work of the crime scene cleaners. As he began his work in the sanctuary, he remembered the many times Monsignor Triplett stood at the altar and celebrated Mass. Monsignor worked hard to make everyone feel welcome in such a large space. He had the charisma to make you think the words he was preaching were directed at you. Hector complimented Monsignor on the powerful message he delivered. Hector sometimes wished God had called him to the priesthood.

The florist arrived unexpectedly with the flowers even after they were notified not to come until 2:00 p.m. Lieutenant Palmer was called to the side door to inform the driver that this was a crime scene, and he would have to return with the flowers at 2:00 p.m. The driver and his assistant were not happy nor was one of the cathedral's volunteers who didn't receive a call informing her of the time change. She wondered what had happened. But like the reporters, she was given no information.

Hector looked at his watch and knew he needed to stop cleaning. He walked down to the narthex to the side door on 50th Street. He noticed the police had set up an area to check press credentials and search any personal bags. Hector was not looking forward to the disruption the reporters and camera crews would create.

As Hector unlocked the door, a canvas of reporters entered, jostling each other to get a story about a terrible murder. He knew that once the news went public of the mysterious life and death of Monsignor Triplett difficult days would follow.

Hector couldn't wait until the press conference was over, so that Saint Patrick's could be properly cleaned and returned to a place of prayer. Although he felt genuine sadness, he held to his faith and was looking forward to the most important day of the Christian faith, Easter, the resurrection of Jesus Christ.

Chapter 15

Lieutenant Palmer could not escape the news media that wanted information. The barrage of questions flew at him as he walked out of the cathedral on his way to meet with the police commissioner at the cardinal's house.

"Who was murdered?"

"Is it only one person?"

"Why hasn't the name of the person been released?"

"Where are the priests?"

"Where is the cardinal?"

"Please tell us something for our viewers."

He reminded them. "A news conference is scheduled for 11:00 a.m., and these questions will be answered."

Police Commissioner Timberbank was the right person for the position of police commissioner for New York City. He had grown up in the city and made his way through the ranks of the police department and was recognized numerous times for his bravery in the line of duty. He was well respected by many within and outside of the department. Palmer knew when the police commissioner was upset, it was best to say nothing for a while.

Arriving at the cardinal's front door, the archdiocese communication director, Donald Armenti, met him and escorted him into the cardinal's conference room. Donald and the lieutenant joined Police Commissioner Timberbank along with the public relations liaison for the New York City Police Department, Karen Zirpoli and Cardinal Flinn who were still working out the details of the press conference.

When the Police Commissioner Timberbank saw the lieutenant, he immediately asked, "Lieutenant Palmer, why didn't you come to the parish house immediately when you came to the crime scene and knew it was the death of one of the priests?"

"There are two reasons: first, the Director of Maintenance Operations, Hector Rivera, needed to be questioned. Second, Detective Sabor wasn't here yet, so I needed to stay in the cathedral to protect the crime scene." Lieutenant Palmer spoke with confidence, but he was also a little annoyed.

"And how much time before you came over?"

"I'd say we came over within the first thirty minutes of my arrival."

"We?"

"Hector Rivera and I. I didn't know where the front door was, so Hector showed me." Palmer continued with assurance.

The commissioner seemed a little more at ease with the answers he received to explain the delay in letting the cardinal and those in the parish house know the situation. Apparently, the cardinal accepted Palmer's answers. Both were ready to discuss the preparations for the press conference.

"Are we all set for the press conference?" The commissioner asked.

"I believe so. The podium is placed where we discussed. We have a sufficient number of police officers to limit the press locations for reporting. The news crews are required to show their credentials at the front door in order to enter. And the doors will open for them at 10:30 this morning."

The cardinal held up his finished statement and an outline the three of them had agreed upon for the press conference. Karen would act as MC for the press conference. Both the commissioner and the cardinal would read statements and not take any questions at this time. They felt it best to present just the known facts, to ask for prayers for the deceased and the parishioners of the cathedral. Another press conference would be held at the police station when more information was accurately known. The cardinal wanted to move the investigation away from the cathedral so the clergy could celebrate Easter Masses with the respect they deserve and not with the media hanging around and questioning every person entering the church about Monsignor Triplett's character.

"Lieutenant Palmer, could I have a few moments with the priests of the parish house once you and the others have finished questioning them?" The cardinal asked.

"Can they meet with you here, in your residence? I need to interview some other people including the only living relative of Monsignor Triplett. Would it be okay to interview them here?" Palmer asked.

"Yes, I also need to discuss the sacramental schedule for tonight and tomorrow. I need to stress that my statement will serve as the official communication from the archdiocese. I want the priests to hear the statement first and to be aware of its importance as they speak with the parishioners and visitors attending the Easter Masses," the cardinal emphasized.

"As head of the church in New York, you set the tone. I have found the investigation always goes better when there is one consistent message spoken to the public," Palmer said.

"That is why I want to stress to the priests the importance of one voice at this unfortunate time and not let their feelings hamper the one voice. We must all pray for Monsignor Triplett. I also want to give them a chance to express their concerns as we get ready for one of the busiest days in the church," the cardinal emphasized.

Palmer thanked the cardinal and then said, "Your Eminence, we've questioned the priests. I don't see any reason you couldn't meet with them. I trust they could use your spiritual counseling, Cardinal."

"I would agree." Cardinal Flinn knew he not only had to give some spiritual counseling, but he also had to provide some direction to avoid speculating or disrupting the work of the police department or their handling of Monsignor Triplett's death investigation. Putting a priest in front of a TV camera without the proper coaching could be problematic.

With everyone in agreement, Palmer excused himself and returned to the parish house. Detective Jabowski had just finished interviewing Father Crumbley in the kitchen and was ready to update Palmer when Detective Pantera interrupted them and wanted Palmer to come to the living room to listen to Monsignor Black's comments on Monsignor Triplett. Detective Jabowski went back to the kitchen for another cup of coffee and waited until the other detectives finished with Monsignor Black.

As Lieutenant Palmer and Detective Pantera entered the living room, Monsignor Black looked tired and exhausted.

"Are you feeling okay, Monsignor?" Palmer asked.

"Yes, I'm fine." Monsignor Black rubbed his eyes.

"Monsignor Black, I would like for you to repeat what you told me about the priests living in the house," Pantera directed.

"I said the cathedral parish house is a house of misfits. We have a gay priest, a priest who was falsely accused of sexual abuse, an alcoholic priest and Monsignor Triplett."

Palmer wanted to know more.

"Would you share again who each of these priests are?" Detective Pantera asked.

"Father Morales is the gay priest. Father Crumbley is the falsely accused priest. I am the alcoholic priest and Monsignor Triplett I think was intimately involved with one of the employees."

"You think Monsignor Triplett was having an affair with whom?" Palmer asked.

"The housekeeper, Emma Pickle," Monsignor Black answered.

"How do you know?"

"Because I overheard one of the former associates, Father David O'Hara, say they met on Thursday at the Women's Republican Club a block up the street."

"What else did you overhear?"

"All I know is every Thursday Monsignor Triplett would leave before noon to go to lunch. Many times, he would not return to the parish house until right before dinner. When he did, he was usually in a relaxed mood."

"Go on," Detective Pantera said.

"Emma did not work on Tuesday or Thursday morning, but came to work each of those afternoons and prepared our evening meal. On Thursday afternoons, she always carried an overnight bag. She also was in a good mood. I had no proof, and I never asked. It was just this feeling I had that they were more than friends." Monsignor Black was suddenly questioning himself for sharing hearsay.

"Are you sure of what you are saying?" Palmer asked.

"No, I'm not sure. That's why I said I had a feeling. You have to ask Emma if it was happening. I tried asking Monsignor Triplett once about it and never got an answer. We all have our individual demons, and maybe this was his. As much as he held things over employees, and those he lived within the house, he was still a good priest. He was well-loved by both the parishioners and priests of the archdiocese. He treated me well and was fair." Tears welled in Monsignor Black's eyes. While he was physically drained, telling these truths was also taking a toll on his conscience.

"Did others know of Monsignor Triplett's alleged affair with the housekeeper... Emma?" Detective Pantera asked.

"If they did, they never said, or at least never said anything to me, but maybe to him."

"You said Father O'Hara told you?" Detective Pantera asked.

"He was the former associate here. It was his first assignment, and he struggled just to celebrate Mass properly.

He always forgot something. I think he was testing me to see if I would take the bait."

"The bait?" Palmer was curious.

"He liked to gossip, and I think he was seeing if I would. I just told him it wasn't any of his business."

"Did you ask the housekeeper?" Palmer continued with the questioning.

"I didn't think it was appropriate. She and I didn't always get along." Monsignor Black recalled the times he complained to her about the cleaning and cooking.

"So no one provided any proof of this relationship?"

"No, and I'm only speculating." Monsignor Black wanted to move off of this topic.

"You said Monsignor Triplett would hold things over employees and all of you living in this house. Would you talk more about this?" Palmer wanted to know if Monsignor Black knew about the black notebook.

"Oh… he wrote everything down in a black notebook. I believed it was a notebook of death for many here at the cathedral. It was his way of holding his staff and priests accountable. The truth was, he wanted everyone to know he was in charge, and I think it was his method of remembering things. He could never get comfortable with a computer or any other electronic devices," Monsignor Black said.

"What other kinds of things do you suppose he recorded?"

"If you were in trouble, he remembered when and where it happened. He remembered the many times he helped you and recorded it in his notebook. He scratched your back if you scratched his, but his back was not personal, it was the church."

"How do you mean helped?" Detective Pantera wanted some clarification.

"If he needed something done, it was his way of getting you to help him."

"Could you give me an example?"

"Last night was a good example, and this has to be in confidence. He told me early, right after lunch that the church tribunal would not grant his brother's annulment because he presented insufficient grounds in the petition. He was mad as could be about it. He was mad at the head of the tribunal, the judicial vicar, Monsignor 'pain in the ass', excuse my French. He's actually Monsignor David Stone. Believe me, he's all stone. So Monsignor Triplett was going to meet with him. He knew his brother would be mad. He didn't want me to say anything about this to anyone. He said he would fix it himself. I kept my mouth shut about his moody behavior and his hostile attitude these last few days, and he overlooked the bottle of Scotch found in my room."

"That doesn't seem too bad?" Palmer stated.

"Remember, I'm an alcoholic. I'm supposed to be a recovering alcoholic!" Monsignor Black explained. "If I had shared Monsignor Triplett's plan to 'fix' his brother's annulment with the cardinal, I'd no longer be allowed to remain here. At my age, I didn't want to go through another treatment program."

"I see. So you're saying Monsignor Triplett would have written that down in the black notebook?" Detective Pantera asked.

"Yes… I believe so. As I said, he kept very good notes on all the priests, employees of the cathedral and even the cardinal and a couple of bishops."

"Did you ever see what was in the black notebook?" Lieutenant Palmer questioned.

"Yes… when I first arrived… he left it out by mistake in the community room. He went to bed, and I stayed up to watch the late news. I was looking at it when he came back in the room. He wasn't at all happy when he saw me with it."

"And what did you read?" Palmer was hoping to learn details that could help solve the case.

"Just that he had a page for what looked like every person who was here and an entry of a date and notes that followed on each. I never really got to read much of it except about Hector, the maintenance director. After that one time, I never saw him without it."

"What did you find out about Hector?" Palmer continued.

"He was a hard worker and dependable, which was nice to know he was putting good things in this notebook."

"Do you think Hector had any reason to kill Monsignor Triplett?"

"No... Lieutenant, Hector's not a killer. He's a lover and a good person. Monsignor Triplett had too many other enemies, and they're all probably in that black notebook."

"Who do you think would be on the list of enemies wanting to kill him?"

"I can think of two. First would be the supervisor of the construction since he was always mad at him. I believe his last name was Quinn. It seemed this project was creating major stress for Monsignor Triplett who already had high blood pressure."

"You said there were two—who else?" Palmer was eager to know.

"Next, I would think it would be the Director of Administrative Services, Sam Tolden. I'm not sure what was going on with him and Monsignor Triplett, but I do know Monsignor wasn't happy with Sam. He would never say why as many times as I asked. I assumed that Sam must have had something on Monsignor, or I don't think he would still be here. Sam wasn't well-liked by the staff or any of the priests. He seemed to feel he was more important than any of us and let us all know."

"How so?" Detective Pantera asked.

"When Monsignor Triplett was away, it wasn't one of the priests who was in charge. Sam always took on that role. It was mostly with the office staff, and you could just feel the tension in the office during the absence of Monsignor."

191

"Is there anything else you remember that could help us with the investigation?" Lieutenant Palmer continued, hoping for another revelation.

"There was a phone conversation I overheard Monsignor Triplett having after the Chrism Mass, and as he ended the conversation, I heard him say, 'I'm going to kill him.' Now I'm only speculating, but maybe it was the other way around, and that person killed him."

"Do you know who Monsignor Triplett was talking to?" Palmer hoped for a real lead.

"I don't. I do know it was about his brother's annulment. It could have been his brother. It could have been Monsignor Stone. At my age and with my hearing, I just didn't hear a name."

"Monsignor Black, you mentioned the Chrism Mass?"

"Chrism Mass... Yes, this is the Mass of the blessing of oils used in our sacraments and the renewal of the priests' commitment to the cardinal. The Mass here this past Tuesday at 2:00 p.m., and most of the priests of the archdiocese attended. The phone conversation I mentioned took place that night. We had just watched the evening news, when Monsignor Triplett's phone rang." Monsignor Black continued to share more details.

Detective Pantera was confused about this information. He looked at Palmer who seemed to understand what he said.

Palmer made a note about the annulment and then asked, "Do you have a telephone number for Monsignor Stone?"

"Didn't Father Crumbley give you the sheet of numbers we had posted on the bulletin board? That's where we keep it," Monsignor Black answered.

Palmer pulled the sheet out and located Monsignor Stone's cell phone number under diocesan personnel. He made a note to call the priest once the interview was over. "Is there any reason you would want to kill Monsignor Triplett?" Palmer looked cautiously at Monsignor Black.

"No! He was a brother priest! Like I said, he was a good priest who may have had something going on once a week on Thursday, but the other times he was faithful, dedicated and inspired others, including me. He was a friend. I would never have thoughts of killing him." Monsignor Black could no longer fight back his tears. His heart was broken. He lost a friend who helped him be a better person and priest.

"I'm so sorry for your loss. You have been most helpful. Thank you for your help and cooperation. Please remain on the property in case I need to talk with you again." Palmer tried to be sensitive to the needs of this priest while moving forward with the investigation.

"I plan on going back to my room and praying for the soul of Monsignor Triplett." Monsignor Black got up slowly from the couch, blew his nose and wiped the tears away.

"I think the cardinal wants to talk with you," Palmer said. Both he and Detective Pantera thanked him again and excused themselves. They went to find Detective Jabowski.

Detective Jabowski came out of the kitchen. She had in her hand the information asked for by Lieutenant Palmer. "Lieutenant, here's the list Father Crumbly made of the staff members and the offices they used." Jabowski showed him the paper.

"Great. Hold on to it. They'll be the next group to interview. I may need to look at it later."

Jabowski folded the list and stuck it in her notepad.

Before Palmer could ask her any more questions, Jabowski's phone rang. She excused herself and returned to the kitchen to answer it. It was her one-year-old daughter's babysitter. Lieutenant Palmer was not happy with the interruption.

After leaving the cardinal's residence, Donald Armenti arrived at the parish house and approached the detectives. He asked if they had interviewed all the priests and if they could meet with the cardinal now. Palmer had no objections, as long as the priests returned and remained in the parish house.

Armenti told Father Crumbley the cardinal wanted to see all the cathedral priests with their breviaries at the cardinal's residence in five minutes.

As the priests gathered with the cardinal in the conference room, he announced the pages he wanted to use for Morning Prayer. It was from the Office for the Dead. The cardinal assigned parts to make it flow, as he acted as a true shepherd to his priests by calling them together to remember the soul of Monsignor Triplett and to pray for God's mercy in judging their beloved priest.

With Morning Prayer completed, the cardinal read aloud the statement for the press conference. Brief and to the point, it announced the death of Monsignor Triplett, the sadness of the loss of the rector, and the cardinal's expectation of full cooperation with the police investigation from all employees and priests at Saint Patrick's. He went on to say the funeral arrangements were pending and would be announced at a later time. He also announced the Easter schedule would remain as planned. The only change that he made was the cathedral would not open until 5:00 p.m. today allowing the necessary time needed for the CSU.

The cardinal gave instructions to the priests to refrain from answering any reporters' questions, but to tell them to contact the Office of Media and Communication for the archdiocese. He asked the priests to focus on Easter with their homilies and to include Monsignor Triplett in intercessory prayer. He expected their full cooperation as the investigation continued. He then asked if they had any questions.

"What about the Masses Monsignor Triplett was to celebrate on Easter?" Monsignor Black asked.

Looking at the schedule Father Crumbley gave him, the cardinal said, "I see he was scheduled for the 11:30 a.m. Mass and the evening Mass. Is that correct?"

"Yes."

"I will celebrate the 11:30 a.m. Mass, and Father Crumbley could you take the evening Mass?" Father Crumbley nodded.

194

"Are there any other decisions you feel we need to make immediately?

Father Morales was obviously nervous, and he wondered if he would be allowed to go to Rome on Monday. While in his thoughts, he heard the cardinal announce, "Juan, I need to talk with you after this meeting, so I'm going to ask you to stay."

"I understand," Father Morales said.

"Do you want us at the press conference?" Monsignor Black asked.

"I do not think that is necessary," the cardinal responded. "When Monsignor Triplett's brother arrives, would you ask him and Lieutenant Palmer to come over? I want to offer my condolences and would like to talk with both of them."

"When do you think the funeral will take place?" Father Crumbley inquired.

"I need to talk with Lieutenant Palmer and Monsignor Triplett's brother to determine when the body will be released from the morgue and the wishes of the family. I would hope at the latest on Friday. If there are no more questions, I think we have covered the business we needed. I will be here the rest of the day, so if you need anything, please give me a call. I will see you about 7:30 tonight. Let us go about this Holy Saturday and Easter Sunday praying for our brother, Monsignor Steven Triplett."

Everyone stood. They filed out of the cardinal's conference room, except for Father Morales. He knew his fate was in the cardinal's hands.

At the parish house, Commissioner Timberbank, Karen Zirpoli, and Lieutenant Palmer, Detectives Jabowski, and Pantera gathered in the living room to discuss the initial investigation.

The commissioner wanted the latest details before meeting with the press. Palmer placed a call to Detective Sabor in the cathedral and put him on speaker.

Sabor reviewed his notes. "The CSU is still at work. Flowers arrived and left. The maintenance guys are limited in what they can do but are working. Hector is cleaning the sanctuary and wants to know if any more areas need to be closed off before the doors open?"

The police commissioner who responded, "I don't think so, but you may want to check with the CSU. Are there plenty of officers to post around the cathedral once the doors open?"

"We're working on getting a few more here. I've already assigned an officer to that task.

"Make sure they are properly instructed." The commissioner insisted, "Limit those reporters to the space in front of the podium. Officers should be in the aisles, so the reporters can't move up the aisles or anywhere near the murder location."

"Will do. I'll take care of it. In the meantime, I finally reached the answering service for the construction company. I found the number on one of their signs in the church. They have more free advertisement than Jesus this Easter. I relayed a message to the construction supervisor—a Mr. Jared Quinn. I gave them my number and asked if he would get in touch with me. They assured me they would call back when they heard something. Also, the wife of the Martinez in maintenance is coming down to explain her comment that Monsignor Triplett 'got what he deserved.' I tried asking her husband about it, but he wouldn't say anything." Detective Sabor hoped he hadn't left out any information. He double checked his notes.

"Thanks for your update Sabor. Stay on the line. I want you to hear from each of the other detectives," Palmer directed.

As the detectives shared the information they learned from those interviewed, Lieutenant Palmer and Detective Sabor agreed the focus of the initial investigation was on four individuals—Sam Tolden, Jared Quinn, Monsignor David Stone and Thom Triplett. They knew that Sam, Jared and Thom were on their way to be interviewed. Palmer wanted two detectives at each of these interviews. Detective Pantera would return to the cathedral and continue the investigation there. Detective Jabowski would remain to assist with the examination of Monsignor Triplett's room.

"Thanks Sabor for your hard work." Palmer said as he ended the telephone conversation. Before he could do any of the interviews, however, Palmer needed to make a call to Monsignor Stone.

Unfortunately, that call would have to wait. The parish house doorbell rang. The police officer allowed a visibly nervous Thom Triplett to come in.

Chapter 16

Jonathan did not respond right away to his mother's phone call asking for him to come home. In fact, he didn't even hear his cell phone. The battery was dead which wasn't unusual for him despite living most nights in his car. It's very hard to keep a phone charged without a car charger. His two friends could offer him only a night or two at each of their houses, and he didn't want to spend the cash he had on a place to sleep. He needed the money for gas and food.

The last thing Jonathan thought about was returning home. As bad as it was to have no place to sleep, and as difficult for him to try to survive, he had no intention of going back home. There was too much drama in his house. He was determined to call in a couple of favors. The first one would be from someone at work last night.

After turning sixteen a little less than a year ago, Jonathan applied for and was given a job at the Michelangelo Hotel. He was thrilled to actually be making some money. He knew how tight money was at his house, and the extra income would help him get what every other American kid wanted his own cell phone.

Working at the Michelangelo was not the best of jobs, but he knew it was smart to keep a positive attitude and avoid complaining about his first job. Jonathan worked in the housekeeping department. He was available for the guests during the evening if they needed anything for their rooms. Guests called housekeeping for extra towels, pillows or any number of amenities. Sometimes Jonathan got a tip, but most of the time it was a courteous thank you.

When he was not going up and down the service elevator, his job was folding towels. When finished with the towels, he used the time to study. As monotonous as it was, he was thankful to be out of the house.

Yesterday, he received a call from room 1260 asking for additional pillows and two wine glasses. He was surprised to recognize one of the guests in the room. He remembered seeing him at Saint Patrick's Cathedral. He thought he knew the voice of the other man and wondered what was going on between them. Surprised, all he could do was give the guest the items and return to the laundry room. While downstairs folding the towels, he just figured they must be lovers, and this was the place they met.

Now it was time to use the information Jonathan had on them to his advantage. While sleeping in the parking lot of Holy Name of Jesus parish, Jonathan prepared to meet one of the guests from room 1260. Jonathan needed a place to stay and thought Father O'Hara could help. He headed up the stairs and rang the doorbell of the parish house. When Father O'Hara opened the door, he was taken aback to see Jonathan on the other side.

"What are you doing here?" Father O'Hara asked.

"So, you know who I am?" Jonathan casually replied.

"Yes, Jonathan, I know who you are."

"Did you enjoy your stay at the Michelangelo last night?" Jonathan uttered with a sarcastic tone. He watched as Father O'Hara's face turned red with embarrassment.

"What do you want?" Father O'Hara demanded, not answering the question he was asked.

"The $20 you gave me isn't enough. I figured out who was with you last night. I'd figured I'd tell the cardinal after I've told my mom. I know you know her. You know… Emma Pickle?"

"Yes, I know your mom. She's the housekeeper at the cathedral. But you're too late, the cardinal already knows."

"How does he know? You mean it's okay for you and Father Morales to do what you did?"

"Not exactly… but he knows. I'm sure we're going to pay a hefty price for our actions."

"I just didn't believe you're like that or would do something like that. I've never known a priest to be like… like… that."

"You mean gay? I'm sorry you found out the way you did. I was shocked to see you as well. You've grown up. How old are you now?" Father O'Hara expressed genuine interest.

"I'll be seventeen next week."

"So… it's been over three years…?"

"Yes, since my dad's funeral." Jonathan quickly added.

"Why are you here?" Father O'Hara asked as he stood at the back door.

"I've been sleeping in my car the last three nights. After seeing you last night, I decided to come and sleep in your parking lot. I wanted to confront you. I figured I'd get some money from you. I also need a place to stay and don't get paid 'til next week."

"How did you know I wasn't still at the Michelangelo?" Father O'Hara was curious.

"Because I saw you going in the house here this morning when I was waking up. I thought maybe you saw me in the car?"

"No, I didn't even see the car. I wasn't really paying much attention when I came back to the house. A lot has happened since last night. When was the last time you talked with your mom or saw her?" Father O'Hara asked as several cars were blowing their horns.

"Three days ago, I left a voicemail. My phone is dead. I need to charge it. No one is going to try and call me except my mom, and all she wants is for me to come home."

"So you don't know what's happened at the cathedral? I think maybe it's best you come in." Father O'Hara opened the back door and invited Jonathan into the parish house.

"No... why?" While Jonathan was curious, he entered the kitchen and wished he had something to eat.

"I have some very sad news to tell you. Monsignor Triplett.... our friend... he.... was murdered last night." Father O'Hara could barely speak the words and worried about Jonathan's reaction.

"O my God!!" Jonathan screamed. And without any warning, he collapsed into the arms of Father O'Hara. He carried Jonathan into the living room, laid him on the couch and propped his head up. He made sure the boy was breathing okay and checked his pulse which was good. He called out his name, and Jonathan attempted to make a noise.

Father McFadden heard the voices and came downstairs to find out what was going on. He was startled to see the boy. Father O'Hara tried to explain, "This is Jonathan Pickle. His mother is the housekeeper at the cathedral. He slept in his car last night in our parking lot. I just told him about Monsignor Triplett, and he fainted."

"Is he all right?" Father McFadden asked seeing Jonathan stir a little.

"I think so. He seems to be breathing okay."

"Let's give him a minute. God willing, we won't have to call 911. Monsignor Triplett was a big help to Jonathan when his father died, so I'm sure this is a big shock to him. Why was he sleeping in our parking lot?" Father McFadden asked.

"He left home, works at the Michelangelo and saw me there last night."

"So he knows about you and Father Morales?" Father McFadden remarked looking at Father O'Hara with sympathy.

"Well, he didn't, but he found out last night. He came here to blackmail me. I think he's a little desperate for money and a place to stay," Father O'Hara said.

"I'm going to get some orange juice for him." Father McFadden walked to the kitchen.

"Jonathan, can you hear me?" Jonathan opened his eyes and slowly focused them on Father O'Hara.

"I think so. What happened?"

"You passed out when I told you the news about the death of Monsignor Triplett."

Jonathan closed his eyes, and the tears began. The news stunned him. Feeling light-headed, he wished he'd been able to see Monsignor Triplett one last time.

"Jonathan, I think you should call your mom and let her know where you are." Father O'Hara checked to see that Jonathan was truly alert.

"I'm so confused. I'm really mad at my mom!" Jonathan saw a priest he didn't know holding a glass of orange juice in front of him.

"Jonathan, this is Father McFadden, the pastor here. He heard you fainted."

"Nice to meet you." Jonathan was polite, but unable to move.

"Here, drink this glass of orange juice. It will help you," Father McFadden said.

"Thanks." Jonathan sat on the edge of the couch, took the glass of juice and without stopping consumed it all. Then he passed the glass back to Father McFadden.

"Do you want another one?"

"Please. I'm really thirsty."

Father McFadden returned to the kitchen for another glass of juice.

"Jonathan, why are you so mad at your mom?" Father O'Hara wanted to provide some guidance to this poor young man. "I remember her doing everything she could to make you happy after your dad passed away. I know Monsignor

202

Triplett even came over to the house and took you to the Jets football games."

"Yes, but Mom... Mom... started seeing someone who's really wrong for her. But my mom thinks he's great!"

"Who is it?"

"You know him. It's Sam Tolden! My mom is dating a married man who has a couple of kids, and he's from the church!!"

"I didn't know. When did all this start?" Father O'Hara couldn't believe what he was hearing.

"I would say about six months ago when Monsignor Triplett stopped coming to our house."

"So... you're angry because Monsignor Triplett stopped seeing you?"

"Yes, when he abandoned my mother, he abandoned me. I... I... wanted to talk with him last Sunday. I... I... even called him to try to understand why, but he was too busy and couldn't or wouldn't see me. That really hurt. I just decided to leave the house. My mom was happy, but I wasn't."

"I don't really know what to say, except I'm sorry for you." Father O'Hara continued to provide support as he listened. "I remember you as a happy boy when you came around the cathedral. Despite the difficult life you are experiencing, I see you as a person with great potential and many possibilities."

"I haven't been happy since my dad died. I miss him so much. I lost my best friend." Jonathan's tears continued.

"And you should miss him. His death was terrible tragedy. Losing a parent is never easy for anyone at any age, especially at a young age. It's horrible. It's unexplainable. But I thought you were talking with different people and getting help?" Father O'Hara seized the opportunity to hopefully help Jonathan.

"You mean the psychologists? They were doing nothing for me except wanting my doctor to put me on different drugs. They didn't listen. They just wanted their money. The only one who really listened was Monsignor Triplett." Jonathan spoke honestly and angrily. He quickly drank a second glass of juice. "Thanks. I'm much better now."

"How about I call your mom and tell her you're here with me? At least she'll know you're okay. I'll be more than happy to go with you if and when you want to talk with her." Father O'Hara looked at Father McFadden to get his approval.

"Thanks." Jonathan responded. "I probably should be the one to call her. You never even talked to me when you were assigned to the cathedral, and now you're willing to help?"

"Like I said, I saw good things in you, and knew with Monsignor Triplett's help, good things would happen. I just didn't know you two had become distant. I'm sorry for the both of you." Father O'Hara sat down next to him.

"So am I. He... he... really tried to help me." Jonathan's tears continued to roll down his face. He felt so alone and saddened by Monsignor Triplett death.

"It's going to be okay, Jonathan. He'll help you from heaven now." Father O'Hara searched for words to help this troubled youth, wanting to put his arm around him

"Thanks for your willingness to help. I think I'd better call my mom. Can I use your phone?" Jonathan asked as he stood up handing the glass back to Father McFadden.

"Sure. Let me show you where you can make the call." Father O'Hara got up from the couch and opened the door to a small office and showed him the phone.

As Jonathan looked at the antiquated phone system, he said, "I may need your help to use this! I don't think I've seen something this old!"

"Funny. Let me get you a dial tone, then you can just dial the number. All you need to do is push the ten buttons of the area code and number. Then you should hear it ring." Father O'Hara chuckled to himself.

"Thanks. I just need to remember the number." Jonathan tried to remember the ten digits of his mom's cell phone.

"I wish I could help." With cell phones, no one memorizes numbers or uses phone books. Father O'Hara didn't even know if they had a phone book.

Jonathan pulled out his wallet and found his emergency information card his mom made him fill out. "I've got it!"

Father O'Hara gave Jonathan a pat on the back and said, "Remember your mom is also hurting with the death of Monsignor Triplett, so do the right thing — agree to go home right now and be with her. You need each other."

"I understand." Jonathan nodded his head.

"If I can help, let me know." Father O'Hara didn't know what more he could do for Jonathan right now.

"Thanks. That means a lot to me."

"Let me give you some privacy. I'll wait for you back in the living room."

"Thanks."

Father O'Hara closed the door and left as Jonathan punched in the ten numbers. He realized Father O'Hara was right. His mother was hurting and feeling the loss of someone who really helped her and him, Monsignor Triplett.

"Hello." The voice on the other end said. "Who is this?"

"Mom, it's me... Jonathan."

Three floors up, Bishop Newsome was unaware of what was happening downstairs. He received an interesting telephone call from a friend and former parishioner of Holy Name of Jesus. She is the front desk manager at the Michelangelo Hotel.

"Bishop Newsome, Gloria Banks here," she began. "I have the information you asked for. It was a little difficult to obtain, but I have the dates of George Newsome's stay here. They were January 12, February 16, March 10 and the last one yesterday, April 19. Does that help you?"

"It certainly does."

"Were there any charges on this account besides the room and tax?"

"That's all I see on each of reservation. All were paid with cash. Each was for one night. O yes... there is one more thing that surprised us..." Gloria added. "Whoever was using your name had also set up an awards point account in your name — and with the four stays, the fifth one is fifty-percent off, so let me know when you want to use it."

"Thank you, Gloria. You have brought a smile to my face. If there's another time a George Newsome registers, could you please flag it and check for ID?"

"Good idea! I'll work on making that happen."

"Happy Easter, Gloria. Thank you for your help."

"Anytime, Bishop Newsome. Happy Easter."

Bishop Newsome had the dates and would again confront Father O'Hara and Father Morales with this information but probably not until Tuesday. He wanted them to stew a little. Besides, there was too much to do for Easter. Even so, his mind was wondering about the punishment he would issue when they all met. He decided to make one more telephone call, and it was to the Abbot of the Gethsemani Retreat Center in Louisville, Kentucky. Maybe this would be the place to send Father O'Hara.

Chapter 17

As Thom Triplett stood at the parish house doorway, Lieutenant Palmer introduced himself and asked Thom to come in as he escorted him to the library. Detective Jabowski joined them.

"Mr. Triplett, I'm so sorry for your loss. I thank you for coming to the cathedral. Is there anything I can get for you before we begin? A cup of coffee or a glass of water?" Palmer asked before he took out his notepad.

"Please, call me Thom, detectives. You said it would be easier for you if I came here, and I'd like to cooperate as much as possible."

"Thank you. I need to ask you several questions first before I update the investigation. Are you sure you wouldn't like something to drink?"

"No, I'm fine, Lieutenant. Please ask your questions." Thom just wanted to get on with it.

Palmer began. "What do you do for a living, Thom?"

"I'm a civil attorney dealing primarily with the mediation of cases. When there's a problem between two parties, I'm the one trying to save everyone's money and bring about a settlement between the two parties to avoid a trial."

"How long have you been doing this?" Detective Jabowski asked.

"I've been a lawyer for twenty years but doing only arbitration for at least the last ten years."

"You weren't doing any negotiations for your brother?"

"Not professionally. I gave him legal advice from time to time."

"Any recently?"

"Not really." Thom was surprised at these questions and wondered what the detectives may have discovered.

"Was there anyone that may have wanted to harm your brother?"

"Not that I know of. My brother had a gentle soul. I was the one who got in your face."

Palmer was eager to find a motivation for the murder, and shifted the focus to the closeness of the two brothers. He stepped in with the next question. "How would you describe your relationship with your brother?"

"Those who knew us... knew we were the best of friends. Even though we didn't always agree on everything, and we disagreed in public a lot, we were still close. We talked almost every day." Thom's voice quivered.

"When was the last time you were in touch with your brother?"

"We... we talked on the phone early yesterday and agreed to meet for breakfast this morning," Thom recalled.

"Is this something you normally did?" Detective Jabowski tried to understand this brotherly relationship.

"Normally, we met once a week, depending on our schedules. Steven was helping me through my marriage annulment, and I was talking with him about some of the issues here at Saint Patrick's."

"Could you explain what you mean by helping you through your marriage annulment?" Detective Jabowski asked.

"Annulment is necessary in the Catholic Church if a marriage ends in a civil divorce. The church, after their investigation, determines the validity of the marriage. If the annulment is granted, it frees a person to marry in the church again." Thom gave the best explanation in the simplest terms to the detectives.

"So you divorce civilly, and then you must go through the church to get an annulment?" Detective Jabowski sought clarification.

"Yes, that's how it works. For many, the process of divorce creates a feeling of guilt. But when the marriage annulment is granted, there is supposed to be a sense of freedom."

"What did your brother tell you about your annulment?" Palmer asked.

"He told me it didn't look good, but he would talk with the priest in charge and see what he could do."

"Do you know if he talked with the priest?" Palmer looked through his notes, locating the name of the priest in charge. "Was it Monsignor David Stone?"

"Yes—that's the priest, Monsignor Stone. My brother said he's as hard as stone with annulments. My brother was hoping to meet with him yesterday." Thom confirmed the information.

"Do you know if they met yesterday?"

"No... no... I don't. I presume he would have told me at breakfast this morning."

"Do you think your brother could affect the decision regarding your annulment if he met with Monsignor Stone?" Detective Jabowski was unsure if she was asking the right question.

"I'm not sure. In my conversation with my brother, he seemed to indicate that there could be a change. He never really told me how, but he felt he could talk with Monsignor Stone."

"Did you meet Monsignor Stone?" Palmer asked.

"Yes, we met once." Thom knew that was a half-truth. "But it was to review my testimony, and my brother was with me."

"So your brother represented you to get this annulment?" asked Detective Jabowski

"Yes. Steven served as my advocate, so he would be the one to go back and talk with Monsignor Stone."

Palmer realized this was the second time someone had mentioned the name of Monsignor Stone in a less than flattering way. He was eager to contact him. The lieutenant needed to confirm the recent meeting of Thom and Monsignor Stone. He then continued with his questions. "You said your brother had issues at Saint Patrick's. Do you know what those issues were?"

"He told me about the problems he was having with the construction company doing the restoration and wondered if he could take any legal action about the delays. The project was costing the archdiocese a lot more than planned. Steven talked about the schedule being way behind, and the contractor making excuse after excuse. My brother oversaw the project and didn't get along well with the supervisor of the construction company. I just know in the last few weeks, his blood pressure went up, and he was concerned about his health. Because of the delays and the loss of income, Steven was going to make some staff cuts to save money. My brother was trying to figure out who he should dismiss. He didn't really say much about it, but I know he and his director were not in agreement. Steven wished he could fire his administrator, but something was holding him back from making that decision."

"You asked him about firing the administrator? Whose name is…?" Palmer asked.

"Sam Tolden… and yes… I asked." Thom responded quickly… He wondered what information the detectives really wanted. He just wanted to know the person responsible for his brother's murder.

"Do you think there was any reason for Sam Tolden to kill your brother?" It was a loaded question.

"I don't know. All I know is their relationship wasn't good." Thom was being honest.

"How about the on-site construction supervisor for the cathedral?" Jabowski asked.

"I would doubt it since everything my brother talked about regarding the restoration was business, nothing personal. It was just not a good relationship between the two of them because of all the delays."

"Is there anyone else you can think of who might have wanted to harm your brother?" Palmer asked.

"I am not sure. I know the parishioners and people of the cathedral genuinely loved my brother. I believe his deacon, priests, the bishops and cardinal were happy with what he was doing here. He never really talked about anyone else."

Palmer carefully chose the words to the next question. "Do you know if your brother was involved in any intimate relationship? Forgive me, but I have to ask."

"You mean having an affair? My brother? There's no way! His dedication was to the church. He was faithful to living a celibate life. Why are you asking?" Thom was thoroughly astounded and disgusted by the question. If anyone else had made this suggestion, it would be cause for liable.

"There was mention he possibly met someone on Thursday afternoons at the Women's Republican Club." Palmer continued.

"Yes, Steven told me once a month he met with the head of the Knights of Columbus for lunch at the club." Thom confirmed the information. He was still upset with the lieutenant's questions.

"Supposedly he stayed there until right before dinner and then came back here to the parish house," Palmer stated.

Thom stood up and went over to the window angry at the questions being asked of him about his brother. He took a deep breath and then faced the lieutenant and speaking with a raised voice. "I'm sorry to disappoint you detectives, but I took Thursday afternoons off, and my brother and I would get together, usually for lunch and then golf when possible, and if not, we played cards. We called it our stress release day. The only Thursday we didn't meet for lunch was on the Thursday he had to meet with the head knight. We rarely missed a Thursday."

"You said you met to golf?" Jabowski was trying to move to an easier question as Palmer processed the new information.

"Yes…" Thom took another deep breath, returned to his seat, "Yes… we met at Cantiague Golf Course. We would meet for lunch in the city before noon and then go out there and play… usually nine holes. Neither of us play well. My brother and I would make some small bets, and he would usually win, providing him with a few extra dollars. I'm sure on those days, he was happy when he returned to the parish house."

"Did you play this past Thursday?" Jabowski asked.

"On Holy Thursday? No, we didn't. Don't you remember all the rain we had? Steven, Monsignor Triplett, called me earlier in the morning to cancel. He was hoping to get a few things accomplished in the parish and wanted to do a little investigating for himself about a couple of his employees."

"Do you know what that was all about?" Palmer was trying to make some connections with the information he had gathered.

"I'm sorry I don't. My brother said he would tell me more the next time we met."

"You have cleared up a few rumors. Just for the record, could you tell me where you were last night until this morning?" Palmer moving the questioning along.

"Yes, I was at dinner with a friend until almost 11:00 p.m. I picked up the check, and I think I still have my receipt in my wallet. Let me look." Thom eagerly thumbed through the papers in his wallet. "Here it is! After dinner, I went back to my apartment, and I'm sure the doorman can let you know I was in by midnight. I haven't left the apartment until I came here."

"I'll need the name and telephone number of your friend."

"It's Jennifer Gibson. I'll get her phone number." Thom knew he had programmed it into his phone.

"Jennifer Gibson, the lawyer?" Palmer asked. The lieutenant had worked with her on several cases. He recalled one in particular where Jennifer, as the young assistant district attorney, was relentless during the trial against the pastor of Blessed Sacrament Parish. The pastor was found guilty of stealing from his own church.

"Yes, that's her."

Palmer remembered the first time he met Jennifer. They were meeting on a Tuesday morning on a case that was set to go to court later that week. It was on September 11, 2001, when the World Trade Center was attacked. She looked up at the television and saw the image she could never erase from her mind. She called her husband who worked in Tower One, but there was no answer. The lieutenant recalled when her husband's body was recovered, Jennifer was devastated—the love of her life was gone.

Just as Palmer was about to ask Thom more questions about Jennifer, he thought better. He knew it was always best to be professional in the police investigation and refrain from personal matters. "I need to ask you one more question. Do you know anything about the black notebook your brother carried around with him?"

"The famous black notebook? Yes, I do. It was his way of keeping track of people and what they were doing. Steven was not too good at the computer, so he used a notebook instead. I never really saw what was in it, but I do know he would keep track of what people said and did. Does that help, Lieutenant?"

"It does. It confirms some of what we already know. Thank you for the information you've shared. It's been most helpful. Let me tell you what we know. While I can't give you all the details, I can tell you that your brother was found a little after 7:30 a.m. this morning in the first pew of the cathedral. It looks like he was struck by a blunt object. His body was taken to the morgue, and the corner must perform an autopsy before the body is released to you. He was killed, we believe, sometime early this morning. Hopefully, the coroner will provide us more information." Palmer knew he couldn't reveal any more details.

Tears formed again in Thom's eyes. He took a handkerchief out of his pocket.

"When you found him, did he have the black notebook and his cell phone on him?"

"We have the black notebook, but we didn't find his cell phone. Why do you ask?" Palmer realized he hadn't thought to ask about a phone.

"Like the black notebook, his phone was always with him. If something was wrong, he would have called me."

"But he didn't."

"To have had his notebook and not the phone—something's wrong." Thom wondered what had happened to Steven's phone. "Do you think the murderer took it?"

"I'm not sure. Finding the phone would help determine the last person he spoke to and it would definitely help with the investigation." Palmer realized he had another clue, but no idea where the phone was!

"Do you want me to call the number?" Thom asked.

"I'd like you to give me the number, and I'll give it a call."

Before they made the exchange, there was a knock on the door. Father Crumbley came to let them know the cardinal was ready to see Thom and Palmer once they were finished.

"Please inform the cardinal we'll be over shortly. I want to examine Monsignor Triplett's living quarters first." Palmer wanted to find that phone.

"I'll let him know." Father Crumbley quietly closed the door to the library.

"Have you been in your brother's living quarters?" Palmer asked as Thom was giving him the number of Steven's cell phone.

"Many times. He has two interconnecting rooms. One is his study and then his bedroom. The study you'll find filled with books on church history, probably papers scattered all over the place, but he knew where things were. And lots of empty coke cans, his favorite soft drink. The bedroom is his place of rest where he put his TV and a nice recliner. He keeps that room neat. He always makes his bed like we were taught as children. He said in making it, he would be sure of one good accomplishment each day. After some tough days, when he returned home feeling as if he had accomplished nothing, he'd see his bed and realized he had done one good thing for the day. He put the TV in there so he could wake up to the morning news and fall asleep to the evening shows," Thom said.

Palmer called the number Monsignor Triplett's phone, and as it rang, he reviewed his notes. The call went to voicemail, so he hung up.

"No answer?" Thom observed.

"It went to voicemail." Palmer put his phone back in his pocket. "So how was your brother's high blood pressure?"

"It runs in the family. Unfortunately, both our parents had it, and they died from complications from it. Thom and I have been on blood pressure medicine since we each turned 55. He was taking a higher dose than I am."

"I'm going to ask you to remain here while I examine your brother's room. If there is anything else you can think of, would you write it down, and we can discuss it when I return. Then we'll see the cardinal and get someone to take you to the morgue."

"I understand." Thom moved to another, more comfortable chair expecting to stay a while longer. He wasn't really in any rush to see his brother's body.

Lieutenant Palmer and Detective Jabowski left the library and closed the door behind them to go and find Monsignor Triplett's room.

In the meantime, as Thom remained alone in the library, he called Jennifer Gibson.

Back at the cardinal's residence, the cardinal showed a side of himself rarely seen in public as he drilled Father Morales with questions. Most people were accustomed to a man deeply admired by the people of New York City, always on the major news networks, smiling and laughing. He was known to have a great sense of humor, charming people of all faiths while explaining the doctrines of the Catholic Church. He pulled no punches on what was expected from those who were Catholic and those who were interested in becoming Catholic.

In private, however, when having to be confrontational, especially dealing with one of his priests, there was a more serious side. Even though it was two consenting adults, the relationship between Father's O'Hara and Morales was wrong in the eyes of the church. Cardinal Flinn did not need another scandal in the church, especially at this time when he was raising millions for the restoration of Saint Patrick's Cathedral. Now face-to-face with one of the errant priests, he was uncertain what disciplinary action he would take.

"You realize the difficult position you've put me in." The cardinal explained to Father Morales.

"I do, and I am sorry for doing so. We made a mistake."

"Does your family know about this?"

"No, they don't. It will hurt them beyond words when I have to tell them."

"Does Father O'Hara's family know?"

"They know he is gay, but they do not know about our relationship."

"If I remember you are supposed to be going to Rome this week, correct?"

"Yes, I'm taking three families over. You were able to get us tickets for the Wednesday audience. I'm really looking forward to hearing and meeting the Holy Father. I wish my parents were going with me." Father Morales spoke nervously. He was still uncertain if he would even get the chance to go.

"I am sure you will have a good time. You can send the pope my regards."

"You mean you're going to let me go?" Father Morales asked with disbelief.

"If Lieutenant Palmer says you can go, I see no problem. In fact, I think it would be good for you to go and stay for a while." The cardinal just realized one possible solution was to let Father Morales stay in Rome.

"I don't understand."

"I am thinking you may need to pursue further studies while in Rome, so you can remain a faithful priest." And with those words, the cardinal decided the consequences of Father Morales's actions.

"Are you telling me, my week in Rome could be longer?" Father Morales was stunned.

"I am telling you to have a suitcase ready, and whatever other personal items you may want us to send you. You need to box up those items you will not need and store them with a friend or family member before you leave. I will reassign you. It was already in the works. Did you know Monsignor Triplett asked for you to be reassigned?"

"He told me about the possibility of a new assignment. But then we had this great conversation where I shared my concerns with him, and we were to have another conversation before I left for Rome about me staying. Did you know about it?"

"No, I did not, but I am glad it was positive for both of you. That should give you some comfort with his death." The cardinal tried to be sympathetic, but he was all business in this matter.

"So you're saying I would have been moved no matter what?" Father Morales asked.

"Yes, you would have been moved." The cardinal leaned forward. "A tentative list of changes is on my desk, and you were to move."

Father Morales was thoroughly disappointed. He could only convey his remorse by saying again, "I'm sorry."

"Now you can tell your parents you are being considered for further studies and await the direction of the cardinal as to where you will go. You will probably stay in Rome for thirty days to meet with several individuals to lay out a plan for you. Are you listening to what I am telling you?" the cardinal asked.

"I believe so." Father Morales was in disbelief. "In less than forty-eight hours, you want me out."

"That's correct! Unless you want me to start the process to remove you from the priesthood?"

"No... no... I do not. I love being a priest. These years have been some of my happiest, sharing the sacraments and preaching the message Jesus left for us. I really do feel at peace and fulfilled." Father Morales leaned forward and looked convincingly at the cardinal.

"Father Morales this has to become your focus. You must leave all your earthly desires behind. This is the sacrifice each of us makes. It is not easy for any of us, and I want to give you this opportunity because I know with guidance and additional education you can be a great shepherd to the people you will have a chance to minister. Do you understand?" The cardinal leaned back in his chair, hoping his words were getting through to Father Morales.

"I'm trying to. I know you're right, but I struggle." Father Morales recognized the reality of his fate and seemed to waver.

"Unfortunately, your struggle is public. Because you are not an asset to me, to the archdiocese, or to the church, I do not think you will be coming back for a while. Is there any reason for the detectives to think you would have killed Monsignor Triplett?" The cardinal was confident Father Morales was not a suspect.

218

"No, I showed him I was nowhere around the cathedral this morning. He saw the hotel receipt, and if he talks with Father O'Hara, he would confirm we were together."

"Then I think you will be able to leave. We will not change your plans. After we finish our talk, I think it would be good for you to call your parents and let them know of this wonderful opportunity your cardinal is giving you. It is my Easter gift!" Cardinal Flinn knew the remark was somewhat sarcastic, but he wasn't entirely concerned with Father Morales' feelings right now. His priority was his church.

"Thank you." These were the only words that could come out of Father Morales's mouth. He knew it was a gift, as well as, a punishment and was struggling to understand fully "the gift" the cardinal had given him. He knew it was his second chance. He wanted to say more to the cardinal, but it was probably best to remain quiet.

"Father Morales, enjoy your week with the parishioners. Are you going with the Quinn and Connelly families?"

"Yes, I am."

"Take in as much as you can of the Vatican and Rome. Make a copy of your itinerary and give it to me tonight. I will be in touch with you sometime this week while you are in Rome, so you will know where to go once the parishioners return home. You will say nothing to them until the night before they are to leave. Make no changes to your ticket, just in case we need you to return. I will let you know. Now go and call your parents. I am sure there is one more call you also want to make...." The cardinal was interrupted when his cell phone rang. He turned away from Father Morales before he answered the call.

Father Crumbley called to inform the cardinal that Lieutenant Palmer had finished interviewing Thom Triplett and would bring him to the residence once the lieutenant inspected Monsignor Triplett's bedroom and study.

The cardinal thanked Father Crumbley and placed the phone back in his pocket. Forgetting Father Morales was in the room the cardinal said, "I wonder what the lieutenant would find?"

As Cardinal Flinn turned his desk chair around, he realized Father Morales heard his last comment. Upset at himself, he said to Father Morales, "Reflect on what I told you..." He stood to indicate the conversation was finished.

Father Morales thanked the cardinal, tried to extend his hand, but the cardinal looked away. The priest walked out of the conference room, closed the door behind him and felt a sense of relief. Their meeting could have gone much worse than it did, but the cardinal, in a diplomatic way, was making everyone look good. The cardinal successfully removed him from the archdiocese while Father Morales remained in good standing with the church and distanced himself from Father O'Hara. While feeling sadness, instead of joy of this unexpected change, Father Morales knew deep within himself this might be the best in the long run and provide him with further studies. But it would leave him almost halfway around the world with no support. Contemplating his situation, he wondered if he could survive. He offered a simple mantra to God "please help me, always be with me."

Father Morales left the cardinal's residence. As he stood outside on Madison Avenue, he heard a fire truck racing up the street with sirens blaring. It was a typical New York morning, one Father Morales was soon to miss. As he entered the parish house, Father Morales went straight to his room. He wanted to avoid contact with anyone he knew. There was one call he had to make before he called his parents. He had to call Father O'Hara.

Chapter 18

"Jonathan, it's so good to hear your voice," Emma said. It thrilled her to know her son was alive. What a relief she was feeling. "Where are you?"

"I'm okay, Mom." Jonathan tried to assure her he was.

"Are you sure?"

"Yes. I'm okay. I'm in a safe place. I know about Monsignor Triplett." Jonathan began to cry. "I'm so sorry."

"How did you find out?" Emma asked while walking around the hotel room trying to get everything repacked in her overnight bag.

"Father O'Hara told me."

"Father O'Hara? Where did you see him?" Emma was surprised at Jonathan's response.

Jonathan wasn't sure how to answer. "It's a long story. I'll tell you when I see you."

"Jonathan, please come home!" Emma begged her son to return.

"I will. I promise. I'll come home today. But Mom, I need one thing from you."

"What is it?"

"He… he can't be there," Jonathan insisted.

"I understand. I promise you. If you come home today, he will not be here." Emma looked at Sam and knew it was over between the two of them.

"Thanks, Mom." There was relief in his voice knowing what drove him out of the house wasn't going to be around.

"When do you think you'll be home?" Emma asked.

"I'll probably be home in a couple of hours. If it's okay with you, Father O'Hara may come too." Jonathan wondered if Father O'Hara would come.

"I would enjoy seeing him. I'm sure he's sad about the death of Monsignor Triplett." Emma was confused at the request for Father O'Hara to come to their house. She could hear the sadness in her son's voice but was thankful he was safe.

"Mom, I'm just shocked, and I know Father O'Hara is too. How did you find out?" Jonathan asked.

"I received a call from a Lieutenant Palmer who wanted to ask me some questions. I'm on my way to the cathedral. As soon as I am done, I'll be home."

"Okay. You should know my phone isn't working. The battery is dead, so hopefully, when you get back from the cathedral, I'll be home." Jonathan wanted to assure his mom she would see him home today and was letting her know why she had not heard from him.

"Do you have to work today?" Emma asked.

"No, I have today off, but I have to work tomorrow," Jonathan said.

"On Easter?" Emma asked.

"Yes, but I don't have to be in until 3:00."

"Will you go to Mass with me?" Emma held her breath and prayed.

"Yes, Mom. We'll talk about it when I come home."

Emma tried to remain composed for the sake of Jonathan, but she could feel the tears coming. "We're going to get through this. There are things I need to tell you that you probably don't know about Monsignor Triplett. He really did love you and was looking out for you. You may have not always thought so, but he did."

"I'm just really confused, Mom. I'm hurting. I wish I could have talked to him one more time."

"I understand. I wish you had a chance to talk with him too. When you come home, we'll talk. I love you, Jonathan."

"I love you too, Mom," Jonathan said as he started to cry again. "I'll see you soon."

Composing himself, he went back into the living room, sat down and looked at Father O'Hara.

"How did the phone call go?" Father O'Hara asked.

"It went pretty well. I'm going to go home. My mom says he won't be there, and we can talk."

"That sounds good." Father O'Hara expressed relief with the news he was hearing.

"It sounds good, but how long will it last. She's in love with him, and I can't stand him."

"You and your mom have some talking to do. Give her a chance. She has it just as tough as you do. She's hurting like you are. You are family, and you need to help each other out."

"But she doesn't always listen to me."

"I'm sure you don't always listen to her. Start with a clean slate, and when she's not listening to you, challenge her. When she listens to you, thank her. Words of affirmation and appreciation to each other help." Father O'Hara didn't know how much Jonathan was understanding.

"Easy for you to say, Father O'Hara. I'll try, but I promise nothing. I might be back."

"I hope you'll come back. Let me give you my cell phone number." Father O'Hara wrote it down for Jonathan to put in his phone.

"Thanks. This means a lot."

"Now don't lose it before you're able to put it in your phone. You can call me anytime, as long as I'm here."

"What do you mean by that?"

"I'm not sure after my overnight at the Michelangelo what my future will be."

"Don't the Scriptures talk about repenting and forgiveness of one's sins?"

"Yes... yes, they do. I think we both have a little repenting to do." Father O'Hara confessed, knowing his form of repentance was being worked on.

"You're right." Jonathan smiled. After the last three sleepless nights in his car, he was feeling thankful to have come to Holy Name of Jesus and confronted Father O'Hara. Even though it did not go as he originally planned, he got a person from his past to help him. He felt entirely lost when he rang that doorbell, but now Jonathan felt he and Father O'Hara were becoming friends.

"Jonathan, you have a lot to live for. You can make something of your life. No matter how tough it may seem, you cannot give up. Have you thought about what you would like to do in your future?"

"I don't know. I love to play the guitar and write music. I'm just not sure I can do something with it."

"I didn't know you played the guitar. I love playing my guitar. It helps me relax. Maybe we can get together and play sometime," Father O'Hara suggested.

"I'd like that."

"Just make sure you have a dream, something to look forward to in your life. Dreams can be achieved. With God's help, who knows what possibilities could be out there for you."

"I sure hope so. What's your dream?" Jonathan asked.

The question caught Father O'Hara off-guard. He didn't know how to answer it, but after everything he had experienced in the last twelve hours, he reflected. "Right now my dream is to be a good priest and see what opportunities come my way as one of Jesus' disciples today."

"That sounds good, but I think you have some things to change in your life," Jonathan advised.

"You're right. I know I have work to do. You do too. Will you work on what you need to change in your life!" Father O'Hara was not sure what else to say to someone so young.

Avoiding the question, Jonathan said, "Maybe you and I can get together and sit and play our guitars. What type of music do you play?"

"I like classical music and then a little of the music from back in the '80s."

"Cool. I thought about classical; I just never had anyone I know play it. I would enjoy hearing you." Jonathan had a new enthusiasm.

"One day we'll get together with our guitars. It would be good to have someone to play guitar with."

Jonathan smiled, wondering if this could lead to the friendship he needed after the loss of Monsignor Triplett. He knew he needed a male adult in his life who could give him some direction. It helped to know they had a common interest in the guitar. "Can I ask a couple of favors?"

"Sure, name them?" Father O'Hara realized this day was not what he was expecting at all but, in some ways, was exactly what he needed.

"Will you come back to the house with me and be there when I talk with my mom?" Jonathan blurted out the question.

Father O'Hara surprised. "Are you sure you want me to accompany you?"

"Yes, my mom knows you, and she says it's okay for you to come over. It would really help, especially talking about Monsignor Triplett." Jonathan hoped that would be enough.

"I think I should check with my pastor before I go with you," Father O'Hara said. He was uncertain if Father McFadden would even let him go knowing he had things to do. "Let me go ask."

As Father O'Hara left to talk with Father McFadden, Jonathan remembered the special times he had with Monsignor Triplett. He also recalled some of the advice Monsignor gave him and remembered him saying, "Always love your mom, for you only have one." Jonathan knew he had to make things right with his mom and hoped Father O'Hara could help him do that.

Father McFadden heard Father O'Hara's request and expressed concern. But since Father O'Hara knew the family and had the approval from Jonathan's mom, Father McFadden thought it would be okay to go, as long as Father O'Hara was back by noon to help set up and prepare for the Easter Vigil liturgy.

Father O'Hara returned to the living room and told Jonathan who was still sitting on the couch. "I'll go with you, but you must be truthful with your mom," emphasizing the last four words.

Jonathan jumped up, "I will. I just need her to be truthful with me!"

"I'm sure if you both sit down and talk to one another from the heart, you will hear the truth."

"Okay. And one more favor. I am starving. Do you have anything for breakfast?" Jonathan felt relief and relaxed enough to ask.

"Sure, come on in the kitchen, and I'll fix you something to eat," Father O'Hara said smiling as they left the living room and walked into the eat-in-kitchen. "There are a couple of different types of cereals in the cupboard, or I can make you some eggs."

Father O'Hara pointed to the opened cupboard, and Jonathan found a cereal he liked.

As Father O'Hara reached for a bowl, his cell phone rang. He looked at the screen and knew he had to take the call. He told Jonathan to help himself to anything else. He would be right back.

When Father O'Hara answered the phone, he heard the person on the other end sound nervous and rambling. He told him to calm down and take a deep breath. He asked for two minutes so he could make it to his room before saying anything more. As soon as he closed his bedroom door, "Juan, you sound terrible."

"I am. The cardinal is sending me packing to Rome for a long time."

"What?"

"I met with the cardinal. He told me I could go on my trip to the Vatican, but I won't be returning. I'll I be staying in Rome! He's sending me back to school! He asked me to pack a bag to take and then pack up everything else and move out before I left. He's arranged for me to get out of the archdiocese in the next 48 hours!"

"I don't know what to say. What can I do?" Father O'Hara was bewildered and frantic.

"I need to pack and move my stuff someplace. Can you help me? Can I give you some boxes to hold onto? I don't know what else to do," Father Morales pleaded.

"Sure. Can you give me some time?" Father O'Hara tried to figure out just what and how he would be able to help.

"Why? Time... that's something I don't have."

"Do you remember the hotel employee who brought us the extra pillows and wine glasses last night?"

"Yes."

"I didn't say anything to you, but I recognized him, and he recognized me. He knew you when you spoke!"

"O my God. I thought we were so discrete. Who is he?"

"He's Emma Pickle's son, Jonathan. He's here right now. He was trying to blackmail me!"

"I know him. He's been at the cathedral. I think Monsignor Triplett was helping him. What does he want?" Father Morales asked.

"He wanted a place to stay. He's been living in his car at least the last three nights because it seems his mom is having an affair, not with Monsignor Triplett, but with Sam Tolden. Did you know anything about that?"

"Not really. There's always gossip, but I didn't believe it. Sam's married. His wife is wonderful. I'm surprised."

"So am I." Father O'Hara echoed.

Father O'Hara continued to explain. "When Jonathan came to the door, he didn't know about Monsignor Triplett's death. I had to tell him. He took it really hard. He was starving, so he just sat down for breakfast. He wants me to go to his house and try to reconcile him and his mom. I'm going, but Father McFadden wants me back in a couple of hours to review and prepare for tonight's Easter Vigil liturgy."

"I understand." Father Morales knew in his heart he really didn't. Knowing what was happening to him, he felt painfully disappointed that Father O'Hara was doing pastoral ministry while he sat alone.

Father O'Hara sensed Father Morales' distress. "I'll try not to stay too long at the Pickles. I don't know how long it will take. Maybe I can come over afterward."

"Do you think you can?"

"I'll try. I can't promise. Get some boxes and start packing."

"First, I have to call my folks and let them know. They're in for a surprise," Father Morales said.

"They'll be so happy for you. Try to think positively about this. I'm happy for you. Call your folks. Give them the good news. Easter will even be more special with the family tomorrow."

"It will." Father Morales struggled with the words.

Father O'Hara looked at this watch. "I need to go. Pray I can help to reunite Jonathan with his mom."

"I need to ask, did the bishop say what he was going to do with you?" Father Morales wondered.

"He hasn't decided. I'm sure I'll be sent someplace. I've got to go. We'll talk more when I see you."

Father O'Hara put the phone in his pocket and returned to the kitchen. Jonathan was finishing his second bowl of cereal.

"Jonathan, did you get enough to eat?"

"Two bowls of cereal is enough. Thanks, Father."

"Are you ready to go home?"

228

"I think so. Hopefully, I can get a shower before my mom gets home. After we talk with my mom, can you stick around and play the guitar?"

"I doubt it, but we'll see. Let me get my wallet and jacket, and I'll be right down." Father O'Hara took Jonathan's dirty dishes rinsed them and placed them in the dishwasher.

As Father O'Hara left the room, Father McFadden came into the kitchen with his own dishes and placed them in the sink. He asked Jonathan if everything was okay.

"Yes. Hopefully, it will be. Thanks again for the orange juice. Thanks for letting Father O'Hara go with me."

"You're welcome," Father McFadden said. "I'm glad you came here to get help."

"I really was desperate, so I'm thankful for you and Father O'Hara helping instead of calling the police," Jonathan said. "What's going to happen to Father O'Hara?

"That's really up to the cardinal and Father O'Hara." Father McFadden was unaware of Father O'Hara and Jonathan's discussion.

"I hope whatever happens will help him be a better priest. He's still a priest and wants to help me. Can he be forgiven?"

"Yes, he can. If we are truly sorry, all of us can be forgiven. Just like you need to be forgiven for the hurt you brought to your mom," Father McFadden explained.

"I know. I need to go to confession. I'll talk with Father O'Hara about that."

"I think you should. Remember, there are consequences to our actions, and I am sure your mom will have some for you. I hope you will accept them."

"I hope I can!" Jonathan looked worried but confident he could face his mom.

Father O'Hara returned and told Father McFadden he would call him when he was leaving the Pickle's but didn't think he would be back in time for lunch. He had tried calling Bishop Newsome, but the call went to voicemail, so he left the

229

bishop a message saying something had come up, and he would talk with him about it the next time he saw the bishop. Jonathan once again thanked Father McFadden. He and Father O'Hara walked out of the parish house and walked briskly to Jonathan's car. It was something that looked like it had been thoroughly lived in. Jonathan began throwing everything that was in the front seat into the backseat to give Father O'Hara enough room to get in.

"Sorry about the mess."

"You may want to clean your car first before you take a shower."

"I just need to throw a bunch of stuff out."

"How did you get a car like this at your age?"

"It was a gift from Monsignor Triplett. He taught me how to drive." Jonathan remembered how patient Monsignor Triplett was with him in those early lessons.

"Nice gift. I'm sure he would be disappointed in the way the car looks. You need to take care of it." Father O'Hara gently admonished the young boy.

"I know." Jonathan knew it would disappoint Monsignor Triplett if he could see his car right now. He was angry Father O'Hara had said anything about it.

Father O'Hara realized the insensitivity of his words. "I'm sorry I hurt you with my words."

"I had it coming. You're right I need to take care of Monsignor Triplett's gift to me." As Jonathan started the care, he felt better hearing the words of apology from Father O'Hara.

Father O'Hara got in the car and buckled his seat belt while his mind returned to the conversation with Father Morales. Juan was leaving. It was all happening so fast. He wondered if Bishop Newsome was working on what to do with him. He was unaware that the bishop was on the phone tracking down the private number for the Abbot at Gethsemani.

Jennifer Gibson enjoyed her Saturday mornings, arriving at her law firm office to catch up on the stack of paperwork neglected after a hectic week with clients. It also allowed her to set the direction for her staff on goals for the coming week. But the real reason she came was to continue to heal after the loss of her husband. Her office view was the empty lots, now the memorial where the World Trade Towers stood. It had been over fifteen years, and even with someone special in her life, she still felt his absence. As she sat at her desk taking a sip of coffee, her phone rang. It surprised her at the name on the caller ID.

"Jennifer!" It was Thom.

"Good morning. I'm surprised to hear from you so early this morning," Jennifer said.

Thom struggled with the words. "I've just received some bad news — my brother is dead."

"O my God, Thom. I'm so sorry!" Jennifer was shocked. "What happened?"

"I'm not sure. I'm at the cathedral to find out."

"Do you want me to come there?" Jennifer asked eager to help but unsure how or what to say.

"No. What can you do? I'll call you when I find out more information." Thom abruptly hung up and immediately regretted he had snapped at Jennifer.

Jennifer put the phone on her desk. As she did, she looked at the two pictures sitting there. One was the last picture of her and her husband. They had just returned from a vacation in Italy. The second was a picture of her and Thom in Central Park. Tears fell for both men so important in her life.

Looking at the number on the phone, the priest didn't recognize it. He speculated it was the call he was expecting earlier in the morning. He debated if he should let the call go to voicemail or pick it up? He decided to find out who it was, but it was too late; it had already gone to voicemail.

Waiting for his cell phone to indicate he had a voicemail message, he stared at his blank computer screen and prayed for some inspiration, so he could write his Easter homily. Nothing was coming to him. He had never felt at a loss for words on something so central in his life—preaching the joy of the resurrection of Jesus. He prayed for the Holy Spirit to help him.

He saw the voicemail. As he retrieved the message, he noticed a little dried blood under his fingernails. He heard, "This is Lieutenant Will Palmer of the NYPD. I need you to call me at this number when you receive this message. It's extremely important."

All he could do was sit there and replay the message. He wondered if he would need an Easter homily after he talked with the lieutenant. He sat and looked at the picture on his desk of his friend and wept. Finally composing himself, he took his phone and touched the callback number.

Chapter 19

Anthony Delfino founded the Delfino Construction Company in 1962. It started out as a small commercial business but quickly grew into one of the world's largest construction companies doing over four billion in the past year. The Manhattan-based company had projects all over New York City including overseeing the $175 million restoration of Saint Patrick's Cathedral.

Anthony Delfino was the honest, well-respected company founder known in the city among some of the most influential individuals. He was highly regarded for his work ethics, and almost everyone appreciated his help in the city's progress. At the age of 75, it was time to pass the responsibilities of the family owned-business on to the next generation. Delfino had, ten years ago, named his oldest son, Joseph, president.

Joseph began working for the company in high school and continued through college, learning everything asked of him. Before he moved into the executive offices, he served as the contract coordinator overseeing some of the company's major construction projects. Joseph sought to benefit both the company and the subcontractors he hired to work for the company. Diligent in making sure the jobs were finished on time and sometimes below budget, Joseph was the natural choice to succeed his father, Anthony.

Unfortunately, as president, Joseph was not his father; he was neither honest nor well-respected. Once in the executive offices, he wanted greater profits each year and found ways to make it happen. His schemes were catching up with him. Recently, the Manhattan district attorney's office started an investigation into the company for inflating customer bills.

The presidency of the company was taking a toll on his personal life as well. Joseph had already gone through two divorces and was preparing for a third marriage to a woman two years older than his eldest son, Anthony Joseph or A.J. She was a knockout model who, allegedly, had fallen in love with Joseph's money, not him. Claiming her devotion to Catholicism, she insisted the wedding take place at Saint Patrick's Cathedral. Joseph was determined to make it happen, not because of his religious convictions but because of his eagerness to soothe his young and beautiful bride-to-be.

At one time, the New York newspapers praised the Delfino family for their contributions to the city. Now the stories were of extra-marital affairs, as well as, the inequality of pay for employees. Despite the publicity, which was mostly negative, the company was surviving. So was the family, except for Anthony who was disappointed in his son.

Cardinal Flinn liked what he saw when he met with Joseph about the restoration of Saint Patrick's Cathedral a little over three years ago. Joseph explained that the extensive work, both inside and out, could take up to five years. The cardinal signed the multimillion-dollar contract on one ambitious condition that the work would be completed before his twenty-fifth anniversary as a bishop which was less than two years away. Unfortunately, the work wasn't even forty percent completed.

At a recent meeting of the Delfino Company, with the cardinal, Joseph outlined several reasons for the delay and the problems they were experiencing. The list was short but serious: the firing of construction workers, the bad weather, and supplies needed were not readily available or had not arrived from Italy. The cardinal didn't want to hear any of it. He reminded Joseph of the reasons they were awarded the contract and became insistent on longer hours to complete the work before the anniversary. Joseph apologized profusely but said he couldn't keep that promise anymore.

After their last meeting, the cardinal asked to meet with Joseph privately. As they sat down, the cardinal said he wanted to talk with Joseph about his upcoming marriage. The cardinal knew Joseph had been married twice. As if brokering a diplomatic settlement, the cardinal said he would personally work with Joseph on his annulment, provided the cathedral was finished by the agreed time. Joseph was both hopeful and fearful in hearing the cardinal's words but didn't know how he could fulfill the request.

"Mr. Joseph Delfino?" The operator began. "This is Sarah… Sarah Herman, the owner of 'No Call, Goes Unanswered Answering Service.'"

"Yes, how can I help you, Sarah? As the owner of the company, what are you doing answering the phone?"

"We're short on help and, as you know, when this happens in a business you own, you have no choice but to work. I'm sorry to call you so early in the morning, but a Detective Patrick Sabor from the NYPD has called and is looking for a Mr. Jared Quinn. He says it's rather important and needs Mr. Quinn to return his call as soon as possible. The only number the detective had was from the construction sign at the cathedral." Sarah looked at her notes. She had just spoken to the detective.

"I'll need some time to get in touch with him. Do you have the number for this Detective Sabor?"

"Sorry, that would help wouldn't it?" Sarah gave the number to Mr. Delfino. "The detective also asked me to give him a call and let him know I had spoken to someone."

"Call the detective and let him know you have left a message with me. Wait about fifteen minutes before you call him back. I want to make sure I can get in touch with Mr. Quinn."

"Glad to be of help." Sara added as their conversation ended.

Sarah was forever a help. Her answering service company had always protected Joseph Delfino.

Always thankful, he showed his appreciation to her with a nice Christmas bonus. He was even more grateful that Sarah had taken the message today giving him time to find Jared before she called the detective back. He knew that sometimes Jared didn't answer his phone, especially on a Saturday morning. As hard as the supervisors worked during the weekdays, they enjoyed their weekends. Joseph knew this when he hired Jared.

Jared Quinn was a fine young man, well-built, and born and raised in New York City. He was lucky to have met Anthony Joseph Delfino, or AJ as he was known, during their high school years. They played football together and were friends hanging out at each other's homes. A.J. had the fancy place, an upper floor, large apartment overlooking the Hudson River. Jared lived in a modest three-bedroom apartment with his parents and four brothers and sisters. Despite the vast difference in the incomes of the families, A.J. spent more time at the Quinn apartment than he did at his own. He liked being around a good family like Jared's instead of watching his own family fall apart. He just got tired of the yelling and screaming between his father and his mom as they moved closer to divorce.

One summer Joseph asked if Jared wanted a job working construction. Jared was thrilled. The job helped him get into better shape for football and provided him with cash, so he could start saving for college. Since he was the oldest, Jared realized that to further his education, he would have to make it happen himself. How unlike A.J., whose father would pay for it all.

The first summer Jared learned all he could about building or renovation in the construction business. He gained a working understanding of blueprint drawings. He was fascinated by the way plans became brick, wood and glass buildings. From this experience, he knew this was the kind of work he wanted to do.

Joseph Delfino could see Jared's potential, as well as the fire in his eyes as he completed his twelfth-grade year. Jared, who was uncertain how he would go to college, was awarded a small scholarship for the role of leadership he had shown during his high school years. The Delfinos, aware of his lack of funds, approached him and offered to help him further his education.

Shortly afterward, A.J. and Jared were accepted to Manhattan College. The Delfinos agreed to cover each of their college expenses. They knew Jared had a positive influence, and they knew A.J. struggled to make the grades. With the two boys rooming together, A.J. had a roommate who would guide and tutor him. In return for his college tuition, Jared promised, after graduation, he would return to work at Delfinos.

During their college years, Jared helped A.J. as he struggled through his classes. However, Jared left A.J. alone to work his way through the bottles of beer and the numerous parties he attended until all hours of the night. Each semester, on the verge of failing, A.J. turned to Jared for tutoring. A.J. realized what a good friend he had, and if it weren't for the help of Jared, A.J. would never have graduated. A.J. told Jared he would always remember this in the years ahead.

When they graduated and started working full time for the company, A.J. was not suited to his new role as a construction site manager. He would rather sit behind a desk crunching the numbers. Jared loved being on the site, and the workers he supervised respected him as their immediate boss. With all the praise and accomplishments, Jared did not like the way Joseph and A.J. Delfino always second-guessed his decisions.

Recently, Jared had gone to Joseph and A.J. about some construction material they received that was below the quality needed for the cathedral project. Both the Delfinos told him not to worry about it. When he discussed the limited number of workers, they blamed it on other jobs that needed to be finished first. Jared was reeling with frustration.

One day after work, A.J. and Jared met for a beer and burger. A.J. let Jared know about the internal problems in the business. Jared learned that for the last five years, clients were deliberately overcharged. A.J. told Jared the savings from subcontractors were not passed on to the customers. Worse yet, the Manhattan district attorney's office was investigating. He also told Jared he confronted his dad about the overcharging, and for a while, it was being covered up. His dad was now trying to correct the mistakes amounting to millions of dollars. After sharing this information, A.J. felt relieved to confide in Jared, his best friend. He hoped it would help both of them — A.J.'s stress, as well as the stress Jared felt as the supervisor for the cathedral restoration.

Jared sat in a state of shock. He had no idea what was happening financially with the business. All he knew was that he was most thankful for the generous salary he was receiving. He knew he was a hard worker, but he was now uncertain of some decisions he had made with the subcontractors. He thought of the impact this would have on his future in the construction industry. Not knowing what to say, he merely listened to A.J. and assured him of his friendship. But now he wondered if the Archdiocese of New York and the cardinal were also being overcharged.

Then the day came when a subcontractor contacted asked Monsignor Triplett to provide a letter that would acknowledge the donation they had made to the cathedral. In this case, it was for over $10,000 in supplies — the amount requested by Delfino Construction. That call was the first time Monsignor Triplett knew of any irregularities. He placed a call to Joseph three weeks ago to find some answers, but he kept getting the runaround. With the evidence Monsignor Triplett had, knowing of the savings and donations from the subcontractors, he decided to use it to his advantage to get some money for the cathedral employees.

While frustrated with the situation, Monsignor Triplett saw this as a way to replenish the loss of the cathedral income. After much discussion, Joseph Delfino and Monsignor Triplett agreed on an amount and would meet in the parish office after the evening Good Friday service. Joseph brought with him a nice briefcase full of cash.

Joseph sat with the phone in his hand and wondered why a Detective Sabor wanted to talk with his best supervisor. He looked for Jared's number and placed a call to Jared hoping it would not go to voicemail.

"Hello?" a groggy, incoherent Jared answered his phone, surprised by the call.

"Jared, sorry to bother you, but I need your full attention in what I am about to tell you," Joseph said.

Alarmed, he propped himself up in his bed and rubbed his eyes several times trying to become more alert battling a terrible headache, "Okay, you have my attention."

"A Detective Patrick Sabor from the NYPD called and left a message for you with our answering service. All I know is he wants to contact you to answer some questions."

Becoming more alert and wide-eyed, he wondered why a detective would be looking for him. "Do you know why he wants to talk with me?"

"It has something to do with the cathedral and some investigation there. I'll give you the number. You call him and then call me back. If he wants to meet with you, I'll go with you and make sure the company lawyer is present."

"A lawyer? Why? I've done nothing wrong. Give me the number, and I'll call him right now." Jared struggled to locate a piece of paper and pencil. Finding the pencil but no paper, he realized, as he cleared his bed of the six empty beer cans, the pizza box top would suffice as Joseph gave him the detective's number.

"I'll call you back as soon as I know what this is about." Jared wondered why he was being called and furious it was on a Saturday morning. Ending the phone conversation, he got out of his bed and walked into the bathroom to throw some water on his face. He found the aspirin bottle, took a couple and sat on the toilet for a few minutes emptying his bladder before making any call. All the while, he wondered what Joseph meant when he said, 'I'll get you a lawyer if necessary.' He knew Joseph worked with a few lawyers in their legal mess, but he had no reason to think he would need one. Returning to the bed, he took his cell phone and made the call. It was answered on the first ring.

"Detective Patrick Sabor."

"Hello, this is Jared Quinn from Delfino Construction. I was told to call you."

"Mr. Quinn, I'm from the NYPD."

"How can I help you detective?"

"I need you to come to the cathedral as soon as possible to answer a few questions for an investigation taking place here. When could you be here?" Detective Sabor didn't want to give him any chance of saying no to his request.

"Am I in trouble? Do I need a lawyer?" Jared expressed concern and uncertainty. He wondered what the investigation was all about as he was tried to locate the remote to his TV.

"I don't believe so at this time. It's just important for you to come to the cathedral. What time can I expect you?"

Looking at his watch, Jared told the detective he would be there before noon. He needed a few cups of coffee and a good shower to get rid of the hangover. As the conversation continued, Detective Sabor once again gave him his name and asked him to come to the cathedral side entrance on 50th Street and to identify himself to the police officer.

"I think I understand." Jared knew the entrance well. This was the same entrance for the construction company. The phone call ended, and Jared found his remote. He turned on the TV to see if there were any breaking news stories about the cathedral. This wasn't the way he liked his Saturday. He thought it would be a nice, relaxing day and then a workout at the gym.

Before calling Joseph Delfino back, he needed to take a shower and get dressed. He was about to go into the bathroom when he noticed a news reporter standing inside the cathedral announcing a press conference for 11:00 a.m. to identify the body that was removed from the cathedral earlier. Someone died at the cathedral? And they want to question me? Jared was feeling some anxiety. Who could it have been? Noticing the time, he quickly took his shower, got dressed and called Joseph.

"Are you watching the news on NY1?" Jared screamed as Joseph answered his phone.

"Calm down…. Yes, I just heard. There's been a death in Saint Patrick's Cathedral? Who was it? You didn't leave any of the workers there did you?" Joseph asked.

"As far as I know, we all left early on Thursday because of the Holy Week schedule. I haven't heard from anyone." Jared knew he didn't even remember Friday except when the pizza arrived. He had finished twelve beers after work on Thursday and fell asleep until Friday afternoon, then ordered a pizza and six more beers.

"When did you tell the detective you'd be there?" Joseph asked.

"I told him I'd be there before noon."

"I'll meet you there at 11:45 a.m.," Joseph said.

"But he didn't ask for you."

"I don't care. You are family, and family sticks together. I'll be there for you."

Jared wondered just how true Joseph's last statement really was given the business problems. Despite the success, they could lose the company if the allegations are true, and Jared would be out of a job. He had been a faithful employee and best friend to A.J., but family? He'd never truly felt that from Joseph. He wondered again why Joseph said it. All he knew with certainty was he needed some good strong coffee and something to eat before he went to the cathedral. Jared looked into an empty refrigerator and decided to stop by the coffee shop on the corner before taking the subway into Manhattan. He found his keys, wallet, cell phone and most importantly, the aspirin bottle. He had what he needed. He didn't know when he would return.

At the same time Jared left his apartment, Joseph was getting a nice strong cup of coffee. He needed to get to the cathedral, and he wanted A.J. to be with him. As he made the coffee, he recalled the meeting with Monsignor Triplett. Joseph could only speculate on the location of the briefcase he had given to Monsignor Triplett. More importantly, how the contents would be explained. If only he had waited until after Easter to give it to Monsignor Triplett. But yesterday morning's call let Joseph know Monsignor Triplett would not wait. In fact, Monsignor Triplett was very insistent that they meet after the Good Friday evening service.

Monsignor Triplett even encouraged him to attend the service. It would help him remember what is important in life. Joseph thought about going, but his girlfriend had made reservations for dinner at one of his favorite steak places — so much for fasting and abstinence on meatless Good Friday.

After dinner, Joseph put his fiancée in a cab, stopped by his office to pick up the briefcase and took the subway down to Manhattan. As he arrived at the cathedral, it seemed the service had ended. The cathedral was dark with one big light focused on the cross lying on the floor. Joseph was struck by the contrast. Usually, the cathedral was filled with tourists coming in and out, lighting votive candles, talking and taking pictures — none of that was happening.

Joseph stopped at the cross and said a prayer to God asking for forgiveness for the wrongs he had done and thanking God for the sacrifice of his Son on the cross. He asked for his crosses to be removed in his life and ended by saying an Our Father. As he walked away, he felt different, unable to explain it in words.

Not seeing Monsignor Triplett in the cathedral, Joseph gave him a call on his cell which he immediately answered. Monsignor asked him to walk out of the church and meet at the entrance of the parish offices. As Joseph was leaving, he tried to find some holy water in the font to bless himself, but it was empty. He remembered that the holy water is removed after Holy Thursday Mass until the blessing of the new water on Easter. He made the Sign of the Cross and said to himself, 'I need to get back to church. I'm missing this.'

As he walked up the steps to the office, he saw Monsignor Triplett waiting for him at the front door. It looked like he was exhausted from the events of Good Friday. Somehow the darkness of the night was evident in the darkness of Monsignor Triplett as they walked down the hallway to his office.

Looking around Monsignor's office, Joseph realized the priest didn't do much work in this place, but used it to meet people for appointments. This was one appointment he didn't want to have and had avoided for a long time. However, with the information Monsignor Triplett had, Joseph needed this meeting to save what was left of his reputation and ask for forgiveness for the wrong he had done to the church.

"Is that the cash?" Monsignor Triplett asked getting right down to business.

"Yes, just like we discussed." Joseph nervously sat in front of Monsignor.

Monsignor sat behind his desk. He opened a drawer and pulled out a manila file folder. He looked squarely at Delfino as he opened it. "I have before me a list of subcontractors. Over the last three weeks, I've made contact with each of them asking what they've supplied to the cathedral in both billable goods and donated goods. Here's the list I obtained. I realized some of your subcontractors said nothing, showing their loyalty to Delfino Construction. I've indicated those on the list."

Monsignor Triplett removed the paper clip from the list and provided Joseph with a copy. Joseph didn't need to see the list. He knew which company had donated to the restoration project for the cathedral. When he saw the monetary total of over $200,000, he realized it was much more in donated goods than he anticipated.

"You've been busy," Joseph said to Monsignor Triplett.

"Why? Why didn't you pass the savings on to the archdiocese?"

"Greed is the only answer I can give. To be perfectly honest with you, I'm faced with my own bills and demons. I just thought the church had all this money—a few thousand here or there wouldn't hurt it."

Monsignor Triplett was angry at Joseph's smugness. He shouted, "This is a $175 million project! Every dollar is needed. Because of this work, the income for the operational expenses of the cathedral is down. I'm being forced to make some layoffs of employees."

"I didn't know." Joseph was alarmed and apologetic.

"The money you're providing will help give a few of them something when their job is terminated. So what you're giving me in that briefcase is for the cathedral and to help those in need. Unfortunately, the archdiocese will have to wait for the next payoff. My conscious is clean with what I am doing," Monsignor Triplett spoke emphatically.

"I wish my conscious were." Suddenly, Joseph felt blood coming from his nose. "Do you have some tissues, Monsignor, my nose is bleeding."

Pulling out a box of tissues, he passed them across the desk to Joseph who was trying to stop the blood flowing from his nose. A couple of drops landed on the armrest of the chair and on the floor. Joseph took several tissues and leaned his head back as his nose continued to bleed. Finally, he got up and laid on the floor to help stop the bleeding. He got more tissues and held onto them until Monsignor Triplett brought over the trash can. Blood was not only on the chair and carpet but also on Monsignor's desk chair and in the trash can. It took about ten minutes before the bleeding finally stopped.

"I'm sorry. Out of nowhere I sometimes get a bloody nose. My doctor says it's related to my stress. Do you have a rag or something I can use to try to get the blood up from the carpet and off the chair?"

"It's late. Leave it. No one will be in here this weekend. On Monday, I'll have one of my maintenance workers clean the carpet and chair," Monsignor Triplett said.

"I'll take the trash with me when I leave and place it in our dumpster. I'm sorry I used a whole box of Kleenex."

"I'll add it to your bill. Speaking of that, I want to make sure we understand each other. I'll be expecting another briefcase next month in the same amount. This time it will go to the archdiocese as an anonymous donation for the restoration."

"I understand." Joseph wondered how he would be able to come up with the same amount of money without A.J. or others in the company knowing about it.

"So the cardinal says he's going to give you an annulment if the work on the cathedral is completed in the next fifteen months before his anniversary?" Monsignor Triplett asked.

Joseph was in shock. "How do you know about this?"

"Let's just say when the cardinal has an extra glass of wine to relax, sometimes, very rarely, but sometimes, he reveals something he probably didn't want anyone to know, but could be of value to me later," Monsignor Triplett said.

Furious that Monsignor Triplett knew of his agreement with the cardinal, Joseph blurted out, "Yes, he did! He also assured me that with his help I would get the annulment."

Monsignor Triplett pulled out a piece of paper from the folder. It contained a statement he wrote explaining that the cardinal promised Joseph Delfino would receive his marriage annulment if the restoration work at the cathedral were done

245

within the next fifteen months. He handed it to Joseph. "I need you to read and sign this paper."

"Why are you doing this?" Joseph was more upset now with this paper placed in front of him.

"Simply to cover the good I'm trying to do with the money you're giving me for those affected by this restoration. They are the innocent ones—the employees who have been faithful in their work. With your signature, the cardinal could be in hot water if he doesn't follow church law. If needed, this statement is a bargaining tool of what some could say is my mistake of stealing from the archdiocese when all I wanted to do was help people."

Again, Joseph was astounded. "So you're blackmailing the cardinal?"

"I wouldn't say blackmail—more like an insurance policy keeping each of us out of trouble." Monsignor Triplett knew this tactic put him in uncharted territory.

Joseph read the sheet of paper. He was more concerned about his fiancé's wishes. "Will I still get my annulment?"

"That's up to you, and the work that needs to be done to make the cardinal happy. When are you starting the twenty-four-hour shifts?"

"You mean you want to help?" Joseph signed the statement and returned it to Monsignor Triplett.

"I want the work completed as soon as possible because it's affecting everything that is and should be happening here at the cathedral. Get whatever permits you need that will allow you to work around the clock. Make sure there's a break every morning to allow an hour for each of the two Masses."

"Jared, my supervisor has already been doing this."

Monsignor Triplett looked at Joseph with surprise. "Well, I've been giving him a hard time since I thought he was the one getting the money from the kickbacks. I'd find excuses, so the workers wouldn't be able to work where they needed to. I yelled about the way the church looked and all the construction mess left around hoping he would respond. Jared simply remained calm as my blood pressure rose. When I finally asked him about the kickbacks, he told me he knew nothing about them."

"Until recently, Jared didn't know about the kickbacks. He's probably my best construction supervisor. He's worked for me since he was in high school. He's very loyal to the company. He told me about the hard time you gave him," Joseph said.

"I need to apologize to him the next time I see him." Monsignor Triplett truly regretted his actions against someone who was trying to do their job.

Joseph tried to explain. "When Jared found out what was going on, he was ready to go to the police. After I talked to him, I said I was working to fix the problem. Jared agreed to stay on until they finish the cathedral."

"You have the right man for the job. You will see about working more hours? I'll try to cooperate more with your supervisor, and hopefully, in less than fifteen months, this will all be behind us, and everyone will be happy, especially Cardinal Flinn." Monsignor Triplett was optimistic.

"Thank you, Monsignor for not taking this any further. I have enough to worry about, and I don't think this would be good headlines for either of us."

"I would agree. I think we've finished our business. Happy Easter."

Joseph got up, pulled the liner out of the trashcan and tied it. He shook Monsignor Triplett's hand and wished him a happy Easter. Leaving through the main entrance of the office, he found the dumpster and threw the bag in. He pulled out his cell phone and placed a call, disappointed he had to leave a voicemail message saying, "He has the money in his office."

Still holding a handful of tissues, Joseph wiped more blood from his hands and nose. He thought just like Good Friday— he had blood on his hands and wondered if he had done enough for God in trying to correct his mistakes.

Before Monsignor Triplett left the office to return to the parish house with the money, file and documents, he needed to make one phone call. He also needed to make a copy of the letter Joseph Delfino had signed and make sure the original was sent to the proper person in case something happened to him. As he turned on the copier, he completed addressing the envelope, ran it through the postage meter and stuck the original with a note on it in the outgoing mail that would be picked up tomorrow. He placed a copy in his safe for his protection. His plan was taking shape and would be exposed sooner than he had expected.

While holding his morning coffee, Joseph looked at his hands. There were still traces of blood on them from last night. He picked up his cell phone to call A.J. and woke him up. "I need you to meet me at the cathedral in an hour. Wear a coat and tie. Delfino Construction may be in trouble." He ended the call before his son could respond. He wondered if he should call his attorney, but with the hourly rates he was charging him, Joseph decided to wait and see how the questioning went. How much more trouble would he and his company face? He was filled with uncertainty and didn't know what to expect when he arrived at the cathedral.

Chapter 20

Walking up the steps to Monsignor Triplett's room, Lieutenant Palmer and Detective Maria Jabowski were speculating on the evidence they might find to help with the investigation. They knew the cell phone was a crucial item. If located, it could provide clues about the last people to speak with Monsignor Triplett. They also knew that when his body was discovered, he didn't have a phone on him. But the murderer could have taken and disposed of it.

Before he opened the door, Palmer pulled two disposable gloves out of his pocket and put them on. With the blinds closed, the room was dark. He located a switch on the wall, flipped it, and a bright fluorescent overhead light started blinking before it illuminated the room. When the light finally came on, he immediately noticed stacks of papers and books randomly placed throughout the room.

Detective Jabowski struggled to get her gloves on as she entered. She noticed coke cans around the room. "It looks like he liked Coke."

"Yes, his brother said it was his favorite soft drink." Palmer scratched his head wondering where to begin as he waited for the CSU photographer and investigator. The wait wasn't long as he heard them walk up the steps.

"He must have loved to read." Detective Jabowski observed the number of books on the floor and papers spread everywhere. She wondered how Monsignor Triplett could find anything.

"His brother said he knew where everything was. This is where he did most of his work. His passion for reading was church history." Palmer welcomed the CSU investigator who started dusting for prints and the photographer who immediately began taking pictures.

Jabowski walked carefully between two stacks of papers and books to a larger leather recliner. She noticed a book on the French Revolution strewn among several telephone messages and more coke cans. "It doesn't look like he threw away much by all the phone messages scattered everywhere."

"We need to collect all the phone message slips, so we can go through them."

"I'll start gathering them," Jabowski got one of the evidence bags from the crime scene investigator.

Reaching the desk, Palmer wanted to make sure the CSU photographer got all the pictures he needed before moving anything else. Once the photographer finished, and everything on top was dusted for prints, the first thing to catch the lieutenant's eye was an envelope with a name on top—"Thom Triplett." Palmer picked up the sealed envelope. He knew it should be placed into evidence, but Palmer wanted Monsignor's brother to open it and see the contents first. He took the envelope, put it in an evidence bag, and informed the CSU investigator he would sign for it and hold on to the evidence until he saw Monsignor Triplett's brother.

Next, he noticed a letter from Monsignor Stone and some papers with Thom Triplett's name on it. All were dusted for prints and bagged. Attached to the papers was a small yellow post-it note saying "6:00 a.m. Saturday." Palmer wondered if that was when the brothers were getting together. It seemed like a strange time to meet. Taking out his notepad, he wrote down the name of Monsignor David Stone, the phone number on the letterhead and snapped a picture with his cell phone of the post-it. He wanted to show this to Monsignor Triplett's brother.

After the photographer had taken pictures of the desk and its contents, Palmer looked through the pile of papers on the desk and found Monsignor Triplett's appointment book. He looked at the entries for Holy Saturday and saw penciled in at 9:00 a.m.—'Thom.' There was nothing else until Mass at 8:00 p.m. He looked at the day before and only saw the scheduled services for Good Friday. It didn't look like he wrote everything in his appointment book. He placed it in an empty evidence bag and sealed it.

As he continued to go through the papers, Palmer saw the beginnings of Monsignor's Easter homily. It was dealing with hope, and Easter being a season of hope. He was impressed with how well it was written. It seemed to be direct and to the point. Palmer thought how sad that this priest could not give it.

"Lots of books, but I don't see a TV in here?" Jabowski remarked as she collected and reviewed the telephone messages.

"His brother said it was in the bedroom," Palmer responded. He discovered Monsignor's various personal bills and financial statements.

"So a reading/work room here and a bedroom to sleep and watch TV… nice." Jabowski appreciated the arrangements in the parish house.

"Jabowski, while going through the papers on the desk, I just found Monsignor Triplett's bank statement. He had less than a $1,000 in it. I also found his American Express and Master Card bills, and it looks like the accounts are maxed to over $5,000 each. It seems besides restaurants, subway Metro cards, a couple of Broadway tickets, there were a lot of charges posted to PayCorp—some charges for $100 and then one for almost $3,000. I'm not sure what these are?" Palmer showed Jabowski and placed the bills in an evidence bag. After shuffling through most of the papers on the desk, Palmer began opening the drawers.

Jabowski noticed something sitting on the side table next to the lazy-boy. "Here's a phone charger but no phone."

"Keep looking. Let me try calling the number. Listen for any ringing." Palmer placed the call from his phone. There was total silence in the room.

"I just keep wondering if the murderer took it."

"Let's keep looking." Palmer looked through the first drawer. He noticed a file saying 'Church restoration.' He opened it and saw lists with multiple dollar figures and names of various companies. He didn't fully understand what he was looking at, so he passed the papers to the investigator to mark as evidence.

"Lieutenant Palmer, I think you need to come see this." Jabowski opened a briefcase filled with stacks of $100 bills.

Palmer walked across the room to look at the contents of the case. There it was—stacks of money. At a glance, it looked like thousands. "I wonder where this money came from?"

"Good question. Wish I had a good answer." Jabowski shook her head in wonderment. "This case is getting more and more mysterious."

"Indeed, it does. We need to get an accurate count of this money. Want to take a guess at how much there is?" Palmer asked.

"I'm wondering how many $100 bills are in a stack. I'll say close to $40,000 is in the case." Jabowski started to count the money.

"I'd say closer to $50,000." Palmer watched as the first stacks were counted. It didn't take long before Jabowski had a total.

"There are eighteen stacks; each stack contains $2,500 — twenty-five $100 bills—for a total of $45,000."

"Odd how the money is bundled." Palmer observed.

Jabowski added. "Maybe that's the way Monsignor Triplett wanted it. But why?"

"Or maybe the person who gave it to him wanted it that way, so it would look like a full briefcase." Palmer contemplated another question to answer.

"So with the $5,000 found in Monsignor Triplett's pocket, he received $50,000. Why?" Jabowski closed the briefcase and gave it to the crime scene investigator to fingerprint, tag and record.

The photographer had moved into the bedroom and turned on another overhead light. What Monsignor Triplett's brother told Lieutenant Palmer was wrong. The room was not organized. Not everything was perfect.

"The way the bed looks, it's as if he got up and left in a hurry. Not only the bed, but dresser drawers and the closet doors are open. And look at the hangers thrown on the bed. Do you think maybe he overslept?" Jabowski suggested.

"He could have. That's one possibility."

"Or do you think someone came in here and ransacked his room? Jabowski asked.

"Yet another possibility, but who?"

"You may want to ask those living here?"

"I will. " Palmer walked over to the nightstand. He wanted to check the clock radio to see what time the alarm was set for. "The alarm was set for 4:00 a.m. Wow... that seems early!"

"It's early for me!" Jabowski exclaimed. "Why would he be getting up so early on a morning when he could sleep in?"

"Don't you remember, he had a 6:00 a.m. appointment with Monsignor Stone?"

Palmer suddenly noticed another charger, possibly for a cell phone, but nothing plugged into it. "Here's his wallet." He showed Jabowski. "I guess he didn't need it when he left."

"Or, if he was in a hurry, he forgot it." Jabowski checked the closet and found the few clothes—shirts, pants, some vestments, and jackets—neatly hanging. Behind the clothes, they found several storage boxes along with a box of family pictures.

"Okay. So Monsignor had $50,000 in cash, was in debt some $10,000 with all his bills, and his wallet had a total of $452 in it along with a few subway Metro cards." Palmer reviewed the information while Jabowski brought over more evidence bags.

Still checking out the top of the nightstand, Palmer noticed a small pill and a glass of water. "Do you know what this is?"

"What does the prescription on the bottle say?" Jabowski returned one question for another.

"There's no pill bottle on the stand. Let me look in the drawer." Palmer opened the drawer to the nightstand and found a box of cough drops and a pill bottle. The CSU photographer took a few pictures before the lieutenant removed it. He read the label which showed Monsignor Triplett was taking 40mg of Lisinopril for his high blood pressure. As he opened the bottle, the pills matched the one on the nightstand. He took the bottle and put it in one of the evidence bags, along with the single pill.

"It looks like someone forgot to take his medicine," Jabowski said.

"Maybe so."

As they continued checking the room, it seemed everything else was in its proper place. The photographer was taking pictures in the bathroom and made another discovery.

Palmer walked into the bathroom, curious to see what the photographer had found. There it was... Palmer hoped his luck would change in this investigation. A cell phone was on the wet counter. He picked it up but realized the battery was dead. He wouldn't be able to look at the recent contacts or hear any voicemail messages. He took the phone, placed it in another bag and went to unplug the charger by the bed to put with it.

"Hey Jabowski, I found the cell phone. It looks like he must have gotten it wet. And the battery's dead. It's going to the crime lab. They can charge it and retrieve the messages and the numbers a lot faster than we can."

"There is a possibility he was in a hurry and dropped it in the water, and it was useless for him," Jabowski suggested. "Didn't you tell us his brother said something about him always carrying it with him?"

"He did. We'll be able to tell more once we get it charged and see who the last person he talked to. He may have made his last call in the bathroom taking a dump. Only there was a bigger dump going to happen," Palmer remarked with a little sarcasm.

"Funny. Are we done here?" Detective Jabowski frowned at Lieutenant Palmer to show her disgust at his callous remark. She reminded him. "I think the commissioner wants to see us before the press conference. Here." She handed him a few more evidence bags just in case he needed them.

"Thanks. Sorry about that last comment. How about helping the CSU with the evidence? I'll make a quick pass through the rooms again and meet you downstairs to see the commissioner. I want you to take Monsignor Triplett's brother to the morgue to identify the body."

"Apology accepted, and I'd be happy to take the brother to the morgue. Maybe they'll have some information about Monsignor's death."

"We'll let the crime scene investigators finish up, and then we may need to return before we remove anything more. Monsignor Triplett's brother will need to get in here." Palmer looked at the CSU investigator and photographer as they continued their work.

"We go through rooms taking pictures in a very systematic manner." The investigator was getting his dig in on how detectives. "You come in, touching, moving and removing evidence that hamper our work if not done systematically."

Detective Jabowski took the hint. As she waited for the crime scene investigator to finish, she reviewed and organized the evidence bags from Monsignor Triplett's room before they moved them to the evidence table in the cathedral.

Taking one more walk around each of Monsignor Triplett's rooms, Palmer didn't see anything more to help him with the investigation. He knew the papers on the desk and in the drawers would have to be examined further, but he felt he had what he needed to continue. He reminded the investigators to seal off the room with the crime tape when they finished. He wanted another chance to question Thom Triplett but knew the cardinal was waiting to see them. Unfortunately, the cardinal would have to come first, and the questions for Thom would have to wait.

Palmer returned to the library and found Thom in tears. The lieutenant wondered if something more had upset him.

"Are you okay Thom?"

"No... no... not... not really, Lieutenant. It's just so hard to believe my best friend and brother is dead." Thom thought this was the best answer to give since he didn't want to discuss his last telephone conversation.

"I understand, and I can only offer my condolences. Will talking with the cardinal help you? I know he's waiting for us."

"Yes. I'm sure he'll want to express his condolences and discuss funeral plans."

"Then we should go to his house." Palmer was ready.

But Thom wasn't. He had his own questions he wanted answered. "Did you find his cell phone?"

"Yes, we did.... It's headed to the crime lab." Palmer had nothing more to share.

Thom was uncertain what to ask next, but was fishing for some information. "Did you find anything else interesting?"

"Actually, we did. There's this envelope for you." Palmer pulled it out of his pocket.

Thom took the envelope and recognized his brothers' handwriting. He stared at it for a minute. "Is it okay for me to open it?"

"Yes, let me see if I can find a letter opener for you." Palmer looked in the library desk drawer and discovered one.

As Thom opened the envelope, a key fell out. Along with the key was a note that he silently read,

'Thom, if you are reading this, then I am probably no longer alive. I am sorry I did not get a chance to tell you how much I loved you. Please know this key holds the answer to many questions and the possible person or persons who may have had something to do with my death. I will see you on the other side. Love, Steven.'

Thom began to weep as he passed the note to Palmer.

The lieutenant read the note. "I'm so sorry." At that moment Palmer realized Monsignor Triplett knew a great deal. As he looked at the key Thom was holding, it looked like the one he saw earlier today. He excused himself and left the library to make a quick call to Sabor.

"Patrick, do you still have the safe key found on Monsignor Triplett?"

"It's with the evidence. We bagged it earlier today and placed it with the other evidence bags in the cathedral."

"Get it and bring it immediately to the house. I need to see if it matches another key?"

"I'm on my way," Sabor responded.

As Palmer went back in to the library, he saw Thom trying to compose himself. "Thom, the key you're holding looks like a safe key. Did your brother ever mention anything about having a safe deposit box or a safe somewhere?"

"He has a safe in his closet in the bedroom. It's not easy to find. I probably should have said something to you about it earlier."

"Do you know where in the closet?"

"It's all the way to the back. If I remember… it's behind some boxes of childhood memorabilia and some pictures he hadn't hung."

"I didn't see it." Palmer remembered that while in the bedroom, Jabowski had seen boxes in the closet but didn't move them. It was a rare mistake on his and her part. He wanted to return to Monsignor Triplett's room.

"One evening early on when he was named rector, my brother showed it to me when I was up in his room. He told me he kept some files in there that he wished he didn't have to."

"Did he say any more than that?"

"No, and I didn't want to know either." Thom now regretted he hadn't asked.

There was a knock at the door. Sabor entered the room holding the evidence bag with the key found on Monsignor Triplett. Thom gave his key to Palmer, and they placed them side-by-side — it looked like a match.

"It's the same key. Monsignor had one on him, and he was ready to give a second one to his brother. Whatever the key opens, Monsignor wanted to make sure his brother could get to it." Palmer returned the evidence bag with the key in it to Sabor.

"Lieutenant Palmer, can I see you outside for a moment?" Detective Sabor asked.

They walked into the hallway, Palmer wondered what Sabor had discovered.

Sabor closed the library door. "Will, I sent you a picture of what looks like two bloody letters written on the pew. Did you look at it?"

"Yes, I saw it. It looks like the letters "S" and "A"." He suddenly remembered three words. He flipped through his notepad and saw what Monsignor Triplett had written on his yellow tablet — *key, stone,* and *annulment.*

"Do you think Monsignor Triplett was trying to write safe?"

"That's a real possibility. We'll find out once we open the safe and look. Thanks for bringing over the key. I need to ask his brother a few more questions." Palmer and Sabor went quickly to the library.

"Did you know your brother had a briefcase in his room with almost $50,000 in it?" Palmer revealed.

258

Thom looked up in disbelief. "I've never known him to have any money—let alone $50,000. He should have been buying the lunches...." Thom had a slight grin of envy on his face.

"You know nothing about the money?" Palmer asked.

Thom was confused. "This is the first I'm hearing about it. Where did he get this money?"

"I'm not sure. Maybe the key holds some answers to those questions, but we've kept the cardinal waiting far too long. Right now, I'm not doing so well staying on the right side with the church, so I think we'd better go see him." Palmer knew he had to return to Monsignor Triplett's room. He hoped the police tape would keep the curious out until he could get back there.

"Do you have any more questions?" Thom hoped he was finished.

"One more thing... I want to show you a picture I took of a post-it in your brother's room." Palmer pulled out his cell phone and showed the picture. "Do you know if he was meeting Monsignor Stone at 6:00 this morning?"

Thom looked at the picture intently. "I'm not sure. I know my brother was going to contact him and set up a meeting, but I didn't know when."

Palmer looked at his watch and knew he needed to end this part of the questioning. The three of them left the library and walked toward the living room. Sabor left them to return the key found on Monsignor Triplett to the evidence table. Palmer wondered where the briefcase of money had come from. He needed to get back into the monsignor's room and locate the safe. As he was trying to figure out his next move, Commissioner Timberbank stopped him in the hallway.

Lieutenant Palmer made the introductions. "Commissioner, this is Monsignor Triplett's brother, Thom Triplett." After an exchange of hellos and condolences, Thom asked directions to the bathroom and excused himself before going to see the cardinal.

"You wanted to see me, Commissioner?" Palmer asked.

"How's it going?" The police commissioner knew Lieutenant Palmer was the best man for this complicated job. He had great confidence in him.

"The mystery seems to get bigger. We just found a briefcase of almost $50,000 in Monsignor Triplett's study. We also found his cell phone wet and the battery dead, so it's on its way to the crime lab. The brother has been helpful, but it's been a strain on him. We're on our way to see Cardinal Flinn to make funeral arrangements, and then Thom will go to the morgue to identify the body. It's not going to be easy. Are you all set for the press conference?" Palmer asked.

"I believe so. I just wondered if we'll hear from Sara before we begin." The commissioner was eager to get the coroner's report.

"I doubt it. You know Sara. If she has something, she will let you know as soon as she can. It's best to let her call one of us. You know she doesn't like to be pressured."

"I agree. I'll wait for her call." The commissioner had experienced the wrath of Sara Brown when he had called her to make inquiries about other autopsies.

Palmer continued to explain. "I'll have Detective Jabowski take Monsignor's brother down to the morgue to officially identify the body. Then Thom would like to come back and go through his brother's room."

"He can only get the clothes needed to take to the funeral home. When the investigation is over, he'll be able to spend time in the room. In fact, once the press conference is over, is there any reason to keep Jabowski and Pantera here?" The commissioner asked.

Palmer looked at his notes. "I'll need them to help interview a few more possible suspects. From the staff, I've got the Director of Administrative Services and the housekeeper coming. Also, the supervisor of the construction is coming. I'm going to ask a Monsignor David Stone, the head of the church court system, the tribunal, to meet me here."

"What's the connection between Monsignor Triplett and this Monsignor Stone?"

"It appears the church gave Monsignor Triplett's brother a negative response to his marriage annulment, and I think they were going to meet to discuss it at 6:00 this morning?"

"Are you sure about the time?"

"Commissioner, at this point, I'm not sure about anything, except there was a note on top of the annulment papers in Monsignor Triplett's study saying 'Saturday 6:00 a.m.,'" Palmer explained.

"Seems like a strange time for them to meet?"

"It does, but I'm not sure if they actually met. I've never understood the Catholic Church's process on marriage annulments. Being Catholic, I was taught marriage is for life. Scripture talks about not divorcing, but the church seems to find a way to allow it."

"It can be painful. My friend got his annulment after doing a lot of paperwork. He had to appear at a church court hearing to be questioned. A few months later, he was informed, based on the witnesses and statements presented, that the church had concluded his marriage would not have lasted "until death do us part." It would cost him $1000 in fees, but from what he said, the Pope recently stopped the church from charging."

"Like I said, the church has found a way to make money on someone's misery." Palmer was surprised the commissioner had shared a personal story with him.

"Enough said, Palmer. It sounds like Detectives Jabowski and Pantera should stay and help you."

"Thanks, Commissioner, if you'll excuse me." Palmer was eager to return to the investigation. He knew the longer the investigation went on, the more likely evidence would disappear, and witnesses would too.

As Palmer walked away, Detective Jabowski walked up to him. "Lieutenant, I made a mistake and forgot to tell you that when I was questioning Father Crumbley, he told me each bedroom had a safe in the closet. While the CSU photographer was taking pictures of the closet, he moved a couple of boxes and found the safe. I came right over to tell you."

Palmer displayed a serious look of dismay. "I know… I just talked with Monsignor's brother, and he told me about the safe. The key in the envelope Thom Triplett received matches the key found on the deceased body. I'm going to take Thom's key and see if it opens the safe after I meet with the cardinal."

"I'm sorry. I should have remembered." Jabowski was sincerely apologetic.

"Let's call it even—after the remark I made in the bathroom." Palmer tried to reassure the young detective of two years there was no damage in her mistake.

Jabowski was appreciative the oversight was forgiven.

Palmer telephoned Sabor to see if everything was ready for the press conference. The lieutenant had a knack for keeping details organized, and this investigation was no different.

"It looks like we'll be ready," Sabor said.

"Once the priests return from seeing the cardinal, I need to get over to see him again. I hope I make it this time!"

"Hey, Boss, is he hearing your confession?" Sabor couldn't resist the jab.

"Yes, and you're next so be ready." Palmer joked. "He's going to meet with Monsignor Triplett's brother and discuss the funeral arrangements."

"After hearing my confession, I'm not sure I'd get a Catholic funeral!" Sabor realized he hadn't been to confession for many years. "I'll see you soon."

Thom Triplett was in the hallway waiting as he watched Lieutenant Palmer on the phone. He motioned he was going to the library to make a phone call and would be right back. He waited for Palmer to acknowledge him. Thom quickly entered the library and shut the door. He looked under favorites in his contacts and placed the call.

"I didn't expect to hear from you so quickly." The voice on the other end compassionately began.

"I'm sorry I snapped you at the end of our last conversation. It's the stress of my brother's death, and you, unfortunately, are the recipient of the anger I'm feeling because of his senseless death."

"I'm sorry. I didn't know how to help you."

"I just need to give you a heads up. Our dinner last night was all lawyer-to-lawyer, correct?"

"Well, almost all of it was."

"Then let's agree it all was. You're going to be brought into this, and I want to be sure it's strictly client-to-lawyer, and nothing can be revealed."

"I agree. If you see the cardinal, tell him I said hello."

"He wants to see me," Thom quickly stated.

"Good. I'm sure he is struggling with the news."

"I'm sure he is."

"Will I see you later?"

"I'll let you know. I've got to go." Thom hung up his phone, thankful he made the call to Jennifer. He hated to end the call, but thought it best to get off the phone in case the lieutenant came in. When Thom returned to the hallway, he was irritated that Palmer was still on his phone.

Thom tried to keep his distance when he heard the words, "Monsignor Stone." Palmer must have just started talking with him. Thom went to the end of the hallway where there was an empty chair for him to sit and wait.

Waiting wasn't something Thom was accustomed to. He decided to call his children and let them know of the passing of their uncle. They needed to hear it from him before it was announced through newscasts and social media.

"This is Monsignor David Stone. You called me?" He tried to sound confident on the phone, but he was as nervous.

"Yes, this is Lieutenant Will Palmer of the NYPD. Sorry to call you on a Saturday morning, but is there any way you could come to Saint Patrick's Cathedral and speak with me? I have a few questions for you."

"Right now? I… I was planning on seeing my 92-year-old mother this morning, as I normally do. Can't this wait?" Monsignor Stone felt the need to go visit his mother. It had been a week since he last saw her, and she was expecting to see him before Easter.

"I'd really appreciate it if you would come to the cathedral now."

"What's this about? Has something happened?" Monsignor Stone knew the answers to these questions, but he acted surprised at any information they told him.

"I think it's best to tell you everything when you come here." Palmer noticed Monsignor Stone's tentative tone.

Monsignor Stone tried to disassociate himself from what he knew. "Is the cardinal okay?"

"Again, it would be better for you to come here." Palmer persisted.

"Of course… I'll try to be there within an hour. I need to let my mom know I won't be coming. This may take some time, but I believe I can be there in an hour." Monsignor Stone knew it was plenty of time. He wanted to compose himself and be ready for any questions they might ask him.

"The sooner you're able to come the better. Come to the parish house, so we can talk." Palmer reiterated.

"Okay. Are you sure you can't tell me what this is about?"

"As I said, I think it would be best for you to come and let me talk with you in person." Palmer realized that in an hour the whole world would know.

"See you in an hour or so."

As he ended the conversation with Lieutenant Palmer, Monsignor Stone finally grasped the possibility he might never return to his residence. But if he didn't go for questioning, suspicion could be on him. Sooner or later he knew someone would come knocking at his door. He wished he could have remembered what happened.

Monsignor turned off the computer, called his mom and told her he wouldn't be visiting today. It was not what his mother wanted to hear. He could hear the disappointment in her voice. He was the only one to visit her.

He then prayed and sought guidance from above. As he was prayed, he was distracted by his own thoughts and wondering if the police had found the person who gave him his headache this morning. He wished he knew who it was. They held each other's fate in their hands.

Chapter 21

Sam had seen her pain and was thrilled to know Emma was talking with her son Jonathan. But as he listened to their conversation, he realized for the sake of their relationship, he wouldn't be able to return to her apartment. Emma loved her son deeply and would do anything to get him to return home. After what he had experienced these last twenty-four hours, he knew it was more important for them to be reunited than for him to continue with this affair. As Emma said goodbye to her son on the phone, Sam saw how happy she looked—the conversation must have gone well.

"Oh, I feel so much better knowing Jonathan is okay." Emma put her phone in her purse.

"I'm happy for you. Did I hear correctly that Jonathan is going to come back home?"

"Yes, he said he would be home today." Emma finished gathering her items.

"I talked with Jean. We're going to put the vacation on hold." Sam was confused and worried what the future held for him.

"I'm sorry," Emma said. "You need to get dressed, pack and leave first."

"Can't we talk Emma?" Sam asked.

"No, I think it best you leave." Emma felt the pain having to say these words.

"You sure you don't want to go first?" Sam asked.

"No, I need a few minutes alone to compose myself," Emma explained. "Right now, I need to focus on Jonathan returning home and helping him deal with the loss of Monsignor Triplett. It sounds like he's taking it rather hard. He will be shocked to find out all Monsignor did for him. I just don't know how I'm going to continue providing for all Jonathan's needs."

Sam finished dressing, packed and looked at Emma. He wanted to give her a kiss but walked out of the room saying nothing. His next stop was the cathedral.... He was scared.

Emma wiped away her tears, not sure whom she was crying for. She double checked the room to make sure nothing was forgotten. She was about to throw some tissue in the trashcan when she saw an unfamiliar small box at the bottom of it. She bent down, pulled it out and discovered a box of over-the-counter sleeping pills. She hadn't brought it and wondered if Sam had. She didn't remember him ever taking sleeping pills before. She would have to remember to ask him.

Emma sat patiently and said a small prayer of thanks to God for the telephone call from her son. As much as she was in love with Sam, her son had to become number one for her. She was so looking forward to getting home and hugging him.

After ten minutes, she left the hotel with her overnight bag and made the short walk to the parish house where she asked for Lieutenant Palmer. She imagined the tension that must be in the parish offices with Sam and the other staff, including the priests. Emma also wondered what questions Sam was facing.

"Your full name is?" Lieutenant Palmer began.

"Sam Joseph Tolden." Sam placed his overnight bag beside his chair.

Continuing with answers to basic questions of address and phone number, Sam could sense the lieutenant was just warming up with his questions. It seemed the politeness suddenly ended at the door, and there was a more serious detective present who was on a mission to solve this case. Sam wondered how long he would be able to answer questions before he would ask for his attorney.

"How long have you worked here at the cathedral?" Palmer turned the page on his notepad.

"I've been working here a little over two years," Sam quickly responded.

"And how would you describe your work here?

"Stressful. As the administrator, the staff comes to me with questions or concerns. I also oversee the maintenance staff and take care of any problems within the physical plant. So... on any given day, I make decisions, and sometimes the cathedral is not always happy with it."

"And how many staff members are we talking about?" Sam counted on his fingers. "I believe there are 25 lay staff. Some full and a few part-time."

"A big payroll?" Palmer tried to read Sam's demeanor.

"Yes, and that's one of the problems," Sam explained.

"Are you involved as the administrator in the restoration that is taking place here?"

"No. The cardinal wanted Monsignor Triplett to oversee that. He was the direct contact between the contractor and the archdiocesan office of construction. The archdiocesan finance office paid all the bills."

"So you had no responsibilities or any relationship with the construction staff."

"Not really... I'd offer advice to Monsignor Triplett when he asked me."

"How would you see your relationship with Monsignor Triplett?"

"He's the one who hired me, and our relationship started off very well. But over the last few weeks, I'd say our relationship was being tested while he had some financial decisions to make."

"What type of financial decisions?"

"Decisions dealing with the number of paid employees on staff and the need to reduce the number because the cathedral's income had dropped due to all the restoration. I had presented him with a couple of possible scenarios to help solve the problem."

"Was he open to the ideas you proposed to him?"

"I'm not exactly sure. We were going to discuss them this week, but it seemed neither of us could find the time to meet." Sam remembered the last conversation with Monsignor Triplett. "I think he was working on a different plan."

"Why do you say that?"

"Because I think the plan he was trying to come up with would have eliminated my position." Sam's tone began to change. He looked a little uncomfortable after revealing this detail and shifted in his chair.

"Did he tell you that?" Palmer detected a possible conflict between these two men.

"No, but he was talking about reducing my responsibilities and hours."

"How did this make you feel?"

"I wasn't happy with that either."

"Do you know when Monsignor was making that decision?"

"Monsignor had to do something before the first of July when our new fiscal year begins. The money wasn't there, and the archdiocese wasn't going to help out."

"You knew this for sure?"

"Yes, Monsignor Triplett informed me he had no choice but to make changes until the income of the cathedral increased. He tried avoiding discussing it with me whenever I brought it up."

"Was there something he had on you?" Palmer wondered about the strain on the relationship between the two of them.

This was one of the questions Sam dreaded. He knew that not only did Monsignor Triplett have something on him, but he also held something over Monsignor Triplett's head. They each had a trump card they could play, and now, with the death of Monsignor Triplett, Sam realized that information would be revealed. He thought hard about the question and decided he wanted some time. "Can I get a glass of water and go to the bathroom?"

"Sure Sam. But don't take too long." Palmer figured this was a stalling tactic but gave him the break he needed to compose his answer. After five minutes, Sam returned.

"Well, Monsignor Triplett discovered I was having an extramarital affair. He even knew the other person..., and I realized I could lose my job because of it. He was very unhappy about the situation, and I think he would have used it to dismiss me."

"And what were you holding over his head?" Palmer asked.

"I had knowledge he was being paid under the table by the contractor to overlook some things being done. Monsignor Triplett had personal money problems. I tried to help him, but he didn't listen to my advice."

"And how do you know the contractor was helping him?"

"I received a call from one of the accountants at my former place of employment — Earnest and Patrick. They reviewed the books and electronic records for Delfino Construction."

"Why would they call you?"

"This anonymous person owed me a big favor and thought it was important for me to know that the construction company paid Monsignor Triplett's credit card bills. It was about to end for him because the Manhattan district attorney was investigating Delfino's company with Monsignor Triplett and the archdiocese were in the middle of it all."

"So that's what each of you held over the other?"

"Yes. That's why I don't think he would have let me go. He knew I knew," Sam said.

"And if he exposed you, would you have exposed him?"

"It was coming to that. As much as I like Monsignor Triplet, and as sad as it would have been, this was the only thing I could find he did wrong."

"Were you getting any portion of the money Monsignor Triplett was obtaining from the kickbacks?"

"Yes... yes... I was." Sam confessed since he knew he couldn't hide this from the detectives.

"How much did you receive?" Palmer asked.

"I received close to $4,000 in cash." As Sam answered, he thought about the last six months knowing what he received in his paychecks. The money he got bought his silence.

"You say you were getting this in cash? How was Monsignor Triplett able to give this to you in cash?"

"He'd get a cash advance from one of the credit cards the Delfinos paid, and then he'd put the cash in my paycheck. I know he kept a record of it all."

"Do you know if others received money?"

"I'm not sure, but I presume so."

"So helping others is what got Monsignor Triplett in financial trouble?"

"I believe so. He was trying to help too many people. One time he told me he had maxed his credit cards and would disappoint a few people because he couldn't help them."

"Were you the one he helped the most?"

"I don't think so. I think he helped Jonathan Pickle more than anyone."

"Pickle?" Palmer was now curious and eager for his next response.

"Emma Pickle is the housekeeper here and the mother of Jonathan Pickle."

"And how do you know Monsignor Triplett was helping Jonathan Pickle."

"Emma had told me."

"And your relationship with Emma?"

"She's the one I was having an extramarital affair with."

271

"I see. And is this why you're carrying what looks like an overnight bag with you."

"Yes, we were together last night." Sam could not believe how easily he was answering these questions knowing the damage it would do to him.

"Can I ask where?"

"At the Women's Republican Club just a block from here on 51st Street."

"Do you remember the room number?" Palmer asked.

"It was 212."

"I have spoken to Emma Pickle. She informed me she's coming here. Do you know if she is?"

"Yes. She was leaving ten minutes after I left."

"How long has this affair been going on?"

"I'd say it started shortly after I came to work for the cathedral. We seemed to have an instant connection, but we didn't really pursue it until about six months ago. She lost her husband a few years ago, and I was having marital problems. We started talking, and lately, with all the stress of the finances, I'd just tell my wife I was working late. But I'd be with Emma."

"How long did Monsignor Triplett know about this affair?"

"I'm not sure, but he confronted me about a month ago and, in so many words, was going to force me to make a choice, even with what I had on him."

"What was the choice you'd have to make?" Palmer asked.

"To end the affair or to resign from my job." Sam then added, "I never told Emma about my conversation with Monsignor Triplett."

"Had you made that choice?"

"I had, but it's all changed now. Emma ended the affair this morning." Sam was heartbroken saying the words.

"Back to last night... were you with her all night?"

272

Sam shook his head up and down before slowly saying the word, "Yes."

"All night?"

"Yes... How many times are you going to ask me this question? We were together from when I got there last night until this morning." Sam frustrated, was stretching the truth a little.

"And what time did you get there?"

"I got to the hotel room before 10:00 last night."

"You didn't leave the room?"

"No. Emma was already there. I arrived with a bottle of wine, and we each had a glass, then watched a little TV and went to bed." Sam knew a few more things were missing from his answer.

Palmer continued to drill Sam with questions. "Did anyone see you arrive?"

"Maybe the person at the front desk, but I knew the room number, I just went to it."

"How often would you and Emma get together?"

"Outside of work, I think in the last six months, we'd see each other at least once a week. It was hard for her since her son wasn't happy with our relationship."

"Did you always meet at the Women's Republican Club?"

"No... this was probably only our fourth or fifth time." Sam lied, knowing that there were more.

"You stayed in all last night?"

"Yes, I didn't wake until I heard my cell phone, and you were calling me." Sam knew his answer was not true, but he would do everything he could to protect himself and Emma.

Palmer wasn't entirely satisfied. He changed the course of the interview. "I'd like to return to your responsibilities at the cathedral if I may. Do you keep track of anyone who has keys to the various buildings here?"

"I'm supposed to. Every key is assigned, checked out and signed for."

"So you would be the person who would assign the key, and the person receiving the key would sign for it?"

"That's correct."

"This would include keys to the parish office, to the cathedral and to the parish house?"

"Yes."

"What about the cardinal's house?"

"Yes, I would assign those as well, but the cardinal would have to give his permission."

"And where are the extra keys kept for all the buildings?"

"They're in a locked box in the parish office safe," Sam explained. "Monsignor Triplett and I have the only keys to the safe. We began this system. We didn't know who had keys to any of the buildings before we came here. With this method, we still had no guarantee who had keys. Even having the keys stamped, 'do not duplicate,' I still found extra keys around."

"Who gave the cathedral keys to the construction workers?"

"We had special keys made for them." Sam remembered what he went through with the locksmith for those keys.

"What was special about those keys?"

"It limited the doors they could enter."

"How was that determined?"

"Monsignor Triplett worked that out with the contractor and supervisor some time ago."

"Do you know what doors they included?"

"I'm not sure of all of them. It was a sub-master key that limited access to some doors."

"I presume the key opened the exterior doors and sacristy?"

"Yes."

"Do you know if the key opened the door for the stairs up to the walkway to the attic?"

"I'm not sure. I'd have to see what the sub-master key opens. Why are you asking about that door?" Sam was confused.

274

"I have my reasons. Would that include the door from the sacristy to the office?"

"No. To get into the office from the cathedral takes another key."

"Do you know how many of these special keys were given out?"

"I don't know. I know they asked me to have six of those keys made. I gave all six to Monsignor Triplett. You'd probably have to ask the supervisor."

"So you don't have a list of those who have these special keys for the construction company?"

"No, I don't. I imagine Monsignor Triplett or the construction supervisor has it. I was just given the task of getting six keys made up, and I don't remember if the words 'do not duplicate' were put on them."

"Sam, is there a list of those who have keys to the cathedral, the parish offices, parish house, and cardinal's residence?"

"Yes, it's in my office." Sam was becoming even more frustrated.

"Speaking of your office, I'd like to ask you a few questions about it. When was the last time you were in your office?" Palmer asked.

"It was yesterday afternoon with Monsignor Triplett."

"You met in your office, not his?"

"That's correct. I needed him to sign a few papers including a couple of checks, so it was just easier for him to come to my office instead of me bringing everything to him."

"So the meeting was just to sign checks and papers on Good Friday. Wasn't the office closed?"

"Yes, it was, but I was taking Easter week off and needed to come in to do a few things." Sam continued to provide information. "Monsignor Triplett told me he would expose my affair with Emma, and this gave him a reason to let me go. He told me it was a hard decision, but because I wasn't going to end my relationship, he had to do it. We had words. I brought up what I had on him, and he said I should do what I had to do. He didn't want to talk any more about it and left. I finished what I needed to do, and I left."

"What were you going to do?"

"I don't know."

"When the crime scene investigators came to your office, they noticed fresh blood on the floor by one chair. Do you know anything about it?"

"Monsignor Triplett got a nasty paper cut looking over a couple of the invoices that needed to be paid. Blood was coming out of his finger. He dropped the invoices, and when he went to pick them up, blood got on the carpet."

"Was that the last time you saw Monsignor Triplett?"

"No, I saw him briefly yesterday evening after the Good Friday service. I could tell by his expression he wasn't happy with the way our conversation ended, so he asked me to come back this morning to finish our conversation."

"Did you?"

Sam cringed at the question. He wondered, did Palmer know.

Palmer waited for an answer.

Sam instead of answering the question, turned the tables on the lieutenant and said, "I think before I answer any more questions, I need to talk with an attorney."

"That would be advisable," Palmer agreed. "Do you have the number to make the call?"

"I believe I do." Sam pulled out his phone looking for the number of his attorney and friend, Kurt Barbertie. He was hoping he would find him home and hopefully sober enough to come and meet him. Even though Kurt drank heavily, he was one of the most successful defense attorneys in the city.

Palmer gave Sam some privacy and stepped out of the library. He walked a short distance to find Thom Triplett asleep in the chair. He decided to let him sleep.

The lieutenant walked back down the hall to call Sabor to send a uniformed police officer over.

"I believed we have the first suspect in the case."

"Who is it?" Sabor asked.

"Sam Tolden."

"The administrator? Are you going to tell the police commissioner?" Sabor asked, excited with the progress of the investigation.

"Yes, the cathedral administrator. Nothing to tell yet. Still questioning."

"I'll send Mark VanDyke over. Nice new officer."

"Thanks."

Palmer opened the door to the library and heard Sam ending his conversation. "Was that your attorney on the phone with you?" he asked.

"Yes, it was," Sam responded nervously.

"Is he coming to the parish house to meet with you?"

"He said he'd be here, but it would probably take a good hour before he could arrive." Sam knew it would take longer.

"What's your attorney's name?"

"Kurt Barbertie."

"I'll tell the officer at the door. When he arrives, he'll be brought to you."

"Thank you. May I have some paper and a pen? I need to write a few things down before he arrives."

"Let me see what I can do for you." Palmer left the library and closed the door behind him. In the kitchen, he found Father Crumbley working hard.

"Father Crumbley, would you be kind enough to bring some paper and a pen into the library for Mr. Tolden? I'd appreciate it. Do you have any coffee made?"

"Just made a fresh pot! Let me get a yellow tablet and pen." Father Crumbley went to his room and within two minutes took the items to the library. He quickly returned to the kitchen. "Lieutenant, Mr. Tolden looks a little worried."

Palmer said nothing as he took a sip of coffee. Immediately Father Crumbley made the Sign of the Cross.

Officer VanDyke arrived and found Palmer who told the officer to take a position outside the library and prevent Sam from leaving and anyone from entering the room until Sam's attorney arrived. Officer VanDyke understood, but by the disappointed look on his face, this was not the assignment he had hoped for.

As Palmer headed to the living room, Emma came up the stairs.

Overhearing the conversation between the two officers, she wondered who the police officer was guarding in the library. She could only think the worst — was it Sam?

Chapter 22

"Excuse me, are you Lieutenant Palmer?" Emma nervously asked as she saw this stranger in the hallway.

"I am. You must be Mrs. Pickle, the housekeeper?" Palmer looked at an attractive lady he guessed was probably in her late forties or early fifties, carrying what seemed like an overnight bag.

"Yes, I'm Mrs. Emma Pickle, the cathedral housekeeper."

"Thank you for coming in. We can talk in the living room." The lieutenant ushered her through the hallway into the living room.

They almost succeeded in closing the door before Father Crumbley entered to speak to Emma. He wanted to see if they needed anything. Emma asked for a glass of water feeling the dryness in her mouth. Palmer was still holding a partial cup of coffee. Father Crumbley returned with a glass for each of them and a small pitcher of water. The lieutenant thanked him and asked that he close the door behind him.

Once they were both seated, Palmer opened his notebook to begin the interview. He thanked Emma for coming in. "For the record, please state your full name?"

"Emma Margaret Smith Pickle. Smith was my maiden name." Emma placed her overnight bag on the floor.

As he had done with the others, Lieutenant Palmer went through a series of basic questions of address, phone number and such. Emma knew the lieutenant had questions he wanted answered, but she could think only about Sam. Had he finished or had he left, or was he the one the police officer was watching?

"I'm sorry. What did you say?" Emma wasn't even listening. She tried not to think about Sam.

"You thought I was calling you about your son. Is he okay?"

"Yes, thank you. He's been away from home these last few days, and I feared the worst. But he called, and now he's on his way home." Emma was eager to get home to Jonathan.

"I'm happy to hear he's okay."

"I want to get home as soon as possible to see him." Emma nervously rubbed her hands.

"Are you okay, Mrs. Pickle?" Palmer noted how vigorously she rubbed her hands.

"I'm just a little nervous. I rub my hands when I get nervous."

"What are you nervous about?"

"I'm just wondering how many more questions you have. I'm not good in situations like this."

"I'll try to get through my questions as quickly as possible. How long have you been employed at the cathedral?"

"Almost six years... Monsignor Triplett hired me."

"Would you say you had a good working relationship with Monsignor Triplett?"

"Very much so! He knew I needed to do something in my life, and this was a great opportunity, especially after I lost my husband."

"How did you know Monsignor Triplett?

"Well, he was the former pastor at Saint Mark's Parish where I go to church. When he was there, I went to him once asking for a job. My husband and I were struggling financially, and I thought if I could get a part-time job someplace while my son was at school, it would help with the finances. He had nothing for me, but he helped me find a couple of jobs. When he came here to the cathedral, there was this opening for a housekeeper. He thought of me, called, and we worked out the details. It's been the best job I could have had for the last six years. I'm very thankful Monsignor Triplett hired me." Emma was looking for the Kleenex in her purse as tears filled her eyes and rolled down her cheeks.

"How was your personal relationship with him?" Palmer knew this was a sensitive question.

"I'm not sure what you mean?" Emma dried her eyes.

"It's my understanding Monsignor Triplett spent a lot of time with you and your son after your husband's death."

"My husband's death was such a shock for us. The only person my son seemed to open up to was Monsignor Triplett."

"Have you and Monsignor Triplett never met at the Women's Republican Club a block away?"

"What? What are you saying?" Emma was shocked at the lieutenant's suggestion. "You think Monsignor Triplett and… and… I got together at the Women's Republican Club?"

"Did you?"

"No, of course not… not in the way you're thinking!" Emma was clearly angry.

"You are familiar with the Women's Republican Club?"

"Yes."

"You've been there?"

"Yes." Emma rubbed her hands again. She wondered what he knew.

"You've checked in there?"

"Yes." She wished Sam was here.

"Alone?"

"No."

"Were you meeting someone there?" Palmer was now dangling the information he knew and wanted to see if Emma would reveal the affair.

"Yes." Emma let him keep questioning as she gave only one-word answers.

"A man?"

"Yes."

"Is the man Sam Tolden?" Palmer decided enough was enough.

Emma paused, dropping her head before she responded. "Yes."

"So you're having an affair with Sam Tolden?"

"Yes... no... I just ended it!" Emma surprised herself by speaking those words with some confidence.

"Were you with him last night?"

"Yes, but it was a mistake."

"At the Women's Republican Club?"

"Yes."

"Do you remember the room number?"

"It was 212."

Palmer checked his notes and found Sam had given the same information.

"Why the Women's Club?"

"Well, for two reasons. One, it's close to the cathedral. And second, I work there a few hours each week helping with the setup of the Thursday banquets. I could easily get a room for us."

"You had two jobs?"

"Kind of. When Monsignor Triplett hired me, I was still cleaning homes part-time and working part-time at the Women's Republican Club, but the hours were not good for me. When I gave my notice to go work as the cathedral housekeeper, they asked if I'd continue to work for them one day a week on Thursdays since they always had the same function. I talked it over with Monsignor Triplett, and we agreed to fix the schedule, and on Tuesdays and Thursdays, I'd come in for dinner. I made arrangements for my son to stay at one of his friend's house those nights."

"So there was a room available last night for you at the Women's Republican Club?"

"Sam booked and paid for the room."

"What time did you arrive?"

"I went to the evening Good Friday Service, and after it was over, I arrived at the Women's Club around 9:30 p.m."

"When did Sam arrive?"

"He got there close to 10:00 p.m. I know because the TV show *Blue Bloods* came on. It's our favorite show on Friday night since it's filmed here in New York. Are you familiar with it?"

"I have occasionally watched it." Palmer wasn't very interested in what she watched. He continued with his questions. "So you saw Monsignor Triplett when you left?"

"Yes."

"He knew about your affair with Sam?"

"Yes. He found out about a month ago. He wasn't happy with it at all, and it created a little friction. It placed both our jobs in jeopardy, and it was wrong. We went against the teachings of the church. I thought Monsignor was going to fire me, but his relationship with my son probably saved my job."

"What do you mean his relationship with your son?" Palmer was curious.

"After my husband passed away, Monsignor Triplett became the friend and role model my son needed. He gave him a car, paid the insurance on it, and helped with the tuition to provide him with a good Catholic education. I never saw a school tuition bill."

"Very generous, of him. Did you ever ask how he could manage such generosity on a priest's salary?"

"I didn't think much about it. I thought maybe he had money in his family." Emma wondered just how much everything cost Monsignor Triplett and what it would cost her now.

"Your son is the one who had the relationship with Monsignor Triplett?"

"Yes. They both enjoyed each other's company. Jonathan trusted Monsignor Triplett, and he became a mentor to him. They even shared a big interest in football, very much like

Jonathan's father. Occasionally, they would go to the Jets games, and, maybe once a week, Monsignor would come over to visit. My is really going to miss him." Emma started crying and was still rubbing her hands almost nonstop. She was unsure how Jonathan was dealing with the loss and worried about Sam.

"Let's take a break and give you a chance to compose yourself. You may want to try to call your son," Palmer suggested. He also needed time to consider the next set of questions with Emma, as well as to go to the bathroom. The coffee was getting to him. This interview was taking much longer than he had anticipated.

On his way out of the bathroom, the lieutenant checked on Sam in the library. He opened the door. "Mr. Tolden, do you have everything you need?"

"I believe so." Sam had been writing a few things down on the paper they gave him.

The lieutenant stepped into the room. "I have Emma Pickle down the hall, and she admitted to the affair. Is there anything else you'd like to tell me?"

"I want to wait and talk with my lawyer," Sam demanded.

"Like I said, when he arrives, I'll make sure the officer brings him to you."

"Thank you."

Lieutenant Palmer stepped out of the library and closed the door. Even though he found out about the affair from Sam, he thought maybe with Emma's admission, Sam would be more open to sharing something to help him with the next set of questions for her. Unfortunately, asking for the lawyer ended any sharing. The lieutenant returned to the living room, closed the door and continued questioning Emma. "Were you able to get in touch with your son?"

"No, he didn't answer his phone. I forgot he told me his battery had gone dead. Can I go home now?"

"If you would bear with me for a few more minutes, I have a few more questions for you. Let's get back to last night and staying in the Women's Republican Club with Sam. Did you ever leave the room?"

"No. When Sam arrived, he brought a bottle of wine, and we stayed in. I needed to take a shower since I was feeling grungy from work at the cathedral. When I came out of the shower, Sam had poured two glasses of wine. I remember I drank a glass, and I must have fallen asleep since I don't remember anything until your telephone call this morning."

"You never woke in the night?" Lieutenant Palmer was surprised by her answer.

"No."

"You didn't hear Sam's phone ring?"

"No."

"So... you don't know if Sam ever left the room?"

"No... but I doubt that he would have left. Why?" Emma was trying to remember last night.

"Would you normally sleep through the night?"

"No, that's the funny thing. I'm a light sleeper, but last night I slept really well. I thought maybe it was because I was exhausted, and the wine did the trick."

"You didn't take anything to help you sleep?"

"No... no... I didn't. I don't ever. But now that you mention it, it was kinda strange." Emma was thinking out loud. "I found an empty box of sleeping pills in the trash this morning. I found it accidentally when I threw some tissues away. I didn't bring pills with me. I was going to ask Sam if he had brought them."

"You didn't ask him?"

"No, he had already left. You don't think he gave me one, do you?" The idea shocked Emma.

"I wish I knew. Would you excuse me for a moment? I need to make a phone call." Lieutenant Palmer quickly left the living room.

As he walked out into the hall, he called Detective Sabor and asked him to get someone over to the Women's Republican Club with a search warrant to collect the trash

285

in a hotel room that was registered under Sam Tolden or Emma Pickle.

"Sabor, check room 212. I'm looking for an empty box that contained a bottle of over-the-counter sleeping pills, probably in the trash. If the room hasn't been made up, get the glasses used for wine and get them to the crime lab for analysis. There's a possibility Sam Tolden may have drugged Emma Pickle."

Detective Sabor said, "I'll get right on it, boss."

Returning to the living room, Palmer apologized for the interruption and assured Emma that he only had a few more questions left.

"You said you worked part-time cleaning houses. Are you still doing that?"

"Only one apartment and that's Monsignor Steven Stone. It was the first job I got thanks to Monsignor Triplett."

"And when do you clean his apartment?"

"Tuesday mornings. It works out well. Once Jonathan goes to school, I take the subway to Monsignor Stone's apartment. Once I'm there, it doesn't take that long to clean, and the pay is pretty good," Emma said. "It worked out for Monsignor Stone too. Many times I'd arrive, and he'd go off to work for a few hours and come back when I was close to being finished."

"How would you describe your relationship with Monsignor Stone?"

"I'm not sure what you mean?" Emma looked at Lieutenant Palmer.

"Was it an employee to employer relationship or was there more to it?" Palmer tried to clarify the question.

Emma wondered what Palmer had heard and was cautious with her answer. "It started out as an employer-employee relationship, but through the course of conversations, it had become more of a friendship—almost like a brother-sister relationship. After my husband died, he was a comfort to me. I enjoyed his company, and he made me feel special, but that's where it stopped for both of us. He's a good friend and a good priest. That's all." Emma was very emphatic.

"Does Monsignor Stone know about your relationship with Mr. Tolden?"

"I'm not sure. He hasn't said, but he has mentioned that I seem happier these last few months. I just told him there is someone special I met at the cathedral, but I haven't told him who it is." Emma was feeling uncomfortable with these questions.

"Did you ever have any physical relationship with Monsignor Triplett?"

"Never! I can't believe you're asking me these questions! Monsignor Triplett was the kindest person I ever met. He wanted Jonathan and me to be happy. He was watching out for us. He was a close friend to me. When my relationship with Sam began, he expressed concern and was particularly afraid it would turn out bad. He was right!" Emma was angry now and hurt. The tears began again....

"But you said Monsignor Stone didn't know who it was." Palmer continued.

"I didn't tell him, but I have a feeling Monsignor Triplett knew," Emma said. She wished he would move on with other questions as she looked at her watch.

"You mentioned Jonathan. Does he like Mr. Tolden?"

"He doesn't. Jonathan could see Sam made me happy, but he didn't want him in my life. Sam and Jonathan never hit it off. Jonathan thought I would get hurt, and he was right. How blinded I was with Sam." Emma hung her head, disappointed that it took almost losing her son to realize this.

"How would you describe Monsignor Triplett's relationship with Sam?"

"When Sam came to the cathedral, it was good at first. Monsignor, from what Sam said, needed someone to oversee the finances. I know Monsignor didn't like the business side of the parish because it took away from what he felt he was called to do as far as the sacraments and the celebration of the liturgies. But as the finances got bad, there was stress on their relationship. I heard it from Sam. Monsignor had to make some tough choices, and from what I understand, he was going to lay off some people."

"Would you have been one of them?"

"I don't think so. If it was me, I think Monsignor Triplett would have told me, and he didn't. Sam said I was never mentioned in the discussion."

"Did Monsignor Triplett ever give you any extra cash?"

"What do you mean?"

"Did he ever give you cash in an envelope or with your paycheck?"

"There was one time... for Christmas. And when I opened my last paycheck, there was $2,000 in cash. He never said anything to me about it, and I didn't get a chance to ask him or even thank him."

Palmer just realized where the rest of the money from the briefcase may have gone.

"Do you still have the money, Emma?"

Emma wondered if she would have to return the money. "I have hidden the money back home."

"When was the last time you spoke with Monsignor Triplett?"

"After last night's dinner, he seemed a little preoccupied. I thought maybe it was just his nerves since he was preaching in front of the cardinal, and he told me he got a little scared. I just wished him good luck. He did great. It was a great sermon, and now his last...." Emma started crying again.

"I heard it was great. I'm sorry I missed it." Palmer tried to comfort Emma. He could empathize with the loss of a special priest. "Just a few more questions. Do you know of anyone who may have wanted Monsignor Triplett dead?"

"I can't think of anyone! He was so well-liked here." Emma found more tissues in her pocket. She could not imagine anyone killing a priest, much less Monsignor Triplett.

"Would you have any reason to want Monsignor Triplett dead?"

"What are you saying? Lieutenant... he was my friend, my boss, a spiritual influence in my life, and a mentor to my son. All that's gone! You don't realize what a void I'll have without him. I'll really miss him. Even though he voiced his strong disapproval of my relationship with Sam, there's no reason I'd want him dead." Emma struggled to gain her composure.

Lieutenant Palmer slowly closed his notebook. "Thank you for your cooperation, Mrs. Pickle. Please stay in town. If I have any more questions, I'll be in touch. I want you to go to the station to make a formal statement, but I think we can wait until Monday." Emma stuffed the tissues in her pockets, picked up her overnight bag, and slowly got up from the chair.

"Would you like me to walk you out?"

"No...no, thank you. I know my way out. Just let me know what time Monday you'd like me to come down to the station." Emma walked out of the living room and saw the police officer still positioned outside the library. She went down the stairs and out the front door thankful to take in some fresh air.

After talking with Palmer, Emma knew she was glad she ended her relationship with Sam. Dodging the small puddles of rain, she watched each step she took on the wet sidewalk to the subway station. She felt the loss of both Monsignor Triplett and Sam in one day. All she could do now was to pray for justice and mercy for each of them.

Chapter 23

Lieutenant Palmer looked at his watch and realized there was a little more than thirty minutes until the press conference. Pressed for time and with more work to do, he needed to get Thom over to the cardinal's residence, so they would have a chance to talk alone. Sitting in the chair at the end of the hall, Thom awoke, looking lost. Palmer hoped the cardinal would have enough time to discuss funeral arrangements and bring some comfort to Thom.

"Thom, let's go to the cardinal's residence. He's going to make a statement on behalf of the church at the press conference at 11:00 a.m. He may not have much time to talk before it, but he wants to see you now."

"Sorry.... I dozed off. I understand, Lieutenant. I just want to see what day he'd like to hold the funeral, and then we can talk more later." Thom stood and made himself presentable for the cardinal.

"I think that would be good. After I take you there, I'll need to come back here and talk with the police commissioner."

"No problem. I want to be at the press conference too."

"By all means. I'm sure the reporters will want to question you."

Thom looked up. "I... I'm not ready to answer questions or make any kind of statement."

"Smart move. We'll keep you away from the press."

"I'd really appreciate that." Thom got up from the chair, and he and Palmer began the short walk from the parish house to the cardinal's residence. As they were about to enter, Thom asked a pointed question. "What will happen to the money they found?"

"That's a very good question. Right now, it's evidence. If it were received correctly, which I find it difficult to believe, it would be returned as part of his estate. If it were obtained under false pretense, it would become the property of the state of New York."

"I was hoping some of it could go to the restoration of the cathedral," Thom said.

"It would be nice, but I doubt the cathedral will see any of it."

Thom and Palmer entered the cardinal's residence and were greeted by the cardinal.

"Your Eminence, I believe you know Thom Triplett," Lieutenant Palmer began.

"We met when I installed your brother as rector here." Cardinal Flinn extended his hand. "I want you to know you have my condolences and prayers. You will have the prayers of the faithful of the Archdiocese of New York when they learn of this terrible tragedy."

"Thank you, Cardinal... Your Eminence. That means a great deal to me." Thom appreciated the cardinal's words.

The cardinal escorted them to the conference room. He was a well-groomed, over-weight individual who commanded ones attention. He thoroughly enjoyed the spotlight no matter what the circumstance or crisis.

"I have been reviewing my statement for the press. Have a seat at the table and we can talk for a few moments before going back to the cathedral." Cardinal Flinn pointed to the chair he wanted Thom to sit in.

"If you will excuse me, Your Eminence, I need to get back with Commissioner Timberbank before the press conference.

I'll see you there. Afterward, I'd like a chance to talk with you alone."

"Yes, Lieutenant, I would also like a few moments of your time. I need to ask you a few questions as well."

"You're in good hands, Thom. I'll be around, Your Eminence, when you're available to talk." Palmer excused himself.

The cardinal looked at Tom with kindness and began his conversation by offering, once again, his condolences. "Your brother was an inspiration to me. I was amazed at all he could get done. He really was trying to pull together not only the physical work being done in the cathedral but also the spiritual work that needed to be done. I will truly miss him, as I know you will."

"Thank you, Your Eminence. He was my best friend. Even though we had our differences, I was very thankful for the friendship, love and opportunity to have someone I could honestly talk with. I'll miss him immensely." Thom reached for his handkerchief and tried to hold back his tears.

"God gave him an Easter gift, and we must still carry our own crosses until we are given the gift."

"You're right. Steven would always say, 'God does not carry our crosses, and we do not carry them alone. God is there to assist us if only we ask.'"

"He is definitely right. Before I make my statement at the press conference, Thom, I want to talk with you about the funeral arrangements. Have you had time to think when you would like the funeral?"

"I was wondering what would work in your schedule."

"Would Thursday or Friday work?"

"Friday would be fine."

"Why don't we say 11:00 on Friday morning here at the cathedral? The church will take care of all the cathedral expenses." The cardinal assured Thom that it was customary for the archdiocese to pay for the church expenses of a priest's funeral.

"Thank you. I'm very grateful to the church. However, in his will, there are certain requests he made for his funeral. I want to do my best to carry out his wishes."

"I'm thankful he did what I requested all the priests of the archdiocese to do, to put their funeral plans and wishes in writing."

"Your Eminence, let me pull it from my brother's file and see what he wanted. When should I get back with you?"

"Thom, let me give you my private number if you would like to call me. Why don't we meet on Tuesday to go over your brother's wishes?"

"That will be fine. What time would be good for you?" Thom was still in a daze from all the events of the day.

"Why don't you come to the chancery on Tuesday, and we can meet at 10:00 a.m. Once you and I have gone over and approved the arrangements, I can make sure to contact those your brother wanted to participate or be involved in the service. The cathedral can work out the necessary details." The cardinal pushed to take care of the details as quickly as possible. He knew the media would want to be present, and they needed to know the details.

"So Tuesday morning at 10:00, at the chancery?" Thom wanted to be sure he had the correct information.

"Yes. I also want to let you know the body of a priest is usually received into his parish church the night before for the viewing and evening prayer. So we would do this on Thursday night."

"Your Eminence, that would be fine. Can we have the viewing from 7:00 until 9:00 that evening?"

"How about starting at 6:00 p.m. with evening prayer followed by the viewing?" The cardinal suggested.

"That would work. I need to mention my brother requested that he wanted to be buried in the family plot next to our parents. Would there be any objection to this?"

"None at all." The cardinal glanced at his watch. "We have taken care of the preliminaries which will help everyone in the planning, but I think I had better get over to the cathedral."

"Thank you again." Then Thom impulsively he added, "I wanted to let you know Jennifer Gibson says hello."

The cardinal was somewhat surprised. But with great experience and keeping his composure under pressure, he just smiled. "How is Ms. Gibson doing?"

"Great. Since she left the DA's office, she has really made a name for herself in private practice. She's taken some high-profile cases. She makes sure all her clients, including those who have a non-profit status follow the law. She wants the book thrown at those who get creative with their bookkeeping."

"Yes, she knows the law." The cardinal was well acquainted with the attorney's passion for discovering the truth. He didn't know how much Thom knew about Jennifer's case against the archdiocese. The cardinal had nothing more to say, and he was eager to end this conversation with Thom. He stood and hoped Thom would realize the meeting was over.

But Thom remained seated. He tried unsuccessfully to make eye contact with the cardinal. "She wants me to join her firm, but I like my independence too much."

"Please give her my regards." The cardinal grew uncomfortable talking about Jennifer and speculated that she and Thom were more than just fellow attorneys.

"I will." Then thinking like a detective, Thom asked, "Forgive me, Your Eminence, but do you know of anyone who would want to harm my brother?"

"As I told Lieutenant Palmer, I knew he had problems with a few people, but I don't think any of those people would kill him."

"I know my brother was having problems with a couple of priests."

"No one gets along with everyone," the cardinal said. "Did he confide in you and tell you who they were?"

"He told me about one. It was Monsignor Stone. I was having problems with him as well."

The cardinal's poker face failed when he heard the priest's name. And Thom noticed the change.

Lieutenant Palmer returned to the cathedral parish house. As he came into the living room, he realized Father Crumbley had designated himself as head of hospitality. He was making sure the needs of the detectives, police officers and diocesan staff were met.

Detective Sabor also entered the living room and was holding the evidence bag with the key found in Monsignor Triplett's pocket.

"Do you know where the safe is in Monsignor Triplett's room?" asked Palmer.

"I believe it's hidden in his closet."

"We have about twenty minutes before I need to go to the cathedral. Let's find it and see if these are the keys?"

"I've asked one of the crime scene investigators to come over and dust the safe for fingerprints," Sabor said. No sooner had he spoken the words, the CSU investigator was standing at the entrance waiting for instructions.

"Let's move to Monsignor Triplett's room once again," Palmer ordered.

"Lead the way." Sabor motioned. Together they climbed the stairs to Monsignor's room. Palmer removed the crime scene tape and opened the door. Turning on the lights, they walked carefully through the study into the bedroom. They stood in front of the closet while Palmer pulled back a group of shirts, moved several boxes and pictures to the side to reveal a safe. It was a small built-in safe that required a key to open. The crime scene investigator began dusting for prints. Once he finished, Sabor handed the key to Palmer who placed it in the keyhole. It fit, and Palmer opened the safe. He locked it and returned the key to Detective Sabor who presented him with the second key. Again, Palmer placed it in the keyhole and turned it. The second key also opened the safe. The detectives wondered what surprises they'd find as they carefully pulled out of the contents of the safe. Six items were discovered as important possessions of Monsignor Triplett: a black leather notebook, three folders and a flat manila envelope addressed to Cardinal Flinn.

"These items need to be dusted for prints and put into separate evidence bags. We're not going to have time to look at them before the press conference. I have a feeling our murderer or murderers may have wanted one or more of these items." Palmer and Sabor pulled out the evidence bags they brought.

"The mystery of the keys is solved!" Sabor was elated as he put the last of the items from the safe into a bag. Then he closed the safe, removed the key and placed it back into the evidence bag.

"Well, now we know what the keys were for." Palmer was pleased with the news. "But the mystery of the cryptic letters written on the pew has not been solved. The cryptic letters looked like an *S* and an *A*. Are they meant to be the first two letters to the word "safe" or "Sam"? Is this why Sam is waiting for his lawyer?"

"I was thinking the same thing," Sabor said. "Do you think Monsignor Triplett wanted to let us know there was something in the safe about Sam?"

"That's a possibility. I just think there's more to what Monsignor Triplett was writing that we might never find out. Are the natives getting restless?" Palmer asked Sabor, referring to the press.

"They're ready to find out who was murdered. They know a body was removed from the church, and it's at the coroner's office. They just don't know the name of the deceased."

"They will in about ten minutes."

As they left the bedroom and study, they passed Officer VanDyke outside the library and asked if Mr. Tolden's lawyer had arrived. The officer reported that the lawyer had not arrived and Mr. Tolden was just sitting, writing and waiting.

Detective Sabor received a call from Detective Pantera letting him know Oscar Martinez's wife was waiting in the church.

"I need to go back to the church. Oscar Martinez's wife is here to confirm his alibi. I need to ask her a few questions." Sabor informed Palmer.

"I'll go with you. I believe everyone who's speaking at the press conference should be there or at least be on their way. I want this press conference to be short and sweet, so we can finish our work." Palmer was emphatic.

"Don't you have to see the cardinal before you leave?" Detective Sabor asked.

"Yes, and I made an appointment for you." Palmer gave it right back. "Seriously, we have a few more people to interview, and I'm convinced we will get a confession. I just have this feeling after interviewing Sam Tolden."

"If we do, there are a few priests around who could forgive the killer for any sins," Detective Sabor offered.

"As I said, you already have an appointment with the cardinal." Lieutenant Palmer wanted the last word.

The detectives left the house and returned to the cathedral. As they walked down the center aisle, it looked as if they were going to the microphones. Many of the reporters and those operating the cameras thought the press conference was going to begin. They were disappointed when the detectives just walked past the mics.

Detective Pantera stood with Teresa Martinez and nodded so Detective Sabor would see him. Sabor walked over to them realizing that they needed to move back up front away from the reporters. At the same time, Oscar saw his wife in the church standing next to a police officer and was worried and unsure why she was here. He stopped sweeping and followed them.

Detective Pantera made the introductions. "Detective Sabor, this is Teresa Martinez, the wife of Oscar Martinez."

"Thank you for coming in," Sabor began.

Teresa looked confused. "I'm not sure why you wanted to see me."

"I would like to know why as well." Oscar reached his wife and stood next to her. "Hi baby, why are you here?"

"If I can explain... She's here to verify your alibi from last night. Why did you say Monsignor Triplett had this coming to him?" Sabor interjected.

"Let me explain." Teresa wasn't going to hide her anger even with the police around. "You need to know Monsignor Triplett was unfair with the pay my husband was getting. We can hardly meet our bills. Oscar told me he had gone to him asking for a raise, and Monsignor Triplett said he couldn't afford one. So we have lived paycheck to paycheck for the last two years. Even with me working part-time jobs, it's been a struggle. I said those words out of anger."

"Why?" Oscar asked.

"The church preaches justice but doesn't show justice by the pay my husband receives. He's a good worker." Teresa looked into Oscar's eyes.

"The only money you knew your husband was getting from the cathedral was from your husband's paycheck?" Sabor asked.

"Yes. Why?" Teresa looked right at Oscar whose face turned red with embarrassment. "Oscar, was there more?"

The detective realized Teresa didn't know about the cash Oscar received.

"I'm sorry baby. There was more. I couldn't tell you about it. No one knows." Oscar desperately tried to explain.

"What, do you mean? Have you been keeping something from me?"

"I got extra money. Monsignor Triplett gave it to me in cash."

"You mean you've been keeping money from me while I've been working my butt off and trying to manage our bills?" Teresa yelled at her husband as she pointed her finger in his face.

"I need you to calm down, Mrs. Martinez." Sabor realized Oscar and his wife were about to fight. The detective needed to control the situation. The press watched intensely from a distance.

"I apologize detective, but when I find out my husband is keeping this from me, the blood boils within me."

Oscar tried to calm her. "I'm sorry baby. I was told I could not tell anyone, or it would end."

"So where's this money? Is there any money?" Teresa demanded.

"I have some hidden. I was going to surprise you with something... nice."

"You've surprised me! How long has this been going on?"

"For about a year, but there won't be anymore. Monsignor Triplett was a good man." Oscar was overwhelmed as tears formed in his eyes.

"How much money are we talking about?" Teresa tried to remain calm and kept her voice down, so the reporters couldn't hear her.

"I think I have about $3,000 stashed away, but now all that ends with his death. Baby... I am so sorry."

"Sorry isn't good enough. We're going to have a talk about this. I just need some time to think."

"So you had no reason to want to kill Monsignor Triplett?" Detective Sabor asked Teresa.

"I never wanted Monsignor Triplett dead. In fact, I wish I could have thanked him for the extra money he was giving to Oscar. If I had known, I would have. I just didn't have all the facts." Her eyes turned to Oscar. It was a look that made him want to run away.

"So do I." Oscar looked at his wife begging for forgiveness.

"The person I want killed is my husband!" Teresa who was still upset, saw how hurt he was and softened as she looked at her husband.

"I think you both can work this out. You've answered all my questions. Thank you for coming in." Detective Sabor closed his notebook and excused himself to join the other detectives who gathered near the center of the cathedral for the press conference that was about to begin.

In the meantime, Oscar once again apologized to his wife. He was sorry he couldn't tell her. He really wanted to make things right with her and realized he could once they got back home. He wanted the trust of his wife again.

Teresa knew she couldn't remain mad at her husband. She loved him. She only wondered how much he had spent without her knowing. She had her own surprise to share. Without Oscar knowing, she had gone to the doctor yesterday and was told she was four weeks pregnant with their first child. She took her husband's hand. "I've got something to tell you." But it would have to wait. The press conference was about to begin.

Chapter 24

As Hector looked out from the sanctuary of Saint Patrick's toward the podium, located temporarily in the middle of the center aisle, it seemed every television and radio news station, along with every newspaper reporter, locally, nationally and even internationally was speculating on the pending announcement. The television news crews had positioned themselves at the best possible angle. Hector recognized the reporter from the local Spanish language TV station WXTV. He thought they had the best vantage point because of their location.

It was unfortunate the news at this press conference was not of a miracle or something more joyful to inspire those whose faith was on shaky ground. Today's announcement would shock and sadden the local faith community of the cathedral and many who heard it around the world. Because of the location and circumstances, there would be pressure for the NYPD to solve the case quickly. As lead detective, Lieutenant Palmer felt that pressure.

Palmer stood with his co-workers patiently waiting for the police commissioner and the cardinal to appear. He knew the press conference was only a formality. Once it was over, rumors would circulate from the media until the case was solved. He was pleased with the investigation. In a short time, he and his detectives had gathered a good deal of evidence and had conducted many interviews. He had a list of possible suspects with one suspect awaiting his lawyer. The detective wondered where the investigation would ultimately lead.

Blinded by the many camera lights, Palmer thought he saw a priest standing near one of the side pillars. He knew the police officers received orders that only those with proper, current credentials were allowed to enter the cathedral. He wondered who this priest was and who he worked for.

This priest was probably in his 60s based on his gray, balding hair. But as Palmer focused on him, he remembered seeing a picture of the man with Monsignor Triplett in his study. He wondered if this priest was Monsignor Stone. Palmer wanted to keep him in sight to see what, if any, reaction this priest would have when the murdered victim's name was announced.

He tried to get the attention of one of the police officers to confirm the identity of the priest, but Palmer was unsuccessful as the two communications liaisons were making their way to the microphone. Quickly the TV news reporters ended their reports and turned their attention to the podium. To Palmer's surprise, the mysterious priest moved from behind the marble pillar into clear view.

After a quick microphone check, Karen Zirpoli announced to the press that neither Police Commissioner Timberbank nor Cardinal Flinn would answer any questions. "Your cooperation is requested in refraining from asking questions." She was not only reiterating it for the reporters but wanted to restate it for the cardinal and police commissioner who were waiting at the side of the sanctuary.

Both Karen Zirpoli and Donald Armenti knew, while they had spent a great deal of time preparing the statements, both bosses would probably go off script. They just didn't want either of them taking questions—no matter how persistent the reporters might be.

As the police commissioner walked toward the center aisle, he stopped by the detectives and police officers and extended his hand to each thanking them for their work. He was doing it all for the cameras. He was also delaying his arrival as the bells in the north tower rang for 11:00 a.m. Approaching Lieutenant Palmer, Timberbank whispered in his ear, "Get this solved quickly, or you'll have a nice desk job waiting."

This just added to the pressure Palmer already felt. He smiled. "I'm doing my best."

Cardinal Flinn followed the commissioner. He looked sharp in his tailored black suit and wore the pectoral cross around his neck, a sign of his position as the head of the Catholic Church for the Archdiocese of New York. His undeniable charisma brought smiles from the press. However, there was a serious look on his face they hadn't seen very often. He took his place beside the police commissioner.

With the cameras rolling, Karen returned to the microphone. "Good morning, everyone. My name is Karen Zirpoli. I am the Public Relations Liaison for the New York City Police Department. I'm here with Donald Armenti, the Director of Media and Communications for the Archdiocese of New York. Also, with me is Police Commissioner, Harold Timberbank, and beside him is, His Eminence, Cardinal Dominique Flinn. Police Commissioner Timberbank and His Eminence, Cardinal Flinn will each make a statement at this time. A written copy of each statement will be available after this press conference. We will issue any further information from city hall. Police Commissioner Timberbank." Zirpoli stepped aside for the police commissioner.

Walking up to the microphone with his notebook in hand, he placed it on the podium and began. "First, I would like to thank you for your patience this morning. I stand before you as the Police Commissioner for New York City to inform you of the murder of Monsignor Steven Triplett, rector of Saint Patrick's Cathedral." He paused as he heard the audience gasp and saw the faces of disbelief.

The commissioner continued. "From the preliminary investigation, this death took place sometime between midnight and seven this morning. Monsignor Triplett was found in the cathedral. The investigating teams have been looking into possible suspects and persons of interest to find who was responsible for this terrible crime the day before Easter. We are uncertain of the motive for this murder. This is an ongoing investigation, so I am not at liberty to discuss any other particular details at this time. As more information becomes available, you will be informed through press release statements from city hall."

The police commissioner double checked his notes and looked to Karen to make sure he had correctly delivered the official police department statement. She subtlety nodded her head affirmatively. Looking slightly smug, he closed his notebook, and as arranged said, "Now I would like to invite His Eminence, Cardinal Dominique Flinn to the podium for the statement he has prepared." He then moved away from the podium for Cardinal Flinn.

"Thank you, Commissioner Timberbank, and to the many detectives and officers here present this morning. I, my brother bishops, the priests, deacons, religious and staff of Saint Patrick's Cathedral are deeply saddened upon hearing of the death of Monsignor Steven Triplett. I know many priests, deacons, religious and laity of the diocese will be shocked and heart-broken. I would like to first offer my condolences to the family of Monsignor Triplett, his brother, Thom Triplett. I ask for your prayers for the Triplett family during this time of loss." The cardinal focused his eyes on Thom Triplett who was standing beside some of the detectives and police working the case.

Cardinal Flinn continued. "Monsignor Triplett was a priest for the archdiocese for almost forty years and assigned to the cathedral for the last six years. He held various diocesan positions showing his leadership ability. For the last two years, he has been my representative for the massive restoration work being done here. He was dedicated to the

304

priesthood and a good friend to me. I… will miss him." The cardinal paused to compose himself after those last words.

Lieutenant Palmer wondered how much of the cardinal's emotion was for the camera and how much of it was real. Would the cardinal's feelings for Monsignor Triplett remain as sincere when he learns about the $5,000 discovered in Monsignor's coat pocket along with the additional $45,000 found in his bedroom?

The cardinal continued. "As you look around this beautiful cathedral, consider that this evening we will celebrate the most joyous day of our faith, Easter. To help the staff and volunteers with the preparations needed for the many who come to church tonight and tomorrow, the cathedral will not be open to the public until 5:00 p.m." The cardinal knew the reporters could care less about this part of his statement, but he made it for the parishioners and visitors who were in the city coming to celebrate the Easter liturgy.

"Tonight's Easter Vigil celebration will take place as scheduled at 8:00. The Easter schedule for Sunday will remain the same as published. All of this information is posted on the cathedral's website." Cardinal Flinn wondered how many parishioners and visitors paid any attention to the website.

"Tragedy has come to this sacred church, and there is much darkness with the loss of Monsignor Triplett. But as we look forward to Easter and the lighting of the Easter candle, our Lord will provide the light we need to help us with this loss." The cardinal looked out at the reporters and caught sight of Monsignor Stone. He was immediately distracted and lost his place for a few seconds before he continued.

"As we move forward to celebrate the resurrection of our Lord, may God bless you this Easter and may Monsignor Steven Triplett's soul rest in peace." Cardinal Flinn ended his statement, deviating little from the speech Donald Armenti had prepared. Donald stood by, ready to distribute the statement to the reporters.

As Cardinal Flinn paused and looked for Monsignor Stone, reporters were yelling questions to him. He didn't hear any of them. The cardinal was only thinking that he wanted to speak with Monsignor Stone before a detective did. He was hoping to make eye contact and get his attention, but he was gone. As reporters continued to holler out questions, the cardinal gently raised his hand in a half-hearted wave, then walked away to stand next to the police commissioner.

The cardinal tried to get the attention of Lieutenant Palmer, but Palmer was focused on the priest who attended the press conference. While the police commissioner and cardinal were making their statements, Palmer noticed the priest showed no emotion or change of expression. Maybe he lived up to his last name and the nickname, "hard as stone".

Karen Zirpoli returned to the podium. "Once again ladies and gentlemen, I thank you for your cooperation in this ongoing investigation. As Police Commissioner Timberbank has indicated, any further statements will come from city hall. Copies of Police Commissioner Timberbank's and Cardinal Flinn's statements are available. We would ask for your cooperation in clearing the cathedral by 11:45 today to allow preparations to continue for Easter. Thank you."

With that statement, the microphones were silenced, and the police commissioner and cardinal immediately walked up the center aisle as reporters once again yelled questions for each of them to answer—both said nothing. The barrage of questions was overwhelming.

"Do you have any suspects?" One reporter yelled.

"What was the priest doing in the church so early in the morning?" Another reporter hollered.

"Do you have a murder weapon?" The questions continued until the cardinal and police commissioner reached the sanctuary steps. The cardinal, for the first time, realized they had removed the front pew. He felt deep remorse for the death of this well-like priest.

306

The commissioner thanked the cardinal for the cooperation he and his staff had received as the investigation continued. The cardinal expressed his thanks for the professional work of the NYPD. It was a chance to share a little small talk and to wish each other a happy Easter. Before the commissioner could say goodbye to the cardinal, he was interrupted by a phone call.

Back at the podium, Karen and Donald stood with a stack of statements in their hands ready to distribute. They were relieved the press conference was over and hoped they had made enough copies.

Many of the reporters quickly repositioned themselves to add their own remarks to the live feed covering the press conference. Other reporters took the written statements but kept their cell phones to their ears as they contacted editors to report the information. For those ten or fifteen minutes, the sacredness of the cathedral was lost amid the noise and discussions. Finally, everyone packed their equipment and left the cathedral through the 50th Street doors they had entered.

Lieutenant Palmer quickly moved to find Monsignor Stone.

"Monsignor Stone?" Palmer shouted.

"Yes?" Confused and visibly shaken, Monsignor Stone was caught off guard when the lieutenant approached him.

Showing his NYPD badge, "I'm Lieutenant Will Palmer."

"Lieutenant Palmer… you said is your name?" Monsignor Stone wondered, "Are you the lieutenant he spoke to on the phone a little over an hour ago?"

"Yes… I'm Lieutenant Will Palmer. I'm sorry it's under these circumstances that we meet. I need to ask you a few questions." Palmer returned his badge to his pocket.

"I'll be more than happy to." Monsignor Stone got up to walk with the lieutenant. They passed one of the duty officers, and Monsignor Stone thanked him for letting him into the cathedral.

Palmer noted the name of the officer.

At Holy Name of Jesus, Bishop George Newsome had listened to the press conference and turned off his TV. As he sat back down, he vividly remembered his last telephone conversation with the friend, Monsignor Triplett. It was hard to believe that conversation had occurred around 12 hours ago.

"George," Monsignor Triplett began.

"Happy Good Friday," responded Bishop Newsome.

"The same to you." Monsignor Triplett coughed into the phone. "I apologize for the coughing."

"Are you okay?"

"I think so. I get this cough now and then." Monsignor Triplett knew it was one of the side effects of his blood pressure medicine. "Was Good Friday good for you?"

"Very much so! The service here was nice and well-attended. How was it for you?"

"I would say mixed reviews. Lots of heartening comments about my homily. Thanks for your input. On the negative side, our organist had his own personal problems that I noticed affected his playing." Monsignor Triplett tried to keep from coughing.

"Glad I can help a friend. Sorry to hear about music problems, especially during Holy Week. So why are you calling me so late?" Bishop Newsome was concerned.

"I met with Joseph Delfino and wanted you to know the results of our meeting. I'm sitting here with $50,000 in cash and a list of subcontractors who have given donations of goods, services, and money to the cathedral. It's over $200,000." Monsignor stifled another cough. "I also have a document you will find interesting about our cardinal and a promise he made to Joseph."

Bishop Newsome sat up straight in his chair. "Please... please... don't.... don't share this with me. I don't want to know. I have great respect for our cardinal, and I don't need you or anyone to harm his name, especially on Good Friday."

"I understand. I just... cough... I just wanted to let you know I'll distribute the money to the staff before I reduce some of their hours, and then I'm dismissing at least two of them. The money serves as a way to give compensation to them. I have made a list of who will get what. I'm putting the two files in the safe in my bedroom just in case something goes wrong."

"What do you mean 'goes wrong?'" Bishop Newsome asked. "Why would anything go wrong?"

"Well, Sam Tolden knows a little, but he'll be fired after tomorrow when I meet with him. He has personal issues that are affecting his work. I can get others to take on some of his responsibilities until I can hire another administrator."

"You sound a little nervous." The bishop sensed it in Monsignor's voice. He had never heard him speak this way before.

"I'm way out of my comfort zone... cough... I just hope the cardinal appreciates what I'm doing for the cathedral. I really don't think he has any idea of the magnitude of the church's financial problems." Monsignor Triplett rummaged through his desk drawer for a cough drop. He popped one in his mouth. His cough was getting worse.

"The work of the church is never easy. I'm sure you have nothing to worry about. Stick to the plan, and everyone and everything will be fine. The construction company will recover and hopefully amend their ways. The archdiocese will get some of its money back, and you have some additional income to help those employees who have been faithful even under the stress of all the restoration. Everyone wins, even though I don't like how it has all come about." The bishop tried to reassure him.

"I sure hope so. I just feel something is going to happen. That's why I'm putting the extra key in an envelope with my brother's name on it. I'm trying to keep you completely out of it."

"Don't let the fear get to you. This will all be over soon."

Monsignor Triplett coughed a few more times. "Your words help my friend. I'll be glad when this is behind me."

"Are you sure you're okay?"

Monsignor Triplett knew he really wasn't. "It will pass."

"Have you gone to the doctor?" After listening to him for the last ten minutes coughing, the bishop wasn't buying his answer.

"I have, and it's being taken care of. Let's get back to the topic we were discussing."

The bishop knew Monsignor Triplett didn't like to talk about his health, so he decided not to pry any further. "As long as you have secured the documents that contain the mistakes you've made, you should be exonerated for the way you've handled getting the evidence needed."

"Thanks, George, for your vote of confidence. I appreciate your support."

"Stop worrying. You're going to be fine. We're all going to be fine. Just realize this is only one problem the other bishops, the cardinal and I face. It's not always easy with some of the crap we have to deal with for the good of the church."

"I hope this is the only time I'm dealing with it." Monsignor Triplett's cough had subsided, and with the bishop's reassurance, he was starting to feel a bit more confident and relaxed.

"I hope not." Bishop Newsome saw great potential with Monsignor Triplett and suggested again, "You could move up in the hierarchical ranks and make a good bishop."

Monsignor Triplett had heard this before and each time responded, "I think I'll pass."

"Not for you to say, Steven."

"Good night, George." Monsignor Triplett shook his head and smiled.

They wished each other a happy Easter and gave a promise to see each other soon.

Tears started to come to the bishop as he remembered that call. He had wanted so much for Monsignor Triplett to be named a bishop. How insightful that last call was. He would miss his friend.

As he turned off the television, the bishop wondered if Monsignor Triplett foresaw his death as he managed this financial mess. He also wondered if he could have done more He felt a terrible knot in his stomach. The best thing he could do now was to say a prayer for him. He knelt, made the sign of the cross and asked God to look kindly on this priest.

After a few moments of silence, the bishop slowly got up. He knew he had a call to make.

Chapter 25

Now that the press conference was over, Lieutenant Palmer hoped to slip into the usher's room to formally interview Monsignor Stone.

The cardinal watched as the lieutenant walked up the side aisle with Monsignor Stone. Monsignor for whatever reason, as he slowly walked he held on to each pew. The cardinal saw this, stopped his conversation with the police commissioner, got Palmer's attention and motioned for him to come over.

"If you would excuse me, Monsignor Stone, I'm being summoned by the cardinal. Have a seat. I'll be right back."

Monsignor Stone found a seat and patiently waited. He couldn't believe the number of individuals investigating the crime.

Palmer reached the cardinal. "Yes, Your Eminence, how can I help you?"

"We want to hold the funeral for Monsignor Triplett on Friday. I presume the body will be released in enough time for this to happen?" The cardinal knew he had to get this decided so that plans could be coordinated.

"There should be no problem. But then again, it all depends on the investigation. The ME decides when the body is released," Palmer explained.

Police Commissioner Timberbank nodded approval as he finished the telephone call with his secretary. "Your

Eminence, I'm needed uptown. You have some of my finest people here to solve this case. Lieutenant Palmer is here to help you." He shook the cardinal's hand and gave a nod to Palmer.

"Thank you for being here and for all the department is doing." The cardinal watched the police commissioner leave.

The cardinal returned his attention to Lieutenant Palmer. "Father Morales is scheduled to leave for Rome on Monday. Would there be any reason for him to delay his trip? He's taking some cathedral parishioners with him."

"That should be okay. His story of where he was last night is plausible. At the moment, I don't believe he would be considered a suspect. I'd say he can stick with his plans provided we have contact information for him while he's away. Do you still want him to take the trip?" Palmer was a bit reluctant to approve of Father Morales's trip, but he felt confident that the priest was not a suspect.

"Yes, I believe he should stick with his plans and go." The cardinal knew he still had work to do to be sure Father Morales could stay in Rome. He didn't share that information with Palmer.

"Is there anything else?" Palmer grew impatient and needed to get back to Monsignor Stone.

"Could I ask why Monsignor Stone is here? Is he okay?" The cardinal was fishing for some information although he already knew far more than he was admitting.

"He's just here for some routine questioning."

"You'd better go back to him. It looks like Monsignor Triplett's brother is with him now and judging by the body language, he doesn't look too happy." The cardinal wished he could ask a few more questions but felt it probably was best not to. He would contact Monsignor Stone later.

"If you'll excuse me, I think I need to get over there."

While Palmer was talking to the cardinal, Thom Triplett found Monsignor Stone and started yelling at him. Palmer

313

quickly walked over and stood between them. "Gentlemen, it seems you know one another."

"Yes, we do." Monsignor Stone was thankful for the lieutenant's intervention.

"Thom, if I could talk with you alone for a few moments. Monsignor Stone, I apologize for the interruptions, but I'll be right back. I'd ask you not to talk with anyone until I return."

"I understand." Monsignor Stone was somewhat frustrated as he once again took his seat in the pew.

"Lieutenant Palmer, thanks for coming when you did," Thom said as they walked past the evidence table.

"I need to ask you a few additional questions. Once we're finished, Detective Jabowski will take you to the morgue."

"You have my attention, Lieutenant. How can I help you?"

"It seems your brother's radio alarm clock on the nightstand was set for 4:00 a.m. Do you know if this is the normal time he got up?"

"I know Steven tried to pray for an hour each morning before he left his room since the business of the day did not always provide him time for prayer. Four o'clock does seem a little early. With tonight's Mass being so late and the busy Easter schedule, I would think he would have tried to get as much sleep as possible last night. I just don't know."

Palmer continued. "We also found the bed was unmade, and his bedroom was disorganized. I was surprised at the appearance of his room, especially after you told me that his bedroom was the one room he kept organized."

"His study was always a mess, but whenever I was there, his bedroom was kept neat. My brother would never have left his bed unmade. As I told you before, we were always taught to make our bed first thing in case nothing else went right for the day," Thom explained.

"In examining his bedroom, it looked like he had gotten out of bed in a hurry. Not only was the bed a mess, but all the dresser drawers were open along with the closet doors, and

314

empty hangers were scattered on top of the bed. Do you think he overslept?"

"He could have, but my brother didn't require a lot of sleep. For Steven to have left his bed unmade and his room in disarray, something was not right... it's all rather tough to comprehend." Thom wished he had a chance to have one more conversation with his brother.

"Your brother also left his bank statement out on his desk along with his credit card bills. His American Express and MasterCard bills were both over $5,000 each, and he had a little over $1,000 in the bank. Did you pay his credit card bills?"

"No... I didn't. He never asked me to. Could I ask what the charges were on his credit cards?" Thom was trying to decipher this new information.

"The charges included a few restaurant bills, subway Metro Card charges and numerous PayPal charges in increments of $100, $200 and $500. One was for $3,000. Do you have any idea what these were for?"

"No. I don't. He rarely talked about his finances until recently when he told me he had a lot of debt and was trying to pay it off. He didn't want to discuss it. I think he was too embarrassed to ask for any assistance," Thom shared.

"When I looked at his bank statement from last month, there was no check written to American Express. The bill from American Express showed it was paid in full the previous month. Do you know how he could pay the previous month's balance which was over $5,000? Do you know if the church paid it?" Palmer speculated.

Thom was frustrated. He had told Palmer everything he knew, and he tried to cooperate, but he wanted to speak with Monsignor Stone before he left. "I doubt it. All I know is money was tight. Maybe his parish finance person would know. Have you talked with him?"

"Not about this."

"I'm just trying to understand all of this. What was my brother up to?" Thom wanted answers. What was really going on with his brother? Some things just weren't making sense to him. Cash in a briefcase, no money in the bank, credit cards to the max, an unmade bed, and up at 4:00 a.m. today. Everything was very confusing.

"I'm not sure. I can only speculate that he was trying to play 'Father Robin hood'—taking from the rich and helping the poor. Your answers are helpful as we keep moving along with the investigation. Just one more question. You talked about the blood pressure pills you and your brother took. It seems one was left on his nightstand. Is it possible he didn't take it? Do you know if that happened often?"

"I'm not sure. He told me he occasionally forgot to take his blood pressure medicine. I know when he did forget, he felt some discomfort."

"Thanks, Thom. As I said, it helps in the investigation. Let me get Detective Jabowski to give you a ride to the morgue." Palmer motioned one of the police officers to find Jabowski.

"Lieutenant, can I come back and go into my brother's room?" Thom became tearful and emotional. He would have to go through everything and decide what would be done with Steven's personal property. He knew some wishes of his brother, but he had to read the will and make sure he carried those wishes out. He wondered how he would deal with items the will covered and items not in the will.

"I'll let you know once the CSU is finished." Palmer thanked Thom as Detective Jabowski arrived to take him to the morgue.

Once Thom had gone, Palmer walked over to Monsignor Stone. "My apologies, Monsignor. Now we can go over to the parish house."

"How's Thom doing?" Monsignor Stone stood up in the pew.

"As well as can be expected. It's a shock to have this happen to someone, especially a brother, a priest, on the day before Easter." Palmer didn't want to discuss the confrontation.

Monsignor Stone calmly added. "Monsignor Triplett received the gift we all look forward to — eternal life. May he enjoy it."

The CSU continued their work as Lieutenant Palmer and Monsignor Stone walked up the aisle where Detective Pantera was waiting. He recommended the interview take place in the usher's room instead of the parish house. The three proceeded to the room and closed the door behind them. Detective Pantera had set the room up with some chairs and a table he found for the three to sit around.

Lieutenant Palmer took out his notepad once again and began the interview with his normal series of questions. He discovered Monsignor David Stone was the Judicial Vicar for the Archdiocese of New York appointed by Cardinal Flinn. He lived in an apartment near the parish of Saint Jerome and, when available, helped with the weekend sacramental schedule. His work for the church was to help priests understand canon law, especially when dealing with non-religious and religious mixed marriages and annulments of marriages. He was the archdiocesan adviser to Cardinal Flinn on matters of church law.

"Since you have brought up your work in handling marriage annulments, is that what you and Thom Triplett were discussing a few minutes ago?" Palmer did not mix words with the Monsignor.

"We were."

"From what I observed, I would say the discussion wasn't going well for either of you."

Monsignor Stone kept his answers as brief as possible. "It wasn't."

"I saw the papers on Monsignor Triplett's desk when we examined his room, and it seems you didn't approve Thom's annulment."

"Yes... it was for various reasons. Earlier this week, I had discussed his brother's annulment with him, and the reasons I could not grant it at this time."

"Can I ask what the reasons were? I assure you, I don't want to breach church law. But the reasons could shed some light on this investigation. However, if you feel you can't or don't want to answer, I'll understand." Palmer hoped Monsignor would provide some missing information.

Monsignor Stone tried to be as vague as possible. "Let's just say more information was needed."

"Was that the reason you were meeting with Monsignor Triplett at 6:00 this morning?"

"How did you know we were meeting?" Monsignor Stone suddenly stiffened and folded his arms. He was more alert now as he looked squarely at Lieutenant Palmer.

Palmer noticed Monsignor's reaction. He realized even as a church lawyer, Monsignor would be tight-lipped and reticent to answer any questions. He gave a little more information. "There was a note on the annulment papers saying 'meeting 6:00 a.m., Stone.'"

Monsignor Stone sat back in his chair and unfolded his arms. He had nothing to hide. "Yes, we were meeting at that time for a few reasons. The meeting was both professional and personal. We wanted it to be private, and since we're both early risers, we set it for 6:00 a.m. We knew by meeting at that time, we wouldn't be disturbed."

"And it sounds like you met?"

"Yes... yes... we did."

"So Monsignor Triplett was alive at 6:00 a.m. this morning."

"Yes... yes... he was."

"You mentioned this meeting was both personal and professional. Could you explain what you mean?" Detective Pantera tried to fully understand the reasons for such an early meeting.

"We were each other's confessors." Monsignor Stone paused and sat back up. "Both of us wanted to be forgiven for our sins by going to confession to fulfill what is asked of us by the church before Easter. That was the personal part of the meeting." Monsignor Stone's voice cracked as he felt the loss of his spiritual advisor.

Detective Pantera then asked, "And the professional part?"

"It was the matter I mentioned dealing with his brother's annulment." Monsignor Stone regained his composure.

"Again, was there anything that could be done?" Palmer inquired.

"I believe so... but I'm not able to share. I need to talk to his brother and inform him first."

"Please don't take offense at this next question, but would the information you have to share give us a reason to suspect his brother?" Palmer was looking for a possible motive.

"No!" Monsignor Stone was adamant with his response.

Palmer noted Monsignor's reaction. "Was there anything else you were meeting for?"

"There was a personal matter I hoped to resolve." Monsignor Stone knew he had to tell the detectives the information his friend held over him. They might discover the pictures.

"I'm not following you."

"This is embarrassing, but Monsignor Triplett had information about an incident I was involved in about thirty-five years ago. He was going to use the information to get his brother's annulment."

"What was the incident?" Detective Pantera asked.

Monsignor Stone was uncomfortable and embarrassed as he told his story. "As young clergy, several of us had gone out drinking late one night and found ourselves in a strip club. I was unaware that anyone had a camera, and someone took a few pictures of me with one of the strippers. I thought all the pictures were destroyed, and it was all behind me until recently. Monsignor Triplett told me he had the pictures, along with the negatives, and would give them to me once I granted his brother's marriage annulment."

Palmer looked up from his notes and scratched his head. "If I understand correctly—Monsignor Triplett, your friend and spiritual advisor, was blackmailing you?" The case just got more complicated.

Monsignor's response was rather nonchalant as he pulled out his handkerchief to wipe his face. "I guess you could say that. I don't know if he would have carried it out. We never got that far."

"What do you mean?" Detective Pantera asked.

"I mean we heard each other's confessions, gave each other a penance and absolved each other's sins. Then we started to talk about the annulment. I said I would be willing to review it again, but I needed additional information to grant the annulment." Monsignor Stone struggled to tell the detectives.

Palmer resumed the questioning. "What happened next?"

"He said he'd talk with his brother and understood that my hands were somewhat tied given that I had to follow church law."

"Did Monsignor Triplett say this to you?"

"Not in so many words. But he knew his brother's petition was not as complete as it should have been."

"Did he mention the pictures?"

"He told me they were in a safe. He had the key, and his brother would have a second key. He was about to show me the key when I was hit on the back of my head. I blacked out and don't remember anything else." Monsignor Stone rubbed his head. It still hurt, but he was more worried about those pictures.

The two detectives were surprised at this news. "Are you okay?" Palmer asked.

"I'm okay. But I still have a headache."

"Do you need to be checked out by a doctor?"

320

"I don't believe so." But Monsignor wondered if he should see a doctor.

Palmer stood and moved closer to Monsignor. "Could you show me where you were hit?"

"Right on the back of the head. There's still some swelling. Do you see? I've already iced it and taken a few aspirin."

Palmer confirmed there was a bump on the back of the priest's head. "You sure you don't want to get it looked at? It looks a little nasty?"

"No, I think I'll be fine. If the headache doesn't go away, I'll go see a doctor."

"You sure we can't get you anything?" Detective Pantera asked.

"No... Let's continue." Monsignor Stone appreciated the detectives' concern.

"Do you know who hit you?" Palmer hoped for another break.

"I never saw who it was."

Palmer hoped for some kind of description. "You don't know if the person was a male or female, tall or short, skinny or fat?"

"No. As I said, I saw no one!" Monsignor Stone was irritated that Palmer kept quizzing him. "Monsignor Triplett and I thought we were the only ones in the cathedral. I was suddenly struck me from behind. The next thing I remember, I woke up lying outside on the steps of the cathedral. I heard the sirens and saw the police cars arrive. I got up and slowly walked away. I don't think anyone saw me. I was disoriented and didn't know what was happening, so I went over to the nearby Starbucks and went to the bathroom to check myself in the mirror." Monsignor Stone stretched his neck and felt the back of his head.

Detective Pantera noticed Monsignor Stone seemed a little uncomfortable. "And you're sure you're okay?"

"I'm fine. I got some ice from the kid at the counter, and I made an ice pack with my handkerchief and held it on my head as long as I could. I sat for a while, and a couple of people asked if I was okay, and I told them I was. The kid at the counter looked worried, so I left. I took my time walking to the subway station, and about thirty minutes later, I was home taking a shower."

"So you never saw who hit you, and you never saw who hit Monsignor Triplett?" Palmer wanted another confirmation.

"As I told you... and I am telling you for the last time. After someone hit me, the next thing I knew I was outside the cathedral. I don't know if I walked, crawled or was carried there. I never saw the person or what happened to Monsignor Triplett!" Monsignor Stone's head was throbbing with all the questions, and he felt tired. "Do you think I could get a glass of water, so I can take an aspirin?"

Detective Pantera left the room to call for a medical assistant to examine the monsignor.

Seeing the small sink and disposable cups above it, Palmer got Monsignor a glass of water. He continued with the questioning.

"Monsignor Stone, you may have been the last person, other than the murderer, to see Monsignor Triplett alive. This question is very important. Do you remember anything else he said to you?" Palmer pressed on.

"I remember Monsignor Triplett said he had another meeting this morning, and he hoped he could make peace with that person. He never indicated to me who it was."

"Did he say anything else? Maybe when you heard his confession?" Palmer knew a priest couldn't reveal information from a confession, but he had to ask. Since Monsignor Triplett was deceased, maybe there were exceptions.

"No, I won't break the seal of confession!" Monsignor Stone wanted to explain. "The seal of confession in the Catholic Church means it can never be broken. It is inviolable. It is absolutely forbidden for a confessor to betray a penitent in words or in any manner and for any reason."

"Can think of anyone who would have wanted Monsignor Triplett dead?"

"I'm sure he had a few enemies. Don't we all? But someone who would kill him? That's just bizarre! And he never mentioned anyone. I know he was under a lot of pressure. Lieutenant, I'm really at a loss. Why would someone murder Monsignor Triplett and not murder me too?"

"That is a good question, and one I can't answer. The murderer probably didn't know you'd be there and didn't want to harm you, just Monsignor Triplett. Or the murderer could have known you and just wanted to spare your life. Hopefully, we'll find the murderer and ask him or her that question." Palmer was uncertain if his answer brought any comfort to Monsignor Stone.

"He should have murdered me and let my friend live." Monsignor Stone felt his own sense of guilt as he rubbed his eyes with his handkerchief.

Giving Monsignor Stone a few moments to compose himself, Palmer reviewed his notes and prepared to ask the next set of questions.

"I need to ask you about Mrs. Emma Pickle." Palmer looked at Monsignor Stone to see his reaction to hearing her name.

Monsignor Stone quietly explained. "Mrs. Emma Pickle has been my housekeeper for the last six years, thanks to Monsignor Triplett. He told me she needed a job. I interviewed her, hired her, and it has worked out rather well."

"Would she have any reason to want Monsignor Triplett dead?"

"Emma? None!" Monsignor Stone was surprised at the question. "Monsignor Triplett was good to her and her son Jonathan. I'm sure the news will devastate them both. Does she know?"

"Yes… I told her, and she's been in for questioning already." Palmer looked at Monsignor Stone's face hoping for some reaction. Again, there was nothing.

Monsignor Stone was worried about Emma. "I remember when her husband died and how difficult it was for her. I should probably call her when I get home."

"That would be good. I know she's feeling the loss too. How would you describe your relationship with Mrs. Pickle?"

"I'd say a good friend."

"Was it always that way?"

"When she started working for me, there was an attraction. You have to admit she's an attractive woman. But there was nothing more," Monsignor Stone admitted.

"There was no hugging or kissing?"

"Hugging… yes…, and I would have loved to have kissed her but never did."

"So, except for some hugging, there is no physical relationship between you and Mrs. Pickle?"

"None! We have a good friendship, and I appreciate the work she does for me. I think of her as my younger sister." Monsignor Stone's voice filled with conviction and some resentment at Palmer's inference.

"Would you say your relationship with Emma Pickle has always been platonic?" Palmer continued to pursue this line of questions.

"It is entirely platonic and always was!" Monsignor Stone was disgusted with the detective's line of questioning. He was certain he would call Emma now and see if she was asked questions like this. "I hope you're finished!"

"Monsignor Stone, as we complete our investigation here, I need you to go to the police station for a formal statement. I'm sorry to do this to you on the day before Easter, but it's necessary for the investigation."

There was a quick knock on the door. Detective Pantera entered with an EMT. The detectives insisted Monsignor Stone be examined before he left. He noticed a small bump on the back of his head, but monsignor's vitals were good. Monsignor was encouraged to get some rest and if he was feeling dizzy, nauseous, or continued with the headaches to go to an emergency room. Monsignor thanked the technician as he gathered his equipment and left.

Monsignor Stone looked at the detectives, "I'll go to the station and provide a formal statement for you. When do you want me to do this?"

"How about 2:30 p.m. today? I'll be at the station by then," Lieutenant Palmer responded. "But before you leave, is there anything else, anything at all, you can tell me to help with this investigation?"

"I think I've told you everything I know." Monsignor Stone put his handkerchief away and pushed his chair back from the table. "There is just one thing—the incriminating pictures. What will happen to them?"

Lieutenant Palmer realized how embarrassing it would be for the priest. "I hope after the investigation, and after we check that you have told me the truth, I can return the pictures to you and help you put closure to your mistake years ago."

"Thank you, Lieutenant. I would appreciate it. I definitely want to put all that behind me." Monsignor Stone was relieved.

"Please do not leave the city in case I have more questions for you. Do you understand?"

"I do." As Monsignor Stone stood, he worried there might be more in the safe that he didn't know about....

"If you think of anything else, please let one of us know. Here's my card with my personal phone number and the address of the police station. Detective Pantera will escort you out to avoid the media. I'll see you at the police station at 2:30 this afternoon. For your protection, I can assign a police officer to accompany you home." Lieutenant Palmer offered.

"No... I appreciate the offer, but that won't be necessary. If the person who hit me wanted me dead, he would have killed me this morning. I'll see you at 2:30 p.m." Monsignor Stone confirmed the time. He was planning a needed telephone call.

Palmer opened the door, the three left and walked toward the north transept of the cathedral.

"Well, maybe those two trying to get in the cathedral can help us." Lieutenant Palmer watched the Delfinos show their identification to the police officer at the door. He recognized Joseph Delfino from the TV ad assuring New York City residents that Delfino Construction was making the city better for everyone. He wondered if one of their workers had been in the cathedral, hit Monsignor Stone over the head and killed Monsignor Triplett.

Chapter 26

Traffic from Holy Name of Jesus Parish to the Pickle's apartment was almost bumper to bumper. Jonathan and Father O'Hara drove over the Queensboro Bridge and up 21st Street into Long Island City. Father O'Hara enjoyed the ride as he felt the cool air through the open windows and watched the sun trying to come out between the stratus clouds. Loving the city, he wondered how many more days he would have here.

As they got closer to Pickle's home, Father O'Hara was very concerned about Jonathon's reunion with his mother.

Jonathan was concerned too. He started to realize his mom would be devastated by the death of Monsignor Triplett. Nervous, trying to hold back his own emotions, he thought about how this loss would affect him. He remembered the day when Monsignor presented him the keys to the car he was driving, and Monsignor Triplett assured him if he made the honor roll, the insurance for the car would always be paid. Now he wondered about his mother, the insurance and the car.

It was usually difficult to find a parking space in this working-class neighborhood, but Jonathan was lucky—one of his neighbors pulled out, and he pulled in. Gathering some of his clothes, he and Father O'Hara climbed the three flights of stairs into the empty apartment. It was a small two-bedroom apartment convenient to the subway station and a few stores nearby. Although a rental, Jonathan and his mom made it theirs. It was their home.

For Emma to get home from the cathedral, she walked up to 53rd Street and Fifth Avenue to take the E line. It could take up to 40 minutes with a few stops. She used the time to her advantage, reading the newspaper or a book. However, today was different. All she could do was pray the Our Father and Hail Mary over and over for her friend and boss, Monsignor Triplett. At the same time, she was thinking and praying about the conversation she would have with her troubled son. As she reached her stop at Queens Plaza, she went down the stairs to cross Queens Boulevard. Traffic was bumper to bumper as she waited for the walk signal. She headed up 27th Street for the 10-minute walk as she passed a bank and a couple of office buildings. She heard the familiar sound of the neighborhood — kids playing, and parents yelling. She quickly walked the few blocks before arriving at her apartment building.

While they waited for Emma, Jonathan invited Father O'Hara to have a seat on the couch.

"I'll be right out." Jonathan took some things he brought from his car and tossed them on the bed in his room. He grabbed his guitar and returned to the living room.

As Father O'Hara looked around, he saw a couple of repairs that were needed. A curtain rod was bent, and some blinds were broken. Also, a wet spot on the ceiling and a front door could use a fresh coat of paint.

"Father O'Hara, here's my guitar. It's nothing special. How about tuning it while I take a quick shower?" Jonathan handed the priest the guitar.

"I'll give it a try!" Father O'Hara took the guitar and strummed it to find just how out of tune it was.

Jonathan went back into his room, found some clean clothes and walked into the bathroom to take the first shower he'd had in three days. Turning on the warm water and feeling it hit his body, he realized how much he appreciated something he had always taken for granted.

Father O'Hara struggled to tune the guitar. It would have been a lot easier if he had brought his tuner. He hoped Jonathan might have one or access to the internet to watch a YouTube video to tune it. He also thought this would be a good time to teach Jonathan how to tune it himself.

As he was tightening the last string, he heard a key in the door lock. Emma walked in with her overnight bag.

"Father O'Hara, what a nice surprise!" Emma looked physically and emotionally drained. She put the bag in the corner of the room trying to conceal it.

"So good to see you, Emma!" Father O'Hara greeted her with a hug. "How are you doing?"

"That's a good question. There's so much going on in my life. I'm not sure. With the death of Monsignor Triplett, I don't know how I'm feeling. I would say right now...'numb' would be the best word," Emma rambled on. "But how about you?"

"I'd agree... numb. But I'm also sad... confused, and uncertain of my future," Father O'Hara replied.

"I'm sorry for you." Emma was polite, but not really listening to his words. As she was talking, Jonathan came out of the bathroom with his hair a mess. He and Emma hugged and cried. The scriptures came alive—the prodigal son had returned home.

"Mom, I am so sorry," Jonathan began. "I know I have a lot of explaining to do, and we have a lot of talking to do. That's why I invited Father O'Hara over... to help. You said it was okay on the phone."

Emma nodded. "It's fine. Maybe with his help, together we can get through all of this."

"Mom, you really look exhausted. Are you sure you feel like talking now?"

"Yes, I think we need to talk things out. I can't have you constantly running away. I love you, Jonathan, and I'm trying my best for you." Emma sobbed.

"I love you too, Mom." Jonathan saw the real hurt he had brought his mother with his actions.

"How about you do something with your hair and let me go to the bathroom, then we can talk." Emma smiled and tousled his hair.

"Sounds good!" Jonathan went back into his room.

"If you'll excuse me, Father, I'll be right back." Emma went to the bathroom to compose herself. She picked up Jonathan's filthy clothes. She wondered if she should wash them or throw them away.

As Jonathan came out of his room, he noticed the rest of the clothes from his car. He quickly picked them up and put them in the laundry hamper next to the washer in the kitchen.

"I think it's tuned." Father O'Hara held the guitar, listened as he strummed it and then gave it to Jonathan to put down.

Emma came out of the bathroom looking much better.

Father O'Hara decided to start the conversation. "How about everyone taking a seat, so we can talk." Jonathan took a seat on the couch, and Emma pulled up a chair from the nearby dinner table.

"I think it's important we begin with prayer." They all bowed their heads and made the Sign of the Cross. "Heavenly Father, we thank you on the day before Easter for bringing this family home. May you guide them in this meeting of reconciliation. May each be open to their mistakes and seek forgiveness from one another. May you allow their love to come through, so together, they may grow as a family knowing you are with them always. We ask for the Holy Family to be with them and help them. We make this prayer through Christ, our Lord."

Everyone responded "Amen."

Emma and Jonathan thanked Father O'Hara for the prayer.

"I know you would like me to be part of this family discussion, and I'm happy to assist. I would suggest for this go as smoothly as possible for one another, you find some paper and a pen or pencil, so we can work on a plan for your future."

Jonathan got up and went to his room and found two spiral notebooks and gave one to his mom with a pen.

"Thanks, Jonathan. Now, I think it would be good for each of you to list three things you'd like to talk about and see if you can agree on three things during this time. Since this is such a difficult day for both of you, I want to keep it to an hour. Is that okay with everyone?" Father O'Hara suggested.

"I think that's a good idea. An hour is probably a good beginning," Emma said.

"I agree." Jonathan had already written his three items down.

Emma was writing hers down wondering how close they would come to Jonathan's. She nodded to Father O'Hara that she was finished.

"Jonathan, why don't you begin and share the three you want to talk about," Father O'Hara urged.

"Mom, I want to talk about your boyfriend Sam, Monsignor Triplett and our money situation," Jonathan blurted. He was glad to express his ideas, hoping she would finally listen to him.

"Fantastic. How about your three Emma?"

"I would also like to talk about Sam, Monsignor Triplett and Jonathan's school grades."

"It sounds like we have a list of four items to talk about. They are talking about Monsignor Triplett, Sam, Jonathan's grades and the family finances. Are you both okay with talking about these four?"

"Yes." Jonathan felt he had already made progress.

Emma knew some of these issues should have been talked about earlier with her son. "I'm fine with these."

"Can we agree to begin with Monsignor Triplett?" Father O'Hara asked.

Jonathan nodded. "I'm okay with that." He knew this topic would be easier than the other three, but more emotional for both of them.

"Okay." Emma remembered many happy conversations over the past years with her friend and confidant.

"Great! Who would like to begin?" Father O'Hara asked.

"I will," said Emma. "Monsignor Triplett loved you like a son, Jonathan. You have to know that, and even though you did not get a chance to talk with him last week when you called him, he was always looking out for you. He was always helping me to make sure you had what you needed. The car, the insurance on the car, money for guitar lessons and the opportunities you had to go to the Jets football games. Those are just some of the things he did for you." Emma couldn't hold back the tears.

"I know, Mom, and I'm sorry I didn't always show my appreciation to him for all he did. I knew he was a good friend, and I needed him since Dad died. I'll miss him, and I wish I'd told him thanks." Jonathan was crying too.

"He knew, Jonathan. He knew." Emma got up from the chair and hugged her son. "We're going to be okay, Jonathan."

"Mom, I needed him, and he wasn't there for me lately. It was like he had abandoned me since he wasn't coming around as much or even talking to me." Jonathan's emotions changed to more anger than loss.

Emma was startled at her son's remark, but she understood. "He never abandoned you. He wanted you to become more independent. That's why he encouraged you to get a job. That's why he gave you the car and only asked for you to get good grades. He saw the potential in you and wanted you to reach that potential as you became more independent." Emma desperately tried to explain this to Jonathan, wondering if he would fully understand.

"He never told me any of that! It just felt like he was distancing himself from me, especially when Sam came around more."

"Jonathan, in life there are things you should discover without someone telling you, and I believe Monsignor Triplett was allowing this to happen. Even though he wasn't coming over as much, he asked about you almost every day, and I know you guys talked during the week. I know maybe you felt it was not enough, especially when you couldn't see him this week. But he was under a lot of pressure with the restoration and Holy Week." Emma hoped Jonathan was listening, really listening.

"Mom, I loved him and never let him know how thankful I was!"

Emma got up from the chair and went over to Jonathan wrapping her arms around him. He let it all out once again.

Father O'Hara was moved to tears as he heard how important Monsignor Triplett was to these two and how much he had helped them with their lives. Now there would be a void, and he wondered how Jonathan would handle another significant loss.

"I loved him too." Emma tried to give her son some comfort. Then with determination and maternal strength, she said, "Jonathan look at me. We're going to get through this loss, but you've got to go back and see the psychiatrist. We both need to see one. You also need to take whatever medication he prescribes. Do you understand? I can't have you living here and not getting the help you need. I love you. Together we'll get through this, but you need help that I can't give. Seeing Dr. Turner is nonnegotiable."

"That's not one of the items we agreed to talk about. I don't think he was helping me." Jonathan pulled away from his mom while still crying.

"He was, Jonathan, but you have to be open and honest when talking with him. Will... will you do that for me?"

"On one condition..." Jonathan knew he needed Dr. Turner's help, but in doing so, he hoped to get something in return from his mom.

"What is it?"

"Sam can no longer come into our home!" Jonathan was testing his mom to see if she loved him more.

Emma said nothing as she returned to the chair.

"Mom, this is my condition. We can talk about Sam, but I'm not going to give in." Jonathan stood and raised his voice to his mom. "You know that's why I left?"

Blinking back tears, Emma finally shared her recent decision. "Jonathan, stop, please. Sit back down. It's... it's over. My relationship with Sam is over. It was wrong. I admit that."

"I hated the bastard!" Jonathan announced with a disdain Emma had never heard before.

"Jonathan, watch your language!" Emma insisted.

"I'm sorry, Mom. When did this happen?" Jonathan asked as he clutched the pillow on the couch. He didn't see the sadness in his mother's eyes.

"This morning."

"Good! He's a married man, Mom."

"Wait, Jonathan," Father O'Hara interrupted. "I know you heard your mom, but did you listen to her? She admitted she was wrong. She's hurting too. Don't you see that?"

Emma continued. "It was all wrong. Love makes you do crazy things. One day you'll learn."

"He wasn't the right person for you, Mom." Jonathan saw his mom's pain. He got up and gave her a big hug. They both returned to the couch.

Holding Jonathan's hand, Emma struggled for words to say. "You're probably right."

"You deserve better, the best. I worried he would hurt you. Did he? Is that why it ended? I worry about you. I love you." Jonathan tried to bring comfort to his mom.

"No... no... he didn't hurt me." But Emma still thought about the empty box that had contained a bottle of sleeping pills.

"Are you sure?" Jonathan asked. "There's something about him that scares me."

"I'm okay... I love you, Jonathan. I am glad you're looking out for me." Emma struggled to find the words to bring comfort to her son.

"Mom, it's going to be okay. I'm home and so are you." Jonathan gave another hug to his mom. He had just received the best Easter gift—not having to deal with Sam Tolden.

"I want you home!" Emma took her son's hand and kissed his forehead.

Father O'Hara was surprised how quickly the one issue was resolved and thankful Emma had ended an inappropriate relationship. He could tell they both needed time together to grieve the loss of Monsignor Triplett. The loss was bringing up painful memories of the loss of Roger too.

He stood and was about to leave when Jonathan said, "Please stay, Father. I'm not sure we're done."

"I think you need time with one another. You've talked about the two biggest areas that needed discussion. If you'd like, I can come back another time."

"I want you to stay," Jonathan said. "I think we should finish our list."

Emma saw the need and put her own feelings aside. "Father O'Hara, I'd like you to stay too. I don't think this will take long, and Jonathan needs to hear about our finances."

"Yes, I would!" Jonathan turned to his mom. "Are we okay with money?"

"No... no... we're not. I just don't make enough working at the cathedral and the two part-time jobs. Things are becoming more expensive. Did you take all the money from the Pillsbury Doughboy jar?"

"Yes." Jonathan cast his eyes down.

"Did you spend the $2,000?" She knew exactly how much money was in there.

"Most of it. I think I've got about $750 left."

"Jonathan, I've always taught you actions have consequences. The car stays put until you pay all the money back. If this means more hours at your job, then you'll do that. You will have to become more responsible for your bills. I can't continue to help you." Emma was now the voice of authority. She was angry. She had to discipline her son so he would feel the punishment. It wasn't fun being a mother and a father.

"Mom, I need my car. I'll pay the money back, but I need the car for work," Jonathan pleaded, but he knew she had made up her mind.

Emma wasn't budging. "The subway will get you there and back. It will also give you time to work on your homework. The grades have to be A's and B's, Jonathan. You can do it, but you choose not to. You'll be a junior next year, and in two years, hopefully, off to college. If you want to make it happen, you need better grades." Emma moved from the family finances to his grades. She was determined to make sure he understood the expectations she always had for him.

"I'm trying my best, Mom." Jonathan knew he could do it, but he wasn't. It was the only answer he could give hoping she wouldn't announce his grades to Father O'Hara. He knew he was lazy and didn't really care about high school or feel totally accepted. Monsignor Triplett had encouraged him to make good grades. Now with his death, Jonathan wondered why bother. There was no money for college. Looking at his guitar, he was just hoping it might be a way to make a living, but he would have to commit to it.

"You're not trying your best. Don't make it sound like you are. Do you want Father O'Hara to hear your grades?" Emma knew it would hit a nerve with Jonathan.

"I'd prefer we keep them between us." Jonathan felt embarrassed.

"I'm expecting better grades, Jonathan. With better grades, more opportunities will come your way. Please help me with this." Emma looked to Father O'Hara.

"She's right Jonathan, and you know she is," Father O'Hara said.

"I'll try, but I make no promises." Jonathan mumbled the words just to appease both of them.

"If you seriously try, you won't have to make any promises—you'll have all A's and B's. Promise me you will do your homework and turn it in on time?" Emma pleaded. Her voice was stronger now.

"I said I'll try!" Jonathan wanted to get off this subject. He went to the kitchen and got a glass of water.

"Jonathan, please come and sit back down?" Emma asked.

Jonathan put the glass in the sink and then sat in the chair. He wasn't happy but nodded his head in acceptance.

Father O'Hara was eager to leave. "It sounds like you two are making progress on almost everything. How are you both feeling?"

"Better." Emma knew it was just the beginning.

"I think the two of you ganged up on me!" Jonathan uttered with a slight laugh. He hadn't felt like smiling or laughing for a long time. He was smart enough to know they were right. But he was still a teenager, and he didn't want to hear it all. "But I'm glad we're talking."

"If you keep talking, it will help." Father O'Hara encouraged them. "You probably won't agree on everything, and there will be more bumps along the way, but can you both agree to keep talking and work out the problem or situation as it comes along? You need each other. Jonathan, your mom is your mom, and she's the adult. You need her, and she needs to know where you are."

"I'll try," Jonathan responded with some confidence.

"That's all I ask son." Emma got up and went over to give him a hug.

337

"I think my work is done!" Father O'Hara looked at his cell phone and tried to determine when he would get to the cathedral if he left now.

"Not until you play the guitar! Mom, did you know Father O'Hara plays?" Jonathan got his guitar and gave it to Father O'Hara.

"I don't remember you playing when you were at the cathedral," Emma said.

"I didn't."

"Play us something!" Jonathan insisted, and Father O'Hara felt obligated since the talk between mother and son went so well.

"It's been a while...." Father O'Hara picked up the guitar. Once he started, it came back to him, and he was enjoying playing a little classical and then a little pop music. Jonathan and Emma enjoyed the private concert. After about ten minutes, he put the guitar down, and they gave him a big round of applause.

"You're fantastic!" Jonathan was surprised and impressed at how well Father O'Hara played.

"It's because my parents insisted I practice and practice. I have them to thank."

"Maybe we can get together and play?"

"First, I need to hear you play." Father O'Hara handed Jonathan the guitar.

Jonathan took the guitar and strummed a few cords. "I'm not good."

"Because you won't practice." Emma remembered the many times she'd yell at him to practice.

As Jonathan struggled to find the chords in the one song, he thought he knew well, he finally admitted, "You're right, Mom. I need more practice! So when can we get together, Father O'Hara?"

"We'll find a time, once you get your grades up, and you pay back the money you owe your mom. In the meantime, practice!" Father O'Hara wondered if he would even be around. "And with those words, I think I'll take my leave." Together they prayed an "Our Father," and Father O'Hara gave them his blessing.

Both Emma and Jonathan thanked Father O'Hara for coming.

Father O'Hara placed his hand on Jonathan's shoulder. "Jonathan, listen to your mom. She's filled with lots of wisdom. She loves you. Don't run away anymore. Talk to your psychologist. And you have my phone number. You can call me anytime."

"I will. You sure I can't give you a ride back to the parish?"

"Thanks, but I think your mom needs your car keys now. I'll enjoy taking the subway." Father O'Hara smiled and reminded Jonathan of the punishment his mom had given to him.

"Father O'Hara, thanks for everything. Happy Easter." Emma was grateful for the help.

Father O'Hara gave her a big hug and whispered, "Love your son. Make him number one above any man in your life for the next few years. I'll be praying for you both." Then letting go, he said, "Happy Easter."

As he left, Father O'Hara reflected on the reunion with Emma and Jonathan. He was thankful to have played a small part in it. He chuckled. He knew he had to pick up his guitar and play more too! He also realized this would help with the changes about to happen in his life.

He approached the subway station and patiently waited the six minutes for the next N line. This would take him close to the cathedral to help another friend. It would not be easy to say goodbye to Father Morales after sharing so much together. But after talking about actions and consequences deep down he knew he had to accept the consequences of his actions last night and so did Father Morales. As he rode the subway, he observed the diversity of the city and felt blessed to be a part of it. He prayed to the Holy Spirit for the strength and guidance he would need when he saw Juan. He knew, for the both of them and their priestly vocation, it was good Juan was going to Rome. He pulled out his cell phone and texted Father Morales to let him know he was on his way.

As Jonathan and Emma closed the door to their apartment, they gave each other a hug, thankful to be together. They mourned the loss of Monsignor Triplett. His death brought them closer to one another. They both realized with Father O'Hara, things would change in each of their lives. Holding each other, both knew they didn't want to lose the love they had as mother and son. Emma's phone rang, interrupting the moment. She pulled it out of her pocket and looked at the screen—it was Monsignor Stone.

"Son, I need to answer this. It's Monsignor Stone." Emma walked hurriedly to her bedroom.

Jonathan knew of the good friendship between his mom and Monsignor Stone. He didn't always like Monsignor Stone because he thought he was very standoffish. He was, thankful he gave his mom a flexible schedule for his school activities.

For the next thirty minutes, Emma and Monsignor Stone filled each other in on their morning's activities. She had no idea he was at the cathedral this morning. He told her Lieutenant Palmer questioned him about their relationship. Emma reassured him she had told Palmer it was a platonic friendship.

Emma told Monsignor she had ended her affair with Sam. She also shared her conversation with her son and how Father O'Hara was a help. He was surprised she had a relationship with Sam and even more surprised to hear Father O'Hara was there until Emma explained how it had all come about.

"Where are you now, Monsignor?"

"I'm on my way back to my apartment. I have to be at the police station at 2:30 p.m. for the written statement."

"Lieutenant Palmer said he would call me when I had to go. I'm going to miss Monsignor Triplett."

"That makes two of us." Monsignor Stone held back his emotions. "Thanks for listening, Emma. Happy Easter."

"Happy Easter, Monsignor Stone. I'll see you on Tuesday." Emma ended the conversation and wondered about Sam. She thought about giving him a call but decided it wasn't worth it. She knew she had to move on.

Emma went back to the living room and saw Jonathan sitting on the couch watching some television show. She went over, sat down beside him and gave him another hug. She had her son home. She felt God made sure of that and maybe Monsignor Triplett in heaven. This is all she needed for a Happy Easter.

Chapter 27

Lieutenant Palmer watched as the Delfinos entered the cathedral. He had instructed the officer at the door to take them to the center of the church and have them sit in eye range of the evidence table. As they followed the officer to the pew, Palmer noticed the sweat dripping from the younger Delfino's face. As much as the detective wanted to interview them, he first needed to review the items discovered in Monsignor Triplett's safe. He saw Detective Sabor talking with one of the CSU investigators and made his way over to the table to speak with them.

"How are we doing?" Palmer asked both Detective Sabor and the investigator.

"We have a few more areas to go over and could be finished with our work in the cathedral within the next hour," the investigator reported.

"That's good news. Have you worked on the items retrieved from Monsignor Triplett's safe?"

"We're still working and about halfway done," the investigator indicated. "We set up an evidence area near the Altar of the Sacred Heart."

Palmer moved to the table where another CSU investigator was reviewing the evidence received so far and checking for proper identification.

"Lieutenant, several items still need to be processed, but we'll complete those within the hour."

"Thank you." Palmer was pleased with the progress. "Judge Kickenbottom signed a search warrant for the contents of room 212 at the Republican Woman's Club. I sent Detective Pantera over with a uniformed police officer. Hopefully, they haven't cleaned the room or removed the trash," Detective Sabor informed Lieutenant Palmer.

"More good news." Palmer turned once again to check on the Delfinos.

"What do you make of the distance between the Delfinos?" Palmer asked Sabor.

"Not sure, but a good time to question them."

"Sabor, I want you to start the questioning of the Delfinos – get the basics out of the way and then interview them individually to see where they were the last 24 hours."

"I understand."

Palmer checked his notes and continued. "If the supervisor, a Jared Quinn, comes in, interview him separately. I want to review the evidence brought over from the safe. I've got a feeling there's something that could provide answers and even a link to the Delfinos. If you need me, come and get me or send one of the officers over."

"Will do, Boss."

"I also need the Delfinos and their supervisor to walk the scaffolding with me, end to end. I want to understand how this restoration is being done, and I'll see how knowledgeable they are of the scaffolding layout."

"So you think they may be involved?" Sabor asked.

"I don't think they're innocent, not with the amount of money we found in Monsignor Triplett's room."

Sabor looked over at the Delfinos. "They must have heard us. They look a little nervous, and I think it's time to find out why."

"They do." Palmer agreed as he looked at the two men. "You better get over there. I'll finish here and be right over. Then he turned back to the evidence.

As Detective Sabor walked over to the Delfinos, the father, Joseph, looked right at his son, A.J. and advised, "Remember say little and listen. After this meeting, I'll fill you in on everything you don't already know. Do you understand?"

A.J. was confused and unaware of all of his father's secret deals. "Understand, Dad? I don't.... I've been trying to clean up some of your mess, but I'll do what you ask—for the family. Hopefully, I want to know the entire truth after all this."

"Believe me, you will." Joseph wanted to tell his son. He hoped his son wouldn't hear it from the detectives.

Sabor approached the Delfinos and introduced himself. "Thank you both for coming. I need to get a few facts from each of you individually, and then my partner will join us for any additional questions."

The detective interviewed each of them separately in the usher's room with the preliminary questions about their duties and jobs. He asked about their whereabouts from last night until they arrived at the cathedral. Sabor discovered they were both at a dinner with fifty people who could collaborate their alibis. Once they finished, the Delfinos returned to the pew to wait.

"Mr. Delfino, were you able to contact your construction supervisor yet?"

"Yes, Detective Sabor. He should be coming. In fact, I can call him again if you want." Joseph noticed Jared had entered the cathedral and was talking with an officer. "There he is."

Accompanied by the police officer, Jared Quinn joined the Delfinos.

"I'm sorry to be late. I'm Jared Quinn."

Sabor noticed Mr. Quinn's red eyes. "Tough night?"

"Just home alone with a few beers?" The remark annoyed Jared as he tried to be respectful.

344

Sabor asked Jared to follow him to the usher's room where he asked the routine preliminary questions and searched for more information. The detective discovered the Delfinos depended on Jared. And because of this, he had the freedom to exercise his responsibilities as supervisor. Sabor and Jared left the priests' sacristy and returned to the Delfinos. The detective thought it best to continue the interview with the three men together.

Sabor began. "How many employees are working on the cathedral project?"

Jared looked around and thought for a moment before he replied. "On Thursday... Thursday... there were twelve workers here and myself."

"You seem rather sure of this," Sabor remarked.

"I remember well the last time I was here working and the number of employees who clocked in and out." Jared was confident. He knew he was correct. Because it was Holy Thursday, there was only a skeleton crew, not the normal 100 or so workers. He remembered it was twelve for the twelve apostles at the Last Supper.

"Was Thursday your last day of work?" Sabor asked even though he already knew the answer.

"Yes. Monsignor Triplett told us weeks ago that we could only work a half day on Thursday and not at all on Friday," Jared explained.

Joseph Delfino added, "But the number always depends on the status of work on each of the projects. We occasionally have to pull workers from one project to go and help at another. Also, some employees don't always show up for work when and where they're expected. Sometimes, we have to fire an employee on the spot for one reason or another."

The detective followed up on Joseph's remark. "You're saying that during any job, you would actually fire someone on the job?"

"Yes, there were." Jared disliked that part of being a supervisor.

345

"On Thursday?"

Jared thought hard about the questions. "Not on Thursday. But I believe on Tuesday or Wednesday, I did let two go."

"And as the construction supervisor, you're able to fire an employee?"

"Yes, I can fire, but not hire."

"I just want to make sure I understand that there were twelve workers here on Thursday with possibly two firings on Tuesday or Wednesday. Since the work started, what's the maximum number of workers you've had here?"

"I'd have to look in the construction office, but I would say... 200. But I'll have to double-check to make sure he was giving an accurate number for the last two years."

"I'll need a list of all the workers who have ever been on this project since it began. I must have the dates when they were hired. For those who've been fired, I'll need those dates and the reason for firing." Sabor wanted as many specific details as possible. Possibly there was someone who had a motive to kill.

Before Jared could say anything, A.J. rose to his feet. "That will take some time. We'll have to go back to the office and review all our records. It could take a while, but we can get you a list." If he was the one who had to produce the information, he knew where to start. He also knew Jared kept it all on a spreadsheet on the computer in his office. A.J. wanted a chance to review the list before Jared gave it to the detective.

"I want it by the end of the day," Sabor insisted.

Jared added. "We keep a record of all employees and firings, so it should be easy to provide you a list." But as he spoke, he felt a deep stare from A.J. Jared realized he probably said too much.

A.J. continued to explain. "Also, our human resource person would have attached something to each of their personnel files showing the reason for hiring and firing. We also have the contact information of all our employees, past

346

and present. We keep them on file for... for... at least seven years."

Detective Sabor interrupted. "Would any of the employees have had any contact with Monsignor Triplett?"

Jared answered. "I would say normally none of them did. For the most part, they did their work and didn't make contact with Monsignor Triplett or any other employee in the cathedral. I was Monsignor Triplett's point of contact."

"I'm presuming these are all union workers who have all their documentation in order and had the necessary background checks?" Detective Sabor looked at the Delfinos, knowing they probably did not.

"To the best of my knowledge, they have!" Joseph stated emphatically. But he knew he made exceptions to try to help individuals out.

"How many of your workers have keys to the cathedral?" Sabor continued his questioning.

"My assistant supervisor, Jamie Avalos and I," Jared replied. "We had keys because sometimes we had to work crazy hours and deliveries were made at odd times."

"Has he been called to come in?"

"I didn't know you wanted him here."

Now Jared wondered if he should have called Jamie, but he never knew what condition he would be in after a Friday night.

"If needed, can you reach him?"

"Yes. Sure... I have his number right here in my phone." Jared was ready to take out his phone and make the call.

"Thanks. I'll take the number down for the time being." Jared gave the detective the number who wrote and circled it on his notepad.

Sabor continued, "Who normally opens the cathedral each morning?"

"Normally, the cathedral staff," Jared explained. "But if we had to work odd hours, either of us could open the cathedral."

347

"Who opened the cathedral this past Thursday?"

"I believe Jamie did," Jared recalled. "Work began at 6:00 a.m., and I was running late that morning."

Detective Sabor thought for a moment and looked at Jared. "I think you should have Jamie come here."

"Let me give him a call." Jared reached for his phone and called him.

"How long is your normal work day?" Detective Sabor asked.

While Jared listened for the call to go through, he answered. "Usually until 4:00 p.m. There's a 30-minute break for Mass in the morning at 8:00 a.m. and then an hour break for lunch which allows for a noon Mass." Jared knew sometimes the guys left early since they didn't always get to take a break.

Jared heard the phone go to voicemail and left a message for Jamie to call him as soon as possible and told him to come to the cathedral.

Back at the evidence table, Palmer put on a pair of rubber gloves to look at each item Monsignor Triplett had kept under lock and key. He wondered if one of these would provide a motive for the priest's death.

Palmer examined the three folders Monsignor Triplett had prepared. One folder held the records of all the payouts he had made with his PayPal account and details of the American Express card payments. As he looked through the list of payouts, the lieutenant wondered if the names were workers or perhaps parishioners who were being helped. The brutal winter probably left many people short of cash, so maybe he helped with their high heating bills. It looked like in his way, Monsignor was doing corporal works of mercy. He was hoping the Delfinos could answer questions about Monsignor Triplett's generosity.

The second folder held records of the money monsignor paid Sam Tolden. Sam had confessed to the nice bonus he received each month. The documents showed the amount was between $500 and $1,000 a month for the last six months. The papers showed the amounts but not the source. Even though Sam had said it came from Monsignor Triplett's cash advances from the credit cards, a thorough examination of the parish financial books was also needed. Lieutenant Palmer needed to bring this up with Mr. Tolden, in the presence of his lawyer.

The third folder was even more interesting. It confirmed Monsignor Stone's story with photographs and negatives of the incident that happened almost thirty-five years ago. The pictures were very grainy. It was hard to tell if it was really Monsignor Stone in any of the pictures. Palmer remembered his own college days and some of his mistakes. He hoped no one had kept photos to blackmail him. He also hoped the court would allow Monsignor Stone to have the folder and bury a mistake from his past.

As Palmer continued looking at the additional photos, he noted one face was younger and more familiar. Monsignor Stone had not mentioned this person. He wasn't sure, but perhaps he thought it was Monsignor Black. He took a picture with his phone before he returned the photo to the folder.

Lieutenant Palmer glanced over to see how Detective Sabor was progressing with the questioning of the Delfinos and noticed another person with them. He assumed the other person was the construction supervisor. He took off his gloves and joined Detective Sabor. He told the CSU investigator that he would return to review the remaining evidence from Monsignor Triplett's apartment.

Palmer walked over to the detective, "How are we doing, Detective Sabor?" Before the detective could answer, Palmer introduced himself to the Delfinos and Jared Quinn. He could tell they were a little edgy as he shook their hands. He wondered how long it would be before they contacted their lawyer.

"We were just talking about the work schedule and the number of workers here. The last time they worked was

Thursday, and there were twelve employees and Jared here," Sabor reported.

"And someone is getting their names and phone numbers, as well as all previous workers?" Palmer asked.

A.J. again assured them. "I'll provide you the information by the end of the day." He felt uncomfortable and wanted to leave.

"How many times did you provide Monsignor Triplett with cash?" Palmer wasted no time in asking the crucial questions as he looked at the three men seated in the pew.

Joseph Delfino looked totally surprised as he stuttered, "I'm not sure what... what... you're... what are you talking about?"

"I know you were receiving kickbacks from the sub-contractors, and Monsignor Triplett found out. You were paying him off with cash. Do I need to interview you separately regarding this matter?" Palmer waited for Joseph's reaction.

Joseph Delfino quickly glanced at his son and Jared who responded, "That won't be necessary. I take full responsibility for the handling of the kickbacks. My son only knows what I wanted him to know, and Jared is just finding out." Joseph didn't know that his son had confided in Jared. Sitting quietly, A.J. wondered if his dad would tell the whole truth.

"So Monsignor Triplett was paid off with cash?" Palmer asked again.

"Yes, he was." Joseph realized Jared's eyes were now opened to the Delfino's troubles.

Palmer pressed for more information. "How much money did Monsignor Triplett receive?"

"Last night he received $50,000." Joseph again saw the bewildered look on his son and Jared's faces.

"I think it's best I continue to question you, Joseph, without your son or Jared present. This is now a legal matter that may go before a grand jury."

"I understand." The senior Delfino stood and winked at his son. "It'll be okay. Remember what I said."

Lieutenant Palmer and Joseph Delfino walked farther down in the church to a pew that would allow them the privacy needed to continue with the questioning. Detective Sabor stayed with the other two.

They reached the empty pew in front of a pillar which blocked any view of A.J. and Jared. Palmer motioned for Joseph to sit. Joseph reluctantly sat down, looked around at the empty side altars and noticed the large metal tool boxes marked 'Delfino Construction.'

The lieutenant made felt he had the privacy needed to continue his questions. "Did you give any money to Monsignor Triplett before you gave him the $50,000 last night?"

Twitching his hands nervously, Joseph responded. "He didn't actually receive any money. After Monsignor told me what he was doing with the money, I paid his American Express and MasterCard bills over $5,000 each month."

Joseph continued with more details. "I would bring the bills to my son. As the financial officer, he would cut a check for credit card bills. He didn't know why the company was paying them, but I'm sure now he is putting the pieces of this complex puzzle together."

"Were you paying anyone else at the cathedral?" Palmer asked.

"Well... I also made sure, Sam Tolden got a check each month."

"What were you paying him for?"

"For keeping his mouth shut about the kickbacks!" Joseph blurted, then looked around to see if anyone heard him. Now he had to reveal all the details. He couldn't hide them any longer. "He had his own financial troubles. As I understand, he was having a little affair on the side."

Palmer was surprised at yet another revelation. "You knew he was having an affair?"

"Yes. Sam indicated he needed the money to be in cash, so his wife wouldn't know. It slipped he was seeing someone."

"Did he indicate who he was seeing?"

"He wouldn't say." Joseph speculated, but he never really knew. He leaned forward trying to see what his son and Jared were doing.

Palmer got his attention. "Do you know if Monsignor Triplett was aware of this?"

"About the affair or the money?" Joseph needed clarification.

"Both."

"Monsignor Triplett didn't know about the financial arrangement made. The arrangement was only between Sam and me. Not even my son knew about it." Joseph explained, realizing as he shared this information that A.J. needed to know the truth.

"How much money have you given Sam Tolden?" Palmer knew Sam had not mentioned the amount when he was interviewed, only that Monsignor Triplett was giving Sam a cash bonus with each paycheck.

"I've paid him $15,000 over the last six months," Joseph spoke without hesitation.

Palmer was surprised at the amount. "Was he satisfied with what you paid him?"

"I believe so." Joseph leaned back to stretch his legs and make another attempt to see A.J. and Jared.

"Do you know if Sam had any other financial arrangements with anyone else?" Palmer thought there may be more people involved in this scheme.

Joseph seemed puzzled with the question. "I doubt it! Who are you asking about?"

"I'm just asking. And the affair—who was he involved with?" Palmer moved the questioning along.

"I already told you! I don't know! He never told me!"

Palmer wasn't bothered that Joseph seemed upset. He needed clarification. "The last time you saw Monsignor Triplett was last night?"

"Yes. I came and met him at his office around 10:00 p.m."

"Is that when you gave him the money?"

"Yes... it was to be $50,000 this month and $50,000 next month. He talked about the first amount going to employees of the cathedral and the second amount going as an anonymous donation to the archdiocese. He said he had a clear conscience in what he was doing." Joseph stopped looking for A.J. and Jared felt better revealing the truth.

"Why was the money bundled in stacks of 25 hundred-dollar bills?" Palmer asked.

"I wanted it to look like a full case."

"Was anything discussed?"

"We talked about when the cathedral would be finished. I said I was hoping to have it completed in fifteen months. We talked about two shifts working on the inside."

"Why was that so important?"

"It had something to do with the cardinal's anniversary celebration."

"Was that deadline going to be possible?" Palmer queried.

"It was possible, but not probable. This project's been very time consuming, filled with unexpected delays and some costly repairs." Joseph knew first-hand about frustrations and delays.

"Is there a bonus if you get the work done on time or before the deadline?" Palmer was curious about the Delfinos motivation.

"Not a monetary bonus, but something that would help me. The cardinal agreed to help me with my marriage annulment because my fiancé wants to be married here."

"Is that possible?" Palmer was bewildered now with these new details.

"I guess it's possible. You'd have to ask the cardinal." Joseph passed on answering the question.

353

"Did the cardinal know of the kickbacks?" Palmer waited for this answer.

"No... Not that I'm aware of," Joseph said. "I don't remember Cardinal Flinn ever mentioning or suggesting anything like that in our meetings."

Palmer looked over his notes to make sure he had asked all the questions. He came to the note about blood in Monsignor Triplett's office. "Joseph, did you and Monsignor Triplett get into a fight while you were in his office last night?"

"No! Not a physical fight.... I'd never hit a priest, for God's sake Why do you ask?"

"There was blood on the carpet in Monsignor's office. Do you know anything about it?"

"Oh yea... now I remember... I got a bloody nose. I mean, my nose started bleeding. It happens a lot, especially if I'm stressed."

"So the blood found on the carpet is yours?"

"Probably so. If it was by the chair closest to the filing cabinet, that's where I was sitting. I'd used quite a few tissues. I cleaned up as much as I could. Monsignor Triplett said I should just leave the rest, and someone would clean it on Monday. When I left, I took the trash in a small white bag from his office and dropped it in the cathedral dumpster."

Palmer realized he forgot to send out a crime investigator to search the dumpster used by the cathedral. He immediately called one investigator over and told him to go with one of the uniformed police officers to the dumpster behind the cathedral and find the small white trash bag filled with bloody tissues. He explained it was possible evidence, so they should be very thorough. If they found it, bring it in, and mark it as evidence.

The lieutenant returned his attention to Joseph Delfino, reviewed his notes and continued his questioning. "When you and Monsignor Triplett finished your meeting, how did you leave the building?"

Joseph thought for a moment, mentally retracing his steps. "Well, I remember I took the trash bag out of the small trash can and left through the main office doors. It was probably close to 11:00 p.m. I walked around to the side of the building where I saw the dumpster and threw the bag in. Then I walked out on 50th Street, over to Fifth to the subway station. I got home shortly after midnight."

"Is that the last time you saw Monsignor Triplett?"

"Yes,"

"Who knows about the kickbacks from the subcontractors?" Palmer continued his litany of questions.

"Me and Monsignor Triplett knew everything. Sam Tolden, A.J. Delfino, and Jared know bits and pieces. Unless they told someone else, those are the only people I know of who know." Joseph felt very self-assured.

"And were you paying anyone else?" Palmer was fishing with this question.

As Joseph was thinking of a response to this question, his phone rang. He glanced at the caller id. "If you'll give me a second, this is my lawyer." Joseph moved down the pew. A moment later, he moved back and informed Palmer, "I'm sorry, Lieutenant, but I've been advised by my attorney not to answer any more questions until he arrives."

"I fully understand." But Palmer wished the call had come a few minutes later. He wanted to hear Joseph's answer to the last question. "If you'll excuse me, I'll let you sit here while I speak with Detective Sabor."

Palmer walked up the aisle to the evidence table where the CSU investigator placed more bagged items from Monsignor Triplett's room. As Palmer passed A.J. and Jared, he heard a cell phone ring.

It was Jared's. He tried to talk quietly as he moved down to the end of the pew. "Jamie, I need you to come to the cathedral now! Monsignor Triplett is dead—he's been murdered."

355

"Murdered! Madre de Dios—May his soul rest in peace." Jamie made the sign of the cross as he spoke. "He was a kind priest."

"Indeed, he was." Jared recalled the few times they had spoken. "Hey, Jamie, did you give your key to the cathedral to anyone?"

"No, you know me. Why would I as an assistant supervisor do that?"

"Just checking. The police want to question you about it. When can you get here?"

"It will take me about an hour. I have the little one. My wife is at work, and I need to find a sitter, and then I'll come." Jamie heard the urgency in Jared's voice.

"I'll let the detectives know." Jared ended the conversation and returned to the group.

"Lieutenant, that call was my assistant supervisor, James Avalos. He said he could be here in an hour."

Palmer and Sabor conferred on the need to separate A.J. and Jared while asking each of them questions about the financial kickbacks.

"Before Jamie arrives, Mr. Quinn, come with me." Palmer directed.

"Please, call me Jared."

Jared followed the lieutenant down the side aisle and sat down in a small pew across from the Altar of Saint Elizabeth Ann Seton that concealed him behind a pillar and beyond anyone's hearing.

Palmer began. "Jared, Joseph Delfino was talking about the restoration work in the cathedral being finished in the next fifteen months. Do you think it could be accomplished?"

"I don't see that happening. We've had problems and challenges, both inside and out. There have been way too many delays with supplies and unexpected surprises in the repair work."

"Even if a second shift was added?"

This news surprised Jared. "What second shift? I don't know anything about a second shift. The work here is not the easiest, and it's not easy finding experienced workers."

"Would any worker have had a reason to be here last night or this morning?" Palmer looked closely at Jared.

"No... no. There was no reason for anyone to be here at all!"

"Did you know anything about the kickbacks being received on this project?"

"I had my suspicions about some kickbacks. One time I received a delivery of some supplies, and on the delivery slip I had to sign, the word 'donated' was stamped across the dollar figure. I mentioned this to Joseph Delfino, and he told me not to say anything. A.J. later told me, confidentially, about some kickbacks. I didn't like what I was seeing or hearing. As much as I love working for the Delfinos, I said once this project was over, I'd be resigning." Jared sounded frustrated with the project and the Delfino's methods.

"Were you given any money for your silence?"

"No. Absolutely not!" Jared quickly answered. He had always been loyal to the Delfinos. But he knew after this job, if he didn't make a career change, he could be in jail with them.

"Did you share this information with anyone?"

"My assistant Jamie Avalos knows." Jared wished Jamie were here.

"I'll be asking him to confirm it when he arrives." Palmer looked at the worried supervisor.

"I'm sure he will confirm what I've told you about the one shipment."

As Palmer finished his questions with Jared, he asked him to remain seated. Palmer walked over to Sabor to learn the details of A.J. Delfino's answers.

Sabor reported that A.J. knew some subcontractors were making monetary and material donations to the cathedral. In addition, A.J. didn't believe they passed the savings on to the archdiocese. He promised to look into additional kickbacks and see if the company owed anything from or to the archdiocese. His father had shared very little information about the kickbacks with A.J. and told him repeatedly, 'best you don't know.'

"Sabor, did you ask A.J. if he was given any additional compensation for his silence?"

"He told me no."

"Did he say he told or discussed this with anyone?"

"He told me his wife knew, and he mentioned it to Jared Quinn."

This latest answer surprised Palmer. "Did he talk with any other employees?"

"I was about to ask him when you arrived." Sabor was pleased with his handling of the questions for A.J.

The lieutenant also seemed pleased, but left the detective and walked back to A.J. to get some clarification. "A.J., you told Detective Sabor you only mentioned the kickbacks to your wife and Mr. Quinn. Is that correct?"

"Yes." A.J. nervously answered.

"You have not discussed it with any other employees?"

"As far as I know, no one else knows." A.J. looked around to see if he could see his father, but couldn't. He remembered his father's advice—wait for the lawyer. "I don't think I should answer any more questions until our lawyer arrives."

The lieutenant made a note to make sure he talked to the assistant supervisor again and A.J.'s wife. In the meantime, Palmer wanted to focus his questions on the placement of the scaffolding.

"Do you or your dad know about the layout for the scaffolding in here?"

"There were some preliminary discussions with my dad and Jared, but Jared was the one who worked out all the details."

Palmer motioned for Jared to come to him. "Jared, did you work the layout of the scaffolding?"

"Yes." Jared was stopped before he could say any more.

Palmer posed a very simple but relevant question. "In a project of this proportion and size, was this the best way to arrange the scaffolding?"

A.J. was quick to answer. "I was present for the first meeting, and Monsignor Triplett was insistent that there had to be as much open space as possible for the many visitors who come through the cathedral. I know my father wanted to grant his wish."

"That was a nice gesture, but it really hampered the work." Jared added, without looking at A.J. "To be honest, it would have been a lot easier to have closed the cathedral completely and done the work. It also would have taken us about half the time. Since the cathedral stayed open, the city fire codes required that all the aisles remained accessible and all the exits. As you look around, what we have here is the best way to install the scaffolding. If the cathedral were closed, we would have had a lot more scaffolding in here. Like I said, unfortunately, we didn't have a choice, so this was the best arrangement."

"And the access points of getting up to the top of the scaffolding, who knew about them?"

"Certainly, all the company workers knew the access points since they were the ones on it. I'm not sure if anyone else knew or even needed to know." Jared wasn't sure why Palmer needed or was asking the question.

"Were any cathedral employees on the scaffolding at any time?"

"Yes… I took Monsignor Triplett up and showed him some of our issues. I also took the cardinal and Sam Tolden. I believe my assistant and I both showed the organist—whose name escapes me at the moment. He was a heavy guy who was talking about the sound system and the organ pipes. He went ballistic when he discovered several of the pipes had been damaged while they were re-installing them." Jared tried to remember if anyone else from the cathedral staff had been up there.

"None of them went alone. They all received the required construction hats for safety." Jared added. It was apparent A.J. was unaware that anyone from the cathedral staff had been up in the scaffolding.

"Did they each begin at a certain point?" Palmer asked.

"Yes, at the point of entrance near the main doors of the cathedral. Because of the complexity of this project, and the number of individuals on and off the scaffolding, we have one point of entry and exit. This is a secured area that is blocked off to the general public. It's also the location for most of our safety equipment." Jared pointed to the location.

"I'd like to take a closer look. Would you show us?" Palmer motioned Sabor to join them.

The detectives followed A.J. and Jared down the aisle to the front church entrance. As they arrived at the foot of the scaffolding, Palmer stopped. "Do the workers just go to a certain area, or do they come up where we are now and walk the length of the scaffolding?"

Jared explained. "Workers have assigned areas to go to, but they all enter and leave from here."

"Do they know about the stairs that went all the way down to the priest's sacristy?"

"I doubt it since we entered and exited from this point of the scaffolding. However, I know about a hidden staircase. Hector Rivera told us it leads to passages that run the length of the cathedral and continue to the attic and two towers. The door is kept locked for safety reasons. The only time it's unlocked is for the firefighters to conduct safety inspections."

"When the organist went 'ballistic,' as you said he did, what happened?"

"I assured him that the construction company would pay for the damages to the organ pipes. He said he'd talk to Monsignor Triplett about it. But he was furious."

360

Palmer wrote down the information down so he could question the organist.

"If we could walk the scaffolding from end to end, I'll have a better understanding of what you're talking about," Palmer suggested.

"No problem. Wait here. I need to get all of you a construction hat and some safety glasses." Jared went to the wall beside the gift shop annex to a huge box filled with supplies. Clearly, this was the entry point. There were signs posted to remind the construction workers of the required procedures. Once everyone had a hard hat and a pair of glasses, Jared gave a few safety instructions. He got a verbal "yes" from each of them to make sure they understood they had to be extremely cautious as they climbed the ladder-like steps of the scaffolding and over some railings to get to the top level. Palmer had Jared lead the way.

Slowly and in and out of the scaffolding, going up several levels, closely following Jared's movements, they made their way to the top level. It was like climbing the monkey bars on the playground during their grade school days. At each level, Jared explained to the detectives the difficulty of assembling the scaffolding so that the cathedral could remain open. He pointed out the extra supports and braces required as they finally reached the top.

With the accumulation of the dust and the daily burning of the candles over the years, the ceiling was coated with soot, and in some places, was almost entirely black. In restoring the cathedral ceiling to its original beauty, the cleaning and the repainting was more time consuming than had been expected, and this was preventing the completion of other work in the cathedral.

As they took their time and carefully observed the work being done, they noticed a portion of the ceiling that had been restored to its original beauty. The wooden plastered ceiling, "The Garden of Heaven" with its 300 "snowflakes" — points where the architectural "bosses" come together. Each

361

snowflake is unique—with a flower, leaves or grapes. All of them took a moment to point out a favorite and marveled at the workmanship.

Almost fifteen minutes later, the four approached the area near the door to the hidden staircase above the usher's room. They stopped and looked out at the altar under the bronze Baldacchino. Jared once again explained the scaffolding's complicated arrangement they devised to avoid hiding the entire sanctuary. Palmer asked about any hidden stairs to the sacristy. Jared reiterated that he was unaware that any of the construction workers used the stairs.

Jared explained that many of the construction workers had been in the usher's room, especially the electricians because most of the electrical panels are located there. Palmer knew what he was referring to. Jared went on to say that the electrical system was one of the problems causing delays. Since it was so old and in terrible shape, the entire system had to be brought up to code and replaced. That also included new wiring for the televisions, updated audio and security systems.

Before leaving the area, Jared told the detectives his assistant said the organist had climbed to this level. Jared noted that Jamie, along with a few of the workers, watched the overweight organist struggle to climb up the scaffolding to look at the organ pipes that had not been removed. The organist told them he had an easier way down. When he reached this area, the organist knew the stairway and used his key to open the door and walk down to the priest's sacristy. With this new information, Palmer and Sabor looked at each other. Without saying a word, they knew they wanted to talk with the organist, immediately.

Jared led them back through the scaffolding to the front entrance of the cathedral. The detectives continued with their questions confirming again that only four people from the cathedral staff had been on the scaffolding: the cardinal, Monsignor Triplett, Sam Tolden and the organist.

Jared said as far as he knew that was correct. "Monsignor Triplett was always checking on the progress of the restoration project."

After they were safely on the cathedral floor, they returned the safety equipment to Jared and thanked him. Palmer turned and noticed Joseph Delfino talking to a well-dressed, white-haired man. His lawyer had arrived.

"A.J., I want you to come with me to your father. Jared, I'd like you to stay with Detective Sabor until I get back." Palmer wanted Jared close if he needed to ask more questions.

"Sure."

A.J. and Palmer walked in silence down the center aisle to the pew to Joseph Delfino.

Joseph quickly made the introductions. "Lieutenant Palmer, this is my lawyer, Emmanuel Fitzmyer."

"Thank you for coming." Palmer extended his hand to Mr. Fitzmyer. "I think we should continue the questioning down at the precinct. We can get formal statements from each of you there. Don't leave the city since we're still checking your alibis from last night.

"When would you like the Delfinos to be at the station?" the lawyer asked.

"How about 3:00 this afternoon?"

Mr. Fitzmyer nodded, as Joseph agreed, "We'll see you then."

"I'll make sure your get the list." A.J. indicated, relieved to be leaving.

"Thank you again for your cooperation." Palmer turned and walked back to the front doors where Detective Sabor and Jared waited. He told Sabor the Delfinos would be at the station at 3:00 p.m.

"I'll get a couple of our detectives to check out their alibis." Sabor walked off to call the precinct.

"Jared, I need you to stick around until your assistant arrives. And you'll also have to come down to the station for a formal statement."

"I understand, Lieutenant."

"Here comes Detective Sabor. While you're waiting would you go with him and get the list of employees who were working on Thursday?"

"Sure, we'll be right back," Jared knew exactly where it was in the on-site construction trailer.

As Sabor and Jared left, Palmer wanted to finish reviewing the items found in Monsignor Triplett's safe. But as he walked over to the evidence table, he decided he needed to question one more person.

He retrieved the sheet of paper with the cathedral staff numbers he had placed in his pocket. Scanning the list, he found what he was looking for... the number for the organist, Brian McManius.

Chapter 28

As Cardinal Flinn returned to his residence through the small private hallway connecting it to the cathedral, he knew if there were any further information on the case, one of the detectives would call. In the meantime, he needed to call Bishop Newsome and discuss his conversation with Father Morales. Once that had taken place, he could finish his homily for Easter.

While waiting for Bishop Newsome to answer his phone, the cardinal reflected on his earlier conversation with Thom Triplett and was anxious about Thom's comment concerning Jennifer Gibson.

"George, how are you doing?" Cardinal Flinn began as he heard Bishop Newsome's voice and shifted his attention to the present conversation.

"I'm doing okay. I'm glad you called. I need to share some news."

"And I want to share my conversation with Father Morales."

"Why don't you fill me in on that discussion first? Then I'll fill you in on my discussion with Father O'Hara." Bishop Newsome graciously invited the cardinal to speak first.

"I don't know if you know, but Father Morales is scheduled to leave for Rome on Monday taking a few of the cathedral parishioners with him for a week."

"I did not know that." The bishop was very surprised.

"I spoke with the lead detective, and he sees no reason for him not to go. In my conversation with Juan, I asked him to pack for a longer trip. I told him he would be leaving the cathedral and staying in Rome for further studies. I'll work out the details this week. The North American College owes me a few favors, so this would be a good place for him to stay." Cardinal Flinn felt confident with his decision.

"You have moved quickly on this," Bishop Newsome commented.

"I think it is for the best. What about Father O'Hara? Have you thought about the possibilities for him?" The cardinal hoped the bishop was doing his part in this matter because he didn't want to intervene.

The bishop explained his plan. "I spoke with David and told him I think it best he takes some time away. I'm going to suggest a thirty-day retreat at Gethsemani. The Trappist monks will treat him well. In fact, I was planning on giving the abbot a call today. I believe David wants to be a good and faithful priest. This time of prayer and work with the Trappist community would be good for him."

"Do you think thirty days will be enough?"

"I'm not sure. It will give him time to think. He may need to stay longer. I also believe he needs to talk with a professional psychologist. I'm making that one of the conditions for his return. I want him to have someone he feels free to discuss his sexuality with... to see if he can suppress the physical temptations and remain a celibate priest."

"And if he can't?"

"Then his actions will have consequences. With all the media coverage on this issue across our country, we have no choice but to let him go."

"I agree. These are the decisions I do not like to make." Cardinal Flinn reflected on the few times he had been placed in this kind of situation.

"Nor do I." Bishop Newsome could easily relate.

"When I talk with Father Morales again, I'll encourage him to see a psychologist in Rome. I think it will help. Hopefully, this will help them live the lives they promised to live at their ordination."

"On another subject, I need to talk with you about Monsignor Triplett and share something that is bound to come out in the investigation." Bishop Newsome struggled to articulate the right words to explain the deceased priest playing Robin Hood with church funds.

"I'm listening." Cardinal Flinn heard the anxiety in Bishop Newsome's voice.

"Steven called me yesterday. He told me he met Joseph Delfino. He received $50,000 in cash from Delfino, as well as a list of subcontractors who made either monetary donations or provided materials to the cathedral project. The dollar amount was over $200,000. Were you aware of any of this?"

"I was not aware of the magnitude of it. Did you say $50,000 in cash?" This upset Cardinal Flinn that there wasn't trust between him and Monsignor Triplett.

"It was his way of trying to get the money that should have gone to the cathedral project."

"I'm surprised he didn't tell me what was happening." Cardinal Flinn tried to remain calm.

"I'm sure he would have, but you know he was feeling a little hurt with the loss of income to the cathedral during the restoration, and he would have to lay off employees. He was going to talk to you... Did he?"

"Somewhat. He wanted financial help from the archdiocese, and I put him off until after Easter. I have seen the financial figures for the cathedral, and they are not good."

"I think he hoped the money he'd received would be used as severance pay to the workers he would let go. I know he wanted to give some money back to the archdiocese." Bishop Newsome shared the little information he knew.

"Good intentions, but look at the results. Who else knew about it? Could this somehow be linked to his death?" Cardinal Flinn was very concerned.

"Possibly. Monsignor Triplett, Steven, said the only one who knew about everything was Sam Tolden, and he was having doubts about his loyalty."

"Where is Sam now?" The cardinal asked.

"Good question. Did you see him around?"

"No."

"I'm sure by now the detectives have called him in for questioning. I would think they've found the money."

"I wonder. I think I will call Father Crumbley and see what he knows," the cardinal suggested.

"Let me know. Dominique, Steven shared with me your promise to Joseph Delfino of an annulment, so he could remarry in the cathedral. Is that true?"

The cardinal hesitates. "I talked with Joseph about working with him on his annulment. In return, he would try to expedite the work done on the cathedral and have it completed before my twenty-fifth anniversary."

"Well, Steven made it sound as if you had promised Delfino the annulment." Bishop Newsom explained.

"George, you know I could never promise an annulment. But I was willing to try and help as much as possible." The cardinal was furious that this private conversation between Joseph Delfino and himself had somehow gotten out. He wondered if Joseph had talked. He had told Delfino he would deny they discussed the annulment. "How did Steven find out?"

"I'm not sure. I hope your words don't come back at you." Bishop Newsome recalled the conversation he had had with Monsignor Triplett who, after one too many glasses of wine, told the story of the promised annulment.

"I hear what you are saying. I'll talk with Joseph Delfino."

Bishop Newsome wanted to change the subject and smooth things over after this awkward phone conversation. "You looked good at the press conference."

"Thanks. Are we finished with our business?" The cardinal wondered what other surprises might be revealed.

"Almost. When is the funeral for Monsignor Triplett?"

"It's scheduled for Friday morning. I am having Donald Armenti send out an email and a tweet to the priests this afternoon with the details. He will be buried in the family plot. I am hoping he asked you to preach."

"I have not heard. That information may be in his file in the chancery or his brother has it."

"I am meeting with Steven's brother on Tuesday to work out the details." The cardinal searched for his appointment book and made sure he had added the event to his calendar.

"Speaking of meeting, do you want to meet with Father O'Hara?"

"George, once you have worked it out with Gethsemani, I'll meet with him. We're going to be down three priests until the ordination of our two transitional deacons. We need to talk about filling those vacancies. I'm going to have to appoint an administrator or a new rector. Are you free for lunch on Tuesday?"

"I can be free for lunch. I do have a couple other issues we need to discuss when it comes to clergy."

"How about Tuesday at noon? I'll have something brought into the chancery." The cardinal was already looking forward to the working lunch.

"Sounds good. Happy Easter. See you on Tuesday." Bishop Newsome ended their conversation.

After that long conversation, the cardinal needed to stand and stretch as the doctor encouraged him to exercise during the day. He checked for any new text messages and was happy there were none. Thankful for the call from Bishop Newsome, the cardinal was still worried about other information Monsignor Triplett might have shared. As much as he trusted and cared for Monsignor Triplett, the cardinal did not know this wheeler and dealer side of him the cardinal did not know. Taking money from the Delfinos to give to the cathedral staff was a great humanitarian decision, but Monsignor was breaking so many rules and could have really gotten himself in trouble with the church, not to mention the civil and criminal laws that he broke. He knew Monsignor Triplett always cared for others above himself, but this time, unfortunately, he had gone too far. He paid for it with his life.

Bishop Newsome decided to give his friend Abbot Choncko a call. Looking at his watch, he thought he could probably reach him now since it was after midday prayer. As luck would have it, after the first ring, the abbot answered.

"Abbot Choncko, this is Bishop George Newsome from New York."

"George, what a pleasant surprise. I just returned from our midday prayer. How are you?" The abbot and bishop had met several times at various meetings and became good friends.

"I'm fine, Sylvester. I need to ask a big favor."

"Doesn't everyone when they call the abbot? Go ahead."

"I need to send one of our priests to you for a thirty-day retreat. Is that possible?"

"All things are possible. Is he in trouble?"

"Nothing dealing with civil or criminal law. He needs an environment to re-examine his commitment to live a celibate life."

"I see…. You're thinking if you send him to the monastery, he can make the decision?"

"Sending him would allow him time for prayer and reflection—to focus in an atmosphere that would remove distractions for him."

"Well, you know this is not our mission to just help bishops with their problem priests?" The abbot was familiar with these requests from other diocesan bishops.

"I know. I just feel that with you, and the other monk's example, he would discern his vocation.... You could put him to work."

"Is he a good worker?" The abbot asked with a little sarcasm.

The bishop responded with a quick comeback. "I'll let you find out."

"And when do you want to send him?"

"How about within the next five days?"

"How about I talk it over with a few of the monks, and I'll be back in touch with you?"

"I understand. How much time do you think you will need?" Bishop Newsome knew the abbot would convince them.

"I'll let you know Monday, but you know we'll help you out anyway we can. I've just been burned in the past by a few bishops when I didn't know or they didn't share all the details. I don't believe you would do that to me but I have others who make me accountable, so let me talk with them."

"I completely understand. I do not think you will have any problems with this priest. When you have reached a final decision, please give me a call. Then we can catch up."

"I'd like to. I need to fill you in on a couple of things happening here." The abbot was facing some of his own problems.

"We will talk soon. Happy Easter, Sylvester and thank you."

Bishop Newsome felt settled about Father O'Hara going to Gethsemani, and he looked forward to a good lunch with Father McFadden. It had been a hectic and unfortunate morning—one he would not quickly forget. Suddenly, he was filled with remorse for the loss of his friend. He returned to the chapel to pray for Monsignor Triplett.

At the Women's Republican Club, Detective Pantera entered the room where Emma and Sam spent the night. He was in luck. They had not cleaned the room. In the trash can, he discovered an empty box for over-the-counter sleeping pills. He bagged the evidence. Once he finished, he and the police officer returned to the cathedral. He told Lieutenant Palmer what they found. Pleased with the good fortune of the discovery, Palmer made a notation of it in his notepad. The investigator took the evidence bag to the lab to check for fingerprints.

As Emma and Jonathan watched television, Jonathan was restless and said he needed to do laundry and organize his room.

"How about doing some homework?" Emma suggested with a grin. She was glad to have him back home and happy he wanted to do a few things for himself.

"I'll get to it."

Emma couldn't forget about Sam. She wondered how he was and if he went home to talk to his wife. She felt the urge to call him. But when she remembered the empty box of sleeping pills in the trash can she was afraid may have given them to her. The thought to call him quickly disappeared. The more she sat there, the more she wanted to talk to Palmer about those pills.

Jonathan walked out of his room with an armful of laundry. "Mom, are you okay?"

"I'm fine now, with you home. How about I help you with your laundry, and you get some homework done?" Emma needed a distraction to stay busy and stop thinking about Sam.

"One hour of homework, for one hour of playing the guitar?" Jonathan negotiated.

"A deal!" Emma smiled as she turned off the television and went to the washer in the kitchen to sort Jonathan's laundry. He was growing up so fast.

Brian McManius the organist employed by the cathedral graduated from Oberlin Conservatory of Music in Ohio sixteen years ago. He returned home to Omaha, Nebraska to be the organist at Saint Peter Parish. After working there for five years, he quit to pursue his dream to one day play in one of the prestigious churches in New York City. Determined to fulfill this dream, he packed his bags, left Nebraska and moved to New York. After three months of substituting at various churches of all denominations, his hope of gaining a full-time organist position did not look good.

About ready to give up and return home, Brian, went to Saint Jerome Church where Monsignor Stone was the celebrant for Sunday Mass. Hearing the beautiful pipe organ there and appreciating the inspiring words from the homily, Brian introduced himself to Monsignor Stone and explained his dilemma. Monsignor Stone looked at this six-foot tall, two hundred fifty-pound young man and thought his story was interesting. He introduced Brian to the organist who asked him to play. After hearing Brian play the organ, Monsignor Stone was so impressed he said he'd make a few calls to other priests who might be looking for a talented organist. Brian was most appreciative to Monsignor Stone, and one of those calls paid off.

About a week went by when Brian received a call from Saint Patrick's Cathedral for an interview. Two weeks later, after playing twice on the magnificent gallery organ, he was offered a position as a part-time organist, playing twice a month and as needed. He was thrilled with the position even though the salary was hardly fair. To supplement his income, he continued as an organist at several other churches. He waited and hoped eventually to have a full-time position in the city he truly loved.

With determination, hard work and the unexpected death of Saint Patrick's principal organist nine years ago, Brian was offered a full-time position. It meant an increase in salary, benefits and the prestige he felt he always deserved. He was living his dream.

Despite the success of his position at the cathedral, Brian was not having success anywhere else in his life. He tried dating, even with online dating services, but he could never find the right person. Depression followed as he became even more agitated regretting his lack of a social life. He also became more and more distant from his family and the few friends he did have.

To bring him some comfort, Brian bought a Siamese cat and named him Bach. Within two years it died, and he never fully got over that loss.

In the past year, Brian quit going to the gym and working out. He gained an additional fifty pounds. He tried various diets with no success. His doctor, his boss, several choir members and parishioners of the cathedral were very worried about him.

Recently, Brian was going through serious mood swings where he would come to a rehearsal all excited, and then at another, he came very depressed. Both moods affected the way he played at rehearsals and Sunday liturgies. These mood swings eventually created additional stress for the choir director.

Brian had gone through this emotional rollercoaster once before while in high school. A psychologist had helped him then, but now he thought he could handle it on his own. As much as he tried, the mood swings continued. The director of music, Dr. Andy DiBrisco, talked with him about it, but he wasn't having any success getting through to his organist. Finally, about three weeks ago, Dr. DiBrisco asked Monsignor Triplett to talk with Brian.

Brian was called to the rector's office for a meeting with Monsignor Triplett. He thought the meeting was to review the music for Holy Week. He was still upset that some organ pipes had been damaged in the cathedral's restoration. Brian was certain Monsignor Triplett didn't understand the damage done to the music and the liturgy itself with broken pipes. He decided to confront Monsignor about the repairs.

But Monsignor had a different agenda. He wanted to discuss Brian's anger issues. As soon as Brian entered the office, he demanded to know about the organ repairs. Before Monsignor could respond, he asked Brian several times to take a seat.

Brian finally sat down, but immediately exploded with anger continually demanding the organ be repaired immediately. Monsignor Triplett's attempts to calm Brian failed. He now saw what others were seeing. Suddenly, Brian calmed down, and the rector told him that unless he sought professional help to manage his emotions, particularly his bouts with rage, he would lose his job at the cathedral.

Without a word, Brian stood up, abruptly turned and left the rector's office, slamming the door behind him. Monsignor Triplett was visibly shaken and called for Brian to return as he had other items to discuss. Brian kept walking toward the front door, he stopped and instead went to Sam's office to talk to him about the meeting with Monsignor Triplett. Sam was the one, true friend he thought he had. Sam told Brian to take Monsignor's advice and get help, but Brian complained he didn't have the money to see a therapist. Sam assured him his health insurance would take care of a good percentage. Brian knew he was probably right, but he still didn't want to hear it.

"This is how I'm treated after eleven years of service?" Brian shouted.

Sam tried to reason with him. "You have been treated well, Brian."

"After talking with Monsignor Triplett, I don't feel appreciated. He just wants to get rid of me. Look at me! I'm fat, going bald, and it would just be easier to let me go!"

"Brian, Monsignor Triplett wants you to get the help you need to continue playing here at the cathedral. You're an outstanding organist." Sam tried to reassure Brian his position was safe but knew his hours would probably be reduced with the cuts to the budget coming in July, no matter what he did.

Brian shouted even louder. "I don't believe a word you're saying, Sam. I thought we were friends!"

"We are, but you've got to want to do something about your attitude and your weight. Monsignor Triplett needs to see you're trying. The tools are there." Sam pleaded, knowing he needed to take his own advice as he looked at his own pot belly stomach.

"Don't give me any of this crap!" Brian stormed out of Sam's office and the cathedral office. Brian wondered what he would do next. Something had to give.

Brian didn't remember much about the days that followed the meeting. He felt Monsignor Triplett and Sam were looking for ways to end his employment. Brian was determined to confront them both when they least expected it. He was working on a plan. He would take control. He'd make something happen. After he overheard a conversation the two men had, it gave Brian the opening to put his plan into action. He wouldn't let the opportunity get away.

Now sitting alone and uncertain of his future, Brian's phone buzzed. He didn't recognize the number and wasn't going to answer it, but then changed his mind.

"Hello?"

"Is this Brian McManius?"

"Yes, it is. Who's this?"

"This is Lieutenant Will Palmer from the NYPD."

"What can I do for you, Lieutenant?"

"Are you the organist for Saint Patrick's Cathedral?"

"I am." Brian presumed the lieutenant already had this information. He stayed calm waiting for the next question.

"I need you to come down to the cathedral."

"I was supposed to be there for choir practice this morning, but then I heard the news broadcast about Monsignor Triplett and was told not to come until this afternoon." Brian knew he had already made other plans.

Palmer insisted. "I think it would be important for you to come now. Whatever plans you may have, cancel them." In the background, he heard a faint PA announcement of a gate change and knew Brian was on the move.

"I'm not sure that's possible." Brian hung up on the lieutenant.

Immediately, Palmer called the station and had them send out an all-points bulletin to the airports, the train, subway and bus stations with a description of Brian McManius. After a quick search, the station officer reported Brian had no prior arrests, and there was no picture on file. The lieutenant needed to return to the parish house to see if the church had a photo in Brian's personnel file, or if there was a cathedral pictorial directory.

"Sorry guys. I've got to leave this for right now. Hold these last two pieces of evidence out until I get back. It shouldn't take long," Palmer instructed the crime scene investigators.

As Palmer left the cathedral, he noticed a man of slight build wearing a Delfino shirt. Even with headphones over the man's ears, Palmer could hear Hispanic music blaring. The man approached the uniformed officer at the side cathedral entrance and introduced himself as Jamie Avalos. Palmer approached that same door and heard it was Avalos. This was too coincidental.

The lieutenant instructed the police officer to contact Detective Sabor and relay the message for him to return to the cathedral to question Mr. Avalos. In the meantime, Palmer went to the parish house, knowing a possible suspect was on the run.

Chapter 29

Sara Brown finished the autopsy on Monsignor Steven Triplett and completed the necessary paperwork. As the chief medical examiner, she collected the essential specimens of the vital organs for the various tests to support the cause of death. Since this was a homicide, lab workers took pictures of the body for the investigators and for the DA to use at the court proceedings, if and when the case went to trial.

Detective Jabowski and Thom Triplett entered the building, and an assistant escorted them to the chief medical examiner's office. Sara introduced herself. "Mr. Triplett, by law, I need to ask you a few questions about the body you're about to identify."

"I understand."

"Are you the brother of Monsignor Steven Triplett?" She began.

"Yes... I'm his only living relative." Thom took out his driver's license and gave it to Sara.

Sara took the license and placed it on her copier to have the information for the records. Once she had the copy, she returned the license.

"Your brother's date of birth?"

"February 26, 1946."

"Any medical condition you're aware of?"

"He had high blood pressure. Our parents both died of heart attacks."

"Was he on medication?"

"Yes, he was."

"Do you know what it was?"

"I don't remember."

"Do you know who his doctor was?"

"Dr. J. Quinito."

"Thank you, Mr. Triplett. Let me take you to your brother." Sara and the two of them walked to the examination room. Thom was feeling a knot in his stomach preparing himself to identify his brother's body. This was not what he wanted to do the day before Easter. He would rather be enjoying breakfast they had planned.

The morgue was a cinder block, gray building that was at least thirty years old. The lighting was poor in the hallway. The building felt damp. The smell of chemicals filled the air. As they walked towards the viewing window, Sara tried to prepare Thom. "I know this will probably be tough for you, but I ask you to take a good deep breath to compose yourself knowing what you will see."

Thom realized this would be difficult. As he stood in front of the glass window, the coroner's assistant slowly pulled back the curtain. He saw a body covered with a heavy white sheet except for one foot and a tag dangling from a toe. Thom fought back the tears. He knew just by the uncovered foot it was his brother. He remembered Steven's feet were always larger, and when they were young, they joked about who would be the taller brother. Growing up, Steven always was.

Sara warned Thom that his brother's appearance would not be easy to see. She explained that because of the loss of blood and the trauma to the head, he would see the cracked skull, with two swollen eyes. Thom took another deep breath. The assistant lowered the sheet, and Thom saw the beaten face of his brother.

"Yes... yes, that's my brother... my best friend." Thom broke down and cried.

Sara gave him a moment to look at his brother and his wounds. This was always the part of the job she hated. It was never easy for a family member to identify the body. With compassion, she waited for questions Thom was sure to have.

Thom turned his back to the window. "Why did he have to die like this?"

"I believe there are two possibilities to your brother's death. Obviously, he suffered a brutal attack. However, my preliminary findings indicate he also suffered a heart attack. Was your brother under a lot of stress?"

"I think he was under a lot more these last few weeks. I know Holy Week is always stressful for him."

"Stress to the heart comes when one is under pressure and not taking medication regularly. Or it may have been triggered by the event that culminated in this trauma. I have ordered some laboratory tests to help determine the cause of the heart attack," Sara explained.

"How long will it take for you to know for certain?" Detective Jabowski inquired as Thom listened.

"I would say probably five days. In the meantime, maybe the detectives will find out more about the assault as they continue their investigation. I'll issue a death certificate indicating the cause of death as 'pending further study' until I get the lab results back. Then I'm not even sure I'll have a hundred percent certainty as to the final cause of death." Sara looked at Detective Jabowski.

"So that's it?" Thom looked at Sara hoping he was dreaming.

"No, I think you should know there is something more." Sara quietly revealed the news. "Your brother probably had cancer."

"Cancer? What?" Thom was surprised. "There's no cancer in our family!"

"Did your brother smoke?" Sara asked.

"In his college years, but he quit when he went into the seminary."

"Did he tell you he had cancer?"

"No, he never mentioned it." Thom shook his head as he tried to keep his composure.

"Do you think he was aware of his cancer?"

"I don't know. He gets a yearly check-up, usually in May."

"Probably just as well if he didn't know," Sara remarked. "I know lung cancer is not always the easiest to detect, and the treatment can be rather painful. Lung cancer cannot be cured. Your brother was probably in stage three. We found indications that it began to spread to the lymph nodes. When, and if he found out, I think he would have required chemotherapy and radiation almost immediately."

Thom was still processing this new information. "I don't know if my brother knew. He never said anything. He was never a good patient, and he would have hated knowing he had cancer."

Sara touched Thom's arm. "I'm truly sorry for your loss."

"So am I." Thom turned to take a last look at his brother's battered face. He placed his hand on the glass window, bowed his head and said a quiet prayer. When finished, he looked at Sarah, who nodded to the assistant to close the curtain.

"Which funeral home you will be using?" Sara asked.

"Frank Campbell Funeral Home. That's who buried my parents."

"If it's okay with you, I'd be glad to call them on your behalf and have them come for your brother's body."

"Thank you... thank you so much...." Thom spoke softly. "How will I get the final test results?"

Sara explained that she would inform Lieutenant Palmer, and then he would be the one to let him know. "Hopefully with the tests results, I can make a final determination of the cause of death and give you an amended death certificate. If you have any questions after that, please give me a call."

"I certainly will. Detective, I need to go back to Saint Patrick's to get a few items of clothing to give to the funeral home." Thom explained.

"Sure. I can take you back to the cathedral." Jabowski then turned to Sara. "I'll let Lieutenant Palmer know you'll call him."

"He's my next call," Sara assured Detective Jabowski.

The three walked back to the front entrance where they said their goodbyes. Thom's phone rang, and he looked at the caller ID to see it was Jennifer Gibson. He let it go to voicemail, knowing he needed some privacy to take this call. The ride back to the cathedral was a quiet one. Thom was deep in thought. He still couldn't believe his brother had cancer and a heart attack. He still wondered who had viciously attacked Steven.

Arriving at the cathedral at the side door entrance on 50th Street, Detective Sabor greeted Detective Jabowski and asked if he could help. Sabor informed Thom that Lieutenant Palmer would be with him in a few minutes and asked Thom to take a seat in a pew close by. Thom sat down, looked at the picture of Our Lady of Guadalupe and knelt. He offered a prayer for his brother hoping that he was with his parents in heaven.

As he sat back down, Thom retrieved the voicemail from Jennifer. "Thom, I wanted to see how you're doing. I'm here for you, and I want to help in any way I can. I'm so sorry for your loss. When you get a chance, call me."

Thom listened again just to hear her voice. It comforted him to know his brother's death saddened Jennifer. Thom knew Jennifer loved Steven too. Her lawyer persona was tough, but realized her Catholic faith was more important to her than the name recognition she achieved when she first confronted the archdiocese in a legal matter. Lately, she was willing to settle cases in mediation to achieve justice and fairness for those involved.

Thom remembered when he had introduced Jennifer to his brother, Monsignor Triplett. It was just a few months earlier. Monsignor told Jennifer he had just received information which could damage the archdiocese. Monsignor Triplett, unsure of how to proceed, sought her legal advice. He shared confidential information with her without revealing the parties involved.

She smiled gave the clergyman some free legal advice. "If it were my client, a feasible solution would be possible provided the cardinal was willing to participate. I wouldn't want someone to decide a case against the archdiocese in a courtroom where it would make the news." Nor did Monsignor Triplett. Jennifer explained that she had a client with a case against the archdiocese similar to what Monsignor Triplett had described and could offer no further advice except to say, "Usually clients want the situation corrected, and when it's resolved, they're willing to drop any other charges."

As Monsignor Triplett listened to Jennifer, he suddenly realized that the information he had was about her client. Monsignor knew he had to speak with the cardinal about the situation, but it would wait until after Easter. Monsignor Triplett hoped the cardinal would correct the situation and settle the matter through mediation.

Now Thom hoped his brother had safeguarded that information in the parish house or in his office. If the information discussed with Jennifer went public, it could cause a scandal in the church, hurting both the cardinal and the archdiocese.

Back at the morgue, Sara returned to her desk and her work. She called Lieutenant Palmer. The call went to voicemail which was unusual. She couldn't recall a time when she had to leave the lieutenant a message. She would try again in thirty minutes.

After leaving the Pickle's home, Father O'Hara finally arrived at the cathedral parish house. The police officer at the door asked Father Crumbley if Father O'Hara could come in.

"Yes, he used to live here." Father Crumbley welcomed Father O'Hara.

"I presume you are here to see Juan?" Father Crumbley asked.

"Is he up in his room?"

"Yes."

"I'll just go up." Father O'Hara didn't want to spend any time with Father Crumbley. Even though there was a brotherhood of priests, he was one brother he had a hard time with socially.

As Father O'Hara approached Father Morales' room, he noticed the door to Monsignor Black's room was open. Father O'Hara knocked on Monsignor's door, and then leaned into the room to say hello.

Monsignor Black looked up from his work at his desk. "David, good to see you! How are you? Come on in and sit for a moment." Father O'Hara entered the room and sat down.

"I'm doing okay. It's very sad about Monsignor Triplett. He was such a good person. Even with him carrying around that stupid notebook, I'll miss him," Father O'Hara said.

"I will as well. Even though I didn't want to come here, he treated me well, and I'll always be thankful in the final days of my priesthood."

"Final days? You're not dying? Are you?"

"No, but one never knows at my age."

"You know your friend is leaving." Father O'Hara was referring to Father Morales. Monsignor Black and Father Morales had a good relationship living in the parish house together.

"I kind of guessed it when I saw him pulling out boxes." Monsignor Black worried for the both of them as he played with the pen on his desk.

"He asked me to come over and help."

384

"And if you're smart…, you'd say goodbye and end this relationship." Monsignor Black emphasized his last three words. Father O'Hara had never heard him speak this way to him before.

"I know, but…."

Monsignor abruptly interrupted… "There is no but. You are a good priest. You have helped so many. This has to be your priority if your priesthood means anything to you. Take this advice from an old man. You're running out of chances. Besides don't you want Juan to remain a good priest?"

Father O'Hara appreciated Monsignor's words. "I want both of us to be good priests. And I know this could be our last chance."

"Then say your goodbyes. You two get the help you need and let God do the rest."

"It's easier said than done." Father O'Hara quickly stood. He said goodbye and wished Monsignor Black a Blessed Easter. Walking down the hall to Father Morales' room, Father O'Hara knew what the old priest said was correct.

Father O'Hara knocked on the door. "Juan, it's David." The door immediately opened. Juan was in his gym shorts and Yankee's shirt. He looked terrible. It was obvious he'd been crying for some time. Entering the room, Father O'Hara closed the door. Juan resisted wrapping his arms around the person he loved.

"Juan. It's going to be okay." Father O'Hara tried to believe the words he was saying.

Father Morales pointed to the boxes, books, papers and clothes scattered about. "Look at my mess!"

"It looks like you're doing pretty good in packing."

"I'm just throwing things in boxes. I don't want to go. I want to stay. I'm not sure I can do what the cardinal is asking."

"Juan, we've got to move on. Staying together wouldn't be good for either of us. My priesthood is too important to me. Your vocation has to be the most important thing for you too.

385

I really think you need to embrace this opportunity the cardinal is giving you to further your studies. You may enjoy it."

"I know what you're saying. It's just all happening so fast. I never thought twenty-four hours ago I would be packing to move out of the cathedral." Father Morales put a few more books into a box.

"Juan, you know deep down inside this is what you need. It's going to help you be a better priest. We've been given a reality check. What we have is not going to last in today's world. And for either of us to think it would, only means disappointment."

"I don't believe what you are saying!" Father Morales was stunned at how easily the words came from Father O'Hara.

"It's the truth. I'm saying it for the good of both of us. This hurts me just as much as it is hurting you."

"So you don't love me?" Father Morales was uncertain why he even asked. He clearly saw the answer in Father O'Hara's eyes.

"Far from it! I do love you and would do almost anything for you, but you know I love the priesthood more. And if you're honest with yourself, so do you. That's why, as much as this hurts, it's time to move forward as priests for the archdiocese."

"I don't know if I can. You've been there to help me so much. I'm going to feel the loss and emptiness."

"And that's why I'm encouraging you to get help when you're faced with that emptiness, loneliness and depression. Each of us has to deal with it—and it will not be in another relationship. If we want to be good priests, God must be first."

"So you've become a philosopher all of a sudden? I'm... I'm sorry. I don't know what I am saying."

"You'll be fine Juan. I was just reminded by a sixteen-year-old kid to put God first. He helped me refocus my priorities."

"How are the Pickles doing?" Father Morales knew the family's situation.

"Jonathan is home, which is good. Emma is trying to work out things in her life. And with the loss of Monsignor Triplett, I'm concerned she doesn't have someone to confide in."

"What about Sam?"

"So you know?" Father O'Hara was surprised.

"Monsignor Black told me."

"I think she ended it today."

"Seems to be a day of ended relationships." Father Morales half-jokingly remarked.

Father O'Hara tried to reassure him. "Juan, ours hasn't ended. I hope we will always be friends, brothers, and good priests to help each other. But we need to have a platonic relationship if we want to remain faithful priests for the archdiocese."

"I hope so." Father Morales tried to compose himself. "You want to help me pack?"

"That's one of the reasons I came over. Juan, I'll always love you." Father O'Hara approached Juan with arms opened.

"I know." Father Morales looked into the eyes of the one who knew him the best—thankful for the hug.

"Juan, when you get settled in Rome, please find someone to help you. See a psychologist, a priest, even a non-believer, but see someone to talk about what you are going through."

"The same for you, David." Father Morales was optimistic that Father O'Hara would.

"Let's get you packed up! There's an empty storage closet at Holy Name of Jesus, and I'll see if your stuff can go there. Don't worry about it. I'll take care of it later this week, just let Monsignor Black know."

"Thanks... thanks so much...." Father Morales placed his personal items in stacks to go in their designated boxes.

"The sooner we get this all boxed up the sooner I can get back to the parish house and help with the preparations for tonight," Father O'Hara urged. For the next thirty minutes, they talked about their independent futures and their hopes to keep celibate lives. With Father O'Hara's help, they slowly organized, and packed Father Morales's room.

Lieutenant Palmer returned to the parish house and found Father Crumbley in the living room, breviary in hand, trying to say his midday prayers. Father Crumbley wanted to continue watching and listening to those who were coming and going in the parish house. He had never had such a busy Saturday.

"Father Crumbley, I'm sorry to bother you, but I need a picture of your organist." Palmer pulled out his notebook to find the name. "Your organist — Brian McManius."

"He should be in one of our pictorial directories. Let me get it." Father Crumbley excused himself and quickly went to find the book.

A few minutes later, he was back holding the directory with a picture of Brian McManius sitting at the gallery organ. Palmer realized Brian was a big person and might have struggled on the scaffolding.

"Do you know his height or weight, Father Crumbley?"

"He is taller than I am, and I'm almost six feet. He is heavier today than when this picture was taken. He's probably over 300 pounds now, but that's only a guess. I say that because I've seen him put on the pounds. He even had an extra fan up at the gallery organ because he really does sweat a lot."

"That helps. Do you know if he would want Monsignor Triplett dead?" Palmer thought if there was a reason, Father Crumbley would know.

"All I know is Monsignor Triplett gave him a couple of weeks off right after the first of the year. Father Morales told me Monsignor Triplett gave Brian the time off because he wasn't taking his medication properly. I'm not sure what medication. Talk with Father Morales about it. He's back in the house," Father Crumbley said.

"Would you mind getting Father Morales for me?" Palmer yawned realizing he needed something to drink. "Could I ask one more favor. Can I get a cup of coffee, black?" "I just made a fresh pot. Coming right up!" Father Crumbley left and quickly returned with a cup of coffee. Then he went to get Father Morales.

Palmer placed the directory on the end table and took a picture of Brian McManius' photo with his cell phone. He immediately sent it along with a brief physical description to the dispatch officer who sent an APB to "…arrest Brian McManius on suspicion of murder. Approach with caution. May become violent…"

Father Morales returned to the living room. He wondered what the lieutenant needed. He thought he had told everything he knew. "How can I help you, Lieutenant Palmer?"

The lieutenant didn't waste time. "Do you know if Brian McManius would want Monsignor Triplett dead?"

Father Morales paused and tried to remember if there was anything that might help. "Well, once I overheard a conversation with Monsignor Triplett and Brian right after Christmas. Monsignor Triplett was unhappy with Brian's unprofessional manner. Monsignor made some reference to taking his medication, and Brian said he wasn't. The next thing I know Monsignor Triplett gave Brain a couple of weeks off. After last night's Good Friday Stations of the Cross service, Monsignor was so angry that Brian had messed up the music for the liturgy again."

"Would you say Brian hasn't been himself for the last few months then?" Lieutenant Palmer asked.

"I'd say that's a fair statement," Father Morales replied.

"Is there anything else you can tell me regarding Brian?" Lieutenant Palmer remembered Thom Triplet was waiting for him, and he had to get back to the cathedral.

"That's really all I know," Father Morales said as Father Crumbley returned to the living room.

Lieutenant Palmer welcomed the second cup of coffee from Father Crumbley. "And you Father Crumbley, was there anything else you can tell me concerning Mr. McManius?"

"Well, a couple of times I hear him when he was in Monsignor's office. Brian would get furious when asked to make changes to the music he had selected with our choir director. Monsignor was extremely patient with him. And unfortunately, too many times Monsignor gave in to Brian. Monsignor told me once, 'it was for the good of the church.' He knew which battles to take on and which ones to let go. You may want to ask Monsignor Black," Father Crumbley suggested.

"Would you mind getting him for me?"

"Not at all. I believe he's in his room." Father Crumbley headed back up the stairs.

"If have no more questions for me, I'd like to return to my room. I have more packing to do in a very short time." Father Morales wanted to be alone.

"Thanks for the information, Father Morales. That's all I need, for now."

While Palmer waited, he reflected on the telephone conversation with Mr. McManius remembering the noise in the background. He felt sure the organist was fleeing the city and possibly the country. Even with the APB, he wondered if it was too late.

Monsignor Black entered the living room and closed the door. He was surprised the lieutenant wanted to talk with him again.

"Yes, lieutenant, how can I help you?"

"I'd like for you to look at a photo I found."

Curious about the photo, Monsignor Black put on his glasses as the lieutenant produced a picture on his phone. Monsignor Black looked at it. "My God, where did you get that?"

Chapter 30

Kurt Barbertie was a successful attorney for Kripp, Pulp, and Hosenbahm law firm. He worked for them for the last eight years and was looking forward to becoming a partner. He carried a full load of criminal law cases in Manhattan which meant often pleading for lenient sentences for his clients. He found reward in what he was doing, but at the same time, it disheartened him with the number of people who ruined lives by taking the law into their own hands.

When Sam Tolden called, asking him to come to the cathedral parish house, Kurt felt somewhat obligated to help his former high school classmate. They had played basketball together all four years of high school. After one of their last games, Kurt and Sam went to a liquor store. Kurt was friends with the owner and had no problem in purchasing any liquor whenever he wanted, but this night the police had the store under surveillance. When the police caught Sam with the bottle, he took the blame for it and was charged with underage possession of alcohol. Kurt avoided any charges. He was thankful to Sam, and now it appeared he had the chance to return the favor.

Kurt worried that Sam needed a criminal lawyer. He turned on the television and listened to the news conference with Police Commissioner Timberbank and Cardinal Flinn. Hearing the news and realizing there was a priest dead, he wondered if this was the reason Sam called. Getting up, he saw the cup of coffee sitting next to the half-finished crossword puzzle from the paper. His wife had been up for an hour and already exercised, made the coffee and solved what she could of *The New York Times* crossword puzzle. She had left the rest for him to finish. After a cup of coffee, he quickly dressed, told his wife his plans for the day, kissed her goodbye and headed uptown.

He arrived at the entrance to Saint Patrick's Cathedral and identified himself. A police officer escorted him to the parish house. He was surprised by the number of officers and detectives on the scene.

Once in the house, another police officer promptly escorted Kurt to the library. As Kurt entered the room, he saw Sam looking tired, worried and scared. He had never seen his friend like this. He thanked the officer and closed the door, took out a legal pad to take notes and set up his phone to record their conversation.

"Sam, I'm sorry you had to wait so long for me to arrive," Kurt began. "This had better be good. It took me two hours to get here. The 1 line had a thirty-minute delay. I heard the press conference this morning about the priest's death here at the cathedral."

"Monsignor Triplett," Sam mumbled his words as he wet his lips. He needed water.

"Yes... so is that his name... Monsignor Triplett? Do you know anything about it?" Kurt asked.

"Will you be my attorney?" Sam quickly asked.

"Well, of course, I'll take your case... if it comes to that. What's going on?" Kurt was concerned with his friend's obvious dilemma.

"I met with Monsignor Triplett this morning. I think I might be responsible for his death." He held his head in his hands and drew a deep breath. He stood and began pacing back and forth in the small library.

"Why do you say that?"

"Because I saw him die, Kurt! I did nothing to save him. Monsignor was gasping for air... and then he was hit over the head with a candlestick," Sam nervously exclaimed.

"Slow down. Slow down. Calm yourself. Take a deep breath. Come back and sit down. I'm not sure what you're saying." Kurt was totally confused and astounded.

Sam walked slowly back to his seat opposite Kurt and tried to explain. "You see... Monsignor Triplett and I agreed to meet this morning... early... since I was trying to leave town with my girls for spring break. As hectic as Holy Week is, Monsignor Triplett was happy to meet at 6:30 a.m. He said he was meeting someone at 6:00 this morning in the cathedral."

"On the day before Easter?"

"I tried several times during the last two weeks to get Monsignor to make some decisions about reducing staff. He procrastinated and finally told me he would have an answer before Easter. That's one reason for the meeting." Sam rubbed his hands nervously as he explained.

"And the second reason?"

"It was dealing with my personal life." Sam looked up at Kurt ready to tell him everything.

"Just take your time."

Sam continued. "The cathedral was having financial difficulties. The income from the Sunday collections was down, and Monsignor thought the restoration was the reason. With less money, Monsignor Triplett had no choice but to cut staff. As for my personal life, I'm... I mean... I was having an affair with one of the staff members, and some parishioners recently found out."

"I can't believe you, Sam!" Kurt exclaimed, again with disbelief. "I thought you had a wonderful marriage with your wife, Jean."

"She is wonderful. We drifted apart, and it's all my fault!" Sam sounded dejected.

Kurt wondered what other information Sam would share. "Continue. You planned to meet...."

"So I arrived at the cathedral a little early. I went straight to my office and picked up the papers I needed, so we could talk about the staff cuts. Monsignor Triplett told me he didn't want to discuss this in the office around staff. Monsignor had struggled with the decision of which staff members would be terminated at the end of June."

"Then what happened after you got the papers from your office?"

"I came into the church through the priest's sacristy. I walked up the stairs, and as I was about to enter the sanctuary, I heard Monsignor Triplett and someone else talking about a safe key. I looked out into the cathedral, and it was Monsignor Stone. Suddenly, I saw Brian come up behind them, and he hit Monsignor Stone over the head with the candlestick from the altar."

"Who is Brian?"

"Brian McManius. He's... he's... the cathedral organist."

"And where did he come from?"

"I don't know. I swear. He just came out of the darkness and was behind him."

"What happened next?"

"When Brian hit Monsignor Stone over the head, Monsignor Triplett collapsed on the first pew. I couldn't see if Brian had hit Monsignor Triplett or not. You have to know... Brian must weigh... 300 pounds. I couldn't see around him. The next thing I saw was Brain dragging Monsignor Stone to the side entrance doors. He picked him up and carried him outside."

"Where were you?" Kurt couldn't believe what he was hearing.

"I was just standing there... in the back of the sanctuary... frozen... I couldn't move." Sam admitted.

"Did you say anything or do anything while this happened?"

"No, I didn't... I couldn't... I was too scared. God forgive me.... I was so scared.... After Brian took Monsignor Stone out, I ran over to Monsignor Triplett in the front pew. He was

394

barely breathing. I wanted to call 911, but I couldn't find my phone. I had left it in the office. I was in a panic. I didn't know what to do. Then Brian came back in the cathedral." Sam was back on his feet and started pacing the floor again.

"And what did you do then?" Kurt listened carefully and watched his friend.

"Nothing, Kurt. I crawled under the pew as quickly as I could to the first pillar, looked out, holding my breath. I didn't know what Brian was going to do. Brian just stood in front of the first pew. Then he took the candlestick and held it over Monsignor's head. Oh God, Brian... Brian... hit Monsignor with the candlestick." Exhausted and distraught, Sam sat down and looked at Kurt. "I... I... ran out from behind the pillar and started yelling at Brian to stop."

"Then what happened?"

"Brian didn't hear me. He was an animal. He hit Monsignor again in the face with the candlestick."

"So Brian hit Monsignor Triplett twice with the candlestick?"

"At least twice."

"Then what happened?"

"I tried to push Brian away from Monsignor Triplett. It surprised him to see me. He took a swing at me with the candlestick and missed. I punched him in the face. I think I broken his nose. I hit him again until he dropped the candlestick. You know, it's like he was suddenly aware of what happened; ...like he finally knew what he'd done. Then he collapsed on the floor with a look of panic on his face staring at the candlestick."

Kurt had already given up on taking notes. "Continue." He let his cell phone record Sam's story. He knew Sam would have to repeat his story.

"I looked at Monsignor Triplett lying in the pew and tried to find a pulse but couldn't. There was nothing. Then I saw blood dripping from his head to the pew and the floor."

"And where was Brian?"

"I looked up and saw him walking toward the front doors. I could hear him crying."

"So, what did you do?" Kurt is stunned by Sam's story.

"Something stupid. I took the bloody candlestick and hid it behind a pillar near the archbishop's chair." Sam saw Kurt's look of disbelief. "I wasn't thinking."

"But...why?"

"Brian was... my friend, and I... I... thought I'd be helping him. I... I wasn't thinking. I had to try and find that key!"

"What key?"

"The key to the safe where Monsignor Triplett had something I needed to get. I knew he had the key." Sam looked at Kurt with a blank stare.

"So instead of calling the police, you were looking for a key! A key that opened a safe that had something you needed?" Kurt tried to put the pieces of Sam's confession together.

"Yes, I'll try... I'll explain." Sam continued. "I needed to find the key... I felt so desperate.... I was thinking maybe it was on Monsignor Triplett in one of his pockets. I tried to get into the front of his coat, but the way Monsignor Triplett was positioned on the pew I couldn't... I needed help. I yelled to Brian but saw him disappear under the scaffolding."

"Then what happened?"

"I heard the side door of the cathedral opening. I took off. I ran through the sanctuary and back down the steps to the priest's sacristy and locked the door."

"And Brian?"

"I don't know."

"Let me get this straight, Sam. Monsignor Triplett dead is dead on the front pew. You have no clue where the other priest, Monsignor Stone went. You touched and hid the candlestick that Brian used. You attempted to find a key to some safe. Afterwards, you hid in the sacristy? Sam, what's in that safe that's so important to you?"

Sam struggled for words. He sat there and listened to his lawyer recount how stupid he'd been. "Monsignor Triplett has... dirt on me. It was information I needed. If I had the key, then I'd be closer to getting it."

"And you know where this safe is?"

"No. I just wasn't thinking. God, Kurt, I'd just seen two men killed by a crazy man, and all I was worried about was a key to a safe and some papers that could ruin my life... and others too." Sam ranted avoiding eye contact with Kurt. "I know I messed up. I feel responsible that Monsignor is dead. I should have done something! Those papers... Those damn papers weren't worth a life. Kurt, I really need your help."

Kurt quickly analyzed the gravity of the situation and spoke honestly to Sam. "Listen to me. They could charge you as an accomplice to a murder. Do you realize that?"

"I know. I... I don't understand why Brian was there."

"He knew about the meeting?"

"Yes. I told him, but I never expected him to be there! He was probably one of the staff members who was going to have his hours cut or even lose his job. He was furious. I said I'd talk with Monsignor Triplett first and see what I could do to help him. He said he'd wait for my call. But he didn't wait... he just showed up!"

"Tell me more about Brian."

"He's the head organist. Been here for about ten or eleven years. Over six-feet-tall and easily a hundred pounds overweight. Lately, there have been some issues with him. He hasn't had the best attitude or been very cooperative. There were concerns about his health and issues with him staying on his meds. In fact, he was so far off his meds a few months ago, Brian got time off to get better. Then, when Monsignor Triplett tried to talk to him about his bad attitude and health problems, Brian just got more upset."

"Did it sound like he was upset enough to kill Monsignor?"

"Why didn't he just let me talk with Monsignor Triplett? When I saw Brian holding the candlestick, I... I just panicked. I was thinking more about myself and what Monsignor Triplett had on me and was going to do."

"That is the least of your worries now!" Kurt was very worried for Sam. "You had better pray a heart attack came before the candlestick."

Sam held his head in his hands knowing his life was destroyed and started crying.

"I take it when you touched the candlestick to move it, your fingerprints are on it?"

"Yes… along with Brian's."

"Sam, have you spoken to Brian since this morning?"

"I haven't."

"And when you left, you went back down the stairs to the priests' sacristy and did what?"

"I locked the door, then went through the sacristy to the office where I had to turn the alarm off! I went back into my office, got my phone and got the papers I wanted to present to Monsignor Triplett. I reset the alarm and left."

"Did anyone see you?"

"I don't think so." Sam didn't remember seeing anything around.

"Sam, do you know anything about the other priest… Monsignor Stone?"

"No… Palmer didn't mentioned anything about him. I don't know if he's dead or alive? I'm really worried, but I was afraid to ask. I need to know. I can't be involved in two priests' death!" Sam was frantic now, beating his hands on his head.

"Sam, calm yourself. I'll ask the lieutenant when he returns. In the meantime, where did you go when you left the church offices?" Kurt needed more information.

"I went back to the Women's Republican Club where I spent the night."

"Alone?"

"No, I wasn't alone. I was with Emma Pickle."

"Who is Emma Pickle?"

"The woman I love, Kurt. She's also the housekeeper for the cathedral."

Kurt thought he had heard everything. But now… this was another revelation. "Sam… Sam… This is getting more… a lot more complicated. Did she hear you leave or come back?"

"No… That evening I crushed up a sleeping pill and put it in her glass of wine. She'd had a rough week and needed to get a good night's sleep. And I didn't want to have to explain my early morning meeting."

"What do you mean?" Kurt couldn't believe what he was hearing. This was not the Same Tolden he knew or thought he knew.

"Let me explain. Her teenage son ran away from home, and Emma really wasn't sleeping well this past week. She didn't know about my meeting with Monsignor Triplett, and I didn't want to tell her. I wanted to be sure she didn't wake up when I left."

"So, you return to the room and find the woman you think you love, that you drugged, still asleep?" Kurt took some notes and shook his head. He wondered how many more shocking surprises he would hear.

Sam was exhausted but continued. "Yes… I took a shower, put my bloody clothes and shoes in my duffel bag and then slid into bed pretending to be asleep until my phone rang. It was the lieutenant calling me to come to the cathedral."

"And what did you tell the lieutenant?"

"When he called, I told him I'd be there in an hour. I needed some time to talk with Emma. My head was spinning. I was so confused and scared. I knew I had to go because if I didn't, it would have looked even more suspicious."

"What time was this?"

"He called about 8:30 a.m. I got to the cathedral shortly after 9:30 a.m."

"What have you told the lieutenant?"

"I told him about the people who have keys to the various buildings, my role at the cathedral, what I know about the budget cuts, how long I'd worked here and about my relationship with Monsignor Triplett. Then he asked me about the last time I saw Monsignor and that's when I asked for a lawyer."

Kurt was in disbelief, tapping his pen on his notepad... "Smart thinking. Sam, I... I thought you had a wonderful wife... and great kids?"

"I have two wonderful girls who are both in college. Since they left, Jean, and I have been distant from one another. Jean reminds me over and over again of her personal wealth. But she is so wrapped up in herself that she hasn't communicated with me for a long time. We've drifted apart. She does her various charity events and enjoys the notoriety, especially at the cardinal's yearly gathering." Sam didn't know where the thought came from, but he suddenly remembered Kurt was at his wedding.

"Sam, let me deviate for a moment and say... Jean is someone you don't want to lose. You need her now with what you're facing. Seek forgiveness.... I believe she still loves you."

"I hear what you're saying." Sam knew the relationship with Emma wasn't going to last. Kurt was right. Despite the problems, Sam still had strong feelings for his wife.

"Let me ask you. Does Emma know you're involved in this death?"

"She knows nothing. I haven't seen or heard from her since she left the hotel. I'm desperate. I need help! Help me! What am I going to do?"

"You will not say anything to anyone unless I'm present. Not anyone. No Emma, not Jean. Do you understand?"

"I do."

"Is there anything you haven't told me?"

"I've told you the truth."

"I want to go back to this key you were searching for. Why is it so important?" Kurt referred to his notes.

"Monsignor Triplett knew everything about everyone. He kept notes in a small notebook he carried with him. He was great at getting what he wanted. He could manipulate people."

"Did he manipulate you?"

"He tried, but he needed me. Or at least I thought he needed me. He worked to protect the church and himself. If you could help him, then you were in. But once you couldn't, he put you aside. I think he was trying to manipulate me at the end."

"Why do you say that?"

"He planned this early meeting and told me I would receive the damaging information he had on me. I had no choice. I had to go. If I pushed back against his attempt at manipulating me and didn't show up this morning, he'd have an excuse to fire me. He already had an excuse anyway—my affair with Emma."

"Another reason to end that relationship." Kurt was wishing that was Sam's only problem.

"Monsignor Triplett normally didn't mess with me. Despite my indiscretion, the headaches with the construction and Brian's problems, I just think something more was going on with him." Sam speculated.

"What do you mean something was going on? Do you know what it was?" Kurt looked at Sam grasping for something that could help his client.

"I wish I did. Like I said, he didn't normally play games with me. All I know is there were lots of appointments away from the cathedral. Some of us thought they might be doctor appointments. Monsignor Triplett just wasn't himself."

"I'm not sure I follow you."

Sam was exhausted and struggled to get the words out—"Lately he was coughing more. I... I think it was from the medicine he was taking. He had medical issues but kept them private."

"Would he have shared them with anyone?"

"Not any of us. The closest person to him was his brother, Thom."

His attorney made a note to contact the brother.

It had been over thirty minutes, and Sara still hadn't reached Lieutenant Palmer. Finally, Palmer answered his phone. Sara explained the findings from the autopsy. She reiterated the information she gave to his brother— preliminary findings showed the assault could have been the catalyst for a heart attack. Even with this supposition, she would sign a death certificate 'pending further study'.

Sara had a few questions for Palmer. "When his room was searched, did they find any medicine?"

"Yes, I'm looking in my notes. He had a prescription for 40 mg of Lisinopril. Did I say that correctly doc?"

"Not bad. You're getting good at this."

"I know one pill was sitting on the nightstand out from the rest of the bottle. Maybe he forgot to take it. Would missing one pill be enough to cause a heart attack?"

"No, but if he wasn't taking them regularly to keep his blood pressure down, then he did increase his chances of a heart attack. Do you have the name of the doctor on the prescription?" Sara asked.

"It is J. Quinito."

"Where is the bottle now?"

"It's with the rest of the evidence in the cathedral."

"You can be a big help Lieutenant if you find the date on the prescription and the number of pills in the bottle."

"I'll do that and call you right back." Palmer immediately contacted Detective Sabor. He asked him to find the bottle, and get the information needed.

Sabor called back within two minutes. "Will, the date filled was April 2 for thirty pills."

"That was two weeks ago yesterday, so he should have 16 pills left. Would you mind counting the remaining pills?"

Dumping the pills on a table, Sabor slowly counted them. "I count 21." He counted again, as he placed them back in the bottle. "Yes, 21 pills left."

"Then he wasn't taking them on a regular basis. I need to call Sara."

Within a minute the chief medical examiner was back on the phone, and Palmer relayed the details to her.

"I'll call Dr. Quinito. Also, the deceased had lung cancer. I'm not sure if the detective who escorted his brother to the morgue passed that information to you."

"Did his brother, Thom know?"

"He didn't seem to," Sara replied. "If I find out anything more, I'll call you."

"Thanks." Palmer knew she was still gathering information to determine the cause of death. He also knew the prosecutor's case would rely in great part on her findings.

The call to Dr. Quinito was answered by his after-hours service who informed Sara he was away on vacation. She briefly explained the circumstances. She asked for the service to contact him and return her call. She hoped the doctor knew Monsignor Triplett well enough and was willing to say how long his patient had been on high blood pressure medicine. More importantly, did the doctor know his patient had cancer?

With a fresh cup of coffee in hand, Palmer went to the library and found a very distressed Sam Tolden with his attorney looking over several pages of notes.

Kurt stood and offered his hand to the lieutenant. "Hi… I'm Kurt Barbertie, representing Sam Tolden."

"Lieutenant Will Palmer." He returned the handshake. "I'd like to ask your client a couple of questions as we move forward with this investigation."

"Go right ahead, but I might tell Sam to refuse to answer."

"I need to ask you, how much money have the Delfinos paid you?"

Sam looked panic stricken. He didn't move or speak. He hadn't told his attorney anything about the paybacks from the Delfinos or Monsignor Triplett. It had slipped his mind. He had been thinking only of the brutal attack and the escape from the cathedral.

Kurt saw the look. "I will advise my client not to answer that question at this time."

"So they did pay you money?" Palmer was determined to get some type of response.

"Again, I advise my client not to answer any questions regarding the Delfinos."

Palmer, displeased, continued. "Let me change to another subject. Why was there an empty box that contained a bottle of over-the-counter sleeping pills and tissues in the trash can in your room at the Women's Republican Club?"

"Again, I'm going to direct my client not to answer your question."

Sam took the glass of water with both of his shaky hands to get a drink before the lieutenant asked his next question.

Palmer was growing more irritated by the non-responses. "Do you know where Brian McManius is right now?"

Sam looked up. "I don't know where he is."

"When was the last time you saw him?"

Sam looked at his lawyer, who gave a nod to answer the question. "This morning."

"Where?"

"In the cathedral."

"And I think that's where we're going to stop," Kurt interrupted. "Unless you're going to arrest my client, he is finished answering questions."

"Would you please stand up Mr. Tolden?" Palmer directed.

"I'm placing you under arrest for the murder of Monsignor Steven Triplett. You have the right to remain silent. Anything you say can and will be used against you in a court of law. You have the right to speak to an attorney, and to have an attorney present during questioning. If you cannot afford one, an attorney will be provided for you. Do you understand these rights?"

Sam looked at Kurt. "I do." With tears falling down his checks, Sam asked his attorney to call his wife and Emma. He had already given the numbers to him knowing something like this might happen.

"Mr. Barbertie, you're welcome to visit with your client at the police station. I'm not sure with the Easter holiday when he'll appear before the judge, but the clerk will be in touch with you." Lieutenant Palmer placed the handcuffs on Sam.

Palmer called for two uniformed police officers to come to the parish house and escort Mr. Tolden to the police station for booking. He knew they would inform Detective Sabor of the arrest. He thanked Officer VanDyke who had been stationed at the library door and asked him to return to the cathedral and escort Tom Triplett to the parish house. Thom was waiting to get a few items from Monsignor Triplett's room to take to the funeral home.

Father Crumbley saw Sam leaving with the police officers, and he rushed into the library. "Is Sam the one who murdered Monsignor Triplett?"

"He's under arrest," Palmer said. "Is there anything you can tell me?"

"No. I wish I knew something, but I don't. I like Sam." Father Crumbley sat down at the table.

Palmer took a seat. "I'd like to ask you a few more questions about the organist. Did you ever see any fighting between Brian and Monsignor Triplett?"

"You mean physical fighting?" Father Crumbley was surprised by the question and wanted clarification.

"Yes."

"No. That's not in Monsignor Triplett's nature."

"Do you know if Brian has family in the city?"

"His family is in Nebraska... I think. I'm not sure. All I know is he lives by himself. Why? Do you think Brian is involved too?"

"Just looking for information." Palmer spoke casually while writing intently in his notepad.

"This is a terribly sad day for the cathedral." Father Crumbley shook his head and said a silent prayer.

"And for the Catholic Church," Lieutenant Palmer added as he got up from his chair and thanked Father Crumbley.

Palmer walked into the hallway to find Thom Triplett with Officer VanDyke. The lieutenant told Thom to remove only the clothes needed for the funeral. To do anything more in the room would have to wait. Thom understood.

"Could I also try to locate his funeral papers? I know in my discussions with him he had done some planning for it." Thom asked knowing he had a copy at the office of the will.

"Do you know where your brother kept his papers?" Palmer asked.

"Yes... He told me had had placed them inside a specific book, *The Code of Canon Law*. As his lawyer, he always told me to look there. And I might want to take a photograph or two to use."

"Interesting... if you find the papers, have Officer VanDyke look at the material and notate the items you take." Palmer directed wondering why Monsignor Triplett put such important papers in a book instead of his safe.

"Thank you, Lieutenant Palmer."

The lieutenant was thinking of the other papers that were found in Monsignor Triplett's safe. He was eager to get back to the cathedral to review this evidence hoping it would help with the investigation.

"Have I answered all of your questions, Thom?" Palmer asked.

"You have, lieutenant. I'll get what I need and be on my way. Thanks again for all your assistance."

As Officer VanDyke and Thom walked towards the stairs, Palmer walked to the front door to leave and left to return to the cathedral. Standing outside, he considered getting something to eat from a side street vendor. He had reached his coffee limit. But before he could step up to the vendor, Sabor walked outside the cathedral door and approached Palmer with the news. They still hadn't found Brian McManius.

Regrettably, both lunch and a look at any more evidence would have to wait. Finding Brian McManius had to come first. The lieutenant's phone rang. He looked at the screen and was surprised at the caller.

Chapter 31

Brian McManius was furious when Sam Tolden told him he was being let go from the staff because of budget cuts. Each of these two robust men loved what the work they did for the church and felt Monsignor Triplett did not appreciate their contributions.

A little over a week ago while they were at lunch, Sam and Brian tried to figure out a way they could save their positions at Saint Patrick's. Sam told Brian of the upcoming meeting with Monsignor Triplett. When Brian found out when they were meeting, he began making his own plans. Brian figured it was time for him to be in charge, to look out for himself. Those plans went horribly wrong as soon as he had put them into action. Now he was on the run.

As Brian arrived at Kennedy airport, he remembered all that had happened. What should have been a discussion between three rational people turned into a senseless tragedy. Why had he snapped like that? He knew he had to get out of town — out of the country — as soon as possible. He took his passport and depleted his savings account at several ATM's. He put his laptop in a carry-on and some clothes in a suitcase. He hoped to slip out of the country on a flight to the Caribbean. He wanted to be sitting on the beach rather than in a six by six-foot cell.

After abruptly hanging up on Lieutenant Palmer, Brian was determined to book a flight to the island of Saint Thomas. Standing in the long line at the Delta counter, crowded with spring breakers, as well as business travelers, Brian tried to appear calm while waiting. In front of him was an international passenger who was taking a great deal of time with the airline representative. Finally, the agent sent the confused tourist to a supervisor who spoke Portuguese. Brian realized Brazil could be another destination to consider if he ever made it up to the counter.

"How can I help you today?" The Delta agent asked with a smile on her face as she signaled him forward.

"I would like a one-way ticket to Saint Thomas on your 2:00 p.m. flight today," Brian tried to remain calm.

The agent immediately checked her computer terminal. "That's Delta flight 1233, leaving here at 2:03 p.m. today and getting you to Saint Thomas at 6:46 p.m."

"That sounds good," Brian was relieved.

"The flight is showing no seats. One moment please." The agent continued clicking on the computer.

Now Brain was worrying. He only had a short window of opportunity, and that window was closing in on him fast. The Delta agent smiled.

"Good news, I can get you on that flight. The total cost is $635.00."

"I'll take the ticket!" Brian presented his passport and paid for the ticket in cash. He checked his old brown suitcase and was one step closer to being on the beach.

"Thank you for flying Delta and enjoy your flight." The agent returned his passport and handed him a boarding pass with his seat assignment and the baggage claim attached to it. She directed him to the security checkpoint informing him the flight would be boarding approximately thirty minutes before departure.

"Thanks for all your help." Brian smiled. He wasted no time as he walked as briskly as he could to get in line to pass through security. Once through, he would be free. The security line was rather long, and things seemed to be moving slowly. After twenty minutes of moving up and down the maze that kept everyone in order,, Brian finally heard the words… "Boarding pass and photo ID."

"Here they are." Brian forced a big smile.

"Saint Thomas." The TSA representative scanned his passport and verified his ticket. When the green light shone on the scanner, Brian could feel the adrenaline rush, as he was ready to pass through the metal detector. The agent looked at "Enjoy your flight."

"Thanks." Brian left the checkpoint ready to take off whatever he needed to get through security. He pulled his laptop computer from the carry-on bag and filled the bin with his shoes, belt and everything in his pockets. He remained calm even with a screaming baby behind him. He placed everything on the conveyor belt as he waited his turn through the body scanner.

"Next!" The TSA representative's tone indicated he was unhappy to work on a holiday weekend. "Hands up, spread your feet please, and stand still." The scan made its way over his body. "Step out. If you would stand over there for a moment," waiting for the image to appear. "Thank you."

He had done it. He was through security. Then he heard another TSA representative call out. "Whose bag is this?" Brian looked up and realized it was his. He froze and felt sweat beading on his forehead and upper lip. His heart raced.

"Would you mind stepping over here? I need you to open it."

Nervously, Brian tried to remember what he had put in the carry-on that was causing concern. Suddenly he remembered! He had put a bottle of coke in his bag and forgot to take it out! As the TSA representative opened the bag, there it was. The representative removed it and informed Brian it had to be thrown away. The bag was closed and placed on the x-ray machine again. This time there was no problem. Brian looked at the time, quickly gathered all of his items and found the men's room.

He took a seat in one of the stalls trying to collect his thoughts and remember everything that had happened in the past few hours. "Why can't I remember those few minutes? Why didn't I listen to Sam and let him try and work things out instead of deciding to go to the cathedral this morning? Why am I running away like a coward instead of facing the police?" All he knew for sure was that he was a killer, and he needed to get out of town.

He looked at his watch. He was fifteen minutes away from the scheduled boarding time. He was ready to feel the sand in his feet, the sun on his face and have a rum and coke in his hand. He wondered what the future would hold for him.

At the gate, because of his size, he knew it was hard to blend in with the crowd. To avoid any attention to himself, he found a seat across from the gate in the corner. He looked at the flight information board — the plane was here. An airline representative came over the PA to give instructions about the boarding procedures. He looked at his boarding pass. Brian realized he would be one of the last to board. All he kept saying to himself was "I've got to get on this plane."

As he looked at the television across from him with the live feed from the local news station, the murder at Saint Patrick's Cathedral was the news of the day. The commentators were discussing and replaying parts of the news conference. The news ticker scrolled across the bottom of the screen announcing the cathedral would not be open until 5:00 p.m. and all the Easter services would take place at their scheduled times.

Brian reflected on the preparation of Easter Vigil services in years past. He had worked with Dr. Andy DiBrisco, the director of music to make each of the services unique and special. He had been looking forward to playing tonight. But he knew that wouldn't happen now.

He thought about the cathedral surrounded by the dark, cold scaffolding, like the dark, cold empty tomb. And then to the beautiful music that would bring happiness to those attending just as those who smiled at that first Easter of Our Lord's glorious resurrection. Brian had worked tirelessly for this year's Easter Service. He knew this was one of the most magnificent celebrations in the church that includes various movements from the blessing of the fire to the lighting of the Easter candle, listening to the Scripture readings of the struggles and faith of so many generations and welcoming those who found their way to the church, witnessing the sacraments of Baptism and Confirmation and ultimately the celebration of the Eucharist. Brian fought back tears, knowing what he had planned, regretting he wouldn't be a part of the liturgy. He wished things were different.

Brian was so caught up in his memories that he almost missed the gate attendant announcing the boarding of all zones. He quickly picked up his bag and with his boarding pass in his hand, walked over to the gate, presented it and walked down the concourse and boarded the plane. Passengers ahead of him struggled to put their oversized carry-on baggage in the overhead compartments. Eager to get to his seat, he stood in silence. Finally, the aisle cleared, and he was able to claim his place. It would be a long four hours. He was seated next to a man about his own size and weight. He quickly stuffed his bag under his seat as he heard the flight attendant announce for the third time the need for everyone to be seated before the plane could take off. He buckled himself in and tried to get comfortable.

"Sorry, I can't help you." The strong, young, tattooed, two hundred pound plus individual seated next to Brian spoke first.

"The feeling is mutual." Brian looked to see if there were any other available seats but with no luck. He remembered the agent said it was a full flight.

The flight attendant saw the cramped quarters that Brian shared with the other passenger. He brought them each a belt extender and found room in the overhead bin for Brian's bag. A little more leg room helped.

"Ladies and gentlemen this is your captain speaking. Once we get our final clearance and finish the paperwork, we can move back from the gate. We have a four hours and fifteen-minute flight from wheels up 'til wheels down. We'll be flying at a cruising altitude of 32,000 feet. The weather in Saint Thomas is sunny with a high of 88 degrees. A bit warmer than New York! We know you have a choice in airlines, so we thank you for choosing Delta. I'll be back later to give you an update. If we can do anything to help make this flight more enjoyable for you, please let one of our four flight attendants know."

Brian looked to his neighbor, and the unspoken truth was that no flight attendant could make this unfortunate pairing comfortable. Glancing at the front of the plane, Brian saw the TSA officer along with two NYPD officers talking with the flight attendant. They all looked towards the back of the plane. He knew he had no place to go, and there would be no rum and coke in a few hours.

"I think I'm about to give you some space," Brian said to his neighbor.

"Lieutenant Palmer?" the voice on the other end asked. "This is Cardinal Flinn. Could I see you when you have a chance? There is something you may want to know."

"Your Eminence, there is something I need to share with you too. I've just walked out of the parish house. Can I come to your residence?"

"Please do. I will wait for you at the entrance."

"Let me make a quick call, and I'll be right over."

"See you shortly."

Palmer called Detective Sabor to let him know of the arrest of Sam Tolden and an APB for the organist, Brian McManius.

"Detective Jabowski is back from the coroner's office, and I have her interviewing the assistant supervisor. Did Sara call you?"

"Yes. I talked with her, and she hasn't determined if Monsignor Triplett died from the blows to the head or from a heart attack. She won't know for sure until after more tests."

"A heart attack?"

"Yes, it seems he's had a heart condition, and after counting his pills, we realized he wasn't taking his medicine. I need to see the cardinal again." The lieutenant announced.

"No problem. Didn't you already go to confession?" Sabor couldn't resist bantering with Palmer to lighten up the conversation.

"Not sure if I need to go. Maybe the cardinal needs to confess. He wants to tell me something." Palmer countered Sabor's remark, but he was curious about the information the cardinal wanted to share.

"This investigation is getting more interesting and more complicated as the day moves on. What about Thom Triplett getting into his brother's room?"

"I've sent Officer VanDyke over to get him. He should be there. Make sure that VanDyke makes a list of the items being removed from Monsignor Triplett's bedroom and signs for it. How is CSU doing?"

"They're almost done. Do you want to see any more of the evidence collected?"

"Yes. Have them wait until I get back. I'll see you shortly." Palmer reached the Cardinal Flinn's front door.

"Lieutenant Palmer, thank you so much for coming. Please come in. Can I offer you something to drink?"

"Thank you, Your Eminence, I'm fine. How can I help you?"

"I think it is how can I help you? I believe in our interview I mentioned that Bishop George Newsome was a confidant for Monsignor Triplett. He gave me some rather disturbing news. It seems Monsignor Triplett was receiving money from the

414

Delfino construction company and was using it to give cash bonuses and severance pay to some cathedral employees."

"Let me stop you, Your Eminence. I know about this. Joseph Delfino told me, and I found a list of the payouts from Monsignor Triplett's safe."

"What else did you find in the safe?" The cardinal was very curious now.

"I know there's an envelope addressed to you that I haven't reviewed yet, but I was wondering if you knew anything about it."

"I am afraid I do, and I am fearful it may bring more bad news to the church if it gets into the wrong hands."

"I don't understand." Lieutenant Palmer was puzzled.

"Remember when you mentioned Blessed Sacrament Parish and the surveillance done by the NYPD? We discovered that over the course of a year the priest there had stolen more than $100,000."

"I remember."

"Do you also remember who the assistant district attorney was at the time?" The cardinal asked.

"I'm not sure?"

"It was Jennifer Gibson."

"Now I remember. She showed no mercy to the priest," the lieutenant recalled.

"I think with what you may have found in the safe, no mercy will be shown to the church or me," the cardinal continued.

"I'm sorry for the church and for you." Palmer wished he had opened the envelope addressed to the cardinal when he reviewed the contents of Monsignor Triplett's safe.

"Jennifer Gibson is the key. She is the one putting together a case against the church and me. I believe what Monsignor Triplett had in the safe is information dealing with a sub-contractor who worked on archdiocesan projects. He discovered the kickbacks they were giving to the archdiocese were not being returned to those parishes."

415

"I see...." Palmer pulled out his notepad. "How does this affect you, Your Eminence?"

"The archdiocese received the savings from the Delfinos, but it was not passed on to the parishes."

"I would think that's something that could be corrected."

"I am sure it can, but I would need some time to make that happen."

"Your Eminence, I'd encourage you to make the time," Palmer advised the cardinal. "I would get in touch with Ms. Gibson."

"I understand." The cardinal was relieved he could correct his mistakes. "May I ask how the investigation is going?"

"I can tell you I've arrested Sam Tolden. For now, he's charged as an accomplice to the murder. There is an APB out for the organist, a Mr. Brian McManius. He may be trying to leave New York. I think he is also involved." Palmer looked at the cardinal waiting for his reaction.

Shocked, the cardinal clutched his pectoral cross in his right hand and could barely speak. "Are you saying these two may have killed Monsignor Triplett?"

"I'm afraid so. I believe they were the last two people to see Monsignor alive."

"May God be with both of them. Are your investigators finished in the cathedral?"

"Just about. In fact, if you will excuse me, I need to get back to them." Lieutenant Palmer said his goodbyes to the cardinal realizing the difficult dilemma the cardinal now faced.

As the lieutenant once again entered the cathedral to review the rest of the evidence from the safe, his phone rang.

"Hello, Lieutenant Palmer? We have Brian McManius."

"Read him his rights, bring him to the station, book him and run his prints. I'll be there in forty minutes," Palmer directed. Despite the two arrests, he wondered if he had the murderers.

Chapter 32

Officer VanDyke removed the two pieces of crime scene tape at Monsignor Triplett's room so he and Thom could enter. As they went into the disorganized study, Thom smiled seeing all the empty coke cans. Thom went to the bedroom and was surprised to see the unmade bed. He could never remember his brother not making his bed.

He opened the closet door. After talking with the funeral director, Thom knew the clothing items he needed to take to the funeral home. He found his brother's good, black pair of pants, a pressed, black clergy shirt and his black loafers. These would be the first items placed on him followed by the vestments Steven wore at Mass.

As Thom moved the sweaters and jackets, he found in a light weighted dry cleaners plastic bag the vestments his parents had given his brother as an ordination gift. He recalled that day forty years ago. Thom was ordained a priest with six other men at Saint Patrick's Cathedral. The family was so proud. Now he was the only family left.

Holding the vestments, Steven, again felt the heartbreak and sadness of today. His only comfort was knowing his parents and brother were reunited. Thom hoped one day, God would take his soul too and bring them all together again.

"Are you okay, Mr. Triplett?" Officer VanDyke asked.

"Yes... just remembering when my brother put these vestments on for his first Mass."

"They are beautiful."

"A gift from the family," Thom informed the officer. "Are you Catholic, officer?"

"I was baptized Catholic, but I'm not really practicing. I'm supposed to go with my parent's to Easter Mass tomorrow though."

"Do you ever feel you're missing something?" Thom asked.

"I do, and I don't. I miss the Eucharist. I don't miss the politics. I miss the community. I don't miss the hypocritical priests."

"Could I ask why you stopped going to church?"

"I left because some priests' words didn't match their actions." The officer shared.

"Sorry to hear that. Did you know my brother?" Thom inquired.

"I'm sorry. I didn't."

"He was a good priest and faithfully served the church. He didn't always like what he had to do, but he was obedient to his superiors. Hopefully, God will reward him for all the good he did."

"That's what we all hope for." Officer VanDyke agreed.

"Maybe tomorrow when you go to church with your family, it won't be so much the priest who will touch you with his message, but just maybe, God will touch you enough, and you will continue to go."

"Maybe."

Thom knew it was time to stop talking. He carefully gathered the clothing and put it into a small suitcase. He went to his brother's bookcase and located the Canon Law book. Sure enough, there was the thick envelope marked "funeral and will." He pulled it out of the book. As he was about to put the book back on the shelf, he noticed there was a file folder marked "investments" and decided to take it with him.

418

Looking around the room, Thom was concerned with the amount of work he needed to do. He wondered who would help him, not only with the paperwork but also with the packing Steven's personal items. He hoped his brother left instructions for what he should do with them.

Thom put the folder and will into the suitcase and closed it. He took one more look around the room that was his brother's home. He knew he would return to begin sorting, packing and distributing his brother's personal property to others. "I think I have everything I need officer. I'm ready to leave."

VanDyke made sure all the items Thom took were put on the evidence list, and Thom signed for them.

As they shut the door to the bedroom, they met Father Morales and Father O'Hara in the hallway, and the two young priests offered their condolences to Thom. Father Morales explained he couldn't attend the funeral since he was leaving Monday for Rome. He expressed his appreciation for the guidance his brother gave him while he was assigned to the cathedral. Father O'Hara offered similar words. They excused themselves as they walked down the hall preparing to leave the parish house.

"That's what I mean by hypocritical priests. Those two priests aren't living the way priests are called to live," Officer VanDyke muttered.

The officer's remarks disturbed Thom. "You don't really know how those priests are living. You've assumed something, and you're quick to judge. God tells us he is the only judge."

"Maybe so, but I get this feeling about the two of them."

"What? As priests, they're not allowed to be friends?"

"I think they're more than friends."

"Even so, the Lord teaches us to condemn the sin and love the sinner. Look at how many sinners our Lord showed his love to. He'll show his love to you if you'd just open your heart to him. Easter is a good time to start... Now I'm preaching like my brother!" Thom just realized how much his

419

brother had helped him in his own faith as he tried to hold back his emotions.

Officer VanDyke said nothing, but he knew the words he heard would resonate with him until he did something about his faith. Perhaps he was too quick to judge those two priests. He remembered when he was judged wrongly and certainly wouldn't want to be judged for some of his past actions. Maybe instead of going with his parents to church, he'd just go on his own. He knew no matter what he decided, it was up to him.

Together they left the cathedral parish house. Thom thanked the officer for his assistance. He headed to the subway station realizing he had not called Jennifer. He hoped she would have a late lunch with him after he went to the funeral home. He decided to give her a call.

"Jennifer. Thanks so much for your message. Are you free for lunch? Thom asked.

"How soon?"

"I'm just leaving the cathedral. I've got to go to the funeral home and make the arrangements. I'm taking the clothes and vestments Steven will wear."

"What funeral home?"

"Frank Campbell Funeral Chapel on E 81st Street and Madison Avenue. That's the funeral home we used for my parents."

"How about I meet you there? Then we find a place to eat. I can be there within twenty minutes." Jennifer said.

"Thanks. I appreciate your help." Thom needed a friend right now.

The cathedral was a place of tremendous activity. CSU was almost finished. Hector and his crew had been working hard cleaning. The place would return to some normalcy shortly.

Hector saw Lieutenant Palmer enter the cathedral and approached him. "Did I hear correctly? You arrested Sam Tolden?"

"I'm afraid so, Hector." Palmer was surprised. "How did you know?"

"I... I was on my way over to see you at the parish house. But when I saw Sam being escorted out and placed in a squad car, I came back here. He couldn't have done it by himself." Hector sneered. "He's too much of a coward!"

"Is there something you want to tell me?" Palmer asked.

"Just making an observation."

Palmer pressed Hector with a few more questions. "I'd like to ask you about the organist, Mr. McManius."

"Well, he and Sam were friends. Has he been arrested too?" Hector was fishing for details.

Palmer changed the subject. "Are you about finished cleaning?"

"Pretty close. The flowers should be here within the hour, and then once they're all in, I can go home. Can I ask, who do you think was in the church this morning?"

"Hector, once this is over, I need to talk to you about what you did — concealing evidence — the black book, remember?"

"I remember...." Hector realized his own sinfulness and hoped one of the priests would be over soon, so he could ask to go to confession.

"We'll talk soon. Happy Easter, Hector." Palmer left to find Sabor and review the items on the evidence table before it was all packed and moved to the station.

"Happy Easter, Lieutenant Palmer." Relieved of his own burden for a moment, Hector watched the lieutenant walk away. He continued cleaning, and a wave of sadness came over him — for himself and for the people of the cathedral parish. They would all be shocked at the news of Monsignor Triplett's death and Sam's arrest.

Palmer found Sabor near one of the confessionals talking on his phone. "You waiting in line for confession?"

Sabor smiled, quickly said goodbye, put his phone away and opened his notepad to give Palmer the update. "Detective Jabowski just finished interviewing the assistant supervisor, a Mr. Jamie Avalos. Mr. Avalos didn't know any more than what his supervisor told us earlier this morning. He opened the cathedral on Thursday and verified the list of workers here. His alibi for last night and this morning checks out."

Turning the page on his notepad, Sabor continued, "Mr. Avalos remembers taking Sam Tolden up the scaffolding and walking the length of the cathedral. He said he was the only cathedral employee he took up there. He also remembers Jared took Monsignor Triplett and the organist. The organist was quite upset when he found several broken organ pipes. The organist also went up one time by himself. Jared talked to him about wearing a hard hat and having a supervisor with him."

"Sabor, do you remember Jared telling us this?" Palmer asked as he checked his notes.

"No."

"Why would Jared fail to give that detail?" Palmer wondered. "Did you ask Jared?"

"I did, and he says he simply forgot to tell us. So the organist was able to climb up and walk the entire scaffolding."

"Did Jared say how long ago?"

"No, he didn't."

"Sabor, call Jared over. I want to ask him."

Sabor instructed Jamie to wait while he escorted Jarred through the center pew to Palmer.

Palmer wanted the correct details. "Jared, exactly when did you assist the organist off the scaffolding?"

"This week, Monday or Tuesday. I... could confirm it with Jamie if you'd like?"

"And is this your organist?" Palmer held up his phone with a picture of Brian McManius.

422

"Yes, that's him. He sure has an attitude. I mean, it really upset him about the broken pipes, and I still don't know how it happened."

"Maybe he broke the pipes," Palmer suggested.

"I don't know what happened. Our men and women worked carefully, and they would have told me if there was a problem, but no one has. I just know the organist was extremely angry and rude. He wanted the pipes fixed immediately."

"I'd like for you to come down to the station to give your statement. I'll send you with Detective Jabowski."

"I can do that. Can Jamie also come along since we were going to get lunch?" Jared asked.

"Sure, we can get his statement too." Lieutenant Palmer motioned for Detective Jabowski and gave her the instructions needed to return to the police station.

Detective Sabor pointed out, "Boss, the Crime Scene Unit is waiting for you with the evidence, and they're ready to leave."

"I need to look at the last items found in Monsignor Triplett's safe—the manila envelope and the leather notebook. Then I'll be ready to go. I'll see you back at the station. Brian McManius should be there by then."

Palmer quickly returned to the evidence table, and picked up the large manila envelope addressed to the cardinal. Inside the envelope, there were three white legal envelopes. The first one contained a letter from the electrical subcontractor doing the work on the cathedral with a list of donations in goods they had provided to the cathedral and two other parishes over the last three years. Someone had stapled a note questioning the invoices. Now Palmer understood what the cardinal was talking about. He placed it all back in the envelope.

The second envelope contained a copy of the letter Joseph Delfino had signed the night before. The letter gave the details of the arrangement made with the cardinal regarding his annulment. Palmer wondered. Where was the original? Had it been sent to the cardinal or someone else?

The third envelope contained the list of employees at the cathedral, the years they worked, their pay and a column marked July 1 with check marks indicating who was staying and who would be leaving. Monsignor Triplett had placed a note at the bottom, "In case something happens to me, I wanted you to know I have prayed hard and long about these decisions. The reasons for the departure of two of our employees can be found in their personnel files." Lieutenant Palmer made a note to get a search warrant for these files.

The last piece of evidence from the safe was a small leather notebook. Glancing through it, he realized Monsignor Triplett kept a list of several priests of the archdiocese and some of their activities that might be considered questionable. Palmer could only speculate on who else knew about this and Monsignor Triplett's reasons for keeping the information.

Finally, Palmer inspected the black book Hector had removed from Monsignor Triplett's coat. He found the pages which detailed dates, times, and actions of Sam and Brian. It was obvious Monsignor was unhappy with them.

The lieutenant looked further in the small notebook at more names. Palmer found very little negative, but more positive statements about many of the employees. Monsignor let everyone think he was keeping a list of their mistakes, but in fact, he was just keeping the book as a reminder of what his staff was doing. Palmer thought for a moment how unfortunate it was that the staff didn't know Monsignor's real purpose for the book.

After reviewing all the evidence from the safe, Palmer saw Officer VanDyke's list of items that Thom obtained from his brother's room. He was glad to know Thom had found the will. Palmer was filled with mixed thoughts about this priest he had admired. He wished he had known Monsignor's reasons for his actions. Keeping secrets and taking matters into his own hands led to his murder.

The CSU placed all the tagged evidence into labeled boxes and prepared to carry the boxes to the police van waiting at the side entrance. The front pew had been taken away just a few hours ago. As Lieutenant Palmer looked around the cathedral, he saw the florist bringing in the spring flowers full of vibrant colors, along with the traditional lilies. Hector, Oscar and Luis helped the florist, making several trips to the van. The older ladies and gentlemen of the parish, probably members of the oldest families of the cathedral, arrived. They immediately noticed the front center pew was gone, and six chairs were in its place. The volunteers reviewed the decorating details from the archdiocesan office of liturgy. They were eager to begin and seemed to know their responsibilities. This year, they felt a particular sense of duty.

Decorating this holy place for Easter had a new significance, another dimension in celebrating eternal life. Palmer finally had the chance to look around the cathedral and experienced a feeling of peacefulness. Even with all the scaffolding and construction material, the cathedral was still beautiful.

As Palmer walked by the volunteers working in the sanctuary, he could see sadness in their faces. He heard it also in their conversations as they spoke of how wonderful Monsignor Triplett was. They were sharing their faith, confident that he was in heaven and hoping they would one day join him. Seeing and hearing their strong their faith, the lieutenant looked forward to celebrating his rekindled faith tomorrow, but he didn't think it would be at the cathedral.

Approaching the side door of the cathedral for the last time, Palmer heard Officer VanDyke and another police officer informing the many tourists gathered outside that the doors would open at 5:00 p.m. Taking one last look around, the detective hoped all would be normal again or at least appear normal — right here, at this time, in one of the world's best-known cities, in this wonderful church with all of its beauty and grandeur — Saint Patrick's Cathedral.

After visiting the funeral home and lunching with Jennifer Thom had returned home alone. Jennifer had agreed to join him for Easter Mass at the cathedral. Now sitting at his desk, he was thankful he found a copy of his brother's will to review. Thom had prepared the will last year, but he had forgotten some of his brother's wishes.

The will was very clear. Monsignor Triplett wanted Bishop Newsome as the homilist at the funeral Mass, and he wanted the funeral celebrated at his last parish assignment. He asked to be buried in his family's section of the cemetery. Thom made a note to call the bishop.

His brother also had a life insurance policy of $50,000 to be given to Jonathan Pickle for the sole purpose of his college education. If he had already gone to college, then the policy was to be used to pay back any of his student loans. Thom was to monitor the distribution of the money to Jonathan. Thom wrote a note "give the Pickles a call."

Monsignor left all his religious items to the last parish he was assigned and hoped his chalice would be given to one of the newly ordained priests who might not have a personal chalice.

Finally, he left whatever cash he had in the bank, along with any outstanding bills to his brother. Thom smiled. He knew, of course, that's what his brother would leave to him—the bills. The will instructed Thom to go through all personal belongings first and take whatever he wanted.

Thom found it all in order. As he returned the will to the envelope, a note dropped to the floor. Thom picked it up and opened it. Dated three days ago, the note read, "Thom, watch for the mail." Thom was a little perplexed with the message and wondered if Steven thought he was going to die soon?

As Thom placed the will in the file, he noticed another sheet of paper with readings and music. This would be important when he met with the cardinal on Tuesday. It was Steven's liturgical plan for his funeral.

Exhausted and emotionally drained, Thom moved to his favorite, comfortable chair. He looked across the room to the bookcase and saw the last picture taken of the brothers together. They had decided last year to take a cruise to Alaska. The picture showed a huge glacier behind them as a piece of it was crushing into the sea. The brothers had huge smiles on their faces. Thom allowed himself more tears. Now, there were no more trips to share with his brother. No more phone calls. No more dinners. He had lost the last member of his family. He pulled out the bottle of Scotch they shared, poured a glass, and lifted it up. "I love you brother. Thanks!" He downed the amber liquor and then another before he finally fell asleep in the chair.

Chapter 33

Brian McManius sat in the holding cell waiting for his attorney to arrive, and Sam Tolden sat nervously with his attorney in one of the interrogation rooms. Detectives Jabowski and Pantera sat at their desks and took statements from Jared Quinn and Jamie Avalos. The Midtown North Precinct was a place of activity this mid-afternoon with phones ringing, detectives talking and cuffed individuals whose fates were uncertain.

Detective Sabor arrived at the station and immediately went to Brian's holding cell. "Brian, did the officer who brought you in read you your rights?"

"Yes, he did." Brian nervously responded

"And you realize you are being charged with the murder of Monsignor Steven Triplett?"

"Yes, I know." Brian mumbled his words without emotion.

"Are you waiting for an attorney?"

"Yes... I am. He should be here shortly."

"I guess we'll wait."

As the detective sat back in his chair, reviewing the little information obtained, one investigator brought the fingerprint report for the candlestick. As suspected, they found both Brian McManius and Sam Tolden's prints. Sabor went to tell Sam and his attorney.

Walking into the interrogation room with the file in his hand, Detective Sabor introduced himself to Sam and his attorney, Kurt Barbertie. With the formalities out of the way, he opened the folder to inform Sam that his fingerprints were on the murder weapon. Sam cried. He knew he would do time in prison as an accomplice.

"I think it's time we get a statement from your client." Sabor slid a yellow legal tablet and pen across the table to Sam. Kurt asked for time alone with his client. Sabor agreed, stepped out of the room, and closed the door.

As Sabor returned to the squad room, he recognized the man coming into the station wearing a dark gray suit. It was Brian's attorney. This case was bound to receive huge media attention, and there was no better attorney than Wade Christy. Sabor asked one of the uniformed officers to move Brian from the holding cell and place him in the second interrogation room.

Sabor walked over to Christy and extended his hand. They were well acquainted with one another.

"Wade Christy, how are you doing this Saturday afternoon, detective? Good to see you. I'm representing Brian McManius. Can I see him?"

"We moved him to interrogation room two. I'm sure he has a lot to say to you." Detective Sabor led Christy to Brian's interrogation room. Before closing the door, he remarked to Christy, "If you need anything... you know the drill."

Returning to his desk, Sabor met detectives Jabowski and Pantera who brought signed statements from the construction supervisors. Both detectives reported there was nothing new since the initial interviews. Sabor walked over and thanked the two construction supervisors for coming in. He assured them if there were any more questions, one of the detectives would be in touch.

As Delfino's supervisors were leaving, Joseph and A.J. Delfino arrived with their attorney, Emmanuel Fitzmyer. Sabor saw them come in and met them.

"Let me put you in one of our interrogation rooms. I'll have Detective Jabowski take your statement."

"Thank you." Fitzmyer struggled to hold his well-worn, oversized leather briefcase.

Jabowski escorted the attorney and senior Delfino to an interrogation room. She asked A.J. to take a seat outside the room, and she would take his statement next.

Once the Delfinos finished their statements, Jabowski thanked them. As the Delfinos were walking out, Monsignor Stone entered. Joseph looked frustrated and wanted to say something to Monsignor Stone, but the priest ignored them.

Monsignor observed the activity in the station and wondered how much was related to the murder. Detective Pantera saw Monsignor Stone and escorted him to an interrogation room to work on his statement. Monsignor was uncomfortable with this unknown detective. He asked if Lieutenant Palmer could be present for his statement. Pantera told him Lieutenant Palmer was running behind, but he was on his way.

Palmer entered the squad room carrying a foot-long sandwich and large drink. Sabor saw him first and quickly brought him up to date on what was going on in the station, letting him know of the statements they had, including the report of the fingerprints on the candlestick. He also informed him they still had not heard from the crime lab on what information, if any, was retrieved from Monsignor Triplett's cell phone.

"Well, that's not good, Sabor. It would be so nice if these two guys would confess. It would make for a pleasant Easter. I think in a few minutes, we're going to try to rattle them to see who will turn on whom." Palmer walked with Sabor to his office.

"Both are still with their attorneys," Sabor said.

"And who did you say was the attorney for McManius?"

"Wade Christy."

"He'll love the media coverage he'll get. I predict he'll add a few more custom-tailored suits to his closet." Palmer couldn't help being sarcastic. He'd dealt with Christy's clients too often.

Sabor chimed in. "And probably a couple of trips to the tanning salon. The man always has a tan even when it's snowing!"

As Detective Pantera escorted Monsignor Stone out, he noticed Lieutenant Palmer had arrived and was now in his office. "Monsignor, Lieutenant Palmer is here. Would you like to speak with him?"

Monsignor Stone stopped. "Yes, if I could. I just need to ask him a question."

Detective Pantera took Monsignor to Palmer's office with his signed statement.

Palmer stood up in front of his desk. "Monsignor, I apologize for not being here." Palmer took the statement. "We appreciate you coming in."

"I was just wondering, Lieutenant, if you will be at Monsignor Triplett's funeral?"

"At the moment, I'm planning on it."

"I'll see you there. Thank you again for all your help." Monsignor Stone shook Lieutenant Palmer's hand and made direct eye contact with him. They each understood these words.

As Palmer sat back down, put his sandwich in a drawer and asked Sabor to call the team in. The lieutenant was confident about the work they had accomplished in a few short hours.

"Now that we're all here. I'd like to thank each of you for your work and your response during this investigation. We now have conclusive evidence linking both Sam Tolden and Brian McManius to the candlestick. I believe we can show motive. According to a file found in Monsignor Triplett's safe, they were both going to lose their jobs at the end of June. The only thing pending is the medical examiner's final report. The district attorney needs it to determine first or second-degree murder charges against the two suspects."

"Do we know who's coming over here from the district attorney's office?" Jabowski asked.

"I believe one of the assistant DA's," Sabor responded.

"Great. I hope they realize this will be a high-profile case."

Pantera added, "We all should. They're going to need someone to take on the media."

"And everyone needs to double-check and recheck your work. We don't want to face the police commissioner for any errors!" Sabor emphasized.

"Thanks again for all the hard work. We're still waiting for the attorneys and DA. For now, finish typing and organizing all the statements you've taken." The detectives left Palmer's office and went back to work.

It was almost 3:00 p.m. when Lieutenant Palmer finally took his sandwich out of the drawer, a foot-long steak and cheese hoagie he had picked up from the sidewalk vendor outside the precinct. He opened the sandwich and smelled the juicy grilled steak. He was hungry, but he was more concerned about the case. He wondered which suspects' attorneys would walk out first. He hoped the assistant district attorney arrived soon. No sooner had he taken the first bite of his lunch, sure enough, she showed up in a professional style navy suit.

Katie Rozzelle made a name for herself in the short time she had been working in the district attorney's office. She took on some of the biggest cases in the city. With great courage and conviction, along with the evidence needed, she successfully convicted a few of New York City's feared murderers, drug dealers, and embezzlers. She wasn't afraid to take on any case and wasn't afraid to bring anyone to justice.

Palmer remembered one of the last cases he testified for. She was the lead prosecutor and sought the death penalty for a multi-millionaire who had an affair with his housekeeper, discovered she was pregnant and arranged her murder. Katie

432

prosecuted the case with class, methodically outlining the evidence to the jury. The defense was weak and had refused a plea deal. The defendant was found guilty and sentenced to a minimum of 25 years in prison. His money didn't provide him his freedom.

The district attorney knew the ADA was the right person for this case. Katie was familiar with the precinct and walked right into Palmer's office.

Grabbing another bite of his sandwich, Palmer realized he really enjoyed working with Katie. He hoped there could be even more between them. He felt they had good chemistry. Ambitious, bright, both single—he asked her out on a date once, but she had refused. He couldn't even get her to have a drink with him after one of her many wins in the courtroom. She lived for her job. She had aspirations of greater things. And the way she was going, she would be noticed and probably become a judge for the state of New York one day.

"Katie, so good to see you!" Palmer quickly swallowed a bite of his sandwich. "Are you here about the murder of Monsignor Steven Triplett?"

"I am. What do you have for me?" Katie was ready to hear the evidence and details of the investigation.

"So much for the pleasantries." He knew it would be all business as Katie took a seat beside his desk. He took another bite of his sandwich before bringing her up to date on the investigation. As he looked at her, he thought just maybe he would try again and ask her out. All she could do was say no, as she had before.

Palmer took a sip of his drink and began. "Our two suspects are in each of the interrogation rooms with their attorneys. The first one is Sam Tolden, and he's working on a written statement with his attorney Kurt Barbertie. The other suspect is the main cathedral organist, Brian McManius. His attorney is the well-dressed, tanned, Wade Christy who arrived about fifteen minutes before you did."

"I've been on the other side of the table from both of them." Katie smiled but offered no opinion of their work.

"We'll give them another five minutes and then it's time to get down to business." Palmer casually leaned back in his chair and took another sip of his drink.

"What evidence do you have?"

"We believe the murder weapon is a candlestick from the altar that has the prints of both the suspects. The motive behind the murder was their belief they would lose their jobs at the end of June."

"I'll need the DNA report on Monsignor Triplett's blood type to make sure it matches the blood on the candlestick and to confirm the candlestick is the murder weapon." Katie mentally went through her own check-list of information and items were needed to build a case.

"It'll be a few days before we get that." Palmer wasn't sure if Katie already knew that.

"And the coroner's report?"

"It's pending further tests. Monsignor Triplett had high blood pressure, and Sara says he could have died from a heart attack before or during the assault. Here's the fingerprint report on the candlestick and the preliminary coroner's report." Palmer pulled them out of his file while trying to get another bite of his lunch.

"Go ahead and eat. I'll read over these. Then I want the attorneys to know I'm here."

Palmer watched Katie review the reports. He wanted to take her out for a drink and see if there was someone who laughed outside the DA's office. As he ate the last bite of his sandwich, he gave it another try.

Palmer leaned forward as he wiped his sticky hands. "So do you have plans for Easter?"

Katie didn't look up. "Yes, and no. My dad is with my sister, and her family wants me to come over for dinner. I'll probably go after I've gone to church."

There was the opening he needed. "Where will you go to church?"

Katie realized she'd be going alone. Before her mom died last year, she made her a promise to go to church on Christmas and Easter. She wanted to keep that promise. "I'll go to Holy Name of Jesus. I like the bishop and the two priests there."

"Would you like some company?" Palmer looked for a positive response, but since she had said no in the past, what would stop her from saying no now.

"You want to come with me to church?" Katie was uncertain how to take his offer.

"Yes… believe it or not, I do go to church! I was just at the cathedral yesterday for Good Friday services," Palmer acknowledged with pride. He hoped that would give him a better chance for a yes from her.

"Really…" Katie was surprised to hear he had been at the cathedral's Good Friday service. Maybe she had been too hard on him. She thought again about sitting in a pew alone tomorrow. "Okay, let's go together. Which Mass do you want to go to?"

Palmer was leaning back in his chair when she answered. He looked at her and almost fell out of his seat. "Let's see what time they have Easter Mass!" He leaned forward, opened Google on his computer, typed in Holy Name of Jesus, found their website with the Easter Mass schedule. "Masses are 7:30, 9:30 and 11:30. When would you like to go?"

"How about 11:30?" Katie surprised herself with the answer and responded in a soft voice. She smiled. She was delighted to have someone to sit with at Mass. "I'll meet you out front."

"Eleven-thirty it is! I'll be there by 11:00. I'm sure the place will be crowded with those Catholics and visitors who just show up on Easter." Palmer grinned as he controlled his excitement and wondered what tomorrow would bring.

"You're right — 11:00 a.m. would be a good time to meet. You should know though that I'm the prosecuting attorney for first appearances tomorrow. Depending on how many individuals have to appear before the judge, I could be late." Katie hoped there would only be a few as she returned the file folders.

"I'll wait." Palmer took the folders and smiled.

"It's time we get back to work." Katie returned to the business of being the assistant district attorney.

No sooner had she said those words, attorney Barbertie came out of the interrogation room looking concerned. Seeing Katie, he introduced himself. "My client is ready to talk."

"And what is he going to tell us?" Katie asked.

"The truth. And he's asking for leniency. He didn't kill Monsignor Triplett, but he was there when the priest was killed and is willing to cooperate with the police."

"Is that his statement?" Palmer saw the yellow pad filled with notes.

"It is, and I'll give it to you after you've questioned him."

"Let's see what he says." Katie motioned for the three of them to enter the interrogation room.

The door opened, and Sam felt drained having told the story to his attorney again. He had just finished writing it all down. He recognized the lieutenant who first questioned him. He knew more questions were to come.

"Hello, I'm Katie Rozzelle, the assistant district attorney for Manhattan. Your attorney has told me you're ready to talk. Is this true?"

"Yes, I've given my written statement." Sam was exhausted.

"And this statement... what's it going to tell me?"

"It says... I mean... I was present when Brian McManius killed Monsignor Triplett. I was at the cathedral to meet with Monsignor Triplett, and I saw it all."

"Let's hear just your story."

Once again, he told his story... starting with Brian McManius striking Monsignor Stone over the head with the candlestick and carrying him out the side church door. "I ran to Monsignor Triplett in the front pew. I wanted to call 911, but I couldn't find my phone. I panicked when Brian came back, so crawled under the pew to the first pillar. Brian picked up the candlestick and held it over Monsignor's head. I couldn't see Monsignor. He was down on the pew. Then Brian hit Monsignor with the candlestick. He hit him again with the candlestick."

Sam continued. "I ran out and yelled at Brian to stop. He didn't hear me. He was crazy! Blood was slowly dripping from Monsignor Triplett's head. I tried to push Brian away from Monsignor. Brian was surprised to see me and took a swing at me with the candlestick. When he swung at me, I punched him in the face. I punched him again until he dropped the candlestick. Brian suddenly seemed aware of what had happened, and he collapsed on the floor. Then I tried to find Monsignor's pulse but couldn't get one. I took the bloody candlestick and hid it behind a pillar near the archbishop's chair. I looked for a key. I asked Brian to help, but he was useless. Then I heard someone at the side door and told Brian we had to go. Next thing I knew, Brian disappeared under the scaffolding. I went back to my office, got my phone and headed to the Women's Republican Club."

Katie sat across from Sam and listened stoically while he shared his story. "And this is what you've written as your official statement?"

"It is."

"You know, if your story holds true, you are an accessory to the murder?"

Sam, exhausted, pleaded. "But I didn't kill Monsignor Triplett."

"No, you didn't kill him, but you were present and didn't stop it either."

"I tried! You've got to believe me... I tried. It... it all happened so fast." Sam was begging for mercy.

"I need to hear what Mr. McManius says." Katie then told the Palmer, "Once you have Mr. Tolden's statement typed up have him sign it."

"Please, I told you the truth. I didn't kill Monsignor Triplett!" Sam shouted hysterically as tears came down his face.

"That will be for a jury to decide." Katie indicated.

"Lieutenant, can I ask you a question first?" Sam struggled with his words.

"Sure." Palmer was curious what Sam wanted to know.

"How is the other priest who was with Monsignor Triplett? I saw Brian carry him out." Sam was unsure if he had told the detective who the priest was.

"Alive." Palmer realized Sam disclosed information that he didn't have.

Sam was relieved with the news.

Katie walked out of the interrogation room with Lieutenant Palmer. "Do you think he's telling the truth?"

"Time will tell. I think this is the story he wants to believe." Palmer instructed Sabor to type Mr. Tolden's statement.

"What's so important about this key that he mentioned?" Katie asked.

Palmer offered a quick summary. "Monsignor Triplett kept evidence about a lot of things happening in and outside the cathedral. He placed it all in a safe in his bedroom closet. He wasn't a holy saint either, but neither were the two employees we have here today. You can read all the details when the reports are completed."

"Should we bring our dear friend, Wade Christy out and see how he's doing with his client?" Katie asked sarcastically.

Palmer knocked on the door and entered the second interrogation room. Katie wasn't looking forward to going up against this Brooks Brothers suit who would use every legal trick with not only the judge and jury but also with the media covering the trial. She contemplated a gag order if the case went to trial.

The lieutenant motioned for Christy to step out of the interrogation room. When Christy greeted Katie, the friction between the two of them was apparent. As they stood beside the two-way mirror, Christy began bargaining. "My client will plead not guilty to the murder by reason of insanity."

"That was quick. And you want to go with that defense?" Katie was surprised. She thought for sure she was going to hear the words 'my client is not guilty.'

"That's what my client has asked for."

"I'll have to ask the judge for a 501C psychological evaluation at first appearance. Do you think he's suicidal?" She was concerned about Brian's mental state.

"I do."

"We'll put a 24-hour watch on him." Palmer volunteered to make the arrangements.

"I agree. But I want a statement from him as to what he remembers and the role Sam Tolden had in all of this." Katie demanded.

"He remembers nothing except that he hit a priest over the head and carried him outside. The next thing he remembers he was up in the choir loft, and he heard the maintenance man yell 'He's dead.'" Christy recounted his client's recollection.

"If that's his story, let's get it down in writing," Katie insisted.

"Who is the judge for first appearance tomorrow?" Christy asked as he saw attorney Kurt Barbertie walk out with his client and give a friendly nod.

"I believe it's Judge Kickenbottom," Katie answered. "He's usually good about psych evaluations, and I'm sure with as much publicity as this case is will get, he'll do everything within his power to make sure the proper steps are taken."

"Fine. I'll see you tomorrow." Christy returned to his client.

As he left, Lieutenant Palmer felt good about the case. He believed he had the murderer and his accomplice. Katie agreed.

"Send me the paperwork!" As Katie prepared to leave, she remembered her earlier discussion with Palmer. She turned to him. "See you tomorrow morning at 11:00 in front of Holy Name of Jesus."

"See you then!" Palmer looked forward to what he hoped would be a happy Easter. But he still had some work to do.

Sam and Brian signed their statements a short time later. They were placed in separate cells, away from each other, waiting for first appearance. Brian who was put on suicide watch had confessed to what he remembered but did not know the role Sam had played in the murder. All Brian knew was he would never play an organ again. Sam was shattered. He wondered what his wife and children were doing now that their trip had been canceled.

Police Commissioner Timberbank heard the latest developments in the case from Lieutenant Palmer and held a press conference at 4:00 p.m. at city hall. With the mayor, Lieutenant Palmer, several detectives and police officers gathered around him, the commissioner read a formal statement to the media explaining the arrest of two suspects in the murder of Monsignor Triplett. He named them and said they were in jail awaiting first appearance. It was a very brief statement and no questions. The press was shocked at how quickly the suspects were apprehended and more surprised at who the two suspects were.

Preparations for the Easter Vigil liturgy at Saint Patrick's Cathedral were complete. The florist and volunteers had done their best to make the sanctuary look beautiful. The volunteers missed Monsignor Triplett's words of encouragement and felt the need to honor him. On the table near the statue of Saint Patrick, they placed a small picture of the priest alongside a book of blank pages for parishioners to leave messages.

As announced, the cathedral doors opened at 5:00 p.m. At each entrance, there were two standing signs. The first was to remind the parishioners and guests of the importance of silence in this sacred place. The second was a picture of Monsignor Triplett with the dates of his birth and death and a request for prayers for him. Moved by the loss of the rector, the faithful, and even the camera-laden tourists respected the request. For the next three hours there was complete silence in the cathedral.

Amid the scaffolding and construction materials blocking many of the twelve altars, individuals from various cultures and countries found a pew or a chair for the 8:00 p.m. vigil celebration. The center section of seats was reserved for those catechumens to be baptized, and those candidates to be received into the church, along with those adult Catholics to be confirmed. The announcement came that the liturgy would begin outside and if possible everyone should gather at the front doors. Many just stayed in their pews.

Moments earlier, Father Morales, in his black cleric suit, went to the cardinal's sacristy to leave an envelope that contained an itinerary for his trip to Rome and numbers where he could be reached. The cardinal thanked him, said he would be in touch and would pray for him. He reassured Father Morales the time in Rome would be for the best. Father Morales promised to remember the cardinal in his prayers. With nothing more to say, Father Morales wished the cardinal a happy Easter and went to join the other priest for the vigil.

At precisely 8:00 p.m., the bells rang from the north tower. The 19 bells, each named after a saint, varied in size with the smallest weighing 173 pounds and the largest over 6,600 pounds. People along the street stopped to check their watches as they listened for the repeat of the one bell seven times.

The sun set between the skyscrapers, and an unanticipated light rain shower began. The faithful and tourists gathered outside on the front steps and received votive candles while the front bronze doors were opened for this special night.

441

With their name tags on, members of the Rite of Christian Initiation class stood with their sponsors and family members waiting patiently. Their faces expressed the excitement and anticipation of the sacraments and blessings they would receive. All waited in silence for the cardinal.

Cardinal Flinn joined the procession down the center aisle with the priests of the parish and several visiting priests from all parts of the world to stand next to the deacon holding the five-foot Easter candle. The cardinal began the celebration with the service of light. He lit the fire, symbolizing the glory of the resurrection. Then he lit the new Easter candle as a reminder of that light. Once he finished, the cardinal, with his lit candle, invited all to pass the light of their candles to others as they entered the church. The deacon then carried the Easter candle to its holder next to the ambo. The cardinal walked to the archbishop's chair, *the cathedra,* representing the dignity and authority of the cardinal. As each candle was lit, the faithful found their seats. The mass of flickering candles created a brilliant glow in the church.

Father Crumbley stepped into the ambo to sing "The Exsultet," the Easter Proclamation. He did a wonderful job with this beautiful hymn of praise. Once he finished, the cathedral lights were turned on, the handheld candles blown out and placed in the pew book racks.

The cardinal welcomed everyone and asked for a moment of silence for Monsignor Triplett.

The whole three-hour celebration was one of light, fire, incense, water, and most importantly, the Eucharist. Hector Oscar, Luis, along with their families were among the many worshipers attending the Easter Vigil. For them, this night strengthened their friendship and their love for the Catholic faith. As they prayed in silence for Monsignor Triplett, none of them would ever forget this day.

Chapter 34

As the sun rose the next morning, the temperature outside was a chilly 55 degrees with clear skies. What a difference one day had made—from the gloomy overcast, rainy skies to an Easter Sunday with sunshine over the city.

It was a different day for so many.

The first court arraignments were at 9:00 a.m., and Judge Kickenbottom wasn't happy he was scheduled for Easter Sunday. He wanted to move the cases along quickly. He was surprised there were any cases at all, much less six cases this morning.

Katie Rozzelle reviewed the material Lieutenant Palmer provided. The district attorney told her he thought she could handle all the first arraignments when he talked with her late last night. Four additional people were booked yesterday, and based on the information, she would ask the judge to remand without bail.

As she looked at the docket, Brian and Sam were number three and four. After reading Brian's statement, she had serious doubts Brian committed the murder on his own since he couldn't remember anything. The insanity plea was his only hope.

The bailiff called the courtroom to order as the judge entered. He then directed everyone to take their seats. The judge heard the pleas, agreed with the assistant DA and quickly had the first two defendants remanded without bail.

The court clerk called the next case. "Case number 265458037 the City of New York against Sam Tolden. The charge is involuntary manslaughter."

"How does your client plead?" Judge Kickenbottom asked.

Kurt Barbertie responded, "Not guilty, your honor."

"Your Honor, this case is just unfolding, and at this time, we ask for the accused to be remanded," Katie requested.

"Bail?"

Katie held her breath. "Your Honor, we recommend $1 million."

"Bail is set at $1 million." Judge Kickenbottom concurred and slammed his gavel.

Kurt went through the motions to protest the exorbitant amount claiming Sam is an upstanding citizen, has never been in trouble before and was an innocent bystander.

The judge listened, paused, glanced at Kurt and denied the motion as he slammed his gavel.

The defendant was returned to custody and escorted back to jail. Kurt escorted Sam's wife and two daughters from the courtroom. They were in tears and total disbelief. He talked to them about contacting a bondsman for the $100,000 needed for bail.

"Case number 265459263 the city of New York against Brian McManius. The charge is second-degree murder."

"How does your client plead?" Judge Kickenbottom asked.

"Not guilty by reason of insanity, Your Honor," Wade Christy responded.

"Your Honor, we request a psychiatric evaluation, and the accused be placed on suicide watch," Katie said.

"So ordered." Judge Kickenbottom slammed his gavel.

Katie looked over at Brian who appeared more confused today. He seemed unaware he was standing before a judge. She looked back to see if there was anyone in the courtroom for him but found no one. As Brian was escorted out of the courtroom, he turned and yelled, "I want to see a priest!" She hoped Christy would call the chaplain.

Katie quickly returned to the proceedings in the courtroom. She had two more cases. As instructed, the last two offenders were to be remanded without bail. She didn't even open the file but went through the motions as the judge concurred with every one of her recommendations. His final words to those present while looking at Katie were "Happy Easter." Then he said, "Ms. Rozzelle, can I see you in my chambers please?"

"Yes, Your Honor." She gathered her notes and placed them in her leather briefcase. She nervously walked to the entrance of the judge's chambers, unsure why he wanted to see her. The security guard was waiting to open the door for her.

Katie cautiously entered the judge's chamber, "Your Honor?" The judge was taking off his robe and putting on his suit jacket.

"Ms. Rozzelle, I know you were struggling with that third case—involuntary manslaughter. You may have to rethink the charge. Do you understand by using involuntary manslaughter, you are saying the person had knowledge of the crime?" Judge Kickenbottom advised.

"I'm aware of that. This case is a little complicated with the mental state of the alleged murderer. I hope it won't go to trial."

"I would agree. I'm not sure the judge who hears the case would agree with the charge. I suggest you talk it over with the district attorney."

"Your Honor, I understand and thank you for your input." Katie spoke politely and walked out of the judge's chambers.

Katie was relieved the first arraignments were over, and she finished in less than an hour. She checked her watch and realized, thankfully, she had enough time to go home and change from her courtroom attire into something more spring-like and still meet Will Palmer at 11 a.m.

445

Will Palmer was getting cleaned up after a demanding day yesterday. He was finding this a good day already—the sun was coming into his apartment. He turned on the news. A reporter stood across the street in view of the main entrances of the cathedral watching the crowds enter wearing their Easter clothes. Since she wasn't allowed to stand at the church entrance, the reporter had a difficult time getting anyone's reaction to Monsignor Triplett's death. Many who did speak with her didn't know who he was. The few parishioners who stopped did express sadness for a priest they admired.

Palmer knew there was still paperwork to finish at the station and wondered if he should work on it after Mass or wait. He was hoping Katie would invite him to her family's dinner. He wanted to spend some time with her. It was the Easter wish he was praying for.

Father Juan Morales had just finished Easter Mass at the cathedral. His family sat in the first two pews. He was happy to see all their smiling faces as they looked their best. His sisters and brothers were with their families to give him support as they had done each Easter since he became a priest. When he reached them after Mass, he told them he would be over in two hours. He knew when he arrived, he needed great courage to break the news to them about his one-way trip to Rome and the opportunity the cardinal was giving him for further academic studies. He thought about giving David a call to wish him a happy Easter but realized the best thing to do was just text him.

Father David O'Hara heard the ping on his phone letting him know he had a text message. He was getting out of bed. He had worked hard the night before with Bishop Newsome and Father McFadden on the Easter Vigil that concluded at midnight. He spent time at the reception for those received into the church. It wasn't until 2:00 in the morning that he was finally able to go to bed. He was thankful he had been assigned the 11:30 a.m. Mass. As he looked at his phone, he realized he had two new messages. One was from Jonathan Pickle asking which Mass he was doing (he never liked the word doing—for it was more than doing—it was celebrating), and the second was from Juan wishing him a happy Easter. He texted Jonathan to say he was celebrating Mass at 11:30 a.m. and to Juan only the words 'Happy Easter.' He wanted to say more but knew it wasn't prudent to do so.

When Jonathan received the text message from Father O'Hara, he told his mom he wanted to go to Holy Name of Jesus Church for the 11:30 a.m. Mass since Father O'Hara was 'doing it.' Emma was so happy he wanted to go to Mass, and Holy Name of Jesus was probably a good idea. She had heard the news about Sam being a suspect in the murder of Monsignor Triplett. She wondered if his wife and children saw him today. Now all Emma could do was pray for him and for his family. She told Jonathan they'd leave by 10:00 a.m. to get to the church, and he gave no resistance. He knew she liked to be at church early.

Father McFadden and Bishop Newsome were sitting at the breakfast table at Holy Name of Jesus. They shared how wonderful everything came together at the Easter Vigil celebration. The music was exceptional, the catechumens and candidates were well-prepared, and the bishop felt he had given one of his best Easter homilies. Of course, the bishop, after any Mass, assured himself it was one of his best homilies. Father O'Hara walked in and wished them both a happy Easter.

The bishop was glad to see him. "Thank you, David, for all your help."

"I think all went as planned," Father O'Hara commented.

"It did indeed," Father McFadden agreed.

"This morning's 8:00 Mass was packed!" Bishop Newsome exclaimed.

447

"That's good to hear. I'll leave you two, so I can get myself over for the next Mass." Father McFadden excused himself, rinsed off his dishes and placed them in the dishwasher.

"David, how are you?" Bishop Newsome asked. "You look a little tired."

"I'm okay. I've ended my physical relationship with Father Morales. We both agreed to keep it platonic. Our priesthood is too important, and we decided it was best for both of us. I'm sure by now you know the cardinal is sending him on a one-way ticket to Rome." Father O'Hara struggled with the words.

The bishop tried to provide some comfort and guidance. "David, it's for the best. I can't tell you it will be easy. It will feel like a loss, but I want to help you with it.

"And what are you saying?"

"I've spoken to the Abbot at Gethsemani, and he's open to you coming for a thirty-day retreat. "Would you be open to that?"

David's mood shifted from one of loss to one of uncertainty and anger. "So you want to send me away for thirty days and then what?" He pushed his chair back as he got up to get another cup of coffee avoiding eye contact with the bishop.

The bishop quietly responded to David's anger in a softer, gentler voice. "How you approach this, David, will help you get back on the right track with your priesthood, and I want that for you."

As David sat down, he wasn't sure what to say next. "I... I know. I'm just not sure that what you're offering will help."

The bishop quickly responded as he leaned forward. "I think it will give you the opportunity to clear your head, spend some time in prayer, do some reading, recharge your spiritual batteries and come back here ready to be an even better priest."

"You mean you want me back at Holy Name of Jesus Parish?" David was surprised he would be welcomed back by the person who is sending him away.

"By all means!" The bishop assured him. "I want you to come back, but I also want you to work with a psychologist, so you'll stay on the proper path for your priesthood."

"When do you want me to go to Gethsemani?" David was now more receptive to being away for thirty days.

"Your departure date will be determined by the cardinal and the abbot, sometime within the next ten days. The cardinal wants to see you after Easter." The bishop knew this decision was difficult for them to discuss on Easter.

"I have to meet with Cardinal Flinn?"

"Yes, probably Tuesday, so don't make any plans. It's a formality, and also his way of making sure something is in your file that he did meet with you. If you like, I can be there with you."

"I understand—protect the archdiocese." David had to stifle his anger.

The bishop wanted to avoid more discussion. He quickly changed the subject. "Are you seeing your family today?"

"Yes."

"It would be good for you to tell them you're going on a thirty-day retreat."

"Okay." Father O'Hara tried to absorb the last ten minutes of his life and the future that was ahead of him.

"David. This is will be good for you. And hopefully, when you return you will thank me." The bishop got up to turn on the television to catch the cardinal's Easter homily. It was a tradition in New York for a local TV station to televise the cardinal's Easter Mass. Millions of Catholics, non-Catholics, believers and non-believers saw it. Watching the screen, he saw the Easter Gospel had just been proclaimed by the deacon who carried the Book of Gospels over to the cardinal to kiss as a sign of reverence for the sacred word. The cardinal went up the steps to the octagonal shaped prestigious marble ambo to begin his Easter message.

"My brothers and sisters, today Saint Patrick's Cathedral rejoices as we come together for this Easter celebration. Yet at the same time, it is saddened that my representative for the cathedral, our rector, Reverend Monsignor Steven Triplett was found dead in this sacred place yesterday morning. I want to offer my condolences and prayers to his brother, Thom Triplett, who is sitting in the front pew and to the many friends of Monsignor Triplett. Monsignor is celebrating today the Easter we all look forward to, the one of everlasting life with our risen Lord, Jesus Christ." The cardinal looked to Thom Triplett and recognized Jennifer Gibson sitting next to him. For just a moment, he lost stride, and his voice faltered slightly, but he quickly recovered.

"Very well done." Bishop Newsome knew the cardinal well and noticed the unexpected pause.

"Today, we, as a community of believers, gather here or listen at home with great reason to celebrate. Having completed our own Lenten penances and sacrifices, this day should be joyful for all. Look at those around you. Amid the scaffolding and dust, or the chaos or hardships you may be facing, we stop on this day to remember what it is all about — at the end of the sacrifice, there is joy. Jesus Christ teaches us this today."

"He has found a way to tie in the restoration to Easter." Bishop Newsome marveled. He stood up and put his dishes in the dishwasher. "Happy Easter, David."

"Happy Easter, Bishop. I'll talk with you more after I've spoken with my family."

"I always look forward to our conversations, my friend. Give your family my best regards." With that, the bishop left as he prepared to go visit his mother.

David sat alone now. He wasn't interested in listening to the cardinal. He stood slowly feeling a great uncertainty about the bishop's decision and the talk with his parents. He walked over and turned off the television. He looked at the kitchen clock and realized he didn't have much time to pull his homily together. He quickly returned to his room asking the Holy Spirit to help. As much as the stone had been rolled away, and Our Lord had risen, he felt as if he was in the tomb, and the stone was being placed back in front and sealing him away at Gethsemani. This was to be his homily — we can live a life buried in the tomb — or we can celebrate the risen life Christ has given to all believers.

As Father O'Hara came out of his room, he almost ran into Father McFadden who proudly announced, "The biggest congregation I have ever seen at the 9:30 a.m. Mass."

"I'm sure it will be just as crowded at 11:30 a.m. We do have a lot of Easter Catholics." Father O'Hara tried to feel the joy of the day.

"Indeed, we do. Are you going to be with your family after Mass?"

"Yes... in fact, they should be here for this Mass."

"Give them my best. Happy Easter, David, and thanks for everything."

"Happy Easter, Matthew, and thank you for your support." Father O'Hara reached for the door to go to church just as the clock in the hall sounded 11:00 a.m.

Outside Holy Name of Jesus, Lieutenant Will Palmer looked sharp in a light, grayish-blue suit, white shirt, complemented by a blue and green striped tie. Katie noticed his well-chosen Easter attire and was pleased to see him looking amazingly well-dressed.

"Happy Easter!" Without thinking, he gave her a kiss on the cheek.

"Happy Easter to you!" And without thinking, Katie returned the kiss.

Will was pleased.

They walked up the fifteen steps to the huge, wooden ten-foot front doors being open by the ushers. They entered the narthex and could smell the aroma from the array of flowers. They were surprised to see Detective Patrick Sabor, his wife and their two small children in front of them.

451

"Wow, this is a pleasant surprise! Happy Easter, Palmer remarked.

Sabor stopped and turned. He grinned. "Boss, I overheard you talking about coming to Holy Name of Jesus for the 11:30 Mass, and I caved into my wife's request to come to church this one Sunday. I only made the request to go to Holy Name of Jesus because I would know someone—you! I wanted to see if you'd really be here."

"Enough with the Boss. We're not on duty. Let's see if we can all sit together." As much as his partner joked about his faith, Palmer knew Sabor had a deep love and devotion to it even though he might not always publicly practice or express it. He was happy to see him after the long day they had yesterday.

Walking in right behind the Sabors were Jonathan and Emma Pickle. Jonathan wore his favorite button-down blue shirt and his dad's Notre Dame tie. Emma couldn't be happier, thankful Jonathan was at Mass with her.

Fifteen minutes before Mass, the usher came to the ambo and made the announcement. "Would you please move to the center of your pew to help with those who are still looking for seats?" Palmer, Katie, and Sabor with his family were trying to make additional space on the pew as they recognized Officer VanDyke standing in the aisle looking for a seat.

"Happy Easter, Officer." Palmer extended his hand and invited him to sit in the pew with everyone. "Glad you're here."

"You clean up nicely, Lieutenant."

Palmer just smiled. "Thanks, and so do you. Is this your parish?"

"Today it is..." and before they could say anything more, the entrance hymn began, and everyone stood to sing "Jesus Christ is Risen Today."

A little over an hour and fifteen minutes later Mass ended. As the massive crowd of people left through the various doors, Palmer and the others waited. They stood in the pew and looked around. Emma and Jonathan Pickle approached, and Emma introduced her son to them. Jonathan asked his mom if he could go light a candle for his dad. After Emma gave him a couple of dollars and watched him walk over to the votive candles, she thought she should be with him, but instead she got the courage to ask Palmer about Sam.

"He was booked this morning as an accessory to the murder of Monsignor Triplett."

"I can't believe he was involved." Emma had tears in her eyes.

"I'm sorry. Knowing Sam gave you the sleeping pill, you have a right to bring assault charges against him." Palmer knew he shouldn't say any more since she would very likely be called as a witness for Sam's trial.

"I need to think about that."

"I think the best thing to do is to pray for him, and I hope you did this morning. You have my num...." Palmer was interrupted by Jonathan's return to the group.

"Mom, let's go say hello to Father O'Hara," Jonathan blurted. He saw her tears and wondered why she was crying, but questions would have to wait.

"Thank you detectives and Happy Easter. I'll be in touch," Emma promised. She followed Jonathan to the front of the church while the others looked on.

Father O'Hara was surrounded by his family, but when he saw Emma and Jonathan approach, a big smile came across his face. He was happy to see them. He took a few moments and introduced Emma and Jonathan to his family. Within a few minutes, someone in the family invited the two of them for Easter brunch. Emma wondered if Father O'Hara had said something before they arrived. It didn't really matter because Emma was thrilled with the invitation. She didn't want to return to the apartment. If she did, she would just dwell on the last two years with Sam and the big mistake she made by becoming involved with him.

453

As his family said their goodbyes, Emma and Jonathan were about to leave when Father O'Hara called them to the side. "I need to tell you two something. It looks like I will be away for a thirty-day retreat starting in a few days. The bishop just informed me of his decision. The good news is I am coming back to Holy Name of Jesus."

"That'll be great... then we can get together!" Jonathan realized if he could do well while Father O'Hara was away, they'd be able to jam one day on their guitars!

"I hope you can find peace in your time away." Emma tried to hold back her tears.

"I pray you will also find peace and happiness, Emma." Father O'Hara tried to console her.

Emma looked for a tissue in her purse. "I'll be fine. I just need some time."

Jonathan wasn't paying much attention to the conversation between Father O'Hara and his mom. Instead, he went to get a Sunday bulletin.

Father O'Hara needed to return to his family waiting in the church. "Emma, I'll see you at my parent's house soon." .

Emma nodded. When Jonathan returned, she wrapped her arm around her son. He was with the most important man in her life now, and she was looking forward to enjoying being with Father O'Hara's family. He gave her the address and said come whenever they wanted. He would try to be there within the hour.

Palmer, Katie and the Sabors watched the church empty. "Happy Easter, Will. We're off to lunch with my in-laws."

"Sabor, glad you came today!" Palmer extended his hand.

"Honestly, so am I."

"Looks like you have your hands full, Patrick." Palmer watched his colleague's three-year-old daughter pulling on her father's suit coat.

"I wouldn't have it any other way!" Sabor laughed as he was dragged away by his two children.

"Happy Easter, Patrick. How blessed you are."

"I should be going too." Officer VanDyke said. "Lieutenant Palmer, thanks for letting me sit with you."

"Glad you came." Palmer gave VanDyke a pat on the back.

"After yesterday, it was good to come on my own. It's what I needed and need," Officer VanDyke admitted.

Palmer flashed him a friendly smile. "Enjoy the day. Happy Easter."

"Thanks." Officer VanDyke walked down the side aisle.

"Well, it looks like it's just you and me." Palmer looked at Katie. "Do you have any plans?"

Katie took Will's hand. "How would you like to come to my parents' house for Easter dinner? You'll have to put up with my sister and her family!"

"I thought you'd never ask. I'd love to." Palmer knew the rest of the paperwork and whatever else he was considering today could wait.

Easter was a day of celebration for almost everyone. It wasn't about death—it was about the life that came from Jesus' death. For those who were able to enjoy the day, it was one filled with laughter, joy and being with family and friends. This Easter, Will Palmer realized this as he held Katie's hand.

The Delfinos had all gathered together, along with Jared and Jamie. Even though there were problems and uncertainty, the Delfinos treated these supervisors as family. Today wouldn't be any different. Jared and Jamie both knew they had a good thing with this family and didn't want to be alone. They were glad to be invited to a meal of baby back ribs, chicken and steak. They wouldn't worry about their future for one day. It might be the last Delfino gathering for a while.

After dinner, Father Juan Morales and his family sat at the table and talked. His parents were so pleased to have Juan home, but they could see something was troubling their son.

"Mom and Dad, I need to tell you something. When I leave for Rome tomorrow to visit the Vatican... I... I won't be coming back with the group." Father Juan stopped as tears formed in his eyes.

"What do you mean, you won't be coming back?" His mom grabbed her son's hand.

"The cardinal wants me to stay and pursue further studies. He feels this is a good time for me."

"And you are just letting us know now?" Juan's dad was annoyed and confused.

"I'm sorry. I honestly just found out yesterday."

"Son, is this what you want?" Juan's dad asked.

"I'm trying to see it as a good opportunity." Juan tried to convince himself this was true.

"So, this is goodbye?"

"It's not goodbye. It's more like until I see you again. Maybe you can come over."

As tears rolled down her cheeks, Mrs. Morales shouted "How can we come over? We don't have that kind of money!"

Juan knew he needed to reassure her. "I'll be back at Christmas." But he wasn't sure that would happen.

"What are you going to study?" Mr. Morales demanded more information.

"I'm not sure, possibly Scripture."

"Did you do something to upset the cardinal which caused him to make this new assignment so quickly? I just don't understand, especially with the death of Monsignor Triplett." Mr. Morales grew more upset.

"Dad, calm down. Since I was already going, Cardinal Flinn wanted me to have some time to get acclimated to the area, possibly to take some classes in Italian before I start the academic classes in the fall." Juan tried to figure out what else he could say to help them understand the cardinal's reason for doing this now.

"We love you son." Mr. Morales gave his son a big hug and then returned to his wife who was crying hysterically.

"Mom, Dad, it's going to be all right. I'll make sure you have a computer with a webcam, so we can communicate with each other. With all the gadgets we have, it won't seem like I'm so far away." Again, Juan wanted to comfort his parents. But no matter what he said, his mother was still devastated. He hugged her and let her cry while he did the same.

After a few minutes, Juan thought it best to say goodbye. His parents insisted on going to the airport tomorrow to see him off. Juan told his parents the group would not know he was staying until the last day of his trip, and his parents must not say anything. He hugged them both and left. As he walked back to the subway station, he felt all alone.

At the O'Hara house, everyone had said their goodbyes, and David was left alone with his parents. He took a few minutes then sat them down to tell them of his indiscretion with Father Morales and the consequences of it. His dad was furious. His mother was in denial. All David wanted to do was to leave and let them try to come to terms with it on their own. His dad wouldn't let him go without sharing one of the strongest lectures he had ever given his son. He told David to look seriously at his life and decide whether his priesthood mattered. David knew his father was right, and he knew he needed more than a thirty-day retreat. He also needed to discuss his messed-up life with someone on a regular basis. After the lecture, the tears and the hugs came. Now he could leave knowing his parents would always be there for him. But the walk back to the subway station was one of the loneliest, and instead of falling into the temptation from the devil, he pulled out his rosary to pray. He knew he was blessed with his faith, his family and his friends. And one friend, in particular, he would deeply miss after tomorrow.

Chapter 35

With the Easter Sunday celebrations over, Monday after Easter normally was an exodus of priests from the parishes hoping to take a few days off. For some, it was going home, and for others, it meant taking off with friends for a few rounds of golf in a warmer climate. Pastors were first to get days off, and associate priests, if lucky, would get one or two days after the pastor returned. With Monsignor Triplett's funeral scheduled for Friday, many of the priests adjusted their schedules to attend. Most of the priests appreciated the late Monsignor wanted to take part in the vigil and funeral.

As beautiful as the weather was on Easter in New York City, how miserable it was the next day. The darkened skies, the blowing winds and the sudden bursts of lightning foretold another spring storm. While trying to remain dry during these storms, umbrellas took on their own ritual and eventually flipped and inverted in, surrendering to the fairly strong wind. These colorful, broken, umbrellas would lay lifeless at the subway stations.

Emma Pickle's emotions were much like the weather — gloomy and dark. Having had one day of peace and joy with her son yesterday, she was feeling a knot in her stomach as she prepared to go to the police station to give her statement. She thought about what the lieutenant had said to her after

Easter Mass and wondered whether she should press charges against Sam for drugging her.

When they arrived home last night, Emma had told Jonathan that she had to go to the police station first thing in the morning and didn't know how long she would be there. She knew Jonathan probably wouldn't be up before noon, so she planned to leave a note on the counter for him listing a couple of things that needed to be done.

After breakfast and her morning prayers, she blew out the candle on her corner prayer table and decided it was time to leave. As the thunder rumbled, Emma picked up her umbrella and left the quiet of her apartment. The rain had not started as she entered the subway station, but by the look of the sky, it was not far behind. Emma realized as she sat waiting, that this was the beginning of a new chapter, alone, uncertain and nervous of what the future would bring. It would take a good forty minutes to get to the police station. For now, she had time to think and write some questions she wanted to be sure to ask the lieutenant.

Lieutenant Palmer was all smiles as he walked into the police station. He had a wonderful Easter with Katie and felt she enjoyed his company too. He was hoping he would have some reason to call her today just to hear her voice and try to plan a real date.

Detective Sabor was right behind him carrying his donut, coffee and a broken umbrella. He looked right at Lieutenant Palmer. "Greetings! Someone seems to be in a good mood."

"Yesterday was a good day. How about yours?" Palmer gave another smile.

"It was good. The weather was good. The family was lots of laughs. Great food, and I even got along with the in-laws!"

"Good to hear."

"What can I do to help with the cathedral murder case?"

"Do we have all the statements we need?" Palmer knew some were missing.

"No. We need Mrs. Pickle's? Is there anyone else's you want? What about the priests?"

"I don't see any need to get any more than we have." Palmer remembered he wanted to talk with Monsignor Black about the photo he had shown him yesterday. He hoped he could eventually get it and return it to him.

"You sure?" Sabor asked.

"You said you checked everything out, and the information provided seems to coincide with what everyone has been saying. Correct?"

"I believe so."

"All the evidence has been recorded properly?"

"I want to double check the list of evidence."

"I believe once we get the statement from Mrs. Pickle, we are all set." Palmer looked at the files stacked on his desk.

Not five minutes later, he was sitting in his office taking Emma's statement.

As they were finishing, Emma shared a concern. "Lieutenant, I'm confused and hurt. I don't know if I should file assault charges against Sam."

"What Sam Tolden did to you was wrong. Only you can decide what to do. I can ask one of the department's psychologists to talk with you if that would help."

"That may be a good idea." Emma took a deep breath, relieved with this information.

"You don't have to file the charges today. You can wait."

"Lieutenant, how... how is Sam?"

"I'm not sure. I know he's still in jail, and the family hasn't posted bail." Emma said nothing. She signed her statement and thanked Lieutenant Palmer for allowing her to wait until today to come in. Palmer got up from his desk and went to see if he could arrange for Emma to see one of the department psychologists.

Looking out the window, Emma was pleased to see the sun trying to come out as brightness was slowly returning to her life. She wanted to get home to be with her son. When Palmer returned, he gave her a card with a name and a number for her to make an appointment. She promised to give the psychologist a call. She excused herself and returned to the subway station to begin her journey back home.

Since he found an excuse to go and see her, Palmer picked up the phone to call Katie. "I have another statement for you on the Monsignor Triplett murder. I would be happy to bring it to your office."

"Sure, come on over about noon."

"I get hungry for lunch about that time of day." Palmer hinted.

"And so do I!" Katie remembered how special yesterday was with him.

"See you then." Palmer hung up the phone feeling good about the first part of his day.

As he sat back, his desk phone rang, and it was the medical examiner's office.

"Lieutenant Palmer, Sara Brown calling. How was your Easter?"

"Wonderful!" Palmer was caught off guard. "And yours?"

"It was nice. I've reviewed the tests on Monsignor Steven Triplett, and in talking with his cardiologist, I can confirm my assumption. I won't bore you with all the medical details, but the test results show he had a heart attack before the assault with the candlestick. It's unlikely he would have survived the heart attack even if he had received aide. The trauma to the head occurred several minutes later. Medically, the head wounds occurred postmortem."

"So, no first-degree murder charge?"

"No, and I'm even wondering about second degree?"

"So am I." Palmer knew the attorney was going for an insanity defense. "Thanks for your update. I'll pass the information on to Ms. Rozzelle." So much for the good day he was having.

461

At the cathedral, Father Morales was still trying to sort out what he would need. He had marked a couple of boxes to be shipped to Italy, and he had quite a few that would have to go into storage. Even though Father O'Hara had helped with a lot of the packing, there were still so many loose ends. Who would ship the boxes? What about his mail? Would he need to do anything with his phone? Was Father O'Hara coming to say goodbye? Would he hear from any of the parishioners once word got out? All he knew was he had to be at the airport by 3:00, and it was already noon.

He turned on his television to listen to the noon news. The lead story was still Monsignor Triplett's murder and details of the two suspects. He felt hurt and saddened if Sam and Brian had committed the murder. He wondered what could have provoked them to end the life of Monsignor. Father Morales had not talked with any of the office staff and could only speculate on what they thought. He was disappointed he wouldn't even get to say goodbye to them. Knowing the effect the murder was having on him, he wondered if someone from the archdiocese would be brought in to help the rest of the staff cope with this crisis or were they left to try to manage alone. He hoped the cardinal would do so.

Father Morales was shocked at the next story. The Delfino Construction Company was charged with falsifying business records. They showed a very worried Joseph Delfino with his attorney preparing to enter a plea of guilty to one count of first-degree falsifying business records. In a statement read by his son, A.J., he insisted that the plea would have "no impact on our ability to complete existing and future projects." The camera showed the cathedral still covered with scaffolding.

Father Juan turned off the television. He had heard enough. He was looking forward to meeting his parents for lunch after celebrating the 12:30 p.m. Mass. He knew most of those going to Rome wanted to begin their pilgrimage at this Mass.

Thom best dealt with grief by keeping busy. He decided the best thing for him to do was to go to his office. When he walked in, his staff was surprised to see him. They offered their condolences, and Thom thanked them. But he was eager to get to his desk to work and eat his lunch. He sat for a moment. Work could wait; first he called Jennifer. "Good afternoon. Did you see the news?" Thom took a huge bite from his meatball sub.

"Well, hello, and no I didn't." Jennifer moved the papers aside on her desk and opened her lunch. "What did I miss?"

"The Delfinos pleaded guilty to falsifying business records."

"I think it's the beginning of guilty pleas." Jennifer hoped. "How's your day going?"

"Not bad. I called the Pickle's residence and left a voicemail to call me. I want to let them know about the life insurance policy. It's going to be a nice surprise for that kid."

"Hopefully, he'll be thankful. Do you know him?"

"I never met him, but my brother always spoke well of him. I also contacted Bishop Newsome and let him know my brother had asked him to be the homilist for his funeral. He was very honored with the request. My brother chose the scripture readings, so I provided all that information to him. He was very conciliatory and wanted to know if there was anything he wanted me to mention specifically about Steven."

"What did you say?" Jennifer picked at her spinach salad.

"I just said he was my best friend. I couldn't say any more than that." Thom tried to get another bite of his sandwich in before Jennifer asked another question.

"Bishop Newsome will do an excellent job with the homily. I don't think you have anything to worry about."

"I agree." Thom's secretary brought him the mail, and he was very curious about the top letter. It was from his brother. He put down the sandwich, took out his letter opener, slowly opened it and began to read.

"You still on the phone?" Jennifer wondered why there was such a long period of silence.

"You're not going to believe this! Are you free? I need to show you something?"

"My next appointment isn't until 2:00."

"I'm on my way over!" Thom folded the letter and placed it back in the envelope, took a few more bites of his sandwich, put on his jacket and informed his secretary he would be back by 2:00. Jennifer's office was a good twenty minutes away—no matter if he took a cab or the subway. As he walked out of his building, rain was lightly falling from the dark sky, he hailed a cab.

Thom arrived at the office of Jennifer Gibson. He just walked in and was a little concerned there was no one at the front desk.

"Jennifer, where is everyone?" Thom asked as he opened her office door.

"Probably out to lunch." Jennifer knew four other people worked in her office. She was making a note to discuss at her next staff meeting the importance of someone always being at the front desk.

"I'm just surprised no one is around."

"I'm here, so what's so important you had to come all the way over here to see me?"

He pulled the letter from his pocket and gave it to Jennifer. Bewildered, she looked at Thom, opened the envelope and began reading.

She couldn't believe it. Joseph Delfino had signed a statement detailing the arrangement he had made with the cardinal. Would the cardinal really provide an annulment for him if he could get the cathedral done in time for the anniversary celebration? She only knew it was one more thing to add to her file on the cardinal.

"Thom, can I make a copy of this?"

Thom knew she was working on a case that could be damaging to the cardinal. "I thought you might want the original."

"Do you mind?"

"Only if you make a couple of copies for me. I'll see him tomorrow." Thom realized the importance of the letter.

Jennifer made copies and scanned the image into the growing computer file about the cardinal. Before going home, she backed up her files for extra security.

"Do you really want to present this to him when you see him tomorrow?" Jennifer gave Thom three copies of the letter.

"If it will help get my annulment, I do. I want to marry you." Thom waited to see her reaction as he got up from his chair and went over to her. It was the first time he had said those words to her.

Jennifer stood, put her arms around him... "I want to marry you, Thom—in the Catholic Church. But I'm not sure this will help. If the cardinal gets upset, it might delay your annulment. Your brother may have had good intentions to help you, but this might just backfire."

"I'll wait to see if there is an opportunity to discuss it with the cardinal. I wish I had been able to ask my brother why he even sent me this."

"He must have known something or felt you could use it somehow."

"I'll be a happy man when I can marry you." Thom kissed her.

She kissed him back and then looked into his eyes... "I'll be praying for you." The moment didn't last long. Her secretary and paralegals returned from lunch.

"I need to go!" Thom put the copies of the letter into his jacket. I'll give you a call later."

After Thom left the office, Jennifer considered the letter he received from his brother. A case was building, and she was confident that charges would be brought against the

465

archdiocese and the cardinal. She had hoped Monsignor Triplett's efforts would resolve the case out of court. With him gone, she would have to set up an appointment with the cardinal and the attorneys for the archdiocese. Now she was worried she'd have to battle an institution that had been in existence for over 2,000 years and one she loved.

Thom returned to his office where his secretary gave him two messages — Emma Pickle and the cardinal had both called. He knew what his conversation would be with Emma, but he wondered what the cardinal wanted. Curious, he decided to call the cardinal first.

"Your Eminence, I didn't realize the number I was calling went directly to you. Is this a bad time?"

"No, I am at the television studio doing my weekly message for the shut-ins of New York. I thought I was to do this on Wednesday, but I discovered this morning it was today." It disappointed the cardinal not to have the day off to be with friends.

Thom was unsure why the cardinal was giving him this information. "How can I help you?"

"It was good to see you at Saint Patrick's yesterday. Sorry I didn't get a chance to say hello to you and Ms. Gibson. Were you able to find any papers concerning your brother's funeral?"

"Yes. Yes... I did." Thom cautiously responded.

"With everything that is going on at the cathedral, I'm trying to help with the preparations. I was asked to see if your brother had selected music or readings."

"He has, but I left the information at home. I'll bring everything tomorrow. Are we still meeting at 10:00 a.m.?"

"Yes, at the chancery. Do you know where it is?"

"I've been there before." Thom remembered the time he had met Monsignor Stone in the Tribunal office about his own marriage annulment.

"Did your brother name a homilist?" The cardinal asked.

466

"Yes... he named Bishop Newsome, and I've called him." Thom was thankful his brother had named someone he trusted and respected.

"I'm surprised it wasn't Monsignor David Stone." The cardinal waited for Thom's reaction.

Thom understood the remark, but he didn't respond. "No, my brother was very specific in designating Bishop Newsome. I'm sure Monsignor Stone will be one of the pallbearers."

"By all means, Thom. We can review this tomorrow. You have helped ease my mind knowing your brother had made plans. I wish all my priests would do the same. I will see you tomorrow." With that, the cardinal abruptly ended the conversation.

"See you tomorrow." Thom wondered why the cardinal had called. Was the cardinal searching for something from him? ...but what? Did the cardinal know his brother had a copy of the incriminating letter? He wouldn't think about it until he was with the cardinal tomorrow.

Thom's secretary suddenly interrupted his train of thought. "Excuse me. Ms. Peggy Richard doesn't have an appointment, but she wants to know if you could see her."

"Certainly, I'll see her. Have her wait in the conference room." Thom was disappointed. His telephone call to Emma Pickle would have to wait.

After Mass, Father Morales said goodbye to Monsignor Black and Father Crumbley. He thanked them both for their support and friendship while at the cathedral. They both expressed their concern for him and promised to keep in touch. But each was wondering what would happen at the cathedral with half of the priest staff gone.

Father Morales with his suitcase in one hand, a passport, airline ticket and itinerary around his neck, left the cathedral parish house for the last time. His parents met him outside the back door. Together they walked to the subway station at 51st Street and boarded the 6 train where they got off on

Spring Street in Little Italy and walked the four minutes to one of their favorite restaurants, Benito One on Mulberry Street. The crowds and noise prevented his parents from asking more questions and shedding more tears. At lunch, they talked about everything. He saw the tears in their eyes knowing in just a couple of hours their son would be away for several months. It was just happening too fast for all of them.

After lunch, they walked the three blocks to the Canal Street subway station. They took the J line from Canal Street and transferred to the A train at Nassau Street which took them to JFK International Airport. The crowded subway pulled into the station where it seemed 200 passengers with their luggage disembarked. The bustling, crowded airport was always going through some sort remodeling. Today was no different. The family stayed close to one another as they slowly walked to the Delta ticket counter.

Father Morales recognized the small group going to the Vatican with him since they were holding a banner saying "Saint Patrick's Cathedral, New York City." They hoped to wave the banner at the Wednesday Papal audience, and if they were lucky, the Pope would see it. They also wanted others to know they were on their way to the Vatican.

The Delta agent checked Father Morales in, gave him his boarding pass and checked his bag. Then the young priest pulled his parents aside to tell them how much he loved them and would be praying for them. As they said their goodbyes, and each gave him a hug and a kiss, they were all crying. Without saying another word, his parents finally turned and walked away to return to the subway station.

Standing with the tour group, Father Morales heard them all try to get his attention with some statement or question. The voices seemed to merge together with him not responding to any of them. There was only one voice he was hoping to hear, and it was Father O'Hara. He realized Father O'Hara would not be there. Father Morales had to accept this trip as the beginning of a new chapter in his life. He closed his eyes and asked for courage and strength. He was determined to make the best of the next few days. He opened his eyes, walked with the group to the TSA security check-in and talked about the opportunities they would have.

Sitting alone in his room, looking at his watch, Father O'Hara realized Juan was at the airport. He wanted to pick up the phone and call him and wish him well but decided it probably was best not to. Instead, he looked up to heaven, made the sign of the cross, bowed his head and offered a prayer for safe travels and blessings on Juan's first trip to the Vatican.

It was now close to 4:00 p.m. At his office, Thom sat quietly still at his desk, blankly staring out the window, thinking about his brother, and surprised by another afternoon shower. He had one more phone call to make before he could end for the day. It was to the Pickle residence. This time someone answered the phone.

"This is Thom Triplett. I am Monsignor Triplett's brother. Who am I speaking to?"

"This is Jonathan Pickle."

"Jonathan, is your mom at home?"

"Just a moment." He yelled, "Hey, Mom, Mr. Triplett. Is on the phone."

"Mr. Triplett. How are you today?" Emma began.

"I'm doing the best I can. And you?"

"I'm doing okay. This morning I had to go to the police station and give my statement. It's just so sad knowing who may have killed your brother."

"It's all very sad. I lost my best friend." Thom felt the loss every time he shared something about his brother. "Well, I'm calling because I have some good news."

"What's that?" Emma said.

469

"My brother left a life insurance policy of $50,000 to your son for his college education."

The news shocked Emma. "You're kidding me!" Unable to say anything more, she just looked at Jonathan who was trying to find something to eat in the kitchen.

"I can give you more details later on how he'll receive the money, but I wanted to end my day by sharing some good news with you," Thom explained.

"Thank you. Thank you so much…. This is great news for Jonathan. I'll let him know. I… I… just can't believe it…. We'll see you at the funeral." She ended the conversation and shared the great news with her son. He had the biggest smile on his face, as he hugged his mom. Jonathon would never forget the friendship Monsignor Triplett had shown him.

Chapter 36

The cardinal woke by 5:00 a.m. each morning to begin his day. Today was no different. It was his usual routine. With the coffee pot set the night before, the first thing he needed was a cup of strong black coffee. Then he forced himself on the treadmill for at least thirty minutes. The doctor ordered him to use the treadmill an hour a day and change some of his eating habits. If he didn't lose some weight, he'd become a diabetic. He wasn't losing weight but was listening to the Spanish lessons hoping to become more proficient in the native language of the pope.

After a quick shower, he put on his black clerical suit that was tailored to fit his size. He went into his chapel for his holy hour which included the universal prayers of the church: The Office of Readings, Morning Prayer, and some quiet time for reflection. Afterward, if he wasn't celebrating a public Mass or at a parish for the Sacrament of Confirmation, he celebrated a private Mass.

He usually finished around 7:15 a.m. and went to his kitchen to prepare breakfast which included a bowl or two of one of his favorite sugar cereals, usually Frosted Flakes, a glass of juice and his second cup of coffee. The calories burned off while on the treadmill were put back on by consuming this unhealthy breakfast. His other ritual was finding *The New York*

Times at his door. He looked forward to a half hour of reading and watching one of the morning network news shows.

Around 8:00 a.m. he heard his doorbell ring. His driver arrived to take him to the chancery. The cardinal chose his own driver, a priest of the archdiocese. The driver also served as the cardinal's personal secretary. The job was not as glamorous as everyone assumed. The priest had to follow the cardinal's schedule and that could mean some fourteen to sixteen-hour days. Usually, the young priest assigned lasted two years before he would burn out or request a change in assignment. Father Peter Unser served in the position for almost two years and was still doing a good job.

As the cardinal got into his car, his schedule to review for this Tuesday was on the seat beside him. As he looked at it this particular morning, much of his day was dealing with the situation at the cathedral. His first appointment was at 10:00 a.m. with Thom Triplett to work out the details for the funeral. That was followed by his meeting with Father David O'Hara and the decision to send him to Gethsemani for a thirty-day retreat. At noon it was lunch with Bishop Newsome to discuss the vacancies at the cathedral and Holy Name of Jesus. He recognized the need to talk with his director of media and communications over the issue of the Delfino Construction Company and whether to make a statement concerning the charges against the company coordinating the cathedral restoration. Donald Armenti would have a draft of a press release ready for him to review.

The cardinal gave Father Peter Unser time off after the Holy Thursday celebration. He hadn't seen him since that evening, so after looking at the schedule and putting it aside, he inquired, "How was your Easter?"

"It was wonderful, Your Eminence. Thank you for the time off. I'm thankful you asked Deacon Wise to be your MC at the cathedral, so I could watch my future brother-in-law come into the church. It was special to give him the Eucharist for the first time. We are fortunate to receive the graces that come from the sacraments."

"Glad you were there. I have told you many times that family comes first."

"Your Eminence, I'm very sorry to hear about Monsignor Triplett. I always liked him." Father Unser knew the close relationship the cardinal had with the rector.

"We have lost a good priest." The cardinal looked out the window to another overcast gray day in the city realizing his own somber mood. He began making mental notes about the priests in the archdiocese who would be good candidates as the next rector of Saint Patrick's. He knew by moving one priest, the domino effect of having to move others could happen.

"Is there anything special you want me to focus on today, Your Eminence?" Father Unser asked as the traffic inched along.

"I will give you a list of a few priests I need to speak with in person. See if we can set up some appointments. Hopefully, they are in town. I also want you to sit in on the first part of my meeting with Monsignor Triplett's brother for the funeral arrangements. Once you have the information for the funeral service, then you can put the programs together." The cardinal then asked, "So how long have you been at Our Lady of Rosary Parish?"

"You assigned me there two years ago."

"Are you happy there?"

"Yes, I get along very well with Father Zansiski. Why are you asking?"

"I may have to move you." The cardinal looked at the rearview mirror to see if he could see the reaction from his secretary.

Father Unser felt a knot in his stomach at the thought of moving, but he knew what obedience meant in the Catholic Church. The cardinal looked after the needs of the archdiocese. Despite the demands of being the cardinal's secretary, he enjoyed the living arrangements he had at Our Lady of Rosary and the relationship he had with Father Mike Zansiski. He decided not to say anything more about it as he pulled into the underground garage and parked the car in the cardinal's reserved spot.

After hearing the elevator announcing the cardinal's arrival to his office suite, his administrative secretary, Mrs. Ruby Bermaten poured a cup of coffee and placed it on Cardinal Flinn's desk. The cardinal went directly into his office, sat down, and after taking a sip, he asked for the spreadsheet of the priests of the archdiocese and their assignments. Ruby, his secretary for ten years, knew him well. She anticipated this request and handed him an updated list with two copies. He took the list, gave an appreciative smile and then asked not to be disturbed.

He looked up to the cross and prayed. He asked for guidance from the Holy Spirit as he reviewed possible candidates for rector of the cathedral. He knew he needed a list of suggestions ready to discuss with Bishop Newsome when they met for lunch. He also knew the bishop would have his own thoughts on the changes.

Thom Triplett approached the front desk where he was given a visitor's pass to the chancery. Father Unser greeted him and escorted him to the cardinal's conference room and asked if he could get him a cup of coffee or something else to drink. He returned with bottled water and said the cardinal would be with him momentarily.

Thom removed the paperwork from his pocket regarding his brother's funeral along with a folder and placed them on the table. He was looking over the papers when the side panel door opened, and the cardinal appeared.

"Welcome, Thom. How are you doing?"

"Your Eminence, I'm doing better. It hasn't been easy these last few days." The cardinal extended his hand. Thom tried desperately to remain strong as he took his seat next to the cardinal at the conference table.

"You know Father Unser, my secretary. I've asked him to take notes on the first part of our meeting as we go over the details and wishes for your brother's funeral."

"I understand." Thom wondered what the second part of the meeting would be about. "As I said to you on the phone yesterday, my brother had chosen the readings and the songs."

Thom provided the choices, and the cardinal did not have any objections. Like any Mass in the Catholic Church, many people helped with the various liturgical responsibilities, and the cardinal and Thom clarified who would fulfill each role. Names were placed beside readings. Priests' names were given as the honorary pallbearers, and the gift bearers would be Emma and Jonathan Pickle.

Father Unser explained the customary funeral practice for priests was to receive the body at the cathedral the night before and to celebrate Evening Prayer prior to visitation. Thom was not familiar with any of this but trusted the young priest.

Thom had a few questions. "Will there be any kind of program for those attending? Since I'm not familiar with this, I can only imagine how many more won't be familiar."

"Yes, there will be a liturgical program for both days." Father Unser knew it was part of his responsibility to prepare the programs, thankful there were templates for these.

"Thom, do you have any other questions about the funeral?"

"I think we've covered everything."

"Do you have all the information you need?" The cardinal directed the question to Father Unser.

"I believe I do." He then excused himself leaving Cardinal Flinn with Thom Triplett.

"Thom, I want to once again express my condolences for the loss of your brother. He truly was a good priest and friend. As much as I appreciated his priesthood for the archdiocese, I am finding there were irregularities regarding some decisions he had recently made."

Thom was puzzled. "What decisions? Are you talking about the money he received?"

"The money? Yes... that is one example."

"Lieutenant Palmer informed me of my brother's intentions for this money."

"The issue of the money may very well come out to the media, and I just want you to be aware of this," the cardinal said. "It is not up to me or the archdiocese to make any statement, except to say that the archdiocese is cooperating with the NYPD as they continue their investigation. As a lawyer, I am sure you understand."

Thom realized by the cardinal's tone of voice that he would distance himself from the relationship he had with his brother. Thom recognized his brother handled the situation terribly. The money was connected to the restoration of the cathedral and not his personal property to disperse. Despite his brother's good intentions, it should have been routed through the cathedral or archdiocesan finances. Thom was beginning to understand the second part of this meeting was to let him know Cardinal Flinn would not protect Steven's memory. It was a disappointment to hear the words from the cardinal, but Thom knew he had a trump card sitting on the table.

"I understand what you're saying, Your Eminence." Thom realized it was best to say as little as possible.

"You know the cash found eventually will be returned to the Delfino family. It really didn't belong to your brother."

Thom now felt the second blow. "I would imagine a judge will make the determination of the rightful owner of the $50,000 in the court of law." Thom didn't want to pursue any legal issues with the cardinal.

"Yes, we should leave it up to the courts. I thought it would be important for you and me to have this discussion." The cardinal felt confident and glad he was direct with Thom.

"Your Eminence, I need to let you know something about my brother's health." Thom leaned forward.

"His health? If I remember... the last time we spoke, he seemed to have a persistent cough. But I didn't know he was sick."

"Nor did I—no one I talked to knew. The medical examiner told me my brother had lung cancer." Thom quietly revealed. "I'm just wondering if his health had a greater effect on the decisions he was making."

The cardinal sat back in his chair. "Lung cancer? I had no idea. Did he smoke?"

"Only in college."

"I... I am so sorry." The cardinal didn't know what to say. He looked at Thom, and they both had tears in their eyes.

"Your Eminence, if you wouldn't mind, I'd also like to bring up a church ethical issue." Thom noticed the cardinal was a little off balance with the news of Steven's cancer.

"By all means." The cardinal quickly composed himself.

From the folder, Thom slowly pulled out a copy of Joseph Delfino's signed statement acknowledging the agreement with the cardinal.

Thom handed the cardinal the paper.

The cardinal quickly read the statement. "Where did you get this?"

"My brother sent it to me. Is this agreement true?"

The cardinal's face turned white. "I think it best not to say anything about this. Do you... do you... know where the original is?"

"Yes, it's very safe."

He quickly tossed the letter back to Thom and became defensive. This is not my signature!"

"Are you denying the deal?" Thom demanded.

"It's more complicated than it looks."

"It doesn't look complicated to me." Thom stayed strong as he looked directly at the cardinal. "I wonder how you may be able to help me."

"I'm not sure what you are asking!" The cardinal saw Thom tense up.

"When we met on Saturday, the day my brother was killed, I mentioned that he was having problems with Monsignor Stone. You were obviously upset when I said that. Why was that?"

"I've had some concerns with Monsignor Stone about a number of annulment decisions."

Thom remained calm. "So did my brother and so do I. Monsignor Stone refused to give me an annulment!"

"I am sorry to hear this. I am sure there is a good reason. I would be more than happy to intervene and see if anything else can be done about your petition."

"I realize the church is in the business of selling annulments. I know that much about you and the church I love. I'd like to offer you a swap—this statement in return for my freedom to marry. But I have a conscience and can't do that. All I can do is pray for it to be reviewed again. I'll see you on Thursday when my brother, who faithfully served the church, is brought back for his funeral." With that, Thom stood, folded the statement left it on the table and walked out of the cardinal's office.

"May God be with you…" the cardinal began to say, but the door quickly closed before he finished.

The cardinal hurriedly got up from his seat, grabbed the folded paper and put it in his coat pocket. He slung open the door, and without stopping at his secretary's desk, walked right into Father Unser's office. The cardinal demanded, "Get Monsignor Stone on the phone for me and if he's in the building, I want to see him in my office right away." He quickly returned to his office, slammed the door and called Joseph Delfino.

"Joseph, I need to see you this afternoon. Meet me at my residence at 4:00 p.m."

478

Joseph felt the weight of his own business problems, and he didn't like the tone of the cardinal's voice. His response was simple. "I'll see you then."

The conversation ended, and the cardinal took a few deep breaths to calm himself down.

Father Usner knocked on the cardinal's office door.

The cardinal took one last deep breath. "Come in."

"Your Eminence, Monsignor Stone is not in the building, and I left a voicemail for him to call you on your cell. I checked with his secretary, and he was going to take this whole week off. He may be out of town," Father Unser explained.

"He didn't leave town. I'm sure the detectives wouldn't allow him to leave town while the investigation is going on, and he was one of the last to see Monsignor Triplett alive." The cardinal was disturbed by the information and was not satisfied. "Go to his apartment, check around to see if anyone has seen him and wait until he returns."

Father Usner calmly responded. "Yes, Your Eminence. I'll go. I know where he lives." Father Usner knew when the cardinal was extremely upset. He remembered the time a few months ago when he forgot some envelopes at the office and failed to deliver them to Monsignor Stone. The cardinal was more than just upset. Father Usner recalled the harsh admonishment he received from the cardinal.

"Give Ruby the funeral information to work on. Do you have his address?" The cardinal ordered. "Call me every hour! Check with Saint Jerome Parish and see if they've seen him."

"I'll let you know when I find him." Father Unser acknowledged the request and realized the best thing he could do was to find Monsignor Stone's whereabouts soon.

Alone and worried, the cardinal wondered about the original statement. Did Thom have it? That paper could permanently damage his reputation. His cell phone rang. He glanced at the screen, it was Bishop Newsome.

The death of Monsignor Triplett finally registered with Monsignor Stone. Shortly after celebrating the noon Easter Mass at Saint Jerome's, he got out of the city and spent time at his place north of the city along the shore of the Hudson River. He called Lieutenant Palmer and left a message he was at his place on the river. Sitting out on the porch and watching the sun hiding behind the clouds, all he could do was cry. He had so much more he wanted to say to his friend Steven, and now he wouldn't get a chance to do it. He was reminiscing about the times they came to this quiet place and talked as friends. Now that had been taken away.

Looking at his own life, he realized he was very hardheaded when it came to annulments. He felt like a dictator when dealing with canon law — the law of the church. He realized he was not happy, did not want the role of dictator, and needed to talk to someone about it all.

When he woke up this morning, he planned to return to the city to talk with the only person he could truly open his soul to. Four hours later, he exited the subway station on 96th Street and walked to Holy Name of Jesus Parish. He checked his phone for the first time. He had missed two calls — one from his office in the chancery and another from the cardinal. These would have to wait. He needed to speak to Bishop Newsome.

When he arrived at the parish house, Father McFadden called the bishop to announce the visitor.

"You have a visitor. It's Monsignor Stone."

"I don't have an appointment with him." The bishop was both surprised and annoyed at Monsignor Stone's unexpected visit.

"He says it can't wait."

"Could you tell him I'm supposed to be going with Father O'Hara to the chancery?"

"I just did. He still wants to see you now. What can I do to help?" Father McFadden asked.

"Let Father O'Hara know I can't go with him. Let him know I'll call the cardinal with the information we discussed. Once I've talked with the cardinal, I'll come down and see Monsignor Stone."

"He looks worried...." Father McFadden knew this was not the hard-core priest coming for a friendly chat.

"See if he'll talk with you," Bishop Newsome suggested.

"I'll see what I can do." Father McFadden went downstairs.

Bishop Newsome picked up his cell phone and called the cardinal.

"George, Happy Easter. Are we still on for lunch?" The cardinal tried to sound upbeat after his unsettling meeting with Thom Triplett.

"Yes, at noon. I know you're getting ready to meet with Father O'Hara, and I wanted to give you an update. I thought I could be there with him, but I'm not going to make it. I'll explain when I see you. I spoke with Abbott Choncko, and he informed me Father O'Hara is welcome at the abbey for thirty days. I suggest he leave a week from today. I've also talked with him about seeing a psychologist. He's open to everything I've suggested." The bishop added, "Upon his return, I'd like for him to stay here at Holy Name of Jesus."

"Thank you for the information. It will help when I talk with Father O'Hara. I will see you for lunch." The cardinal hung up without responding to the request to keep Father O'Hara at Holy Name of Jesus. The cardinal wasn't thinking about his next appointment. He was more concerned with the location of Monsignor Stone.

In the downstairs sitting room at Holy Name of Jesus Parish House, Bishop Newsome greeted Monsignor Stone, and he could see by monsignor's face something was wrong.

Father McFadden excused himself. His only remark to the bishop was, "My prayers." Bishop Newsome then escorted Monsignor Stone up to his study.

Monsignor Stone spent the next hour talking about the many issues he had shared with the detectives: his strip club experience—over thirty-five years ago, the problems he faced with Thom Triplett's annulment, the concerns he had about the work he was doing for the cardinal, his meeting with Monsignor Triplett on Saturday morning and his own assault. Bishop Newsome knew about some of these issues but very puzzled by was very puzzled by what Monsignor Stone wanted.

Finally, Monsignor Stone came to why he was there. He pleaded with the bishop. "I want out of the Tribunal. I've done it long enough. I just want to be a simple parish priest."

Bishop Newsome began, "I think it would be good for you to take some time away from it all. I can see the pressure you are under, especially losing your friend, Monsignor Triplett. What if you took a month off?"

"With all due respect, Bishop, it will take more than a month." Monsignor Stone spoke with a sudden return to his stoic self.

"How about three months? Then the new parish assignments will come out." Bishop Newsome tried to find a quick solution. He didn't always agree with Monsignor Stone's ideas and recommendations for the archdiocese, but he knew canon law. He didn't want to lose this highly educated and articulate priest. He hoped three months would give Monsignor the break he needed.

"Things are going to get... messy in the archdiocese," Monsignor Stone admitted.

"When are they not messy?" Bishop Newsome knew it was a rhetorical question. The archdiocese was always dealing with lawyers—civil, criminal and even canon lawyers. But the bishop knew at lunch, he would have a couple of items he would have to discuss with the cardinal.

Monsignor Stone got to the point. "When can I start my three-month sabbatical?"

"How about in a week?"

"That quickly?" It surprised Monsignor Stone the bishop could make it happen so soon.

"Let me talk with the cardinal. He needs to know what we've discussed. The information you've shared will remain between us and the cardinal." Bishop Newsome explained.

"How are you going to handle the information on Jennifer Gibson and the cardinal?"

"He will know, I know. Let's see how he responds." Bishop Newsome could only speculate.

"Thank you for taking the time to listen." Monsignor Stone felt relieved.

"You will be hearing from me, David. Thank you for all you've done for the archdiocese." Bishop Newsome was genuinely grateful to the monsignor and walked him downstairs to the front door. As he returned to his suite, the bishop stopped in his chapel. Prayer was one thing he needed to do more of—for himself, the cardinal, the Archdiocese of New York, Jennifer Gibson, Joseph Delfino and Monsignor Triplett.

After leaving the bishop, Monsignor Stone didn't want to return home or go to the tribunal office and answer any of the phone messages. He opted to get a quick bite to eat and then go to one of his favorite places, the Metropolitan Museum of Art. It had been several months since he had been, and he wanted to check out the new exhibits. Hopefully, he made the right decision in confiding in Bishop Newsome.

Cardinal Flinn was told his next appointment was waiting in his conference room. "This won't take long," he told Ruby. "If they locate Monsignor Stone, let me know."

As the cardinal entered the conference room, Father O'Hara stood, unsure of what he should say.

"Please be seated, Father O'Hara. Bishop Newsome and I have talked, and he has told me of your indiscretion and his proposal for the consequences of your actions. Are you aware of what he has proposed?" The cardinal spoke to the young priest with his authoritarian tone.

"He would like me to go to the Abbey of Gethsemani for a thirty-day retreat."

"Yes. I think this would be beneficial for you." The cardinal wasted no time in outlining what he expected. "You will leave in a few days. Bishop Newsome is still working out the details. I also want you to get psychological help and support when you return."

Father O'Hara struggled to make eye contact with the cardinal. "I understand." Once he did, tears filled his eyes.

"Understand this, Father O'Hara. I won't tolerate this another time." The cardinal abruptly stood, thanked him for coming and said he would be in his daily prayers.

Surprised at the briefness of the meeting, Father O'Hara didn't know what to do. Finally, he wiped his tears, got up from the chair and thanked the cardinal for seeing him. As he walked out of the chancery, Father O'Hara felt a great sense of relief. He wondered since nothing was mentioned about staying at Holy Name of Jesus, the bishop and cardinal may not have discussed it.

The cardinal waited a few minutes before he returned to his office. He suddenly realized that Monsignor Walter McBrien, the president of the North American College had not contacted him with approval for Father Morales' stay at the college. He quickly buzzed his secretary on the phone and asked her to place a call to the president to check on the availability of a room for Father Juan Morales for the next six months or so. The cardinal then asked, "Have we heard from Father Unser?"

"Nothing," Ruby replied.

"When Bishop Newsome arrives, please ask him what he would like for lunch from the local deli down the street. As much as I would love a good Reuben sandwich, I better stick with the chef salad with oil and vinegar."

"Are you sure you're okay?" Ruby asked knowing he wasn't.

"It is one of those days where the cross is feeling a little heavier." The cardinal wished he were twenty pounds lighter, twenty years younger and back at the parish enjoying administering the sacraments—not dealing with the stressful issues of the archdiocese.

"Let me see what I can find out from the college. Do you want to talk with Monsignor McBrien if I can get in touch with him?" Ruby asked.

"Only if he asks. I will see him next week, correct?"

"Yes, you're leaving a week from Wednesday for Rome." Ruby looked at the cardinal's calendar on her computer to confirm.

"Thanks." The cardinal knew he had his secretary's support but also the distance he had to maintain. Some things he could never discuss, and this made his role as chief shepherd so difficult. He looked at all the paperwork on his desk and returned to the list of priests on the spreadsheet. He knew, without even looking at it, the few priests who could handle the responsibilities of Saint Patrick's. He quickly wrote down three names and looked at how long each had been in his present assignment. He would have to convince one of these three to move. He also looked at the associate lists which was much smaller. With so many priests from different parts of the world, he had to be prudent in deciding who could assist with the growing Spanish community while getting along with those in the parish house. Again, there were only a few choices. He had his thoughts but wanted input from Bishop Newsome. The final step—the cardinal presented the recommendations to the clergy personnel board for approval.

Ruby knocked and re-entered the office to inform the cardinal of her conversation with Monsignor McBrien. A room was available for Father Morales. They would work the details out when the cardinal arrives in Rome next week. She also told him Bishop Newsome had to stop by his office first and would be in the cardinal's conference room at noon, and lunch is on its way.

"Still no word from Father Usner?"

"He called and said Monsignor Stone hasn't been seen since Easter. The secretary at Saint Jerome thought he may be at his place on the Hudson since he wasn't going to be available to help for the coming week," Ruby explained.

"Do we have the address of his place on the Hudson?"

"I'll check." Ruby left and closed the door to the cardinal's office.

Looking at his watch, Cardinal Flinn wanted to see the beginning of the noon news before sitting down with Bishop Newsome. He turned on the television in his office. He was shocked at the opening news story. The reporter standing in front of Delfino Construction reported, "In the latest twists with Delfino Construction, the President, Joseph Delfino, was found dead in his office at 11:00 a.m. this morning."

The cardinal slumped into his chair. He felt the breath knocked out of him, put his hands to his face, made the Sign of the Cross and offered a silent prayer.

Chapter 37

"Your Eminence, are you all right?" As soon as Ruby opened the cardinal's office door, she saw the face of a man who looked like he'd seen a ghost.

The cardinal could barely utter the words. "Joseph Delfino is dead. I just heard it on the news."

"What happened?" Ruby couldn't believe the reporter as she looked at the television. "I just saw him here... about a week ago!"

The cardinal was worried and stunned. "The reporter only announced it — no details."

"I'm so sorry for the family and for you. I know you worked closely with him. Are you okay?" Ruby knew he had both a professional and personal relationship with him. She also knew Joseph Delfino brought envelopes to the cardinal on a regular basis.

"The poor family. I can only imagine what they are going through. If any of them call, please let me know."

"Bishop Newsome is in your conference room. The deli delivery boy is on his way up with the order. I'll bring the lunches in and some water," Ruby said.

The cardinal turned off the television, straightened his suit jacket, and proceeded to the conference room. He greeted Bishop Newsome somberly. "Have you seen the noon news?"

Bishop Newsome looked surprised and responded with a nonchalant, "No. Why do you ask?" as he found a comfortable chair at the conference table.

"Joseph Delfino is dead."

The bishop stood up straight and almost lost his balance. "What? How?"

"The reporter did not say."

"Do you think it had anything to do with the charges he was facing with the business?" Bishop Newsome asked.

"I do not know." The cardinal struggled to sit down in his chair. His mind wondered. He recalled the many times he and Joseph had met for social and business activities.

Bishop Newsome sat back down. He didn't know what to say. This event put a whole new light on what he would share. Seeing how distracted and upset the cardinal was about this news, the bishop wondered if he should share any information he had learned this morning.

Ruby knocked on the door, entered, and placed a tray of with two chef salads and water on the table. As she turned to leave, she noticed how quiet it was in the room. She asked if they needed anything else. When they said no, she excused herself and closed the door leaving them to eat their lunch.

"Let us pray and eat, George." The cardinal spoke softly as he made the sign of the cross, offered a prayer for the food to nourish them both, and then he remembered the deceased — Monsignor Triplett, Joseph Delfino and their families.

They each took a plate off the tray. The salads were stacked high, but they had no appetite. They tried to make small talk about Holy Week and Easter. They exchanged the usual accolades, and there was even a little laughter. They respected one another, but Bishop Newsome always knew it was he who served the cardinal, and he remembered his place. Finally, the cardinal pushed his lunch aside and went back into his office to gather the spreadsheets on the clergy and the possible replacements. When the cardinal returned with his papers Bishop Newsome knew lunch was over. It was time to work. He took out his own notes. The first sheet he slipped to the back. It was the information Monsignor Stone shared with him.

The cardinal began the conversation hoping that it would be easy to find the next rector of Saint Patrick's. "What about moving Father James Elderidge to the cathedral?"

"He's 65, and I believe he has a couple of health issues. Do you think he could handle the stress?" Bishop Newsome offered some obvious facts. This wasn't his first choice, but he was not ready to make any suggestions yet.

"Good point. What about Monsignor Paul Irby from Corpus Christi?" "He is only 54 and has been there for five years. Every time I visit, he seems to have an active parish, and the liturgies have been good."

"I agree. He would make a good choice. Unfortunately, the problem with him is his poor money management skills. His parishes seem to accumulate a lot of debt. Corpus Christi is a small parish where the spending can be limited. At the cathedral with a larger budget, I would be concerned." Bishop Newsome once again patiently offered facts the cardinal might not be fully aware of.

"The safest decision would just be to move you," the cardinal surprisingly suggested.

"I thank you for the consideration. If it would help, I will go. But you and I both know, one day the pope will move me. And it would be in name only since you would have me helping out all over the archdiocese. Who will do the daily work?" Bishop Newsome was finding excuses not to be considered.

"I just wanted to see what you would say. Who do you think I should consider as rector?" The cardinal felt frustrated and wasn't focused entirely on the task at hand. But he still had one more name on his sheet.

Without hesitation, Bishop Newsome blurted out, "I think you should consider Monsignor Stone. He has the experience and could handle the responsibilities. And he has no parish at the moment. Besides, he wants out of the Tribunal. More importantly, he has been loyal to you, and I think he would remain loyal to you knowing what may come your way." Bishop Newsome hoped he had chosen his words carefully to present his candidate. He was laying the foundation for Monsignor Stone to be named the new rector.

The cardinal sat motionless… he said nothing as he looked at the bishop…. he wondered what Bishop Newsome knew.

Finally, the cardinal concurred. "You are right. He could be a good rector. I tried to locate him, but he is not answering his phone. Have you talked with him?" The cardinal tried to understand the bishop's push for Monsignor Stone.

"Yes, he came to see me about two hours ago. He's been at his place on the Hudson. He's feeling the stress of his position and asked for some time off." Bishop Newsome didn't want to reveal their entire conversation.

The cardinal probed for any information the bishop might have. "And what did you tell him?"

"I told him I needed to talk with you. He wants three months off." Bishop Newsome hoped the firm tone of his voice would influence the cardinal to grant Monsignor Stone's request.

The cardinal shook his head. "I would like three months off! I can't leave the position of rector open for three months."

Bishop Newsome offered no response.

"Did you discuss being named rector?"

"No, I didn't. I wanted your thoughts. Regarding his time off, I think I could get him down to one month – if he were actually named rector of the cathedral. Of course, his knowledge of the Delfinos and his awareness of Jennifer Gibson's work were discussed."

The cardinal now realized that Bishop Newsome had the upper hand in this discussion and probably knew about the money the Delfinos put in the archdiocese account, but the cardinal also had his own trump card to play.

"Did Monsignor Stone mention anything about how the Delfinos helped him? His home on the Hudson was not purchased on just his salary." The cardinal watched for the bishop's reaction.

Bishop Newsome responded quickly. "I'm sure it wasn't. But the stress of it all, considering his own friend's death, has made him rethink what is really important. As Scripture says, the truth has set him free, and he's willing to do whatever it takes to rectify the situation." The bishop waited cautiously for the cardinal's reply as he fiddled with his pen.

The cardinal avoided a direct response. "It would be nice to talk with Monsignor Stone."

"Do you want me to locate him and ask him to come back into the city?" The bishop knew Monsignor Stone was already in the city.

"As mentioned, I have tried to contact him. I even have Father Unser sitting outside his place. Monsignor Stone could be a good rector. Are you sure I can get his loyalty?"

"You will get his loyalty, and he would need your total honesty. The archdiocese and you, Cardinal, may face some charges over the paybacks you received from other jobs the Delfinos did for you." Bishop Newsome just hit the jugular on the cardinal revealing his knowledge of the paybacks.

The cardinal pushed his chair out and stood. "What are you saying?" In a sudden burst of frustration and anger, he walked toward the window.

"I know about the money you received from the Delfinos."

Cardinal Flinn turned to the bishop. "I am to blame for the stupid mistake. I did not think my decisions would hurt anyone. But after these last forty-eight hours, I discovered they have. One priest was killed because of the money that should have gone back to the cathedral. When it comes out that two more parishes should have received money and did not, it will put a dark spot on my role as shepherd. I can only ask forgiveness."

Bishop Newsome stood to approach the remorseful cardinal. He had never seen him like this before and felt moved to give advice.

"Your Eminence, you have a chance to make amends for your mistakes, your greed. With the untimely death of Joseph Delfino, and the charges against Delfino Construction, you can go to Jennifer Gibson with the truth. Return the money to the parishes, and hopefully, this will stay out of the press and hearings. Do we have the money?"

"Readily available? I am not certain. I am sure our CFO can show the money in the parish savings account, but it may have to come from some of our archdiocesan reserves." The cardinal knew the archdiocesan finances were stressed due to the cathedral restoration.

Bishop Newsome laid out a possible plan. "The key will be to get Jennifer Gibson on board with this. From what Monsignor Stone shared, she wants justice for the sub-contractor who knew about overcharging the parishes. She knows the archdiocese benefited."

"I know she knows!" The cardinal was gaining his composure and sense of responsibility. He returned to the table and then slowly sat down. "I have talked to her, but I had hoped the lawyers were working it out."

The bishop finally asked the hardest question. "My understanding is the archdiocese has received over $100,000 in kickbacks. Is that correct?"

The cardinal hesitated, "I… I am… not sure. I have all of it in a file." He lied. He knew it was over $200,000.

Bishop Newsome looked him straight in the eye waiting for him to change his answer, but the cardinal avoided any direct eye contact. Bishop Newsome said nothing.

"George, I would like to speak with Jennifer. I saw her with Thom Triplett on Easter at the cathedral. I believe they must be seeing each other. Do you think Thom knows about this situation?"

"I'm sure he knows something."

"Well, he knows Joseph Delfino wants my help with his annulment." The cardinal took the paper out of his coat pocket for the bishop to read.

"Didn't you help Joseph with his first annulment?" Bishop Newsome asked, even though he knew the answer.

"Yes... I did. That's how this all got started!" The cardinal looked away.

"What did Thom want by showing you this statement?" Bishop Newsome knew this could cause a huge scandal

"Thom is just a man full of righteous anger and simply wants me to talk with Monsignor Stone about his refusal to give Thom an annulment. He wants to see if anything can be worked out. I do not think he would intentionally harm the archdiocese, but he might make life difficult for me for a while." The cardinal confided.

"So what did you tell him?" At that moment, Bishop Newsome felt sorry for the cardinal.

"I told Thom, I would review it with Monsignor Stone. It was the least I could do." The cardinal took the paper and put it back in his pocket.

The bishop now understood the situation better. "Let me see what I can do. If Monsignor Stone will review the case, and we can reason with Jennifer Gibson, maybe we can save face and protect you and the archdiocese."

"You will help?" The cardinal softly asked.

"There are a lot of ifs, but you know I will." Bishop Newsome assured the cardinal. "What about the vacancies at the cathedral?"

The cardinal felt a great burden lightened. "If we can put Monsignor Stone as rector, I will ask him which priest he would like to have as his parochial vicar."

"Sounds good. Let me get in touch with Monsignor." Bishop Newsome took out his phone and realized they had been talking for over two hours. He sat back down.

"In the meantime, let me go to my office and try calling Jennifer Gibson." The cardinal stood. "Before I go, I... I just want to say thank you, George." Without waiting for a response, he opened the conference door and left.

When the cardinal returned to his office, he saw a curious announcement on his desk. It was a press release from his director of media and communications about the charges levied against the Delfino Construction Company. The carefully worded statement also included the cardinal's condolences and prayers on the death of Joseph Delfino. He needed to sign off on the announcement before it could be released.

"Ruby," the cardinal pushed the intercom button, "would you come in here for a minute." As she entered, he was all business and much calmer. "I need you to do three things for me. First, call Father Unser and have him come back to the chancery. Next, take this press release down to Bishop Newsome in the conference room and see what he thinks. If he sees no problem, then I will sign it. Then call Jennifer Gibson and see if she has time to see me this afternoon. Thank you."

He picked up the phone and called the attorney for the archdiocese. The cardinal knew when he made the call himself, one of the partners would be available. Cardinal Flinn wanted to know if there could be any charges of inappropriate distribution of funds for receiving the kickbacks and putting them into the archdiocesan accounts instead of the parish accounts. He knew the answer but wanted to hear it from an attorney, and he needed to know how to correct it.

"David... Can you hear me?" Bishop Newsome felt as if he were shouting, trying to speak over the horns honking on the other end.

"Yes, I'm here." Monsignor Stone responded.

"I need you to come to the chancery."

"Can this wait? I'm just now walking up the steps to the Metropolitan."

"No, it can't. I have a proposition I believe you'll like, but it will require a bit of cooperation from you."

"Can you give me a hint?"

"I'd rather tell you in person." Bishop Newsome really wanted Monsignor Stone to talk with the cardinal.

"Give me thirty minutes, and I'll be there." Monsignor Stone said a quick prayer asking for guidance and for what he was going to be offered.

After talking with Jeremy Walsh, senior partner of Stuber and Anchors Law Firm, the cardinal knew exactly what steps were necessary to avoid taking the fall for his own indiscretions.

Before he could put the plan into motion, Ruby returned. "Father Unser is on his way back. He was going to stop and get something to eat. Bishop Newsome is looking over the press release, and Jennifer Gibson is on line three."

"Jennifer, thank you for returning my call. I hope you had a Happy Easter. I saw you at Mass with Monsignor Triplett's brother, Thom." The cardinal was unusually cordial.

"How can I help you, Your Eminence?" Jennifer wondered why the cardinal had called.

"Did you hear Joseph Delfino was found dead in his office this morning?"

"Yes. I did. A sad day for the Delfino family." Jennifer was as brief as possible, still uncertain what this call was all about.

"I am calling to see if we can get together and discuss your work concerning the Delfinos and the steps the church and the archdiocese can take to make things right. With the death of Monsignor Triplett and now with the charges against the Delfinos, the church does not need any more publicity — especially negative."

"I'm bound by client-lawyer confidentiality. I would need to check with my client first." Jennifer knew the client wanted a cleared name and all the attorney fees paid by the

495

archdiocese. "Let me give them a call, and I'll be back with you."

"Do you think we can work to resolve this today?" The cardinal asked.

"No promises but have someone ready to write me a check." Jennifer knew she could easily submit a hefty bill to the archdiocese to make this matter go away. "And Your Eminence, I would clean up a few marriage annulments for the good of the church."

The cardinal understood. The Delfinos benefited from the church with two annulments granted by the archdiocese, and Jennifer knew it. He now needed Monsignor Stone's help.

"I will see what I can do," the cardinal replied. An appointment was set for the cardinal's office at 4:00 this afternoon.

The cardinal contacted John Hassel, Chief Financial Officer for the archdiocese and discussed the issue with him. The cardinal hoped they would resolve the matter with a few transactions. A simple transfer of the proceeds he received for the cathedral's restoration to the archdiocese's reserved accounts. Then another transfer of funds from the reserves to the parishes that deserved the proceeds. Despite objections from the CFO, the cardinal insisted the transfer of funds between accounts be done by the end of the day.

An hour later, the CFO called to report the account balances had changed, and he had notified the pastors of the parishes receiving the additional money.

Monsignor Stone waited in the cardinal's conference room seated across from Bishop Newsome. The cardinal felt confident over his recent accomplishments as he entered the room. He greeted them in his same cordial manner as he took his seat. Now he wanted to make things right with Monsignor Stone.

"David, thank you so much for coming in. Let me get right to the point. I know I asked you for some personal favors for the Delfinos. Specifically, I am talking about their annulments. I am thankful for what you did."

Monsignor Stone was enjoying the moment. "You realize, Your Eminence, those annulments would have been granted if all the steps had been followed properly. And I wouldn't have taken so much heat from the Tribunal staff and others for fast-tracking them." Monsignor Stone spoke with the cold resolve for which he was known.

"Thank you, Monsignor, for sharing this with me once again. Now I need you to review those files and take the necessary steps to make things right. Do you understand what I am asking?"

"I can review the files." Monsignor Stone clearly understood what Cardinal Flinn was asking.

"I would appreciate it. Once that is done, I understand you would like to be relieved as Judicial Vicar for the archdiocese."

"Yes... I would."

"Then, I will grant your request."

Monsignor Stone smiled and took a deep breath of relief, but before he could say anything, the cardinal continued.

"I want to name you the next rector of the cathedral. I need you here to advise me as well as take on the responsibilities of being the rector. I ask for your continued honesty and loyalty no matter what decisions I make." The cardinal waited for Monsignor Stone's answer.

"Bishop Newsome already discussed this with me. Are you sure you want me to become the next rector?"

"I believe at this time, with all that has happened, you are the right person."

"I want the next sixty days off to make the transition." Monsignor Stone bargained.

"How about thirty?" The cardinal offered.

"It was worth a try. Okay, I'll take the thirty days."

"I see no problem with your request after you have taken care of those files."

"And what about Thom Triplett's marriage annulment?" Monsignor Stone asked.

"Are there grounds for the annulment?"

"Yes, and I'd like to get it taken care of before I leave the Tribunal as a parting gift for Steven." Monsignor Stone knew it could be done, and there was no better way to remember his friend than by doing the right thing for his brother.

"I agree. Could it all be done within a week?"

"I believe so... if I can get Thom's cooperation."

"I do not think you will have any problem." The cardinal knew Delfino's signed annulment paper was worthless now. It was Thom's annulment that could bring some happiness.

Monsignor Stone was relieved and excited. "I accept the change and look forward to the challenge as the next rector. It will be great to get back into parish ministry."

"We must talk about a new parochial vicar for you since Father Morales will not be coming back. You can let me or Bishop Newsome know your thoughts. Father Crumbley and Monsignor Black will stay at the cathedral. You are friends, correct?"

"Yes, Monsignor Black and I even lived together at one time, so it will be good to connect again."

The cardinal sealed the decision with a handshake and words of thanks. "I have one more bit of news to share with both of you that I learned this morning about Monsignor Triplett. His brother shared with me that the autopsy showed he had lung cancer. Did either of you know this?"

"I didn't." The news shocked Monsignor Stone. "I had just seen him that morning, and he said nothing."

"Nor did I," Bishop Newsome responded. "I'm shocked. That could explain some of his actions."

As Monsignor Stone and Bishop Newsome walked out of the office, Ruby informed the cardinal that A.J. Delfino was on the phone.

"I'll see you both on Thursday night." Monsignor Stone left return to his office at the Tribunal. He had to pull the two Delfino annulments.

"My condolences A.J.," the cardinal began as he Ruby transferred a call from A.J. Delfino. "What happened?"

"Your Eminence, we believe it was an overdose of drugs. The problems of the business just got to him." A.J. struggled to find a reason his dad would take his own life.

"I am so sorry. May God be with him now and with you and your family. I will definitely remember him in my prayers tonight and offer Mass for him tomorrow morning. How can I help?"

"Would you do the funeral?" A.J. made the request, but he wasn't sure how the cardinal would respond knowing his father had committed suicide. He knew his dad would want a Catholic funeral and what better person to celebrate it than the one he had helped.

Monsignor Stone returned to his office, picked up the phone and called Thom Triplett to schedule an appointment to talk about the annulment. He knew Thom wanted the process completed as soon as possible. They agreed to meet at 4:00 p.m.

At 4:00 p.m. Jennifer and Thom arrived separately and met at the chancery. Quickly, they compared notes then agreed to meet afterward at the Italian place just up the street. Wishing each other good luck, they both hoped their issues would be resolved, and they could begin planning a future together.

Thom was escorted to the Tribunal office of the Judicial Vicar. Monsignor Stone offered his condolences immediately and then informed Thom of the meeting with his brother early Holy Saturday morning. He explained that if the grounds could be strengthened, Thom could petition again for a decree of nullity. There was a good chance the tribunal would grant your annulment. After sharing the news with Thom, Monsignor Stone was overcome with emotion as he recalled his last conversation with his dear friend.

Relieved to hear the news, Thom got up from his chair and thanked Monsignor Stone. He embraced Monsignor, aware both were still hurting.

After they wiped the tears from their eyes, they returned to their seats. Monsignor Stone continued. "Your brother said he sent you a letter, but he wished he hadn't. Did you get it?"

"I did."

"I never knew what the letter was about. While we were talking about it, our conversation was interrupted."

"We'll, the letter was actually an agreement between the cardinal and Joseph Delfino, that Joseph's annulment would be granted if the restoration was completed in time for the cardinal's anniversary."

"Thom, do you still have it?"

"I do."

"I have to tell you, Thom, I don't think your brother intended to damage the church by sending that to you. We both knew him well enough to know that was not his plan."

"Now that we've talked. I... I do agree with you." Thom paused for a moment and looked at the letter. "Steven wouldn't want to hurt the church. I think I should destroy it and any copies."

"You're doing the right thing." Monsignor Stone felt a sigh of relief but also sadness. "I will miss your brother."

"So will I." Thom got up to leave. "I'll see you on Thursday." He was filled with mixed emotions as he left Monsignor Stone. There was joy in having the hope of his freedom to marry, but deep sadness that he would neither share the good news with his brother nor be able to ask him to preside at his wedding.

Monsignor Stone wanted to speak with Thom about his last conversation with his brother, but it would have to wait for another day. Understandably, Thom's emotions were close to the surface. It would have been unkind to push the discussion. After Thom left the office, Monsignor Stone realized how good it felt—that small moment of pastoral concern in the midst of the business side of the church. Returning to parish life would be good.

One floor up, Cardinal Flinn welcomed Jennifer. She politely declined his offer of coffee and presented the written list of her client's demands.

"My client wants an apology from Your Eminence for not acknowledging the savings he has provided for the archdiocese. He wants to be 'strongly considered' in any future projects the archdiocese has for the services from his company."

The cardinal accepted all the terms and would have the archdiocesan attorney's review the documents as a formality before signing. Jennifer explained that there was a 48-hour window.

Having settled the demands of her client, Jennifer presented the cardinal an envelope containing a bill for her legal services totaling over $20,000. She informed him she wanted $10,000 to go anonymously to the poorest Catholic elementary school in the archdiocese.

"What school would that be?" Jennifer asked.

"I would have to check, but I would say it is Saint John Bosco."

Jennifer looked at her file and saw it was the school where her client had gone and where his children go. "My client will be pleased." Jennifer was also pleased.

The cardinal assured her she would have a check within a week and a letter notifying the school of the donation. As they concluded their business, she thanked Cardinal Flinn and left the chancery with a smile of victory on her face. She couldn't wait to talk to Thom.

At 6:00 p.m., Cardinal Flinn left the chancery and was driven back to his residence where he poured a Scotch and water. He sat in his comfortable chair looking at his treadmill with no desire to get on it. He still needed thirty more minutes of exercise, but he was too tired. Instead, he opened a bag of jellybeans and turned on his television to watch the evening news. After finishing his drink, eating the bag of candy and watching the news, he went to his chapel for Evening and Night Prayer. As he offered his prayers, he hoped he had dodged a bullet, uncertain if anything would be revealed to the public. He was glad to know at least some of his problems, and the archdioceses, were resolved. Yet he was unsure what the next day would bring.

Chapter 38

Saint Patrick's Cathedral was filled beyond capacity on the Friday after Easter. Despite the scaffolding, mourners gathered along the outer walls in reverent silence out of respect for the late rector. Monsignor Triplett had ministered to and celebrated the sacraments with many of those present. He was a vital part of their lives. Now they mourned him and tried to come to terms with the circumstance of his death.

Hector and his maintenance crew had added every chair they could find, even placing chairs around the outside of the sanctuary normally the aisle that access to Our Lady's Chapel. With so much scaffolding in the church, and the volume of Easter flowers covering much of the sanctuary, an additional hundred chairs were placed in this area for the archdiocesan priests, but it still wasn't enough. There were over two hundred vested priests, including Father David O'Hara taking their seats.

Monsignor Triplett's body arrived at the cathedral on Thursday night when the cardinal received his remains for the greeting and evening prayer. The casket was placed in front of the huge Easter paschal candle at the steps of the sanctuary just a few feet away from where he died. Monsignor Triplett was vested in the liturgical vestments he wore for the celebration of Mass — an alb, stole, and chasuble.

Three items were laid on the casket. The first was a long white pall that recalls the deceased's Baptism. The second item was a crucifix to serve as a reminder of having received the sign of the cross at Baptism and the promise of sharing in Christ's victory over sin and death. Finally, the Book of Gospels, acknowledged the deceased cherished the Gospel of Christ in his earthly life and now was blessed to share in eternal life.

The church was left open throughout the night for family, friends, parishioners and visitors to pay their last respects and offers prayers. The Knights of Columbus stood as the honor guard. NYPD officers were both inside and outside the cathedral the entire time serving as security for the church and mourners.

This morning the cathedral staff filed by the casket to say goodbye one more time. Feeling the loss of their friend and boss, they knowing two valued employees were in jail. As they were escorted to their reserved seats, they also knew today's funeral was the beginning of the healing process.

For Emma and Jonathan Pickle, it was the end of a friendship that stopped too soon. They appreciated and gave thanks for the blessings Monsignor Triplett brought into both their lives. Jonathan had a better outlook for his future, and Emma was grateful she would maintain her job at the cathedral.

Monsignor Stone was given a special seat in the sanctuary. It was the first time he had been back to the cathedral since the press conference. He looked distraught. He thanked God for his friendship with Monsignor Triplett and asked for help with his new responsibilities.

Mrs. Sue Kimberland, was now the principal organist. The cathedral hired her three years ago from the Episcopal Cathedral down the street. As a cradle Catholic, her faith wavered over the years, but Monsignor Triplett helped her return to the church. She and Brian McManius made a good team until his recent behavior changes and now his arrest.

Sitting at the gallery organ, this was not the way she expected to receive this position.

Thom Triplett sat in the front row opposite the place of his brother's death. On his right were his children and ex-wife. On the other side of him, holding his hand was Jennifer Gibson. He already went through two handkerchiefs the night before, so he placed three in various pockets for today.

Behind him was the Mayor of New York and several other highly prominent city officials.

Thankfully, the weather was warm, and the sun was shining through the windows not covered by the draping of the scaffolding. With all the flowers, there was an inescapable redolence of new life and joy, even on this heartbreaking day for so many. Unlike flowers that just die, one day all lives will end, but a future awaits those of faith.

The Delfino family sat among the mourners to avoid the media covering the funeral. They were still waiting on the official cause of death from the coroner, but the preliminary investigation indicated Joseph had taken his own life. The family was disappointed the cardinal would not preside over Joseph's funeral since he would be in Rome meeting with the pope next week.

The media reporting on the funeral was limited to space across the street near Rockefeller Center. Thom didn't want any of the media in the church. Many reporters tried to get comments from the usually outgoing, charismatic and beloved cardinal, but he was advised not to say anything since he still faced with his own circumstances.

Father Peter Unser, serving as the master of ceremonies, gave the signal to the director of music for the funeral Mass procession to begin. The procession entered with the altar servers carrying the incense, cross, and candles followed by the deacons, priests, and bishops from within the archdiocese and from the neighboring dioceses. The cardinal entered last.

Each of the clergy made their way to the altar, properly reverenced this sacred table with a bow and were directed to their seats. The bishops sat near the archbishop's chair. Monsignor James Black and Father Luke Crumbley served as the chaplains to the cardinal and sat on each side of him. When Cardinal Flinn arrived at the foot of the sanctuary steps, he removed his miter and gave it, along with his crosier, to the two seminarians serving as acolytes. He was then handed the thurible, the vessel containing the incense, and placed two spoonfuls of incense in the incensor. The cardinal ceremoniously incensed both the altar and the casket. The altar where the sacrifice of Christ is remembered and the casket where lies one who lost his life doing good for others. Monsignor Triplett loved to use incense at funerals, and today would be no different for a priest who had served the archdiocese well. Cardinal Flinn proceeded to the archbishop's chair for the opening prayer.

After the reading of the Scriptures selected by Monsignor Triplett, including a passage from the Gospel of John assuring us that there are many rooms in the Father's house, Bishop Newsome surprised the congregation and stood at the steps of the sanctuary in front of the casket. He took a few moments in silence and looked out to everyone assembled. Then he turned and looked at all the deacons, priests and bishops who gathered around him, many still standing. He had the attention of those who could see him. He wanted his words to be heard.

He focused his reflection not on the accomplishments of Monsignor Triplett's life but on Monsignor Triplett's priesthood. He spoke about the importance of the celebration of the Eucharist in his life and the importance it should have in everyone's lives. He talked about the wonderful gift that is always available for all because of men who respond to the call from God to the priesthood. The priests thought he would talk about vocations to the priesthood, but instead, he turned around and reminded the priests of the gift they have to

506

celebrate the Eucharist for whatever parish or institution they serve. It was 'their earthly room', and he urged them to appreciate this room, knowing the Lord was preparing 'their heavenly room.' Monsignor Triplett always appreciated this service at the altar. He reminded them it is the center of life for the faithful who enter through the church doors.

There was not a dry eye among those gathered for the congregation was absorbed in his words of wisdom. Bishop Newsom had one more point to make that he hoped all would hear and remember.

"One day the Lord will be the true judge for each of us. Even though there are those on earth who bear the title, and there are those who pass judgment without the title, we are not to judge. Monsignor Triplett lived and grew in his faith, always looking for the good in everyone. We are called to do the same. I know he never wanted to judge or be judged. Always remember the good he did and let God take care of the judging. For he will rest in peace, and we too will join him in the great room where the greatest celebration around the altar takes place, in the Kingdom of everlasting life."

Bishop Newsome ended his homily. "Remember the words of Jeremiah, 'Mercy triumphs over judgment'."

As Bishop Newsome returned to his seat, he was startled to look at the congregation and suddenly hear clapping. It was Emma and Jonathan Pickle who began, and then the entire church erupted in applause that lasted a full three minutes until Cardinal Flinn stood. He smiled and turned toward Bishop Newsome and thanked him for his fine words knowing his friend, this rector, would be given a place at the great altar in heaven. He looked forward to or hoped he too would one day join him.

Mass continued with the Liturgy of the Eucharist and an endless line for the reception of the Eucharist. During communion, the cardinal recognized Will Palmer and Patrick Sabor and a few others involved in the investigation.

The detectives had smiles on their faces. Prior to coming to the funeral, the crime lab confirmed the DNA on the candlestick was Monsignor Triplett's and the fingerprints belonged to both Sam Tolden and Brian McManius. The case was one step closer to being solved.

As Communion ended, the priests and bishops returned to the altar and put the remaining consecrated hosts in one ciborium and placed the vessel in the tabernacle. The cardinal sat in his chair and offered his own private prayers and reflection, thanking the Lord for the opportunity to serve the people of New York City despite the problems and struggles faced within the archdiocese.

After the closing prayer, Cardinal Flinn moved and stood in front of the coffin for the final commendation and farewell. He then asked for the congregation to be seated. Cardinal Flinn expressed simplistically his own condolences and thanks for all those present, especially to Monsignor Triplett's brother, Thom. He asked for prayers for his priests, the bishops, the cathedral's families and himself. He looked around at his priests and the congregation and realized that Monsignor Triplett's presence was still at work bringing a great sense of peace in the cathedral. Knowing this, he concluded with the words heard so many times at Catholic funerals reminding all that no one knows when life will end on this earth,

Eternal Rest, Grant unto him O Lord.
And Let the Perpetual Light Shine Upon him.
May the soul of Monsignor Triplett, and the souls of
    all the faithful departed,
Rest in Peace.
    Amen

Rejoice in hope, be patient under trial,
and persevere in prayer.
Romans 12:12

Author's Note

I must say something about the people, places and events in this novel.

Saint Patrick's Cathedral, "America's Parish Church", in New York City exists, and the location is described with accuracy. The cathedral went through a major restoration in 2014. However, in any work of fiction, some liberties have been exercised to help the story.

Regarding other locations mentioned in New York City, those who live or visit will know or discover which are real and which are not. I wanted the focus of the book to be Saint Patrick's Cathedral.

The Catholic clergy represented in this work are not based on actual persons. Some of these characters may seem familiar for I have used traits and habits I have seen in priests and bishops I have encountered.

I have fictionalized the hierarchical structure of the archdiocese of New York with the help of their actual website.

The New York Police Department (NYPD) officers and other agencies represented in this novel are not based on real people. Research, and my own limited experiences knowing those who work as detectives, crime scene investigators, and officers, has helped me with the development of these characters. I am thankful for those who dedicate their lives for the safety in whatever city they may serve.

Any other persons mentioned have been fictionalized.

Finally, regarding events during Holy Week and other sacramental celebrations in the Catholic Church, I have tried, with great accuracy, to explain these, and show not only how meaningful they can be, but beneficial. No matter your faith, visit a local Catholic church and experience these beautiful liturgies.

Book Club Discussion Questions

1. Now that you have finished reading the book, what was your initial reaction?

2. Which character do you relate to and why?

3. The Catholic Church has had to face some difficult issues, some presented in this story. Do you think these were depicted realistically in the novel?

4. The hierarchy of the Catholic Church had to make some tough decisions throughout the book. Do you think Cardinal Flinn responded properly? How about Bishop Newsome?

5. Talk about the life of Monsignor Triplett. How would you say he did in handling the church business affairs? How about his own affairs?

6. Do you see Emma as one with a weak or strong personality? What made Emma's behavior authentic?

7. Various characters are at different stages in life with their faith. Who were the strong ones, who were the doubters, and who were the ones searching?

8. Do you think the detectives were believable in their handling of the murder case? Why or why not? Where did they show a more human characteristic? Where were they vulnerable?

9. Who had more self-confidence – Father Morales or Father O'Hara?

10. What surprised you in the book? What upset you?

11 Throughout the book, much is shared about the various Sacraments and Sacramentals. What did you learn about the Catholic Church?

Anthony P. Mikle has served the Catholic Church for over 35 years in parish and diocesan positions. He has always loved a good mystery story, and so for his first novel, he turned his sights on a murder within one of the most famous churches in America and known throughout the world.

anthonypmikle.wixsite.com/site

Made in the USA
Monee, IL
30 November 2019